Caitlin's

FIRE

BY MARY ANN KERR

THINK WELL BOOKS

thinkwellbooks.com

Published in part by Thinkwell Books, Portland, Oregon. The views or opinions of the author are not necessarily those of Thinkwell Books. Learn more at *thinkwellbooks.com*

Design and cover Illustration by Andrew Morgan Kerr
Learn more at *andrewmorgankerr.com*

Published and printed in the United States of America
ISBN: 978-0-9891681-2-0
Fiction, Historical, Christian

BOOKS BY MARY ANN KERR

A WOMAN OF ENTITLEMENT SERIES:

Book One
LIBERTY'S INHERITANCE

Book Two
LIBERTY'S LAND

Book Three
LIBERTY'S HERITAGE

CAITLIN'S FIRE

Dedication

I dedicate this book to Jesus Christ
The Alpha and Omega, the beginning and the end.
I also dedicate *Caitlin's Fire* to my sons,
David, Peter, Stephen, and Andrew Kerr.

ACKNOWLEDGEMENTS

CAITLIN'S FIRE is one of those stories that unfolded day by day. I have felt God's anointing on me as I write. He is the author of creativity and has blessed me with the ability to write stories. It is a gift for which I shall be forever grateful. A quote from Stephen Charnock, who was a Puritan theologian in England in the 1600s, has resonated within me since I read it. "The secret touches of God upon the heart, and inward converses with him, are a greater evidence of the existence of a supreme and infinitely good Being, than all nature." Isn't that the truth? When we focus on God rather than self-helps, He touches our hearts with love, joy, and peace, and I must include creativity, in almost tangible ways. I give Him all the glory.

There are so many of you who kept begging for a fourth book. To you, my readers, I am thankful. I pray God's blessing on you and may you grow closer to Him day by day. *Caitlin's Fire* is my fourth book and although not in the series, many beloved characters are in it.

I have many I could acknowledge who have encouraged or blessed me in so many ways.

Dori Harrell at *Breakout Editing* has done a wonderful job editing *Caitlin's Fire*. I am grateful!

I thank my son Stephen Kerr for helpful insights, always improving the content. I'm grateful for him taking the time to read *Caitlin's Fire* and telling me he really enjoyed it.

Andrew Kerr, my youngest son and author of *Ants on Pirate Pond*, has again designed and illustrated a cover that is distinctive and striking. Thank you for all your help with publishing through *Thinkwell Books*. To Shari, his wife, I thank God for you and your sweet spirit and cheerful manner, for always looking at the bright side of a situation.

Peter Kerr, my second eldest son, professor at Asbury and owner of KerrComm, I thank you for always encouraging me in my writing. Your book, *Adam Meets Eve*, is a book every believer, especially those looking for a mate, should read. Your sci-fi book, *The Ark of Time*, is a great story. Well done, Peter! Rebecca, what a blessing you are and such a great daughter-in-law. I see you growing in Christ and admire it.

David and Rosie, how I do love you. As I write this, you are here visiting us. Although you've been in and out these past couple months, it's been a joy to have you here.

I'd like to thank a friend we've known for years, Phil McHaney, who my husband was stationed with in Goose Bay, Labrador, Canada. You've been such a "Barnabus" to my writing; "Son of Encouragement" is what you are. Thanks! Bill Taylor...you encourage me, too!

Once again, I thank Allan Thomlinson for marketing my books. What a blessing it is to me. Phil and I both treasure your and Karen's friendship.

Jamie Lee, you've become a friend as well as an encouragement to me.

To my cousins, Carl Grub, Cathy Kiki, Starla Peterson, Cheryl Piersol, Jean Ahlefeld, and Lillian VanHouten—thanks for being part of my fan base! I love each of you!

Twyla Vimont, Sandy Falter, Delva Lantripp, Lori and Roy Barrett, and so many others, I so appreciate your encouragement and the question, "When's the next book going to be out?" Thanks!

I thank my husband, Philip, who gives me time to write and encourages me. Thank you for your love and understanding support.

I want to give God all the glory. He has given me this gift, and I am so grateful to be able to write stories that are interesting as well as inspiring. Thank you, Lord...

Holy, holy is the LORD God Almighty, who was, who is, and who is to come!

List of Characters

PREFACE

"HYMN OF PRAISE"
Sometimes faith comes like a trickle.
Sometimes faith comes like a flood.
It streams at me from heavenly places,
It's beginning rooted in the blood.

Jesus how I thank you for it,
Jesus how I praise your name.
Faith as little as a mustard seed
Is all I need for Godly gain.

Praise your name, oh blessed Jesus,
Praise your name, oh God above.
Praise you Holy Spirit leading,
Leading me with infinite love.

Bless, Oh Lord, Thy Name Most High,
Bless You, oh my soul Rejoice.
Bless the One who gives us life,
Bless the One who gives us voice.

May our voice be one of praise,
May our voice be clear and true,
May we use it for Your glory,
May our voice be all for You.

MARY ANN KERR

PROLOGUE

*And Jesus answering said, A certain man went down from
Jerusalem to Jericho, and fell among thieves, which stripped
him of his raiment, and wounded him, and departed,
leaving him half dead.*

LUKE 10:30

THE HEAVENS, SPRINKLED with twinkling stars and nearly a full
moon, lit the road from Santa Rosa to Sonoma. It was early February
of 1885 and cooler than normal. The damp air, coupled with a breeze,
chilled the man on horseback. He pulled his collar up closer around his
neck. He hadn't planned to be out this late, but the Hendersons hadn't
been home. He'd thought to see the type of casks they used, how they
aged their wines, and to ask about marketing. Hendersons had a good
product. Planning to spend the night there, he'd been disappointed to
see they weren't home. Even though it was early evening, he'd decided
to ride south.

Reckon I'll spend the night in Petaluma, he thought. *Tomorrow I'll ride
for Frisco.* He pulled up suddenly from a canter to a halt. "Whoa! Whoa
there, sweetie pie."

Someone lay, nearly face down, in the road. The man on horseback slipped quickly from his saddle and knelt on one knee. He turned over the man, who had suddenly become very alive. The once-prone man aimed a pistol at his rescuer's face.

The kneeling man heard a movement behind him and started to turn, but a club slammed into his back and head. He dropped like a stone.

"Is he dead?"

"I don't know, an' I don't rightly care. Let's get his coat. It's a beauty."

Quickly divesting him of coat, satchel, and watch, one of the two took the man's gun. The robber also felt a money belt and untied it.

"Look, a money belt! And can you see the butt of this gun? It's a nice piece."

"Yeah, but we need to get his horse and get outta here. This road's heavily traveled, 'specially on a night as bright as this one."

The two men headed for the horse and made a grab for the reins, but the animal backed away. They tried several times, but the horse wouldn't let them closer than three feet.

One said, "We'd better go. Someone's likely to come along any minute."

They mounted their horses, which had been tied to a tree, and rode north, heading toward Santa Rosa. With a good gun, expensive coat, and the money belt, it'd been a lucrative night.

The horse stood over its owner, nosing him, but there was no response.

CHAPTER 1

And thou shalt speak unto the children of Israel, saying,

'If a man die, and have no son, then ye shall cause his

inheritance to pass unto his daughter.'

NUMBERS 27:8

"And last, but not least, I thank my youngest daughter for her support and loving care during my long illness. Maisie Marie, Aidan Eve, you are precious to me. I have given you enough to be well provided for all your natural lives"—the lawyer cleared his throat before continuing—"even without the provision of your husbands."

The attorney, Mr. Brandon, looked up at the people seated. He knew about Mac's feelings toward Mr. Hart. He provided nothing for his wife, Aidan, he only took. Again, the lawyer cleared his throat and continued to read the last Will and Testament of Mackenzie Macleby McCaully.

It was late afternoon, and the February sun cast long shadows across the lawns in its last bid for life. Lamps had been lit, and their reflected glow in the mahogany framed mirror over the mantelpiece gave the impression of peace and serenity in stark contrast to the atmosphere that pervaded the room. A tight feeling of tension prevailed. The parlor had chairs lined up in rows, and all the servants and ranch hands were seated. Each had been recognized by Mackenzie McCaully.

"The property of McCaully Ranch, the house and all its environs, horses, stables, and cattle, I bequeath to my youngest daughter, Caitlin Kendall McCaully."

Cait heard a concerted gasp from her brother-in-law, Jared Hart, and her sister, Aidan. Her heart sank. *Jared will not be content until he has it all. I'm glad I had the foresight to make plans. My life won't be worth the paper the will is written on by tomorrow. What was Da thinking? Jared'll probably contest the will saying Da was out of his mind. I wonder if Aidan has any idea how evil her husband is. I'm certain she must.*

She heard Aidan whisper into Jared's ear but couldn't hear what was said.

Mr. Brandon continued to read. "All of you know Caitlin is the only one of you girls who invested herself body and soul into the ranch. I have made the will incontestable. Please be satisfied with what I've given you."

The lawyer finished and asked, "Are there any questions?"

"Yes, there most certainly is. When you say the will is incontestable, does that mean there's no possibility of breaking it? I understand that's what the old man said. I simply want to know if there's any way it can be broken." Jared spoke bitterly, and Gavin turned to glare at him. They were brothers-in-law but not friends.

"Of course you can't break it, Jared. You just heard it out of Mr. Brandon's mouth. We'll abide by the reading and honor our wives' father. This is what Mac wanted. Aidan has enough to keep even you comfortable for a very long time."

Gavin was disgusted. Every time he encountered Jared, he became more incensed with the younger man's cavalier attitude. The entire family knew Jared was lazy with no work ethic, no job, and was a leech on his wife. How Aidan put up with him was beyond their understanding.

Gavin didn't approve of Aidan, either. He was thankful Maisie was of a different ilk. She was sweet tempered and beautiful as well as intelligent.

Mr. Brandon responded, "No, Mr. Hart, there's no way this will can be changed or broken. The only way anything could possibly change is if Miss Caitlin should predecease her sisters. The provision, then, is that the estate would be split between Mrs. Galway and Mrs. Hart. But, in the event Caitlin marries, it would go to her husband and any progeny." Mr. Brandon looked at Aidan and Maisie as he spoke.

Maisie was content. She had loved her father with a passion. She'd prepared her heart for the past eighteen months for this day. Maisie had dreaded it but knew it was coming. Gavin would see her through this. Her da had more than provided for her. She would invest half of it in the stock of her husband's company, and with the other half, she would diversify. Maisie sat and squeezed Gavin's hand. She was proud her husband wasn't afraid of Jared. She was. She felt he was wicked and couldn't see how Aidan could stand him, let alone marry him. She knew Caitlin warned her not to. So did her da.

Maisie's cloud of jet black hair was like silk and wrapped up in an intricate knot at the back of her head. Stunning, dressed all in black, her hazel eyes turned the color of whatever she was wearing. Right now, they were slate gray. Maisie was Caitlin's eldest sister by four years and married to Gavin Galway, who adored her. He'd inherited a gem mine in the Sonoma area from his father and was a man to reckon with in the world of precious and semiprecious stones. Sometimes, Maisie worked at their gemstone store in San Francisco. They'd been married three years but had no children.

Maise now watched as Cait, in obvious distress, arose from her chair.

Cait stood and turned to face her sisters, tears standing out in her clear gray eyes. Her rich auburn hair, a braided crown of glory around her well-shaped head, gleamed brightly in the lamplight. A confection of black satin and lace covered her from throat to floor, fitting over a figure of perfection, which was also striking because one rarely saw her in a dress. Jet earrings glittered in her ears. Slim and lovely, she had no idea how elegant she looked. She blinked away the tears and glanced at the ranch hands, embarrassed they should see her in such a weakened, vulnerable state. It was a man's world, and a man's world was hard.

"I didn't know he was leaving me the ranch. He never spoke of it," Caitlin said softly. She daren't look at Jared. She didn't care to see his beautiful eyes, now a flat, pale blue. His face darkened with hatred and Aidan snorted in contempt.

"You really expect us to believe that?" Aidan asked. She sat with her slim legs crossed and had the sleek look of a cat. Aidan wore black, as befit someone in mourning, but her dress was cut low over her bosom and was as tight as a second skin. A long ruffle from just below the knee to the floor rustled when she moved. Her sapphire blue eyes glittered with anger. Black hair held highlights of red and was pulled tightly back, held in place by an onyx comb studded with diamonds. She looked haughty and sophisticated.

"But, it's true," Caitlin said. "I didn't know he'd ever changed his will. I thought everything was written up years ago and it all went to Mother. I've never seen Mr. Brandon come here to the ranch since Da's been sick."

"That's because Mac didn't want you to know, Miss Caitlin. He arranged for me to come on a day when you were out riding fence," said Mr. Brandon, smiling kindly at Mac's youngest daughter. When he finished reading the will, the ranch hands filed out and the servants headed for the kitchen. Only the family, Ewen, and Mr. Brandon stayed in the parlor. Ewen was nearly family.

Jared stared at her, his eyes full of hate. *I hate you, Cait,* he thought. *You cautioned Aidan about marrying me and all over a little misunderstanding. Just because I tried to kiss you in the barn when I was seeing Aidan. You slapped me, and I've done my best ever since to destroy Aidan's relationship with you. Your relationship has always been tenuous, at best. For some reason, my sweet little wife is jealous of her younger sister.*

The day after her da died, Cait had overheard one of the ranch hands talking with Jared, at least she was fairly certain it was Jared. She couldn't tell by his voice which ranch hand it was. She'd been on her knees in a stall tending an early calf whose mother couldn't nurse. Neither man had known of her presence.

They'd discussed how to get rid of her. An accident could happen while she was out riding, or maybe they'd hit her over the head with a horseshoe and put her in the stall with her stallion. Caitlin shuddered hearing Jared's plans for her. She didn't know whom she could trust beside Ewen Carr, her da's foreman and best friend. *Who in the world, on this ranch, is in cahoots with Jared? I almost feel as if my mind is playing tricks on me. It was Jared, wasn't it?*

After hearing the conversation, she'd told Ewen that she'd be riding out after the reading of the will. Not telling Ewen where she was headed had made him extremely angry, but Caitlin didn't want anyone to know. That way, she wouldn't have to worry about Jared ferreting out the information of where she'd gone.

Ewen spoke in a strident tone. "Why in tarnation would you leave here? Your da just died. You need to stay to keep things runnin' the way we're used to. It's not a time for you to go galavantin' around the country. The men need to know you're boss. Why the devil would you be a wantin' to ride out now?"

"I need to get away, that's all. I nursed Da for quite a spell, and I need time to get myself back together before taking over the responsibility of McCaully Ranch." Cait's lips had been set in a stubborn line. She didn't want to tell Ewen about the threat she'd overheard in the barn. She couldn't prove anything. Her heart was breaking over her father's death, and the last thing she wanted was to leave the ranch, but she'd heard of a mission in San Rafael that took in women who were in straitened circumstances. *Well,* she thought, *I'm in desperate circumstances.*

Ewen promised to keep things running until she returned, but she could tell he was unhappy with her decision. When she'd gone to town to buy some black clothes, she'd ridden over to Napa and set up a post office box for herself. Ewen could communicate with her if he needed to.

She'd also told Mr. Brandon to handle the ranch's financial affairs until she returned. He'd been displeased with her decision to leave, too, having no idea how evil Jared could be. Caitlin was not used to explaining herself to anyone. She knew Mr. Brandon felt she was shirking her responsibilities.

Caitlin forced her mind off Jared and to the present. When Mr. Brandon finished reading the will, she talked with him in the foyer.

"Would you care to stay for dinner, Mr. Brandon?"

"Normally, I'd take you up on that, Miss Caitlin, but I have an engagement this evening I can't fail to attend." Caitlin handed him his coat and once he'd donned it, she handed him his hat.

"Thank you for your calming presence, Mr. Brandon, and for soothing things over."

"You're most welcome, my dear." He put his hand on her shoulder and gave it a gentle squeeze. "The best of luck to you." He walked out the front door and set his top hat onto his thick gray hair. "I'm most sorry for your loss, Miss Caitlin. We will all miss Mac but none more than you." He added in a whisper, "You think I disapprove your going away, but I don't. I think you need some time alone to get your heart settled. No matter how much you anticipate and know someone is going to die, its finality is still a shock. I know how much you loved your da. But, you come back soon, you hear?"

"Yes, I hear and I'll come back soon, Mr. Brandon. Thank you." She kissed his cheek.

The lawyer gave her a quick hug. He'd been a friend of Mac's for years. He turned away but not before she saw the tears in his eyes.

Cait closed the door and leaned her back against it, tears filling her eyes. She wondered if she could get away this night without Jared knowing she'd left.

He entered the wide foyer, a sneer on his face. "So, you got it all didn't you, Caitlin? You sweetened up the old man and got him to sign everything away to you. Well, I'm not going to let it rest until it's split up and we all get a share of the pie. Do you hear me, Cait? I'm going to get this ranch cut up into three big chunks."

He began to advance on her, hands outstretched, as if he wanted to choke the life out of her.

"Gavin!" Caitlin yelled at the top of her lungs.

Gavin came running into the front foyer. "What is it, Cait?"

Jared's face was black with rage.

"Leave her alone, Jared. You can't change anything. If anything happens to Caitlin, I'll have the sheriff down your neck fast, investigating every move you've made since you were a baby! Now, get out of here!"

Jared shook his fist at Caitlin. "I'll make you pay. You've taken much of Aidan's inheritance, and believe me, I'll make you pay." He strode back into the parlor and told Aidan to pack their bags. They were going home.

Caitlin turned to thank Gavin. "I'm sorry about that," she said, "but he scares me."

"He scares Maisie, too." Gavin gave his sister-in-law a quick hug and hoped his presence would give her some added courage. It was not going to be easy for her to run this huge outfit by herself. He held her away from himself and looked into her shadowed eyes.

"You sure you're all right, Cait? Are you going to need extra help? I want you to watch your step, little sis. I've been thinking of putting a Pinkerton onto Jared just to keep him honest."

Caitlin's eyes widened as the import of his words sank in. "I've decided to go away for a while. I overheard Jared talking to one of the ranch hands, and I'm not being overly dramatic when I say Jared wants to get rid of me...permanently."

Gavin stared at her a moment before replying, "I'm sure you're not exaggerating. Where will you go?"

"I'm not telling anyone where I'll be, but I'll be fine. Once things settle down here, I'll come back. Leaving for a bit would be the best thing for me right now."

Gavin squeezed her shoulder. "Well, I have no doubt you can take care of yourself, but perhaps you should come with us. You'd be more than welcome. Maisie adores you, in case you haven't noticed."

"Thanks, but I'll be fine. I've already made some arrangements." Cait bit her lip as the lie slid out. It wasn't true. She didn't even know if the mission would take her. She knew it was in San Rafael, which was a bit of a ride south from the ranch, but she was used to whole days of riding and knew it wouldn't be a problem.

Pre-dinner drinks were being readied and Caitlin wanted to freshen up. She went up the wide staircase, glad that Jared and Aidan would be leaving before dinner. She went to her rooms.

Caitlin had little in the way of black dresses or any dresses, for that matter. The day after her father died, she'd ridden into Santa Rosa and purchased a couple dresses off the rack for mourning. She'd also bought two cheap black split skirts, black blouses, a hat, and inexpensive leather boots. She didn't wish to appear at this mission looking as if she had money. She bit her lip, thinking about Fire. He definitely was worth a lot of money, but it couldn't be helped. No one else could feed him, not even Ewen. She'd have to take him with her. She'd decided earlier to ride out after the evening meal, her bag already packed. Now that Jared was leaving, she wasn't quite sure.

She checked the leather satchel she and Sweeny had put together, hoping she hadn't forgotten anything. She sat down to make a list and checked the satchel against what she'd written. *I think that's all I'll need. Stockings, oh, I almost forgot to pack stockings. What else?*

CHAPTER II

Be not forgetful to entertain strangers:
for thereby some have entertained angels unawares.

HEBREWS 13:2

BEFORE THE READING OF THE WILL, Caitlin had hidden some things in a saddlebag under the straw in Fire's stall. Her stallion was a big roan that let no one near him except Mac and herself. She knew her things would be safe there.

Now sitting in her room, Caitlin teared up as she thought about her da. She picked up the daguerreotype of him off her nightstand and sat in a rocking chair covered in plush yellow material. Kicking off her shoes, she curled up her long legs and opened the glass case, staring at the likeness of her father as tears ran down her cheeks.

He looks so stern. So many people were afraid of him. They didn't realize he only had a rough exterior. Oh, how I'm going to miss him. We had such wonderful talks, and he taught me so much about life. I'll miss our chess games and reading together from our favorite books. Oh, Da... Cait began to cry in hard, racking sobs, as if her heart was broken, which, indeed, it was. It was the first human death she'd ever experienced. Her mother, Ryanne, had died in childbirth when she'd been born, and Mac had never married again. Cait had seen beloved dogs, cows, and horses die but hadn't realized how deeply the heartache over her father would be, particularly because she'd been expecting his death. Her sorrow cut deep.

She wondered again why Mac came to America. He'd said it was because of the potato famine in Ireland. He'd called it the great hunger. Everyone, he'd said, was hungry. There was such misery he couldn't bear it anymore. He never had shared much about the family he'd left behind. She wondered if he had gotten the money illegally to come to America and thus never spoke about it. She'd read about the potato famine and the dates were wrong for when her da had immigrated. She smiled through her tears, remembering she and her sisters had spoken exactly like him as youngsters. Their mother was the only one who had spoken correct English.

He'd always been happier in the saddle than anywhere else. Maybe I inherited that from him. Oh, Da… She walked to the bed and curled up into a ball of misery. She cried herself to sleep. Even as she slept, the tension did not leave her body. Caitlin was exhausted.

Sweeny, her maid, peeked into the room but saw Cait asleep and withdrew quietly.

She knew all about Jared. After hearing the threatening conversation in the stable, Caitlin had hurried to her room and, while dressing for dinner, had told Sweeny everything she'd heard. The maid was loyal, but Cait didn't even tell Sweeny where she was going after the reading of the will. Normally, she shared everything with her maid.

Sweeny went downstairs to tell Cait's sister and brother-in-law she was asleep. Unless Caitlin needed her, she found other work to do and never sat idle. She chewed on her bottom lip, anxious about Caitlin riding off by herself.

Working on a huge ranch, Cait met few girls, and Mac had treated her more like a son than a daughter. She could do just about anything a man could except heavy lifting. She loved to rope cattle, but branding them wasn't her favorite. She had a few friends, but no one close. Sweeny was her only confidante.

When Mac had the house built, he'd had suites put in on the second floor so that each of the girls had a private sitting room, bedroom, and bathing room replete with bathtub, sink, and porcelain chamber pots that fit into a commode. Caitlin's sitting room was light and airy and had French doors that opened to a large balcony over the gardens below. A small water fountain poured its contents into a huge bird bath, and the sound of the moving water was soothing. Her walls were done in a light yellow wallpaper with sprigs of daisies scattered here and there. All the trim was stained cherry, matching the darker centers of the daisies. It was a friendly looking room, and a couple plush yellow chairs and the cushion of the same material on a rocker completed the decor and gave it an inviting air.

Caitlin awoke as Sweeny entered the bedroom.

"I'm sorry to wake you, Miss Cait. I came in to help you get ready for dinner. I know you needed the rest, but Miss Maisie and Mr. Gavin are waiting for you in the parlor."

"It's all right, Sweeny. I need to get up anyway. Have Aidan and Jared left yet?"

"Yes, they left about twenty minutes ago. My goodness, I had no idea your da would leave each of us so much money, Miss Cait. It's over a year's salary. Oh miss, I will be desolate without you. You will take care, won't you?"

"I'll miss you, too, Sweeny, but I'm not leaving until later. We'll say our good-byes then. I'll change into one of those new split skirts. Thank you for packing my things." She grabbed Sweeny's shoulders and gave her a big hug, which was returned in full measure. Then her shoulders began to shake in grief and tears poured down her cheeks. She wiped them on her sleeve, trying to get her emotions under control as Sweeny continued to hold her.

"I'm going to miss you more than you will me," Sweeny said sagely. "I think it'll be harder for me. You'll be doing new things and keeping busy, somehow, I reckon."

"Oh, I have no doubt Duffy will keep you busy, too. Trust me, she keeps this house shipshape and she'll have you doing things other than waiting on me." Caitlin took a deep breath, smoothing her wrinkled dress.

"Well, Miss Cait, let me help you get dressed for dinner." Caitlin's room was not cluttered. Almost everything was functional, yet somehow, utterly feminine.

She stood patiently and let Sweeny change her dress. It was difficult to let another person dress her. She was usually up at the crack of dawn and dressed herself in denims and chaps. She had no idea how lovely she looked in the denims. It was an unheard of outfit for a woman, or even a girl, for that matter, to wear trousers. Caitlin argued with her da about it when she was twelve and won, a rarity in the McCaully household. Nobody won arguments with Mac. Cait had, but only because she talked about how dangerous it was to work on fencing and with barbed wire, with a skirt that could get snagged. Mac acquiesced with a grunt...which meant yes.

Sweeny didn't redo Cait's hair, which was still in a braided crown. Caitlin usually did her own hair. The maid merely smoothed it back where Caitlin had mussed it on the pillow.

"Reckon I'll go down for dinner." She took a deep breath and made her way to the parlor. Maisie and Gavin were already there having pre-dinner drinks.

The lamps, which had been lit for the reading of the will, still reflected their glow in the mahogany framed mirror, but the feeling of peace was now a reality. The tension that had pervaded the room earlier was gone. The lined-up chairs had been removed, and the room gave off an air of contentment and serenity.

Maisie turned toward her younger sister and assessed her change of clothing.

"You changed your dress?" She walked swiftly to Cait and gave her a hug filled with love but laced with regret. She wished she'd spent more time with her youngest sister when they were growing up. "You looked pretty before. Now you're stunning."

"Oh, Maisie, thank you. My other dress got wrinkled up...I took a nap."

"Well, it's nice to see you in a dress. I can't remember the last time." Maisie smiled warmly.

"The last time was the last time you were here for Sunday dinner," Cait said drily.

Gavin asked her, "What would you like to drink?"

"Oh, just some of that raspberry juice would be wonderful."

Maisie asked, casually, "So, where are you going, Cait?"

Caitlin pressed her lips together before answering softly, "I'm not disclosing my whereabouts to anyone. That way, I don't have to worry that Jared or anyone else, for that matter, will come looking for me."

"All right, all right. I just don't like the thought of you going off without someone knowing where you're going. It's a bit frightening to me. I love you very much, Cait. I don't wish to see anything bad happen to you, that's all."

"I know...I love you too, Maisie. I'll be careful, I promise." Her heart warmed toward Maisie, who never seemed to have time for her in the past. "I have this planned out pretty well, I think. I'm worried at this point that Jared might come after me. At least this way, it'll give him time to cool off. I sure can't understand why Aidan married him."

"We know what you mean," Gavin said. "Maisie and I were discussing that very thing a little while ago. I wonder if she realizes she's made a big mistake in judgment. Knowing you McCaullys the way I do, it'll be a cold day in hell when she admits she's made a mistake."

Maisie turned and punched her husband on the shoulder. "Oh, and you're the one to talk, me luv. I've yit ta see you admit to a mistike, and we've been married these tree yirs." She spiced her speech with an Irish brogue she'd learned from her da.

"That's because I haven't made any mistakes yet."

The three of them laughed. He grabbed his wife's hand, and they walked into the dining room.

The man awoke slowly, his head spinning. The sense of whirling brought bile to his throat. He started to turn his head, but it was too painful. Swallowing, he opened his eyes and heard, as if from a long distance, a voice talking.

"Doctor, he's comin' around. I think he's a gonna wake up this time."

"You said that last time he opened his eyes." The doctor was filling out some paperwork as he talked. "Are you willing to keep him here, or should I find someplace else for him to recover?"

The woman wasn't paying any heed to the doctor's words. Her attention was fully focused on a pair of deep-set blue eyes that looked at her coherently for a moment. The expression drifted into a look of nothingness as he closed his eyes again.

"Oh, Doc, I hain't be a thinkin' he should be moved, do you?"

"Well, now, I don't rightly know. Most likely he'll be fine. You and Zebidiah don't have to feel as though you need to keep him here. You have a house full with all your children. Mayhap he can be moved tomorrow. Let's wait and see, Lindsey May, how he does when he wakes up. He may be able to ride on to where he was headed in the first place. I'll say one thing, though. It's a miracle some bone wasn't broken with the wallop he took on his back." Doc Addison stood and stretched before going to the sofa. He touched the man's forehead, which felt cool and clammy. "I'm pretty sure he's out of the woods, but we'll wait and see."

"Would ya like some tea? I jist made some zucchini bread this mornin'."

"Well, ma'am, I do believe I'll take you up on that. I've been hoping the patient would wake up so we can see where he hails from."

The doctor looked around at the comfortable room. It was good sized and served as kitchen, living room, and dining room. A faded braid rug brought some color to the pine flooring, which was darkened with age. The walls were made of pine logs, stripped of their bark, and faded to a dark patina. The cradle in a corner always seemed inhabited by a baby. The doctor had delivered five of the eight children who lived here.

Lindsey May Pindar, twenty-five years old, had been married for eight years. Her husband, Zebidiah, worked in the gemstone mine just two miles from their house in Sonoma County. The three older children, Mini Louise, Saidy Helen, and Lettie Lynn, were Zeb's by his first wife, who'd died having Lettie. Lindsey May loved the three girls as if they were her own.

She lifted the hot water off the wood stove and poured it into the two teacups. Scooping tea into a metal ball, she placed it in the doctor's cup. The zucchini bread smelled wonderful. Deftly, she buttered two slices and put a large piece on the luncheon plate for the doctor and a small piece for herself. She smiled at him over her shoulder.

"Seems strange, don't it, when a body's ill or hurt ya lose track a time? It's been two days now, hain't it?"

"Yes, ma'am. Your husband found him night before last on his way home from work. It was already dark and a wonder he saw 'em. I'm glad the man's horse didn't wander too far. Someone must have robbed him. There's not a piece of identification on him, no coat, no money, no pocket watch, even. His clothes seem to be of quality cloth. Guess we'll just have to wait until he wakes up. Waiting for him to awaken has enabled me to get caught up on my paperwork and how much I owe my creditors."

The two of them sat comfortably at the large round table. It was a good piece of oak that had seen better days. Scratches and stains marred its surface. Lindsey May stirred her tea water with the used tea ball still steeping in it.

"Wonder iffin he's married? What iffin his wife's a worryin' about 'em?"

"Now, don't go borrowing trouble for yourself. It won't do you any good to fret, nor your milk, for that matter. Umm, I do declare, your zucchini bread is the best in the county, Lindsey May Pindar!"

She grinned at him and said, "Thank you. I'm a gonna be needin' ta get busy here a fixin' dinner, right soon. The girls tooked all the children out for a tramp in the fields. Did ya know Zebidiah taught Mini Lou how ta shoot, and she carries a gun now? Shot a rattler last August, she did. We ate 'em. It was dee-licious."

"I've never eaten snake. I've heard it tastes like fried chicken. Is it true?"

"Better'n fried chicken. It's so tender, it jest melts in yer mouth."

The man on the sofa stirred again and Lindsey May hurried over to look at him.

"He's awake, Doc. This time he's awake. How're you feelin', sir?"

The man lay for a minute looking up at the woman bent over him.

CHAPTER III

Lo, children are an heritage of the LORD:
and the fruit of the womb is his reward.

PSALM 127:3

"**DO I KNOW YOU?**" The man's head pounded with pain and he closed his eyes, swallowing to fight the nausea. He opened his eyes and felt as if he were going to be sick. He started to sit up, but the woman pushed at his chest. He made a grab for a large metal bucket sitting beside the bed with a wet cloth in it. Dumping it, he vomited and lay back, shutting his eyes against the pain.

"Here," Lindsey May said. She picked up the cloth and handed it to him, turning helpless eyes toward Doc Addison.

The doctor walked to the sick man, who was wiping his lips with the cloth, his hand shaking. Lindsey May held a glass of water out to him and trembling, he took it. Putting the rim to his lips, it rattled against his teeth. He took a big mouthful and swished his mouth out, spitting it into the pan. He took a goodly drink, but his head hurt abominably and everything seemed blurry.

The doctor pulled up a chair and sat gazing at the man. His kindly brown eyes, warm as melted chocolate, met bewildered blue ones.

"Feeling pretty rough, eh? You took a nasty one on the back of your head, son. Do you remember what happened?" Doc leaned forward with his elbows on his knees, observing the young man while he talked.

"Why yes, I was riding to…to…I can't remember where I was going. I saw a man in the road. It was dark and I got off my horse, and I…I don't remember anything else."

"What's your name? Where do you hail from?"

"Name's ah…" He looked at the doctor with incredulity in his eyes. He blinked, trying to clear his vision. "I…I don't know my name! I don't know where I'm from." He started to shake his head in frustration but stopped. It pounded as if a drum beat inside it.

"You don't know who y'are?" Lindsey May had heard of such things, but she'd never actually encountered such a thing.

"You have my trousers, don't you? Is there anything in them that identifies me?"

Lindsey May looked a bit mournful at the poor man. "There hain't nothin' in your denims, nothin' in your shirt, nor vest neither fer that matter. We hain't gone through the things on yer horse."

"I have a horse?"

"Uh-huh, a fine piebald. She's a gorgeous horse," Lindsey May replied.

"It took quite a few stitches to close up the wound on your head," the doctor said, gazing at the younger man with sympathy.

At that moment, the door banged open and eight children trooped in. They came in noisily, but when they saw the man on the sofa sitting up, they made a semicircle around him and stared.

"Can he talk, Mama?"

"Mama, is he gonna to be all right?"

The children began to chatter all at once. The man, who already felt as if hammers were pounding in his head, felt he couldn't bear the noise.

Doc Addison realized being in this household wasn't going to help his patient.

"Do you think you can ride?"

"Yes, my back aches, but it's my head that hurts. It feels like hammers pounding in there."

Doctor Addison turned to his hostess. "Lindsey May, I'm going to take this man home with me. I think he's fit enough for that. Mini Louise, can you go saddle up our horses?"

"Yes, sir, I kin, an' I'll be a doin' it right sharp."

"I'll help her, Doctor Addison," Saidy said as she looked at the sick man, sorry he'd been ill. She hated throwing up.

Lindsey May handed Mini Lou the metal bucket. "I want you ta take this out an' dump it in the outhouse then rinse it out at the pump." She turned back to the man, realizing he needed to dress. He was wearing one of Zebidiah's night shirts.

"All right, children, let's all go out and help saddle up the horse while the doctor helps the man get dressed." They left noisily, waking baby Jonah. She picked up the baby, who'd begun to cry, deciding she could nurse him in the barn. The children were outside, but Jonah was screaming his lungs out. Lindsey May grabbed a small blanket and went out, banging the door shut behind her.

"Whew, that's a handful," the doctor said as he turned to his patient. "Your head aches, but I think you'd be better off going with me, where it'll be quiet."

He helped the nameless man get Zeb's nightshirt off, pulling it carefully over his head so as not to disturb the dressing. A wide bruise showed across his back and the doctor poked at it again, to see if any ribs might be broken.

The man flinched but didn't complain. He asked, "How long, sir, until I remember who I am? Oooh, my head hurts."

"Do you think you can ride?"

"Yes, but I reckon I'm not used to children. That was a hullabaloo. Don't believe I could handle it for overlong." Buttoning his shirt, he slipped his arms into his leather vest but still felt woozy. Everything was still a little blurry but not quite as bad as when he first sat up.

The doctor looked carefully at the man who had no memory and thought, *He's a man of means. His speech is educated, and his clothes aren't cheap. They're of fine material, and the leather vest looks custom made. His gun belt is tooled leather. Bet he's going to miss his gun.* He took the man's hands into his own and looked at the palms. They were calloused a bit, but the nails were even and clean.

"Well, son, let's be going. We'll stop at McCaully Ranch. Mac's got cancer, and I need to check on him. Haven't seen him since last week. I've been down to Vallejo taking care of some business for my mother. Stopped by here day before yesterday on my way home. Good thing, too, seeing as how Zebidiah found you on his way home from work. If we're lucky, we'll be invited to dinner at McCaully's. You ready? Let's go." They walked out the door and found their horses tied at the hitching post.

"How you doing, Piggypie?" *Now, where did that come from? My horse's name is Piggypie? I rather doubt it.* The top of his head felt as if it were ready to explode. The constant pounding made him feel sick to his stomach. He automatically checked the girth and tightened it.

The doctor laughed. "That seemed to come out quite naturally. I think, with time, you'll remember who you are, but don't strain at it. So, your horse's name is Piggypie. I'll bet there's a little story there." He waited for the man to get on his horse, ready to catch him if he couldn't, but the man stepped into the stirrup, swinging his leg over with the ease of habit. He gritted his teeth against the pain in his head, but the rest of his body, although sore, felt fine.

The doctor thanked Lindsey May for her wonderful zucchini bread. He turned to his horse, Blondie. The palomino had seen better days, but Doc loved his horse. She was fifteen but still going strong. He patted her neck, speaking softly to her before he looked down at the Pindar family.

Doc Addison tipped his hat to Lindsey May. "Thanks for your help and hospitality, ma'am." He turned his horse away and started out at a slow trot.

The nameless man turned to follow. He knew one thing for certain. "Either we walk or we canter. I can't handle a trot."

The doctor lightly touched a whip to his mount's flank. The nameless man touched his heels to Piggypie's sides, and they were off at a canter, smooth and steady.

Liberty Bannister sat in the great room, legs curled up underneath her. She leaned her head back against the leather chair and closed her eyes, reminiscing over the past eighteen months. She swallowed, feeling nausea rise from her stomach. *It's amazing that I could go from being married to a dishonest crook and have a thief and murderer for a father, to being married to a wonderful man and have a father who is full of integrity and truth. I was an only child, and now I have a twin brother who is more than I could ever ask for…quite a change in circumstances. I've been married nearly seven months, I'm thirty-one, and I don't think I could be happier.* Her thoughts turned into a prayer, *Thank You, Almighty Father, for changing my entire life.*

Liberty wondered if she should have gone with Matthew to San Francisco. He'd left two nights ago, saying he would ride to Santa Rosa the first night and then catch a train to San Francisco. She, for some reason, had a nagging feeling something wasn't right. *Father, why do I feel this way? Is there something wrong? I lift Matthew up to You and ask for Your protection and care to hedge him in. Help him, Father, to be wise as a serpent and innocent as a dove. Now, why would I pray that? Thank You, Holy Ghost, for interceding on my behalf.* She opened her green eyes but closed them quickly as she felt her mouth water up with nausea. *I've felt this way all week. Perhaps I have—* Liberty ran to the bathroom and was sick in the chamber pot. Conchita had heard her running footsteps and followed her down the hall.

"Mees Libertee, I geet some honey an' crackers to settle your tummy." Conchita was the Rancho's cook and main housekeeper. Although she deferred in all things to Liberty, she was a stanchion in the Bannister household. When Liberty had first come west, it was Conchita who had welcomed her with open arms, making her feel at home and a part of the family. Since her first night, Liberty and Conchita had been kindred spirits.

Conchita came back with crackers and honey. She was a short, rounded woman with glossy black hair that always hung in a braid down her back. She felt everything was solved by eating honey.

"Mees Libertee, thees ees good for you an' the baby."

Liberty smiled. "Conchita, I'm not pregnant…I can't have children. I was married to Armand for thirteen years and never could have a baby."

"Eet muss not be you, Mees Libbee, you carry Meester Bannister's baby. Trust me, I know eet ees truth."

Liberty sat back on her heels, stunned, her eyes rounded in surprise. She munched on a honey-coated cracker as she stared at Conchita. Counting back in her mind, she wondered, *Can it be true, Lord? Am I expecting a baby? How can this be? Was it Armand and not me? Oh Lord, can I really be pregnant? Can I?* Excitement began to bubble up within as her thoughts jumped here and there. *Can I really be?*

She licked her fingers of the excess honey and stood. "I'll get my journal, Conchita. I've believed for over fourteen years that I was barren. Was it truly Armand and not me?" She went back to the great room, Conchita trailing after her, and began to thumb through her journal. She looked back several pages and realized it'd been two months since her last menstrual flow. Never missing once since she was twelve, she looked in wonder at Conchita.

"But, I never thought to have children…oh Conchita, can you believe it?" She arose, grabbed Conchita by the arms, and danced around the great room. The two women laughed and danced until breathless. Falling onto the sofa, Libby's face looked full of wonder.

"Matthew's going to be so surprised. We'll fix up one of the bedrooms and…oh Conchita! I need to ride over to Liberty's Landing and tell Granny and Papa." She strode down the hall to the bedroom and sat in a chair, pulling on her long leather boots. She glanced at the coat tree by the door as she picked up her hat. Matthew had a couple hats hanging on it. *And, why do I still have this nagging feeling about Matthew? Lord, please protect him.* She went outside to saddle up Pookie, but Diego said he'd do it. He was Conchita's husband and foreman of Rancho Bonito. He pushed back his sombrero, letting it fall onto his back, the thong ties snug at his neck.

"Mees Libertee, ees everything all right?"

"Yes, why do you ask?" She shaded her eyes with her hand to better see the expression in his. It was sunny, but in the distance, clouds looked threatening. It had rained off and on all morning.

"I doan noh, Mees Lebee. I just haf the bad feeling. You know...*muy malo*," he replied.

Very bad. He's saying very bad, so he has the same feeling I have about Matthew. "You have this feeling about Matthew?"

"*Sí.*"

"I know what you're saying. I've had it all morning, a bad feeling since I got up. I'm not one to borrow trouble, but something just doesn't feel right. Did Matthew say anything at all to you before he left?"

"He only say to mee, he go north to see the Henerson's vineyard, then he go to San Franceesco. He be gone for seex days."

"Yes, that's what he told me, too. I wonder if we should wire Alex? Matthew was supposed to stay with him last night. Pray for him, Diego. We need to pray, since both of us are feeling something's not right. Thanks for saddling Pookie. I'm going over to talk to Papa and Granny. I'll probably stay there for lunch. No doubt Cook will want to fatten me up."

Diego clasped his fingers together and bent down. Liberty stepped into his hand, and he hoisted her onto Pookie, handing her the reins.

"Thank you, Diego." Libby looked down at Matthew's faithful foreman. "And remember, please pray for Matthew."

"*Sí*, Mees Libbee, I weel do eet."

CHAPTER IV

(I) will give him a white stone, and in the stone

a new name written, which no man knoweth

saving he that receiveth it.

REVELATION 2:17b

THE DINING ROOM WAS PLEASANTLY WARM. Floor-to-ceiling windows lined the east wall and glass doors on either end of the room led to a patio and gardens below. It had started to rain, and fires burned cheerfully in their grates at both ends of the lengthy room. A long mahogany sideboard graced the wall opposite the windows, its entire top made of marble. Walls painted rusty red held lit sconces, and hanging over the long mahogany table two chandeliers, their crystals glittering, lit the room with an elegant glow.

The table was set with china, beautiful crystal, and heavy silver, lending an air of graciousness and refinement. When any family or guests came to visit, Caitlin and her father had eaten in the dining room along with Ewen. If it was just the three of them, they ate in the kitchen, not bothering about the formalities. Every Sunday had been an exception. They invariably dressed up and ate their main meal in the dining room.

This evening was no different, and dinner was being placed on the table; Sweeny and McDuffy were serving. As Caitlin, Gavin, and Maisie were about to sit, the huge cowbell by the front door rang out. Dora McDuffy hurried to get it. She'd been with the family for over twenty years and was a pleasant-faced woman with her own suite of rooms in the McCaully house.

"Doctor Addison, why, how nice to see you!"

"Hello, Mrs. McDuffy. We're riding from the Pindars' and were so close, I thought I'd stop and check on Mac while I'm here."

When the doctor said the name Mac, the nameless man's ears perked up a bit, but then his shoulders slumped. Mac wasn't a familiar name.

Dora McDuffy looked at the doctor, nonplussed and speechless.

Caitlin, who'd been ready to sit down, hurried to the door. As she entered the front hall, a gust of wind blew in from the porch.

"Come in, Doc, come on in out of the rain and your friend with you," Caitlin said. Dora McDuffy went to set two more places at the long table, knowing Caitlin would invite the men in to eat. Maisie and Gavin stood waiting in the dining room for the visitors. They could hear the conversation.

The two men took off their dripping hats. The doctor took off his coat, but the man had only a vest, which he futilely brushed off. Both were thoroughly wet. Doc didn't introduce the man, which Cait thought strange.

"Why don't you come on into the dining room and join us for dinner? We were just about to sit down and there's plenty." She said to the doctor, "I thought it strange you didn't come to the funeral yesterday, but you've been out of town, haven't you? Da died three days ago, Doc. I'm sorry to have to tell you that. We were all hoping for a miracle...that somehow he would recover." Her gray eyes filled with tears, and Doc pulled her into his arms. He was not only their family doctor but a good friend of the family for years.

"I'm so sorry, Caitlin. I know this whole ordeal has been hard on you. I didn't realize he was that close last time I checked on him."

She pulled back and wiped at her eyes. "Well, come on in. The food will get cold."

They entered the dining room and the doctor said hello to Maisie and Gavin and started to introduce them to the man, but he paused and explained.

"I've been down at Zebidiah Pindar's for the past two days. Stayed at the inn in Santa Rosa the last two nights. This man here got bashed in the head and robbed. Zeb found him on his way home from the mine." He nodded at Gavin, who owned the mine. "Lindsey May's been caring for him. Problem is, he can't remember who he is yet. I know it'll come back, but it may take some time."

The people around the table looked a bit askance at the man. None had ever been around someone who didn't know who he was. Caitlin motioned for them to be seated. Gavin sat at the head of the table with his wife on his right and Caitlin on his left. The doctor sat next to Caitlin and the man sat next to Maisie.

Caitlin turned to the doctor. "It's not our custom, but I know you like to say grace, so why don't you go ahead."

The doctor bowed his head; the others followed suit. "Dear Lord, how we thank Thee and give Thee praise. I pray for the McCaully family, that Thou wouldst bring comfort and strength during this time of loss. We also pray for this man who's lost his memory…that Thou wouldst restore him. Thank Thee, Father, for this food. May we give Thee praise for Thy bountiful provision. Amen."

"Thank you, Doctor Addison," the man said for the first time. "Also"—he turned to look at Caitlin— "thank you for your hospitality. Is there a place I could wash up before I eat?" He smiled politely at the people around the table, but his head was pounding with every beat of his heart. All he wanted was to go to bed and sleep to escape the misery.

"Certainly." Gavin got up and led the man down the hall to the lower landing commode room. He pointed to the water and a glassed commode holding the chamber pot. "Please help yourself." He closed the door behind him but waited in the hall for the man to finish. Gavin felt sorry for him. He couldn't imagine not knowing who he was. He'd noticed the man's clothes, items he'd wear himself if out riding here on the ranch.

As the man came out of the room, his gaze focused on Gavin. "Sorry I took so long. My head is splitting, and I tried to wash my face but bending over the basin wasn't worth the effort," he said with a rueful smile.

"I didn't mind waiting. They're just now serving dinner and we're not missing anything. I'm sorry for you. It would be dreadful not to know who you are or where you hail from."

Gavin led him back to the dining room, where they sat down as McDuffy began serving. She had poured water into the glasses and asked, "You don't want any of this do you, Doc?" She waved a bottle of wine at him.

"No thanks, Dora."

"Would you like a glass?" she asked, turning to the nameless man.

"Yes, yes I would, in fact I…" His voice trailed away. He looked embarrassed.

"I suppose it would be nice if you could come up with a name for me."

McDuffy, who was pouring the dark liquid into the stemmed glass as he spoke, looked surprised at the request.

Gavin replied as he picked up his glass, "Let's first toast to total recollection for this man, here, here."

Everyone joined in, Caitlin and the doctor raising glasses of clear, cold water.

The nameless man took a sip. "Mmm, this is a nice Merlot. Whose is it?"

Everyone looked at him and wondered how he could tell what type of wine it was.

He glanced up at the questioning faces. "Reckon I know something about wine."

Caitlin gazed at the man. "You certainly do. I don't care for wine myself, but I know what is served at my table, and this is a Merlot from Henderson's just north of here. I'm glad you like it."

"Henderson's…Henderson's…now why does that sound familiar?" The man still felt nauseated from his headache.

Gavin began to dish up mashed potatoes, and the doctor put a large piece of fried chicken breast onto his plate.

Caitlin was glad Aidan and Jared were on their way home. It was a pleasant meal.

They talked a lot about Mac, laughing at some of the memories. Maisie and Gavin shared their dreams and aspirations for the gemstone company. Gavin pumped Caitlin for information about where she was going, but she wouldn't budge in her resolve to keep her whereabouts quiet.

"So, Caitlin, are you going to continue running cattle?" Gavin was curious as to how his sister-in-law planned to proceed now that Mac was gone.

"Ye-es, at least for the time being. I'm really not sure about the future. Many of the ranches are beginning to convert to produce. I've actually been doing some reading and researching about grapes, oranges, and nuts. Da thought we should begin turning into a vineyard or something besides cattle. Since I don't drink, it doesn't make sense to have a vineyard. I wouldn't know a good wine from a bad one."

"Why *don't* you drink, little sister?" Maisie had always been too busy with her own life to be very curious about her younger sister. She realized she loved Caitlin. She knew her father had been the protector, but now that he was gone, she appointed herself Caitlin's protector.

"I don't like it. I love fruit juices and don't need nor want alcohol." She toyed with the apple pie Mrs. Dunstan had made. Duney, everyone called her.

"I know how to grow grapes. If you want to convert, I'm quite sure I could help you. I'm going to need employment and a place to stay until my memory comes back." The man looked openly across the table at Caitlin.

I'm looking at gray eyes, he thought, so why do I see eyes as green as new moss in my head? He could see those eyes as clearly as if they were in front of him.

"Well, I'm now owner of this ranch, and you're hired. I'd like you to stay here at the house, and I'll have Ewen meet you. He's the ranch foreman and usually joins us for dinner but had to ride into town for something. I know this is a snap decision, but I'd like to put about three hundred acres into grapes. That's what Da wanted, and I'm going to try it." She took a last bite of her apple pie, wondering if she should tell this man of her intentions to be gone.

Gavin looked at Caitlin and grinned. "You are so like Mac it takes my breath away."

"I wonder if that's wise, Cait." Maisie stirred the pie crumbs on her plate. She was as open as Mac when it came to saying her mind. Raising her eyes to meet Cait's across the expanse of the table, she continued. "For one thing, you don't know this man, you don't know if he truly knows about grape growing. He can taste, but how do you know he won't go off and leave you hanging if he remembers who he is? What if he's from back east and just out here visiting? I'd think twice if I were you."

"Well, he *looks* honest. I can tell by his eyes."

Maisie sighed. "Jared looks honest, doesn't he? Look what a bum he's turned out to be."

Caitlin stared at her sister for a moment. "No, Maisie, Jared never looked honest to me, nor to Da either, for that matter. Da, in truth, told Aidan flat out not to marry him, as did I." She turned to the stranger. "So, have you thought of a name for yourself?"

He looked at her blankly for a moment before replying. "N-no, I haven't."

"Conor," the doctor said, "we're going to call him Conor. That way, Ewen will take a liking to him. It's such a good Irish name. Conor... let's see...Conor..."

"Innes," Maisie supplied, "Conor Innes. With a good Irish name like that, you'll fit in just fine." She smiled at the man, satisfied with his new name. He smiled back. Maisie thought him incredibly handsome with his deep-set blue eyes and dark brown hair. The chandelier cast a glow on his head, bringing out some reddish highlights.

"Thank you. It's strange, but I feel better knowing I have a name, even if it's not my true one."

Caitlin gave the man a measured look. "I'd like to talk to you, Conor, in Mac's...in the library." She finished her sentence with tears in her eyes that threatened to spill over. "Doc, why don't you spend the night? It's getting late and we have a comfortable bed waiting for you."

The doctor looked at her gratefully. "Think I'll take you up on that, Caitlin. I'm pretty tuckered out and twelve more miles of riding tonight sounds a bit much to me at this point. Also, I happen to know Conor isn't the first person to get his head bashed on that road. There's been a rash of robberies lately, and I don't wish to be riding after dark." He looked around the table and had everyone's attention.

Gavin asked, "Do you mean the main road? Why, that goes right past my mine."

"Yes, that's where the problem's been."

"Does Sheriff Rowe know about this?"

"Yes, he does, although I can't say I've seen him do anything about it." He added, "Sure was a mighty fine dinner. You tell Duney she's a wonderful cook, compliments of me."

Gavin and Maisie had already decided to spend the night, but Gavin was visibly upset that robberies were taking place, and no one had been arrested.

He spoke again. "I hope Jared and Aidan will be all right. Part of their ride home will be in the dark."

"Well," the doctor said, "so far, all the attacks have been on men riding alone."

"I'm sure they'll be all right, Gavin." Pushing back from the table, Caitlin stood and announced, "I need to spend a few minutes with Conor. We'll forego the customary 'men only' time, and Maisie, you can stay here and enjoy the male company...Gavin, Doc..." She nodded at the two men and led Conor to the library, having neatly dispensed with the practice of women leaving men to drink, talk, and smoke if they so desired. She consciously straightened her shoulders as she walked. Caitlin felt incredibly tired.

CHAPTER V

I will greatly praise the LORD with my mouth;
yea, I will praise him among the multitude.

PSALM 109:30

CONOR TRAILED BEHIND CAIT. As he walked down the hall he thought, *It's interesting, but I don't feel uncomfortable at all...I must be used to comfort and nice things.* Entering the library behind her, he looked around him in appreciation. It was lovely. The walls were a salmon color with dark mahogany for shelves, desk, and door trim. A large carved mahogany mantel graced one end wall over a fire that burned cheerfully in the grate. Four chairs, two facing two, had been placed by the fire, with a low, square table in between.

Conor looked at the books and knew he loved them. He walked slowly past a few shelves, pausing to look at titles. *I have that one,* he thought. *I'm a man of means, or I've come from money. I don't know which. I'm so frustrated. I feel as if I have pressing business to accomplish and what it is, who I am, only God knows. I do know I have faith that God will sort this out. When Doctor Addison prayed, I knew that I have a personal relationship with Jesus Christ. Lord, please help me. Help me to know who I am and where my family is.*

Caitlin gestured to a chair facing her. Conor seated himself and looked across at this beautiful woman. He felt no attraction at all. *She's beautiful but I believe I must be taken. I keep seeing a pair of green eyes full of love for me. I hope my head's not going to pound until I remember who I am. I pray not.*

Waiting until the distant look in his eyes faded, Cait wondered what he was thinking. She sat back and stared at the fire. Glancing at him, she could see he was ready.

She sat forward as she began to talk. "All right, Conor Innes, there is something about you that makes me trust you. I cannot begin to tell you how glad I am that you came here tonight. I'm sure you guessed this evening, Maisie is my sister. We have another sister, Aidan Hart. Her husband, Jared, was upset with the way my father distributed his holdings. The truth is, he was upset even before the reading of the will. I was out in the barn in a stall, down on my knees, bottle feeding a calf whose mother can't nurse. I overheard a conversation yesterday, and Jared, at least I'm quite sure it was Jared, along with one of my hired hands, is planning to do away with me."

Conor fixed his eyes on her, trying to listen to what she was saying. His head still throbbed with a steady beat, but the pain had lessened a bit. His eyes widened at the import of her words.

"You do believe me, don't you?"

"I don't have any reason to disbelieve you…and yes, some men will do anything for money."

Caitlin sat back in her chair, relieved the man believed her. "Well, it's true. I'm quite sure it was Jared. My mind doesn't want to believe it, but my ears and gut say it was him. The problem is, I have no clue who, among the men working for me, would be willing to hit me in the head with a horseshoe or be sure an accident happens when I'm out riding or repairing fence. Is there only one, or more than one? Are they McCaully hired hands? We have fifteen ranch hands and about twenty-five hundred head of cattle. We'll be separating out the yearling calves and branding next week. The rest we'll take to market. What I wanted to say to you is, I need some eyes and ears. I need someone to ferret out who is not amenable to me being boss. I was planning to leave here tonight, but now I'm going to wait until early morning. Jared and Aidan didn't stay the night here the way I thought they would. I'll ride out early tomorrow morning. I have a post office box in Napa that I'll check at least once a week."

"Where will you stay?" Conor was thinking that if an emergency arose, waiting until she checked her box wouldn't be such a good plan.

"I'm not disclosing that to anyone. That way, I don't have to worry about someone letting it slip."

"If this Jared fellow and someone else is looking for you, they'll be checking all the hotels between here and San Francisco, at least I would. In truth, I'd probably set the Pinkerton's out to find you if I needed to know where you'd gone. They can ferret out anything."

"Yes, I understand that. Jared, if indeed it is Jared, will do anything to get me out of the way. I believe where I am going I'll be perfectly safe."

"Well, miss, I'll be praying for you."

Caitlin looked at him, surprised. "Thank you, that's a real comfort and no mistake."

"Now, about your plan to convert to grapes. Do you think that's a wise idea at this juncture? If you do, would you like me to buy rootstalk? Do you want me to start planting? You'll need quite a number of people to start plowing the soil and taking the rocks out, besides doing the planting. It won't be your hired hands that'll be doing that. Men used to running cattle will resent becoming farmers. I don't know how I know that, but I do." He smiled at the woman sitting across from him.

Caitlin smiled back, thinking him handsome, but her mind was racing, doing some rethinking.

"I think you're right. Do you know much about cattle? If I want you to figure out who's involved with Jared, it might be better if you're involved with the men. You can make a better assessment if you're working with them. I know one of them must be involved, I just don't know who, nor if there's more than one. Perhaps it would be better, too, if you stay in one of the bunkhouses instead of in here. That way, you might be privy to more information. I'll pay you well and start with an advance in case you need some personal items."

It was the first time she'd paid attention to his attire. It looked fairly casual, but she could see the vest wasn't cheap, and his boots were beautiful. The shirt and denims were not off the rack. *Who is he? I'll bet he's asking that about himself more than I am.*

Liberty paused on a hill sitting astride Pookie and overlooked her land, which abutted Matthew's. She still thought of it as her land, but she'd deeded it to her father. He, along with Liberty's grandmother, lived in the beautiful house Liberty had built the year before her marriage to Matthew. It was an imposing structure sitting half way up the hill on the other side of a small valley. The terra-cotta blended in well with the surroundings. *My papa has done such a wonderful job of landscaping. The house doesn't have that forlorn new look that many houses just built have. It looks as if it's been there for some time. My, but look at the rows and rows of vines…he's done a lot of work. Lord, thank You again for such a wonderful family. I couldn't ask for more, and yet You've seen fit to give me a baby. My cup runneth over, Father. Thank You for Your bountiful blessings…how great You are.* She continued to sit quietly, praising God and looking at the house He'd given her over a year ago.

Often, the house was full of children. Liberty's twin brother, whom everyone called Alex to distinguish him from his father, Alexander, had a houseful of children. They'd added another girl last October and this past June, Emily, Alex's wife, had announced another baby on the way.

Let's see, this new one will make six—whew, that's a goodly number. What will Matthew think about us having a baby? Oh, Lord…I think Conchita's right. You are blessing Matthew and me. I'm so glad for doing it right. We could have gone ahead and been intimate with each other; after all, neither of us were virgins, but I'm so glad we waited. What a blessing it always is when we do it the right way. Not thinking I could get pregnant, oh, I hate to think that I could have without being married, if we'd made the wrong decision. Thank You for protecting me, for filling me with enough love and helping me to grow in You. I know Matthew's going to be delighted about being a father. He sure enjoys holding Hannah.

Hannah was Sally Ann Brown's little girl. Sally Ann Brown, now Meeks, had been widowed when her husband had been murdered in Boston a day or two after Liberty's late husband, Armand. Sally Ann had come west and had lived with Liberty for more than six months, finally succumbing to Doctor John Meeks' wooing. She'd married the doctor and seemed quite happy. Doctor John had fallen head over heels in love with Sally Ann upon first sight of her. Sally Ann was now expecting a baby. *Let me see, she's not yet twenty-one, and John acts as if he's the only one who's ever been excited to be a father. Wait until Matthew hears. Oh, Father, please protect him. I know with my whole being that something's not right. Father, I trust You with all of my heart. It's easy to make my own plans and then ask You to bless them. It's harder to wait upon You, which is what Your Word says for me to do. I know that You know what is best. May I accept all that comes my way, knowing that Your hand filtered it. How thankful I am that my trust is in You, who will never abuse it.*

Liberty wondered if Diego had told Kirk of his feelings concerning Matthew. Kirk was Matthew's younger brother and lived at the Rancho. *Father, how thankful I am that because of the change Kirk saw in Matthew, he has come to know You as his personal Savior. What a change You have wrought in his life. The selfishness and wild ways are gone. Father, bless Kirk, too.* Liberty loved having a Father in heaven who loved her and answered prayer, not always the way she wanted, but in ways that were best in the long run.

Tapping her heels lightly against Pookie's sides, Liberty descended the slope at an easy canter. She looked where the shack used to stand, glad her father had torn it down. He'd built an arbor of grapes and a little pool of water from the well there as a memorial to God's protection on her life. She was thankful she had no bad memories or distaste of the place in which Jacques Corlay had waylaid her. She'd even been able to sit there and pray, thankful for the protection the Almighty God had given her. What Satan had meant for evil, God had turned to good. The only lasting result from Jacques Corlay's assault was when the weather changed, her arm ached where it had been broken. She'd become quite good at predicting major weather changes.

As Liberty rode down the valley floor, she was amazed at what her father had accomplished this past year. Grapes grew across the flat and up the sides of the hills surrounding the little valley. She rode over quite often, but she hadn't noticed the pool on the right near the base of the hill. She remembered there was a hot spring there. *Papa must have made the hot spring bathing area he's been talking about. Granny will adore that, I'm sure. A spa, she called it.* Liberty grinned. Riding up to the front of the mansion she'd had built, she admired its architecture and symmetry. It was beautiful. The vines she'd planted on the front porch had grown and wrapped the columns in their green loveliness. It was February, but it was not raining. The sun shone palely behind a sky studded with clouds that threatened rain. She could smell it; her arm ached with it.

Liberty dismounted and slapped her reins around the hitching post. She waited as they wrapped themselves around the cross bar sufficiently to hold Pookie safely. She gave the mare a couple pats and stroked her face.

As she walked into the house, she called out, "Granny, Papa, I'm here." She headed for the kitchen. Entering it, she still marveled at its homeyness. Her father and grandmother sat at the oak table, just starting to eat luncheon. They stood as she entered.

"Liberty! How lovely that you've come to visit. We so adore having you. I can't begin to tell you how much your Granny and I miss you living here." Her papa met her halfway across the room and gave her a huge hug. Wearing slender trousers and a white shirt open at the neck, he gave the appearance of being younger than his fifty-two years. Tall and slim, Alexander Liberty had the same coppery hair as Liberty, his sprinkled with gray.

"I love you, sweetheart."

"I love you, too, Papa." She returned his hug in full measure and walked to the table. She hugged Phoebe, her grandmother, and sat down, but got up again when she realized Cook was busily dishing up her meal. Liberty hadn't seen her when she entered. She hugged the faithful cook who'd traveled west just to be with her. Libby stretched her arms around the woman's wide girth and pulled her to herself.

Still holding Mrs. Jensen's middle, she said, "I love you, Cook."

"I luff you, too, Miss Libby, an' I haf missed you, too."

Liberty washed her hands as Cook looked on with loving eyes.

Mrs. Jensen was a superb cook. She patted Liberty on the cheek before retreating to her stove. She loved Liberty as if she were her own daughter.

Alexander Liberty gazed at his daughter, his heart overflowing with love. He hadn't known for nearly thirty years she'd even existed. His beautiful gray eyes drank her in.

"I'm thankful to the Lord for giving me a daughter such as you."

"Thank you, Papa, I feel the same about you. I'm very thankful." She turned to Mrs. Jensen and said, "Umm, I love your stroganoff, Cook. You must have known I was coming over. It smells delicious."

"You yust sit down an' eat. You look too tin, Madam Bannister. What dat Conchita feed you anyway?"

"Liberty, just call me Liberty or Libby. 'Madam' always brings back too many memories I'd rather forget."

"Ja, I like to forget some of dem too."

"Let me pray," Phoebe said. "I want to eat while it's still hot."

They all bowed their heads. "Lord, how grateful we are for Thy wondrous care. We thank Thee for the comfort we enjoy, the friendships and family we love, and we are grateful for food, which gives us physical strength. Most of all, we are grateful for Thy Son who gave His life so that we might have life everlasting. We thank Thee. Amen."

Liberty and Alexander also said "amen," and Alexander crossed himself.

CHAPTER VI

"But he knoweth the way that I take;

when he hath tried me, I shall come forth as gold.

JOB 23:10

ALEXANDER, PHOEBE, AND LIBERTY caught up on news while they enjoyed their meal. Liberty conveyed the uncomfortable foreboding she felt about Matthew and that Diego shared her feelings.

"I've been feeling all morning as if something is not right. Diego told me, just before I rode over, that he is feeling the same way about Matthew…Diego's not one to say anything unless he feels strongly about it."

"When is Matthew expected back from San Francisco?" Phoebe asked.

"Well, not for four more days, but Granny, I never feel like this. I wanted to share with you mainly to ask you to pray especially hard for Matthew because I just know something's not right. It's as if God is impressing that upon my heart."

Alexander nodded. "We'll both be sure to do that. No sense borrowing trouble, but if you're feeling upset and Diego is too, it's not to be ignored."

"Thank you, Papa. I know you're a man of prayer." She patted his arm and he put his hand over hers and gently squeezed.

"I suppose one thing I've learned over the years," Alexander said, "is that I can sit and think and stew over something, or I can take it to the Lord in prayer and lay it at his feet. Sometimes, I pick up the burden again and have to pray and lay it back down. It's not healthy for us to be anxious about things. That's why the Bible tells us not to be anxious about anything. We are to believe God will take care of it when we give it over to him."

"I do know that," Liberty replied, "but it's good to be reminded of it now and then."

Phoebe grinned, changing the subject. "Libby, did you see the pool your papa's putting in where the hot spring is?"

"I did," she said with an answering grin, "bet you're glad about that, aren't you?"

"Yes, and you will be too once you get into it. Alexander's going to plant trees around it and make it a secluded spot. Hope I live long enough to enjoy that added feature." She smiled widely at her granddaughter.

"Oh, Granny, you're not ill, are you?" Libby asked. She'd only known her grandmother for a year and a half and surely didn't want to lose her.

"Pshaw, child, I'm healthy as your horse. I'd just like to bathe in the all-together before I die." She laughed when she saw Liberty's expression.

Liberty, her eyes widening, knew her granny meant, bathe naked. She giggled and the two women laughed together, gray eyes meeting green, both sparkling with humor.

"You would, wouldn't you?" Libby was laughing, holding her sides, thinking about her grandmother soaking outside in the hot water. She giggled again.

Alexander smiled at both women. "It's going to take quite some time before trees can make that kind of privacy. Maybe I'll just grow a thick arbor of grapes there. It'll grow faster than trees and not make quite the mess with leaves." Alexander adored his mother, and if it was in his power to do something to make her happier, he'd do it.

The meal was perfection, and Liberty did it justice. She'd lost all her breakfast. In truth, she'd lost breakfast all week. She leaned her elbows on the table, her hands holding her chin, as she listened to her papa talk about his grapes.

Libby tried to get Cook to join them for dessert, a chocolate confection of almonds, bits of chocolate, and cream. "Well, if you won't join us to eat, I want you to sit here for a few minutes…please?" Liberty patted the chair next to her.

"Get a cup of coffee first. I have something to tell all of you. I want you to be in on this conversation. After all, you've known me for fifteen years, Cook. I am so excited I can scarcely contain myself. I only got the news this morning from Conchita." She smiled and patted the chair next to her again. Phoebe looked at her granddaughter curiously, and Alexander folded his arms across his chest. Cook poured her coffee and waddled to the table.

Liberty toyed with the remains of her dessert. She took a sip of coffee and looked first at Cook, then at her granny, and lastly, she took a long look at her papa. She savored the moment.

"I know what a blessing it is when Alex and Emily come up from San Francisco to visit with their brood of children. I was thinking about them on my way over here. They are now expecting their sixth baby. How blessed I am to have them and both of you in my life. Of course, you all know I thought for over twenty-nine years that Jacques was my father. He, being a partner with the man he made me marry, was awful. They were both so evil."

Cook interrupted her. "Oh my yes…dey vas so evil."

Liberty continued, "Armand's being murdered was horrible, but I was so relieved I couldn't mourn. Armand and Jacques damaged or destroyed many lives. At first, being married to Armand, I was sorrowful that I couldn't have children. Later, when I realized how evil he was, I became grateful to be barren and not have a child of Armand's.

"I suppose you all know Elijah has been disbursing monies from the companies I own and restoring some of the companies back to the men who owned them, or to their widows. I never wanted the companies Armand took by his pernicious ways. I want no part of reaping from a harvest of ill-gotten gain. That being said, I want you to know…" Tears flooded her eyes as she looked at each person around the table. Her gaze fixed on Alexander. "I want you to know I'm expecting a baby."

Phoebe clasped her hands over her heart. "Oh, my," she exclaimed, "oh my! Oh, praise the Lord!"

Cook's head jerked up at the news. Tears of joy rolled down her cheeks. "Dat is da beste news. Oh, Miss Liberty, dat is da beste news!"

"Hallelujah! Praise be to God for this wondrous gift!" Alexander jumped up and swept Liberty into his arms. They began to dance around the kitchen floor. Liberty started laughing. "Oh, it's so good to be alive and…so good to be so happy!"

Caitlin hoped Conor, or whatever his name was, would be able to hold his own. If he could find out who was involved with Jared, it would solve her problems. Jared had made his intentions clear. *I wonder if Conor knows anything about ranching. My ranch hands will wonder what in the world I'm doing if he's not a hard worker. He seems honest, and that's the most important thing. That poor man probably has family waiting for him someplace. Not knowing who you are must be horrible.* Her thoughts swung to the ranch. *I hope he can find out who has thrown in his lot with Jared. Most of my problems would be solved if we could find out who wants me out of the way. I know things are beginning to get rundown around here, not enough money in cattle anymore. I know that's why Da thought we should look to grapes. He didn't want that any more than me, but what is a body to do? The cattle aren't bringing in enough money. I've got to figure something out. Guess I'll worry about that problem later.*

Caitlin had awakened at three thirty and lay there, hoping to go back to sleep. Her mind would not shut off, so she donned the clothes Sweeny had laid out the night before.

She strapped on her leather holster and tied the thongs around her leg. Quickly drawing her gun, she felt as if she'd slowed down a bit. *Perhaps I need more practice, or maybe I'm slow because I'm so tired.* She tiptoed to the kitchen and grabbed some fried chicken left over from dinner. She took some of Duney's wonderful hard rolls and reached into the cooler for some butter. She split them and smeared butter on several rolls. Wrapping them in newsprint, she stuffed all the food into her satchel.

Under the cover of darkness, Caitlin slipped out the back door and ran lightly toward the stable. She filled her canteen at the pump on the way.

She had purloined a few lumps of sugar from the kitchen and took one out of her satchel for Fire, who whickered softly and stomped impatiently in his stall as she opened the stable door. Blowing out his nostrils, he stomped again, his tail flicking. Cait went to the tack room and lifted his heavy saddle off the saddle rack. She carried it to Fire's stall and threw it over the wooden slats. She slipped into his stall and held her hand out flat with the sugar lump in it. She talked to the great horse in a soft voice. Fire was tame but his spirit was not broken. The two had a mutual understanding, a certain respect for one another. He took the lump delicately with his lips, obviously savoring its sweetness.

Fire was gorgeous, a shiny gray with a darker mane, tail, legs, and head. His name came from his fiery temper when he was a colt. It was a wonder he'd let anyone tame him. It had taken much patience on Caitlin and Mac's part. Cait slid the bit easily into his mouth and slipped the reins over his head. He shook his head up and down, and Cait patted him, crooning love words. She threw the saddle blanket over his back and pulled it away from his withers. Hoisting the saddle was the hardest part. Fire stood sixteen hands high. Mac had always been amazed she could throw a saddle over the roan, but she was tall and strong. In grief, she leaned her head against Fire's barrel for a moment. Her eyes filled with tears for the loss of her da. He'd been coherent until a few days before his death. She knew she was overtired and brushed the tears away impatiently. Still, she leaned her head against Fire. *I'm not only mourning Da, I'm mourning a relationship with Aidan that will probably never happen. I sorrow to leave McCaully Ranch. I reckon I'm being a baby, but oh…how I wish things were different. I feel so alone without Da…so alone.* She wiped her eyes again, sniffed, and let out a big, broken sigh.

She grabbed the girth and buckled it tightly, thankful Fire didn't blow himself up the way some horses did, which made another tightening necessary. Caitlin rustled under the hay, found her scabbard with her rifle in it, and brushed the straw away. She hooked it over the saddle horn. She found the saddlebag she'd hidden and checked to see if she'd put a box of bullets in it. She had.

Leading the big roan out of the stable, Cait closed the big door as quietly as she could, sliding the wooden latch into place. *Sure don't want to wake up any of the ranch hands,* she thought as she picked up the satchel she'd dropped by the door and fastened it to Fire's saddle. Cait held the pommel and jumped for the stirrup. Fire held steady and she was up, swinging her leg over. She had never ridden sidesaddle. None of her sisters had either. She walked Fire noiselessly down the long drive of the house. She guessed it must be close to four thirty. Caitlin kicked at his sides. Keeping her heels well down, they rode off at a steady canter.

Jared Hart was angry. He'd gone to bed quite late, even for him— after two in the morning. He woke with a raging headache, having imbibed too much whiskey the night before.

Aidan was asleep beside him on her back, her dark hair spread out over the pillow. One arm was flung over her head, the other crossed her breast. He wished she'd sleep in her own rooms. He liked privacy and he was tired of her clinging ways.

He stomped down the stairs in a vile temper. He wanted another drink or a pot of coffee. He went into the study and looked at the mantel clock. Seeing it was nearly nine, he kicked at an ottoman in frustration, and his toe stung as a result. He cursed and headed toward the kitchen for coffee.

Cassie already finished making breakfast. She tried to keep it warm without spoiling it. Usually breakfast was done by this time of morning.

"Good morning, Mr. Jared." Cassie could see by his face he was in one of his rages. She said nothing more and started to dish him up.

"Leave it," he said harshly, "all I want is coffee." He took the cup she handed him and walked back to the study. He sat by the fire and contemplated his next move. His headache was no better. *I wanted to be over to the ranch early this morning. Got to get my hands on some money... soon. My life won't be worth cow dung if I don't pay back those gambling debts. What'd McGregor tell me? Yeah, I have until the end of the month to pay back at least half of it. The second half is due the middle of March. I've got to find some money in a hurry. What am I going to do?*

Jared sat back in the big leather chair and sipped the coffee. His head throbbed and he couldn't focus on any one thought. His mind jumped from one thing to the next, but none moved him any closer to figuring out how to get hold of some money. He needed cash and he needed it now. Maybe he should just take the money Aidan had inherited. The only problem with that was she wouldn't sign any money over to him. He'd already tried that route. If he took it without her consent, he'd be booted out of the house. Of that, he had no doubt.

How in the world am I going to get my hands on some money? He set his coffee cup down on the end table and reached beside his chair. Feeling around, his hand touched cool glass. He grasped the neck, pulled it up, and peered at its contents. The bottle wasn't empty.

CHAPTER VII

Hear me when I call, O God of my righteousness:
thou hast enlarged me when I was in distress;
have mercy upon me, and hear my prayer.

PSALM 4:1

ELIJAH HUMPHRIES AWOKE EARLY and lay thanking the Almighty for another day. He praised God every single day for healing Abigail, his wife. She was the love of his life and had been dying when they lived in Boston. The Almighty God had seen fit to heal her.

As he lay there, he thought how grateful he was that Liberty wanted to give back the companies to the original owners or their surviving families. Elijah had been Armand's lawyer, not by choice, but by bad luck of the draw among his business partners. Liberty's dead husband, Armand Bouvier, and supposed father, Jacques Corlay, had been evil business partners cheating men out of their companies. A couple men had committed suicide rather than face the ruination of their finances. *Today, I'm going to get rid of that last company.*

Elijah was to ride to San Francisco this morning. The plan was to meet with Alex Johnson…whose name should have been Alex Liberty. *He certainly looks like his father. I look forward to seeing him.* Alex had sent a wire saying there was a snag in the company, and he needed help from Elijah, who had given him all the paperwork he'd found in a secret compartment of Armand's desk. Before sending them, Elijah had gone over the papers quite closely but wanted another set of eyes in case he'd missed something.

Alex was Liberty's twin brother, and after nearly thirty years of not knowing each other existed, they'd been brought together. Elijah planned to spend at least a couple nights in the big city. He looked forward to it...he loved Alex's children and was a surrogate grandfather to them.

Alex Johnson had been practicing law in San Francisco years before Liberty had moved west. He and his wife, Emily, had five children and one on the way. Emily had no parents and Elijah and Abigail had no children. It was a perfect fit, and Alex had asked Elijah and Abigail to step in as if they were Emily's parents, to be grandparents to the children. They couldn't love the children any more than if they were their real grandchildren. They spent many a happy hour playing with the children either in San Francisco or in San Rafael or at Liberty's in Napa.

Elijah reminisced about all that had transpired when Armand was murdered. He'd dropped by Liberty's manse in Boston simply to tell her she was not to inherit anything from her husband's estate except the property in California. He'd wanted to prepare her so it wouldn't come as such a shock in front of the others who would attend the reading of the will. Armand had spitefully cut Liberty, almost entirely, out of his will. Meeting the young woman, Elijah believed, had been ordained by God. He loved Liberty as if she were his own.

He thought of the events that had taken place. He left his practice in Boston, which had been a big step of faith. He knew, without a shadow of doubt, he and Abby had been called by the Almighty to open a mission for women in need of help.

The day they opened the mission, they'd had more than a hundred girls come to stay. What a miracle that had been, to have the mission sufficiently finished to accommodate them all. They now had three girls who had decided to stay on permanently.

Janne Nyegaard had been a huge asset to the mission. Fluent in five languages, she'd been instrumental when it first opened. She'd been one of the girls diverted to the wrong ship, kidnapped, and transported to San Francisco. She, along with the other girls, had sat in a warehouse waiting to be sold to the highest bidder. George Baxter, the chief detective of Boston, had broken wide open the ring of human traffickers. Now George, one of Elijah's best friends, was chief detective in San Francisco.

He thought about Janne for a few moments. Enrico Greenway, the mayor of San Rafael, had taken a real shine to her. Elijah wondered what the Nordic blonde thought of the mayor. He smiled at his thoughts. If Abigail had anything to do with it, Janne would be a married woman before long.

Elijah began to pray. He prayed for the next forty-five minutes. It was as necessary for Elijah to spend time with the Almighty as it was to breathe. He carved out time each day for his Maker. He knew if he didn't set aside time to spend with God, it would never happen. One day a month, he spent a couple hours silent before the Lord…simply adoring Him, or listening for His voice. Every night, before going to bed, he read a chapter in Proverbs that corresponded with the day of the month. In addition, he always had a book of the Bible he was studying. Elijah loved the Lord.

He got up quietly so as not to awaken Abby and padded into the bathroom to get ready for the day. He was ready spiritually. Now he needed to get ready physically. He always felt better when he shaved. He hated shaving, but when he was done he felt as if he'd completed a huge task. He sharpened his razor on the strop, sudsed his face with soap, and began to shave.

Conor Innes awoke slowly. He stretched and reached out his hand for…? He abruptly came fully awake. *I was stretching out my hand to touch someone.* His head felt better than the day before. *Who was I going*

to touch? The owner of those green eyes I keep seeing? Conor had spent the night in the main house but would move into the bunkhouse today. He could tell it was early, the sun not yet up. He automatically reached toward the nightstand for his pocket watch before remembering he no longer had one. It had been stolen along with his money, gun, and whatever else he'd carried on his person. He'd treasured that watch, it'd been his father's. *Ah, how do I remember that?*

He got up and shaved, using someone else's straight razor, strop, and soap. He dressed and went down to the kitchen.

The doctor was not yet up.

"Good morning, Mr. Innes. Miss Caitlin told me last night to take care of you. I have coffee right here, and the procedure around here is that you help yourself to whatever you want to eat."

"Good morning, ma'am, it's the same at my er...ah...well, we do that at my house, too." *So, what was I going to say, ranch? Oh Lord, please help me get back my memory.*

He took the large mug of coffee from her. "Thank you, it smells delicious. What's your name?" he asked as he started to sit down at the large oak table in the corner of the kitchen.

"It's Mrs. Dunstan. Mr. Innes, you need to go into the dining room. This table is for the hired help and family when no one's visitin'...an' folks around here just call me Duney."

"Well, Duney, I am hired help." He smiled as he sat at the scrubbed oak table. "Yes indeed, I'm hired help."

Duney smiled at this easygoing cowboy. "Oh, by the way..." Duney opened a drawer and withdrew a fairly new Smith & Wesson New Model Number Three revolver. She held it gingerly by the butt, her face reddening. She didn't like guns.

"Miss Caitlin put this in here for me to give to you."

Conor stood when she pulled the gun out. *Now, why does that gun bring those green eyes to my mind?* He lifted it but it didn't feel loaded. Checking to make sure, he opened the chamber. *Just as I thought...it's empty.*

"Here's a supply of bullets Miss Cait said you might be needing." Duney reached into the drawer again, glad the stuff would be out of her kitchen.

Conor breathed a sigh of relief that Miss McCaully had been so thoughtful. He had a tooled leather holster, but his gun had been stolen. He knew he didn't use this type of revolver, but he was familiar with it.

"Thanks, Duney, this sets my mind a little more to rest. I'm fairly certain I'm never without a gun. We've a lot of rattlesnakes in this area, you know."

"Well, it sets my mind to rest, too. I hate those things and certainly don't like having it in my kitchen drawer. Now, you get yourself some breakfast."

"Thank you, I'll do that shortly." He took the stairs two at a time and went to the room he'd slept in. He'd forgotten his gun belt. He gave the room a cursory look, but he didn't own anything else in it. Strapping on the holster, he put the gun into it. He drew quick as lightening and knew he was in practice. As he started to descend the stairs, he heard a noise behind him. He turned and saw an older man, probably in his early fifties, closing a door in the hall.

Ewen saw the young man and appraised him quickly.

"You must be the man Miss Caitlin wrote me a note about…you Conor Innes?"

"Yes, sir, I am." *For the time being,* he amended to himself. He stepped back up to the landing.

"Well, son, I'm Ewen Carr, foreman, and your boss, at least for now. Miss Cait didn't leave much of a note. She just said to expect you to be here and that you're moving into the bunkhouse today. I understand you can do the three r's: rope, ride, and repair fence. That's what I need around here." He stuck out his hand, and Conor shook it firmly and looked Ewen straight in the eye.

Ewen liked what he saw and nodded in affirmation. "Yep, it's what I need."

The two men went downstairs.

"Good morning, Ewen, an' how are you this fine morning?" Duney liked and respected Ewen. He was fair with the men and even tempered. He had a fine head of beautiful white hair that at one time had been fiery red. It laid flat with no part, always combed straight back from a long face with serious eyes. She was forever trying to get a twinkle into those frosty blue eyes, and sometimes she succeeded.

She handed him a fresh cup of coffee and turned to Conor. "I dumped yours. Here's a fresh cup for you too, son."

Ewen looked at Duney in surprise. *She must like this young man. She's usually standoffish with anyone new.* He took another long look at the man. *There's something about him that speaks of peace. He'll be a good addition to the ranch. There's been an uncomfortable atmosphere among the men, and I can't seem to get to the bottom of it. No one's talking, that's for sure.*

Caitlin made fairly good time. Dusk was beginning to fall and she saw a lamplighter down the main street when she reached San Rafael. She had no idea where she needed to go so she stopped at an imposing house on the edge of town. She knocked on the door and a pleasant-faced man answered.

"I'm looking for the mission located here…the mission for women?" Her statement came out more like a question. The man looked at her blankly for a second and then a smile lit up his brown face. "The Lord Almighty must have directed your steps, missy. The owner of this house opened the mission. The master, he done gone to San Francisco, but the mistress, she be at the mission right now." His eyes traveled to the hitching post. "We have a stable at the mission, missy, but if you'd like, we can stable your horse right here. He'd be taken care of for as long as you need."

Caitlin stared at the man for a minute, thinking fast. *If anyone traces me, it might be better to have Fire here than at the mission. On the other hand, if I have him at the mission I can make a fast get away if I need to. With Fire at the mission, I'll be able to see him without venturing out myself. He'll also need feeding and won't allow anyone else near him.*

"Thanks for your offer, but I think I'll keep him with me. He's never let anyone else besides my da…my father, ride him." This man had such sympathetic brown eyes that her gray ones filled with tears.

He put his hand out and patted her on the shoulder. "Missy, it'll be all right. I'm certain sure as anything, it'll be all right," he said gently. "Ya'll look straight down this heah street an' you'll be a seein' the mission right there, 'bout four ta five blocks down on the right hand side."

"Thank you, sir, and I'm sorry for losing control. I've been up since early this morning. I suppose I'm just plumb tuckered out."

"Oh, missy, I understand, believe me I do."

Thomas gave her a final pat on the shoulder and pointed down the street.

"You be askin' for Miss Abigail," he said. "Uh hum, you jest tell her Thomas sent you. Go on now."

"Thank you, Thomas, thank you very much."

Caitlin was so tired she had difficulty climbing on Fire. He was tuckered out too, she could tell. It'd be another good half hour of work, grooming, feeding, and watering him before she could rest herself. She found the mission and slipped down Fire's side. Carefully, she tied his reins to the hitching post. She reached up to unhook her satchel from the saddle and gave Fire a loving pat.

"I'll be right back, big boy."

Double iron-grilled gates enclosed the front walk of the mission. Caitlin unlatched one, making sure it closed behind her. It was heavy and clanged shut. She took a deep breath, wondering how long she would stay here.

Taking another big breath that ended in a sigh, she knocked on the door.

Abigail Humphries, who was ready to head home, opened the door and saw the young woman standing there looking tired and forlorn. Dusk was deepening to night, but the lamplighter had already been this way and the light from the street lamps cast a peaceful aura behind the girl. The glow of lamps inside lit the interior of the mission, creating a warm, welcoming atmosphere.

"Come in, child, come right on in. My name is Abigail Humphries, and you are most welcome to stay for as long as you want." She drew the younger woman inside.

"Thank you. Thomas sent me and told me to ask for you. I am going to need to take care of my horse first. He's had quite a day." Caitlin smiled tiredly at the older woman, whose beautiful blue eyes sparkled with warmth but without curiosity.

"Oh, I can get someone to groom him for you. You look pretty much done in."

"Thank you, but I'll need to do it. He won't let anyone else touch him. I don't know how long I'll need to stay, but I can help with food for my horse and for me. If someone could show me where to lead him. Also, Mrs. Humphries, I need to be here incognito. I am afraid I can be traced, but more than me, my horse can be traced."

Abigail could see this girl was dead on her feet. She took her to the kitchen where Bessie, her cook, was sitting at the oak table talking to Janne.

"Janne Nyegaard, this is…" Her voice trailed off.

"Katie, Katie McKenna." The name rolled easily off her tongue, and Caitlin thought, *I made up my name and know who I am…that poor Conor, we made up his name and he doesn't know who he is.*

Chapter VIII

For the ways of man are before the eyes of the LORD,

and he pondereth all his goings.

PROVERBS 5:21

JANNE GOT UP FROM THE TABLE as she patted Bessie's hand. She helped with all the new girls.

"Welcome, Katie. You'll find the mission a good place to live, and no one pries into your affairs. On the other hand, there are good listeners available if you care to talk."

Abigail said, "I'll see you tomorrow, Katie. Bessie and I need to get home. Janne here will get you acquainted with the mission and see that you're settled in." She turned to the Nordic blonde. "Janne, dear, Katie needs to stable her horse, eat, and be shown her room…in that order, I think." She smiled at Janne. "Thank you for being such a wonderful, dependable woman."

"You are welcome, Abby. Come, Katie, I will show you the stable and where the oats and hay are kept." She spoke with a pleasant accent, but her diction was perfect. "Shall we get your horse first?"

Abby eyed the newcomer and sensed something was desperately wrong. The girl had dark smudges under her eyes and Abby could see some kind of deep emotion that put a shadow in the gray of her eyes. Abigail squeezed Caitlin lightly on the shoulder, picked up a satchel, and headed out the door.

Usually, Bessie was already at the house with dinner prepared for Elijah, but since he was in San Francisco, the two women had eaten dinner at the mission. Bessie heaved herself up and smiled at the women still seated.

"Good night," she said and followed Abigail out the door.

Liberty rode home from her papa and granny's, thinking she needed to ride to San Rafael and tell Abigail and Elijah her news. She was so excited about expecting a baby that it had driven some of the worry about Matthew out of her mind. *I need to keep busy. Otherwise, I'm going to sit around biting my nails in worry over my husband. Something's not right, I can feel it in my heart.* She remembered a scripture she had memorized when married to Armand. *Be anxious about nothing, but in everything give thanks…I give You thanks Father. Please, protect Matthew.*

When she arrived at the Rancho, she slid off Pookie and started to lead her into the barn, but Diego was there and took the reins from her.

"I take care of Pookie. Mees Libbee, I congratulate you! Eet ees wonnerful news. Conchita, she tell me, you weel have the *bebe niño,* noh?"

"Thank you, Diego, and maybe *bebe niña.* I don't care, I'm just elated and thankful. Thanks for taking care of Pookie. I am quite tired. Thank you, too, for praying for Matthew. I'm worried about him, but there's nothing you nor I can do." She walked toward the house, her brow wrinkled in worry.

"Conchita, I'm back." Liberty headed to the kitchen where she knew she'd find her. Kirk was sitting at the kitchen table eating cookies.

She smiled at Kirk and scolded in jest. "Kirk, what are you doing eating cookies? Don't you know you'll spoil your supper?"

Conchita was busy telling Lupe and Luce, her nieces who were hired help, exactly what she wanted done for dinner. She welcomed Liberty back with a big hug.

"So, you weel tell the girls your news, noh?"

"Yes, and Kirk, too. All of you, I have some very good news. Matthew and I are expecting a baby!"

"Oh, *señora!* Ah…such wonderful news!" Luce was happy for her. Liberty had said, when she first came west, she wasn't able to have children.

"Si, señora, esa es noticias maravillosas." (That is wonderful news.) Lupe always talked in Spanish when excited.

Kirk was surprised. He stood and gave Liberty a big hug. "I am happy for you, little sister. Matthew had thought you wouldn't have children of your own. He must be delighted. And, I'm going to be an uncle."

"Matthew doesn't know. I guess I'm so excited about the news that I didn't think to keep it secret until he knows. Conchita is the one who told me this morning. I'm so excited I could burst with the joy of it. I'm so happy."

Everyone began sharing stories about babies…dinner was later than planned.

Early the next morning, Liberty set out for San Rafael. Conchita and Diego were a bit unhappy she would go by herself, but Liberty had no such qualms. She loved to ride, and she was quite a marksman. Her gun was a Smith & Wesson New Model Number Three revolver. She'd purchased two before leaving Boston, one for Maggie—her maid and friend—and one for herself. She remembered her first shooting lesson with Matthew and smiled. He'd been quite impressed with her gun. He said it was commonly carried by lawmen. Matthew carried a Colt Single Action revolver. He loved his gun and had a custom made butt put on it that he'd designed himself.

As she rode south she thought about the past and prayed again for Matthew's protection. Liberty knew Diego had premonitions before. He'd felt a storm brewing and thought it might be Jessica, Matthew's first wife, who'd come back home to die. But, he'd recanted and said that was not the storm. The storm had been Jacques Corlay, the man she'd thought was her father for nearly thirty years and who followed her west and kidnapped her. Now, Diego had another one of his premonitions about Matthew. He spoke to her again before she left this morning. His voice echoed in her mind. *"Someting noh good, Mees Libbee, es muy malo. I noh tink Meester Bannister, he make eet to San Franceesco. I go to church early thees morning an' I pray for hees protection, mees."*

Matthew wasn't due home for three more nights, but he was supposed to stay with Alex, her twin brother. Maybe she should ride on down to the city. Liberty didn't know what to do. It would be good to talk to Elijah and Abigail. Elijah would know what to do. She felt as if she'd known him all her life. He'd been like an angel to her when Armand was murdered. He'd helped her get away from Boston and the unhappiness she'd known there.

Liberty heard horse's hooves pounding behind her and was startled to see Kirk riding up to join her.

"You didn't think I'd find out about you taking off by yourself, did you?"

She smiled, her green eyes sparkling. Liberty had let her hat drop down on her back, and her coppery curls glinted in the bright sunlight. She threw back her head and laughed for the pure joy of living *and* enjoying it. Being married to Armand Bouvier had been horrible. Even growing up had been difficult, knowing her father didn't want, need, nor have time for her. She was grateful he hadn't been her real father.

"I didn't even think to ask you to be my escort, but thank you for coming with me."

"You are most welcome, my fair lady." Kirk grinned at her. "I was planning to ride down to San Rafael in a couple days anyway. Abigail wired to ask if I'd come do a few minor repairs at the mission. I haven't seen hide nor hair of them for probably nigh unto six weeks. It'll be good to see them. Elijah, as you know, was instrumental in leading me to Christ. I've admired him from the first day I met him."

"Yes, me, too. I was just thinking about that before you rode up."

The two of them rode comfortably together, chatting about happenings around the Rancho and what was occurring in the nation.

"I wonder how President Cleveland will do running the country?"

"It's interesting to have a bachelor for our president, isn't it? Has that ever happened before? What I mean is, no first lady. I understand his sister hostesses for him." The ride seemed no time at all with the two of them engrossed in conversation.

Elijah was not a happy man. He sat in Alex Johnson's office in San Francisco, drumming his fingers on the desk as he listened to the young man talk about the company that had once belonged to Mr. Jamison. Jamison had committed suicide when he'd lost his business eight years previously. His widow and four children had gone to live with a sister. Armand Bouvier had moved the company to San Francisco not long before his death. The corporation, A & B Construction, bid for road or construction work, all quite legitimate when owned by Mr. Jamison. This information, Elijah had known for months. Now, things were different. In exchange for votes and monetary kickbacks, a prominent politician in the city was giving work to this firm. The roads built were of inferior quality, and A & B Construction gave large amounts to the politician for the bids.

Elijah continued to drum his fingers on the desk beside his chair. A clock ticked loudly in the quiet office. Alex, his head bent, was rereading some of the information. A small potbellied stove in one corner took the chill off the room. A couple of large seascapes hung on the walls. The room was comfortable but free of clutter and everything had a purpose. It looked as if it had recently been painted; the walls were a clean, crisp taupe trimmed in white.

"You do realize we can't give this company back to Mrs. Jamison. It's not the same company as when her husband owned it. It's as crooked as they come."

"Yes," Elijah replied heavily, "yes, I do understand. I suppose our next move is to notify George Baxter. Have you ever met him, Alex?"

"No, I haven't had the pleasure, but I've heard you talk about him."

"He's a fine man and a wonderful Christian. We met when Liberty's husband was murdered in Boston. It has developed into one of those friendships that will last a lifetime. I was thankful when George accepted the position as chief of detectives here in San Francisco. He's had a hard time trying to clean up the department after the last chief had such a crooked ring of men working for him."

Elijah leaned back in his chair and asked, "You've met Cabot Jones, haven't you? He's George's right-hand man."

"Yes, I have. His wife is Libby's best friend. I believe I met them at the wedding."

"Maggie was Liberty's maid in Boston, but they became close friends on their journey out west. She's a fine girl. Cabot's now a happily married man. I've heard they're expecting a baby."

"Yes, they are, and we are, too." He smiled at Elijah. "Let's go have lunch and then we'll make our way over to the police station." Alex looked questioningly at Elijah to see if he approved the plan.

"Yes, yes, I suppose that is what we should do. After all this is over we could liquidate this company and give the proceeds to Mrs. Jamison. If she's careful, it should allow her to buy a modest house and last her for the rest of her life, unless the company ends up folding completely." Elijah hated fraud, greed, and deceit. He sighed heavily.

Conor moved into the bunkhouse. He'd had a bedroll tied on Piggypie behind the saddle. He wondered if he'd been traveling somewhere or if he was a loner and didn't belong anywhere. Yet, within him, he could feel the need to be with those green eyes. He also knew from being in the McCaully library that he was used to and familiar with books...good books.

He followed Ewen into one of the bunkhouses.

"Conor Innes, this is Jethro Hart, my right-hand man who oversees the boys here at the ranch. He's Jared Hart's brother. Jared is married to Miss Caitlin's sister, Aidan."

Conor remembered the conversation with Caitlin the evening before. They had spoken about Jared, that Aidan shouldn't have married him and that Jared didn't look honest. This man was his brother.

Conor shook his hand and looked him straight in the eyes.

Jethro's eyes were a light blue and masked his thoughts, but he seemed pleasant enough to Conor.

"Welcome to McCaully Ranch. Where d'ya hail from?"

"Oh, I think I've been all over the country. Recently, I've been around these parts, mainly north of Frisco."

Jethro nodded but suspicion filled his eyes. Ewen didn't usually hire drifters. He, most of the time, wanted references. *Well, it's none of my business if he changes his policies after Mac's dead. Wonder what Miss Cait thinks about this? This ranch has slowly been going downhill, to my way of thinking. I reckon we'll see what this man can do. If he's capable, I don't really care if he's a drifter or not.*

Ewen, a no nonsense kind of man, said, "Jethro, I want you to get him settled in and working alongside someone today. You can see if he's what we need here." He turned to Conor. "I know Miss Caitlin hired you, but I'm foreman here. If you don't pull your weight…well, you won't be a permanent fixture, understand?"

"Yes, sir, I do."

Jethro said to Ewen, "I'll get 'em started right away, sir."

Ah, he thought to himself, *so Miss Cait hired him. Now, that is interesting. Wonder where she met 'em? Wonder, too, where she is this morning. Usually she's already hard at work.*

"Thanks, Jethro, introduce him around, won't you? Then I want that fence repaired where those cows broke through yesterday. That temporary isn't going to hold."

Jethro nodded respectfully. Ewen nodded back and left.

"You can toss your bedroll up there. Top bunk's empty." Jethro pointed. "This's where we sleep, plan, and play cards. We eat over there…it's the chow hall." He gestured to another smaller building. "We have a cook, a durned good one, too. Goes by the name of Gus. He's a full-blooded Swede, and you don't wanna cross 'em. I've known 'em to do some pretty nasty things to food when a man's made 'em mad." He grinned at Conor, who grinned back.

"I'll be sure to be *very* careful."

Jethro pointed toward a window. "You can see there's two more bunkhouses like this one. Mac didn't want too many men sleeping in the same room…said tempers fly when a man's got too many bodies around 'em." Conor nodded in agreement.

The two went outside and Jethro introduced him to some of the men who were beginning to ride out.

"This here is Manny's crew. Manny, meet Conor Innes, our new ranch hand. Manny's crew is Abbot, Hank, Darren, and Frank." The men rode out after nodding to Conor.

"This is Eli. His crew is Mosey, Jeb, Rhys, and Duke. Boys, this here's Conor Innes, a new hired hand."

Conor tipped his hat and said, "Howdy." Some nodded and a couple tipped their hats in return before they cantered off to the range.

Jethro said, "We try to put men together into small crews. They eat, ride, sleep, and do whatever together. If a man can't seem to fit in, he's put with a different crew. If that doesn't work, he's gone.

"Over here is John, Drew, Sneedy, and Ricardo. Meet Conor Innes."

Conor once again tipped his hat. Sneedy whipped out a rope and snagged Conor's hat with a flick of his wrist.

Conor said easily, "You're in good practice."

"Waal now, I be a likin' yore hat. Think I'll jest make it mine."

Quick as a wink, Conor drew on the man and said quietly, "I like my hat too."

Respect dawned quickly in Sneedy's eyes, and he grinned at Conor. It was the law of the land. A man had to stand up and not be cowed by another.

"Yep, I kin see ya'll be liking yore hat more'n me, so's I'll's be givin' it back ta ya." He nodded at Conor's gun. "Yure purty fast with that thing."

Conor grinned back, holstering his gun, and a mutual respect was cemented between the two men. *Drawing a gun on a man isn't my normal behavior, so where did that come from? Was it to prove to these men I'm not to be trifled with?*

Jethro liked what he saw and said to the men, "You mind if we put Con with you?"

"Nope," John said hastily, "we'd be happy to have 'em. He's a swift draw an thet comes in handy out on the range." He turned to Drew and Ricardo. "What'll ya'll say, you want 'em?"

"Shore do. I got no problem havin' 'em on my side, thet's certain," Drew responded amiably.

Ricardo looked the newcomer up and down. "Hee's a fast draw…I like heem to be weeth us. Eet ees fine theeng."

Conor took a closer look at Ricardo. He was used to hearing a heavy Spanish accent. He said a quick prayer. *Father, I know you have plans for me…I reckon it's to find out the renegade in this bunch, but Lord, I really want to know who I am.*

CHAPTER IX

The labour of the righteous tendeth to life:
the fruit of the wicked to sin.

PROVERBS 10:16

CAITLIN LAY FLAT ON HER STOMACH, awakening slowly. She stretched and rolled over. Sudden realization flooded into her consciousness, and her eyes flew open. She wasn't in her own bed. *Da is gone...forever gone.* She lay there as tears trickled down the sides of her face. She'd known for some time it was coming. Her da had gotten quieter and quieter and was steadily losing weight. He'd begun talking about heaven and dying. She'd gotten the priest to come talk to him. The priest, fairly good looking, had come willingly to the ranch but didn't seem personable and his eyes held no humor. Her da hadn't asked for the priest. She'd simply thought, since her da was Irish, that he was also Catholic. Religion had never been discussed in the McCaully house as far back as Cait could remember.

She smiled through her tears as she thought about his reaction.

"I'll talk wi' ye Faether O'Flannagan, but mind ye, I no be wantin' me last rights. I'm naet a gone yit."

His Irish brogue had become more and more pronounced the sicker he got.

The priest seemed quite uncomfortable, but Cait left the man to talk to her da. After he'd finished and left, Da had told her they'd had a nice chat, but now he'd like to talk to the minister of the small, white clapboard church in Santa Rosa. She'd fetched the man, a Reverend Babcock. She wondered, even now, what the man had said to her da. He'd had the most peaceful expression on his face when the minister had left. Da said he'd got Jesus, but he didn't talk much after that. He sat and cried all that evening and said he'd wished someone had told him years ago...*told him what?* He seldom spoke the next two days. He'd begun to ramble, and then he was gone.

Oh Da, I'm going to miss you. You've been the man of my life for over twenty years. Aidan and Maisie have their own lives to lead and their own men. Ewen's a faithful foreman, but...oh how I'll miss you, Da! She lay there for quite some time and let the memories flood over her as she mourned. Finally, she sat up, wiped her eyes, and blew her nose.

Caitlin swung her long legs over the side of the bed. She stretched again and padded to the room she'd been shown the night before. Cait had never seen a toilet like this. It was almost like sitting in a chair, and the contents washed out at the bottom. *I'm going to have this put into the ranch house, once this is all over...at least I will if we have enough money. What a wonderful invention. No more chamber pots.*

She splashed water onto her face and rubbed away the tear stains. She looked in the mirror and was glad to see her gray eyes weren't reddened from crying. She dressed and did her thick auburn hair in a long braid. She wrapped it around her head like a crown and slipped hairpins into it to keep it in place. She looked into the mirror again and thought, *I reckon I'm presentable enough.* She pinched her cheeks for a little color, took a deep breath, and descended the wide stairs.

Bessie was already in the kitchen making pancakes. The Humphries' cook didn't have to come to the mission, but it did her heart good to talk to the girls. She loved cooking for them and teaching some how to cook. In the beginning, there had been more than a hundred girls. It had taken quite a time to get down to the three who were now housed at the mission. Caitlin made four, but the number fluctuated greatly. A month earlier, they'd had twenty-three.

Caitlin entered the kitchen. The girls were already seated at a large table. Janne was one of them. She looked around for Mrs. Humphries but didn't see her.

"Good morning, Katie." Janne arose and introduced Caitlin to the girls in the room, but she didn't pay attention to their names. It wasn't her intention to get close to anyone. She simply wanted a place to stay and hide away until her ranch was a safe place for her. The girls smiled at her and she nodded her head at each introduction.

"Nice to meet you…sorry, but I need to excuse myself. My horse wants feeding before I sit down to eat." She took an apple from a basket on the sideboard and left the kitchen with a deep sigh of relief. *Women make me nervous. Now, that is strange, since I have two older sisters.* She thought about it and realized she'd been working strictly with men for several years. *I think I like men better than women. I can't stand all that emotional hoopla that seems to come with women. Just give me an even-tempered man who's not moody, and I'm fine.*

Caitlin knew she'd remember to respond if someone called her Katie. Her da had always called her Katie unless he was angry about something she'd done. Then, he'd always called her Caitlin Kendall McCaully. She smiled to herself through a mist of tears and left for the stables by a back door from the kitchen. Big double doors were shut on the front of the stable, but a smaller door opened to the interior on the side near the front. She entered and pulled the door shut with a soft click, but Fire had heard her. He whickered and her heart warmed, delighted that her horse seemed to love her as much as she loved him. The stalls were clean and new looking. She handed the apple to her stallion and got some chopped hay, filling the manger. Fire pawed, ignored the hay, and dropped the apple half eaten, letting her know they were not alone in the stable. Cait saw an older man by the doors. She exited the stall and closed the door carefully behind her. Fire didn't touch his food when someone else was around.

"That's quite a horse you have there, miss," the man said, a soft burr in his voice. "He's a pretty big roan. Wouldn't let me near him this morning, and I knew better than to try."

Caitlin grinned at the man. She stuck out her hand and introduced herself. "My name's Cait...Katie, Katie McKenna."

"I'm Joey McClintock. The Humphries hired me when they opened the mission. I help with horses brought in here or those that stay down at their house. Keep the carriages and wagons in shipshape, I do. I live in the caretaker's cottage along with my wife."

"Well, Joey, it's nice ta be meetin' you, and thank ye much fer not tryin' ta approach me Fire. He's neevir let anyone near 'em 'ceptin' me and me da." Caitlin had slipped quite naturally into an Irish brogue.

"Well, now, me darlin', I be vary keerful 'round him, ta be sure."

"I thank ye." The two grinned at each other.

Joey headed for the caretaker's cottage, and Caitlin returned to Fire's stall to finish feeding him. She wasn't excited to go back inside the mission. *If this is going to be my home for the time being, reckon I may as well be civil.* She took a deep breath and headed for the kitchen.

Elijah and Alex rode out to the western shore of San Francisco. Alex's house was just south of Cliff House, a wonderful restaurant, known not only for its cuisine but also for its relaxed ambience.

Alex stopped his horse on a cliff overlooking the peninsula, as did Elijah. It was windy and overcast. Rain would not be long in coming. Both men sat easily on their horses, not conversing but simply looking at the splendor before them. Sky met ocean in varying degrees of gray. Waves crashed over huge crags, sending walls of cascading water splashing forth with mists of constant, vanishing beauty. Seagulls swooped and soared between them and the rocks, diving into the mists screaming their plaintive song.

Elijah was to spend the night at Alex and Emily Johnson's house. He knew it'd be a noisy evening but looked forward to it. He secretly loved Xander, the oldest boy, the best. *What a little character he is! I love him so much.*

"Alex, you've said nothing about Matthew. Isn't he staying nights with you this week? At least that was my understanding, unless somehow, I've not gotten the information correct."

"No, it's correct. We expected him three nights ago, but he didn't come. I've no doubt something delayed him; however, it isn't like Matt not to wire us and tell us of a change in plans. Perhaps he'll be at the house when we get there." He had to yell to be heard above the crashing waves and winds that snatched the words from his mouth.

As Elijah sat watching the scene below him, a scripture from Job came to his mind. *"Or who shut up the sea with doors, when it brake forth, as if it had issued out of the womb? When I made the cloud the garment thereof, and thick darkness a swaddlingband for it, And brake up for it my decreed place, and set bars and doors, And said, Hitherto shalt thou come, but no further: and here shall thy proud waves be stayed?"*

Elijah prayed, *Almighty God, I've been feeling well down on myself for not catching the information about the A & B company. Father, I'm sorry for letting pride in my abilities affect me this way. Thou hast given me the abilities I have. I've dedicated everything I am to Thee. I cannot change the fact that I missed it, but I will give Thee praise in every circumstance. I thank Thee for the wisdom Thou hast given me. May all I do be for Thy glory, not my own.*

Alex looked at Elijah, his burnished coppery curls whipping around his head in the wind. Neither man wore a hat. It wouldn't have stayed on with the gusts blowing hard around them.

"Shall we go?" he yelled. He grinned for the sheer joy of living.

Elijah nodded, an answering grin spreading over his face.

They headed for the haven of Alex's home, Elijah looking forward to holding the children in his arms. The wind blew hard as the men rode south. Both were wrapped in their own thoughts. Droplets of rain began to pelt them with a sting from the strength of the wind. Alex gave his horse a kick and immediately went into a gallop. Elijah followed suit, keeping his head well down, trusting his horse to follow Alex's lead.

Liberty and Kirk arrived at the Humphries' house in the latter part of the day. Liberty was exhausted and wondered if some of her tiredness came from being pregnant. She'd noticed herself looking forward to naps in the afternoon, which wasn't normal for her. Now she knew why.

They tied their horses to the hitching post and walked up to the stately house belonging to Elijah and Abigail. The door opened before they could knock. Thomas greeted them happily. Unexpected company was a welcome event in this household.

"Miz Abigail, she done be at the mission right now, but she be home soon, I's 'pect. Come in, come right on in."

Liberty started to step inside but Kirk held back.

"I'll get your things, Libby, but I'm going to mosey on down to the mission. I'd like to see just what repairs I'll be making so I can plan out a line of attack." He smiled. "I'll only be here about three days or so, I reckon. When Abigail comes back here for supper, I'll come with her."

"All right, but I'm all done in. I'm going to lie down for a short nap. That way, I'll be fit to visit later. I'm fairly drooping."

Kirk ran down the aggregate walk to get Liberty's satchel. He unstrapped his small valise and let himself in the front door to set their things on the bottom step of the stairs. Glancing up the stairs, he decided to run their cases to the top, taking the steps two at a time. He took them one at a time coming down and entered the kitchen. Thomas offered him a glass of lemonade, which he accepted gratefully. Liberty and Thomas were sitting at the big kitchen table. The juice was fresh squeezed and delicious. The kitchen was unusually large and had everything a cook would want, for Bessie's convenience.

Liberty silently admired the way Abigail had decorated it. The kitchen walls were painted a warm apricot color. The stove was fairly new, built right into a large island in the middle of the room. A huge fireplace stood at one end, with paned floor-to-ceiling windows on either side. In the corner was an alcove that was all windows, where they now sat. An entire counter jutting out from the wall was a cutting board so people could stand on either side and use it at the same time. A large cooler, pie safe, and large cupboards for storage were a boon for any cook. Glass doors led out to an enclosed courtyard.

Kirk sat down and the three talked comfortably together, catching up on news. Thomas was happy to see the two of them. Taking a long drink of the lemonade, Kirk quenched his thirst while Thomas shared his news.

"Mr. Humphries, he done gone to see your brother, Miz Liberty. Left early yestady mornin', he did. Said he'd be comin' back in a couple days." Thomas' face was nearly unlined, yet his grizzled hair was pure white. He looked distinguished to Liberty.

Liberty swallowed her disappointment. She had planned to talk to Elijah tonight.

Kirk took his glass to Bessie's spotless sink and said, "Well, I hate to break up the party, but I need to get down to the mission. Liberty, you need to go take a nap. Our things are at the top of the stairs. I didn't know what rooms we'll be staying in." Kirk nodded at Thomas, knowing the man would get his sister-in-law into a room in short order.

Liberty replied, "I will. I do need to lie down for a bit. Thanks, Kirk, for riding down here with me."

"You are most welcome, and thank you, Thomas. I appreciated the lemonade. It hit the spot after that ride." He turned. "Liberty, I'm taking Pookie with me to stable her with Queenie. You can walk to the mission if you need her or send word with someone."

The sun, which had been shining brightly the entire morning, was now obliterated by a huge cloud that filled the kitchen with shadow.

"I need to go. It looks like rain." He leaned and bussed Liberty on the cheek. "I sure am glad to have you as a sister, Libby Bannister."

Liberty looked up at him, pleased. "I'm glad to have you as a brother, Kirk. What seems strange is that you came into my life before my twin."

He looked down at her. *I'm glad she married Matthew. Jess had been a mistake from the get go. She was a woman who needed the glitz and glitter of life. That doesn't last nor does it satisfy. Now Jess is dead, and Matthew is able to move on in a new life with Christ. I am so glad he's found a woman of worth.*

"Uh hum, now that you have two brothers," he said with a twinkle in his eyes, "you'd better behave and get yourself some rest. I'll most likely see you at dinner, unless I'm invited to eat with a bevy of girls at the mission. Now, that's something I wouldn't turn down!" He laughed and grinned at her.

Liberty laughed with him. "No, I'm quite sure you wouldn't turn that down."

Kirk shook Thomas' hand. "Thanks again for the lemonade, Thomas." He walked to the door as Liberty started up the stairs.

She turned toward Kirk as he started to leave. "And, thank you again, brother," she said, "for riding down here with me. It made the time fly. I do declare, I don't think you ever stopped talking."

Kirk grinned at her and left, pulling the door closed behind him. Liberty went on up the stairs with Thomas trailing behind her.

"You be sleepin' in dis here room, Miss Libby." He opened a door and ushered her into a beautiful, spacious bedroom.

"Thank you, Thomas, I'm sure I'll find everything I need, but all I want is to lay down on that bed. By the way, Thomas," she whispered, "I'm expecting a baby. Can you believe it? I'm thirty-one years old and expecting my first baby!"

"Oh, missy, I'm happy for you. The Lawd be praised!"

CHAPTER X

He shall die without instruction;
and in the greatness of his folly he shall go astray.

PROVERBS 5:23

AIDAN AWAKENED SLOWLY, surprised Jared was already out of bed. He usually got up much later than she did. She lay there and thought about how she was raised and what she had to put up with being married to Jared.

He's drinking more and more. Is he so unhappy with me that a bottle of liquor is better company than me? Am I such a disappointment to him? I know he's becoming a huge disappointment to me. He treated me so special before we were married, and now…it's as if I'm nothing to him. I'm a noose around his neck. I don't even know if he loves me.

She sat up. Her cloud of black hair gleamed in the morning light with red highlights. She pulled her gown strap back onto her shoulder and rose with a huge sigh. *I'm so unhappy. Da warned me against Jared, but of course I wouldn't listen. Caitlin warned me, too. Why do I resent her warning and not Da's? Am I that jealous of her? She's been such a hard worker. I reckon I love her more than I've ever let on—to her, anyway, or even to myself. Well, I'm sorry about that. Now that Da's gone, we McCaully girls need to stick together. I'm done with trying to please Jared and his warped way of thinking. I plan to be a straight shooter from now on.*

She wrapped a robe of green silk around herself, tied the belt around her slim waist, and descended the stairs. She peeked into the study and saw Jared, but instead of going in to talk to him she headed to the kitchen for a cup of coffee. Feeling she couldn't handle a confrontation before having some fortification first, she carried her cup up the stairs to her room. Aidan sat for a while in a rocker and looked out her window. She sipped the brew and thought about her options. She stood, stretched, and got dressed to go riding, which was a way for her to release pent-up emotions that were fast becoming overwhelming. She sat back down to finish the rest of her lukewarm coffee and stared out the window. When she finished, she went downstairs to confront Jared.

Jared was trying his best to be patient with Aidan. He sat in a drunken stupor, striving in his dulled mind to figure how to get some money out of her. *It won't do for her to get angry with me. I need money, and somehow, I'm going to get it.* He suddenly had a flashback of Mac putting a satchel into the left bottom desk drawer. *I know Mac had a goodly amount of money in that satchel of his. I've seen cash in it before. I wonder if it'd be enough to cover my gambling debt? What am I thinking? Stealing from a dead man?*

On the other hand, I heard the Hendersons were going on a trip south. I could, perhaps, get some of their valuables and sell them. Their vineyard is doing quite well. They have many bibelots that look like they'd fetch a hefty sum. There's a lot of danger in that. What if I were caught? He held his aching head in his hands. *What am I going to do?*

Aidan came into the study with a determined stride. Her hair was neatly French braided into two pigtails and she was fully dressed, ready to go riding. She wore a slim split skirt. She and her two sisters had never ridden sidesaddle. Mac never allowed it, saying it was a good way to break one's neck.

She looked at Jared disgustedly. "You're drunk, aren't you? It's nine thirty in the morning, and you're drunk."

"I'm not drunk, not drunk a'tall, my sweetums."

"You smell, Jared, and you reek of alcohol. What's wrong with you, anyway?"

"Nothin', sweetums, nothin' a'tall. All's right with me and th' world." He got up and walked unsteadily toward the doorway of the study. His shoulder hit the doorjamb and he cursed before heading up the stairs.

Aidan sat down heavily in the chair Jared had vacated. *I made the biggest mistake of my life marrying him. He's either drunk, angry, or running up debts all over town. He was such a charmer. Da and Cait were right. He's lazy and has no thought of working for what he has. What am I going to do? I thought I loved him. What's sad is, I think I still do. I thought he loved me but he doesn't. Jared only loves himself. Maybe I should go back home and live for a while. Perhaps if we were separated things will work themselves out. I think I'm finally beginning to grow up. I don't believe I even like who I've become.*

Aidan knew she was fooling herself. *How can something be worked out, if we're not talking about it and about solutions to the problem? Oh well, I'll think about it later. I'm going out for a ride, or maybe I'll have breakfast first.*

Conor was enjoying himself and the day. He was used to physical labor and leant himself fully to the task at hand. It felt good to work with his hands. The sun was out, but it wasn't a very warm sun. The wind tried to steal his hat but the breeze felt cool on his face, which was warm from exertion. Sneedy and Conor worked side by side the entire morning. Repairing fencing was not too difficult, but Conor figured he was not familiar with it. The barbs were sharp, and he'd gotten a few cuts on his hands.

Sneedy was full of information and did most of the talking.

"Ya knows, we keep the fences up not only ta keep our cattle in, but ta keep free-range cattle out. They's got regular wars goin' on down thar in Texas; men cuttin' the fences down to let range cattle roam where they wants. Some don't like seein' th' cows die fer lack of forage. Winters kin be hard on th' durned animals. We don't have thet thar problem around here. Them animals kin always find food cuz we don't be havin' such cold weather here." He worked, stretching the barbed wire around the post as he talked.

"Thet's a purty nice ride ya got thar. Air ya interested in sellin' 'er?" Sneedy had been eyeing Conor's piebald mare all morning. She was a beautiful horse. Large patches of black and even bigger areas of white made up her coat. Below the knees, her legs were covered in long white hair. Her mane, tail, and both sides of her face were black. From Piggypie's poll, down her forehead to the muzzle, was a wide blaze of white.

"Nope, ol' Piggypie and me, we go a long way back. She's been my horse for over six years now. I helped deliver her." *Now, how do I know that? I do know that, don't I? Reckon if I start second guessing everything I think, I'm going to end up not remembering anything.*

The two men worked steadily, repairing the entire area the cows had broken through. Every once in a while Sneedy would give Conor a tip on how to make the job a bit easier. When it was time for lunch, they joined up with the rest of their crew and headed back to the chow hall. All the men ate together for every meal except Ewen, who ate in the big house.

Gus, the cook, squinted his eyes, looking Conor up and down. "You da new man?"

"Yes, my name's…uh Conor, Conor Innes."

"Ah, another Ireesh. Huh, I see yous the man Miss Cait hired. Uh huh, yes, yous handy with a gun, I hear. Uh huh, yous a quick draw. That's a mighty good ting in these here parts. We have the rattlesnake around here."

Conor had a flashback at the word rattlesnake, seeing in the blink of an eye a man writhing on the ground, his neck turning blue from a bite on the juggler. He felt no emotion at the knowledge of the man dying, no connection, but right next to the man was another person, but the memory faded as quickly as it had appeared. It was gone, but who was that other form? He felt, somehow, he knew the other person and wondered if that person was alive...who was it?

"Yes," he replied to Gus, "I know the Pacific Northwest Rattlesnake is deadly. I believe I've killed more than one in my lifetime, but to change the subject, I hear you're a mighty good cook. What's that smell, anyway? It's making my mouth water."

"That's my Gus's Stew. I named it after me. It's that and the biscuits I made. That's what yous smelling. Help yerself."

"I will, and thanks." Conor grabbed a dipper and scooped up a big bowl of stew and took two biscuits. They looked really good. He was hungry. Sitting next to Sneedy, he looked across at Drew and Ricardo. John sat on his other side.

Evidently Drew had just told a funny anecdote to Ricardo and Sneedy, who were both holding their sides from laughing.

"You ees so amusing, Drew...you one rib-tickling hombre."

"Rib-ticklin' ain't th' word fer it. Yore downright side-splittin', Drew." Sneedy was gulping for air from laughing so hard.

John said, "How's it going for you, Con? Sneedy here says you're a hard worker. Have you worked barbed wire before?" John was glad they hadn't asked a loafer to join their crew. All his men worked hard and he was proud of his crew. It looked as if Conor was going to fit right in.

"Nope, can't say that I have...not much anyway. Mostly I brand cattle and separate the calves from their sweet little mamas. I've done some work in vineyards and haven't yet had the desire to work sheep." Conor wanted to get the men onto a subject other than himself. He knew talking sheep to a cattle rancher would get a conversation going in no time.

"I understand several of the cattle ranchers in the area are moving toward grape vineyards and nut groves. Is that correct or is someone blowing smoke my way?"

There was much talk about sheep eating not only the grass but the roots and ruining the range for cattle, and then the subject of grape growing was discussed. After a tasty meal, the men rode out to their respective jobs. As he climbed onto his horse, there were a few harshly spoken words between John and Rhys, but Conor couldn't hear what they said. Sneedy looked on with tightened lips but didn't enlighten Con as to what the trouble was. The wind had picked up and rain was coming, but it was still light and the men worked until nearly sundown before coming in for supper.

Alex Johnson and Elijah Humphries arrived at the large house overlooking the Pacific Ocean. Alex had named his house Liberty House, after his middle name, not realizing Liberty should have been his last name. He was contemplating legally changing his last name to Liberty and going without a middle name.

Matthew still hadn't arrived, and Elijah began to worry. *What can have happened to him? If there had been a change in plans or something has delayed him, Matthew is responsible and a man to let people know he can't make it.*

Emily told Elijah that Matt was supposed to be a guest and was due to have arrived three days before. They had prepared for him to come, but Matthew never showed up.

Elijah decided to send a telegram to Liberty and to his own dear Abby on the morrow. *Perhaps something important came up, and Matthew simply hadn't had time to contact the Johnson household.*

All the sudden he felt as if the wind had been knocked out of him as Xander cannonballed his young body into Elijah's stomach.

"Granpajah! Granpajah! I knew you were coming. I've been waitin' and waitin' for you to get here. I have something I want to show you!"

He hugged Elijah, who hugged him right back. Xander began to push him from behind, toward a little room off the kitchen. As he pushed, Elijah tried to say his hellos to the rest of the family. Laughing, he was being propelled rapidly across the kitchen. Emily smiled and Penelope laughed delightedly.

Penelope had helped raise Alex. Looking at Xander brought back a host of memories of Alex as a child. Xander looked much like his father had as a youngster, with his winged eyebrows and bright, gray-green eyes. Burnished coppery curls covered his head the same shade as Alex's. Penelope was still amazed at the resemblance, even though she encountered it every day. She leaned against the countertop to watch as Xander pushed Elijah across the floor, memories flooding into her mind.

Penelope remembered when she first met Sarah Johnson, Alex's mother. Alex had been nearly two months old when Sarah had happened upon Penelope's house. Sarah moved back to Boston after discovering her husband's unfaithfulness. Looking for a place to live, she'd seen Penelope Weaver's house and had, at first, thought it empty. When she pushed open the front door it was an answer to Penelope's prayer. Penelope had tripped over her sewing basket and broken her leg and hadn't been able to get up. Sarah's arrival may have saved her life. Sarah moved in that day and it had been the beginning of a lifelong love. Penelope loved Alex as if he were her very own flesh and blood.

Alex felt Penelope was his real grandmother. He'd always felt a stronger attachment to her than to Sarah. When Madam Violet Corlay had given birth to twins—a boy and a girl—Violet had given Alex to the doctor, Sarah's husband, who delivered them. Liberty was Alex's twin, and the two had met about eighteen months before when they were nearly thirty years old. Both felt a closeness only a twin could fathom.

Xander continued to push Elijah toward the room off the kitchen. He threw open the door and made an announcement as if he personally were responsible.

"Here's Daffy the second, and look!" Xander knelt and picked up a little puppy. Daffodil was a yellow labrador, but her puppies were half Australian shepherd. Alex had been upset because he'd wanted to breed her with another yellow lab, but the shepherd had jumped the six-foot fence to their back yard. The puppies were darling.

"Mama says it's time to find homes for them. Would you like one, Granpajah? I know it'd have a good home with you. Maybe Aunt Libby would like one, too. Oh Granpajah, I know Abigran would *love* to have one of these darling puppies. What d'ya say? Will you take one, please?"

Elijah wasn't sure what Abigail would think of a puppy, but Xander was a child he couldn't resist. He wasn't sure how he'd feel having a dog in the house. They'd never had one in Boston.

"Well, young man, I'll think about it while I'm here. What do you say to that?" Elijah was a lawyer and knew how to circumvent answers until he thought them through.

"All right, Granpajah, but I really, really want you to have one. You'll love it."

A puppy, its white coat mottled with black, climbed out of the box and headed straight for Elijah. She wagged and he picked her up. Elijah was won over in that minute.

"Okay, I'll take this one. What is it?"

Xander turned the puppy over and said, "It's a girl, Granpajah. You picked one of my favorites. Actually, she picked you. She has good taste, doesn't she?" He grinned widely at Elijah, excited he would take one of the puppies. "Mama said we can't keep any of the puppies unless we get rid of Daffodil, and I could never, ever do that. Daffy is the bestest dog in the whole world."

"No, I don't suppose you could. Which one would you pick out for your Aunt Libby? My, they sure are sweet. How many are there?"

"There's seven of them. Umm…I think I'd pick this one. There's this one, and see that one? They look the most like yours. These two are males, but I think Uncle Matt and Aunt Libby would love one, don't you"

"Yes, Xander, I do." He stroked the puppy in his arms. *What will Abby think? What will Libby think?* He smiled, thinking about the two women he loved so much and knew both of them would love having a puppy.

CHAPTER XI

My lips shall not speak wickedness,

nor my tongue utter deceit.

JOB 24:7 (NEW REFERENCE)

KIRK HEADED TOWARD THE MISSION after leaving Liberty at the Humphries' house. He knew Thomas would take good care of her and that she'd get the rest she needed. He thought about having a niece or nephew. *It must have been Libby's dead husband who couldn't have children. Matthew is going to be so thrilled. I thank You, Lord, for allowing this to happen. It's a miracle to Liberty. She will make a wonderful mother. Thank You for protecting me from Consuelo. That would have been a huge disaster...same as Matt made with Jessica. Help me to please You in all I do.*

Consuelo was Conchita's cousin and a selfish woman. He'd sought her out, enamored by the charms she so readily displayed. *Plain old lust, that's what it had been. How thankful I am that my eyes are not drawn to her anymore. I don't lust for her. All that is gone, taken away when I accepted You, Jesus. It's not that I'm not tempted. It's simply that I make the righteous choice because I want to please You. I am responsible for what I look at or where I allow a glance to turn into a gaze. Help me to be on my guard. Help me to be pleasing to You in all things, Lord.*

Clouds darkened the sky. Kirk could see the day, which had been so fair, becoming sullen. *Rain is on its way.* The weather usually came in from the coast. Dark clouds scudded their way across the horizon, blotting out the blue, and without the sun, he felt chilled.

He rode Queenie, a sweet-tempered Appaloosa, slowly down the main street to the mission and held Pookie's reins lightly. He thought about how they'd come to have Queenie.

Matthew had gotten two horses when Jacques Corlay had died, Queenie and Cloud. Matthew thought they were probably rented horses, but paperwork had been found in Corlay's belongings, proving he had purchased them. Matthew had then traded horses with Liberty: Pookie for the two mares that had been Jacques'. Jacques had been Liberty's step-father and because of all that had happened, she didn't want the horses. Although Pookie had been Matthew's horse, Kirk had always ridden her. When Matt traded Pookie for Queenie and Cloud, Kirk had chosen Queenie to ride and loved the mare. He rode her at every opportunity. She had a great smooth stride and an easy, even temperament. Kirk loved her. *Well, looks like I'm here.*

He climbed down from the saddle and took both horses around the mission house to the stable. Unlatching the wooden slide out of its pocket, he opened the large barn doors. Light flooded into the dimness. As he entered, he immediately noticed two things: The stable was still as clean as the first day he entered it, and a beautiful roan had taken up residence in one of the stalls. He led Queenie into the stall next to the roan and Pookie into the one after that. He closed the main double doors.

The huge roan whickered softly, and Kirk reached into a pocket, offering the big horse a piece of sugar in a flattened palm. The horse blew out his nostrils and gently took the sugar out of Kirk's hand. He stroked the beautiful head through the slat and suddenly noticed the roan was a stallion, not a gelding. Kirk was surprised the horse was so friendly.

He unsaddled Queenie and Pookie. He crossed to the tack room and hung the saddles and blankets and then put some hay in the mangers of both horses. He grabbed a couple brushes and went to the stall and thoroughly brushed down Pookie while she enjoyed chomping on the hay. He hummed a song as he brushed her. When he was finished, he went into the stall with Queenie. He heard the side door to the barn open and kept brushing. He supposed it to be Joey McClintock, Elijah's groom.

The stallion whickered, and Kirk heard the latch on the stallion's stall open. He peered between the slats and saw a girl enter it. She was tall and utterly feminine looking. He was surprised she'd go into the stall of the stallion but quickly realized the horse must belong to her. He didn't mean to spy, but he saw her take the stallion's head and lean her own on his. She stroked his neck and crooned love words to him. As he watched, he was surprised to see a gun strapped to her hip. It made him smile to himself.

Kirk turned back to Queenie, beginning to brush her coat and said aloud, "That's a mighty friendly stallion you have there, miss."

Caitlin was startled. She stooped under Fire's head and climbed up two slats to get a better look at the man who had spoken. Fire nudged her back with his head.

"An' jist how would you be a knowing that, sir?" she asked softly, the Irish burr sounding thick in her voice.

"Why, miss, he's as gentle as a lamb. He whickered when I entered the stall here with Queenie and took sugar from my hand like a baby."

Caitlin raised her eyebrows in disbelief. *Of all the gall, ta be a lyin' ta me an' he niver mit me afore in me life.*

"He's niver taiken a ting from a body, 'ceptin from me an me da." She flat out didn't believe the man. She climbed down and exited the stall, going around to the other stall to have a better look at the man who lied so easily. Caitlin was tall for a woman, but he topped her by at least five inches. She saw a man who had deep-set blue eyes that twinkled even in the dimness of the stable. His hair was a honey blonde color. For some reason, he looked vaguely familiar. To her surprise, he plopped the brushes into her hands, which she took without thinking.

Kirk always carried about five lumps of sugar in his pocket. Knowing the girl didn't believe him, he went around and entered the stallion's stall, talking softly.

"Be keerful, sir, he'll…" Her voice trailed off as the big roan didn't move or quiver but breathed through his nose softly as the man began to speak to him.

"Hello there, big boy…bet you'd like another one of these, wouldn't you?" He held out the sugar cube in his flattened hand, and the stallion, after shaking his head up and down a couple times, blew softly against his palm as he took the sugar. Kirk gingerly stroked the beautiful neck and Fire stood there eating it up as if he had known the man all his life. His tail twitched appreciatively.

"Why I niver! I wouldn't hiv believe dit if I hadn't seen it. Why, I'll be owing ye an apology, Mr.….?"

"Bannister, Kirk Bannister. Pleased to meet you Miss…?"

"McKenna…Katie McKenna," she supplied readily. She was sorry for having distrusted the man. She simply had never seen Fire take to anyone. It astounded her and she stared at him as if he were an apparition.

"You have a beautiful stallion, Miss McKenna." Kirk went around the stall to Queenie's.

"I know. He was a yearling when my da gave him to me for my sixteenth birthday. Fire's only six years old. He's only ever let my father and me close. He won't even eat if someone else tries to feed him." Katie's brogue had dropped, and she spoke English with no accent.

Kirk noticed it and missed the sweet sound of an Irish burr. *Sixteen… ah, she must be about twenty…twenty-one?*

"Are you staying here at the mission?"

"Yes, I arrived last evening. I don't know how long I'll stay, but I think I'd like to see if Fire will let you ride 'em. Are you interested?"

"Are you jesting? Of course, I'd love to have a chance to ride him. There's not a man I know who'd turn down an invitation like that." He grinned at Caitlin, who grinned right back.

"I'm here to make a few repairs around the mission. Have you met Abigail Humphries yet?"

"Yes, she seems a very sweet woman. Are you a repairman then? Is that your profession?" All the sudden, Caitlin realized why the man looked familiar. There was something about him that put her in mind of the man they had named Conor Innes two evenings before.

Kirk replied, "Well, I guess you might say I'm an all-around help." He didn't mention he was part owner of a vineyard that promised to become one of California's best in years to come. Kirk had been saving his wages since he graduated from college. He'd bought land that abutted Matthew's and had planted more rootstalk, doubling the Bannister holdings. *Matthew was so proud of me last year.*

Caitlin felt comfortable knowing the man repaired things. It was the kind of man with which she was familiar.

Before getting up, Elijah spent some time praying for Matthew. He was concerned and had awakened several times during the night to pray for the young man. He also prayed for Liberty and that she would handle the news about Matthew with God's peace within her. He prayed for each of the Johnson children and for Emily's pregnancy and for Alex as the spiritual head of this family. He prayed for Penelope, who was Alex's Nana and the real matriarch of the Johnson household. Elijah prayed for his servants and own household and his law partners. Last but not least, he praised God for Abigail, for her continued good health, and for the blessing she was as his lifelong companion. He was a grateful man.

Planning to leave the Johnson household early the next morning, Elijah intended to spend this last day enjoying the children. The day before, he'd spent a considerable amount of time talking with his friend, George Baxter, the detective. Elijah and Alex were going to leave the problem of the A & B Construction Company in the capable hands of the San Francisco chief of detectives. It looked as if George was going to assign his right-hand man, Cabot Jones, to the case. Elijah felt easier knowing the problem would be taken care of in an expedient manner. He got up, washed, shaved, and was ready to face the day having finished his prayers.

Emily, Alex's wife, was dishing out breakfast for the children. Alex and Elijah looked on with smiles on their faces.

"Mama, I don't want any butter on my pancake, please." Penny sat next to her Nana, Penelope, who was busy on her other side helping Jonathan cut up his pancake.

Ally was sitting with her hands neatly folded in her lap, waiting to be noticed.

"Ally," Alex said and looked at his second eldest daughter, "you can cut up your own pancakes. Don't sit there and wait for someone else to do it. You're old enough to do it yourself."

"Yes, she is," piped up Xander, "she's older an' me an' I kin cut up mine, see?"

"But I can't cut it in straight lines like Nana does. I want Nana to do it. She's doing Jonny's."

"You heard me, Ally. Cut up your own." Alex tried to look sternly at his daughter. It was amazing how much she resembled his twin. Her moss green eyes looked at him pathetically.

"She always wants everyone to wait on her." Penny looked at her younger sister disgustedly.

"Do not!"

"Do too!"

"That's enough, girls." Nana put a stop to the argument before it could escalate.

Emily felt exhausted. Her ankles were swollen and she ached all over from a lack of sleep. *I feel as if I could fall asleep at the breakfast table. This pregnancy is the most difficult I've had yet.* Shadows were dark under her eyes. Phoebe Lynn lay in the nursery asleep. She had cried most of the night. Nanny Jane was watching over her, but it was Emily who'd spent the night caring for the sick baby.

Alex took a good look at his wife and decided he would take the day off and care for the children. He'd take them all, along with Nanny Jane, to the park and let his wife have some peace and quiet.

"One-four-three, my dear girl." He looked at his wife tenderly.

Penny spoke with authority in her voice. "We all know that means I love you, Papa. I is one letter and love has four letters and you has three. One-four-three equals I love you!"

"Yes, and it also means that today, I am going to take you on an outing and let your mama get some rest. We'll get Nanny Jane to take Phoebe Lynn in the stroller with us."

The children began to talk excitedly, all together and all at once.

"One-four-three, Granpajah," Xander said excitedly.

"One-four-three back," Elijah said to the little boy. He looked at him with love in his eyes. *What a blessing Alex's children are to Abby and me. Thank You, Lord, for giving us the joy of children.*

"I've thought about it and thought about it. Tell me, Xander, how am I supposed to get those two puppies home? I need at least one hand to guide my horse. I certainly can't carry two puppies in one hand."

"Aw, that's not so hard. You just have to put each of 'em in a satchel or in your saddlebags or sumptin'. They're not too big yet, but they'll be as big as Daffy or bigger. At least that's what Papa said." He looked serious as he talked to Elijah. "I know what you kin do. You put each one in their own satchel and hook the handles over your saddle horn. That way you kin keep an eye on them while you ride."

"Well, I suppose that will work." He looked at Xander doubtfully. Wriggling puppies wouldn't stay in satchels…at least he didn't think they would.

Elijah rode out by himself right after breakfast, heading for the nearest place he could send a telegram. He promised to be back as soon as he sent messages off to Liberty and Abigail. He looked forward to spending the day with Alex. He'd help with Penny, Alley, Xander, Jonathan, and Phoebe Lynn.

The children were sorry Elijah would be going home on the morrow. He planned to leave before anyone was up in the morning.

CHAPTER XII

A merry heart maketh a cheerful countenance:
but by sorrow of the heart the spirit is broken.

PROVERBS 15:13

LIBERTY SLOWLY CAME OUT OF A DEEP SLEEP. She hadn't taken her normal ten-minute snap. A snap was what she called a short nap. She felt groggy and disoriented. She stretched and rubbed her hand over her flat tummy, thinking about the miracle growing within. *How happy Matthew will be! He loves children and to have his own…he's going to be elated. I can't wait to tell him.* She rested her hand on her stomach, feeling as if she already had a special connection with the baby.

Liberty lay thinking about Matthew and the worrisome feeling that wouldn't go away. She was sorry Elijah had gone to San Francisco. *I wonder how long he plans to be gone?* Thomas told her Elijah was staying with her twin, Alex. *Maybe I should ride down to the city and see if Matthew is there. It would be fun to see Maggie, too. I think I just might do that. I'm already halfway there. Wonder if Kirk would go with me?* She lay there for a few more minutes, praising God, thanking Him for who He was…grateful for His mercy and grace.

She began praying for Matthew and other people in her life. She prayed for the minister of the small church they attended in Napa. Matthew had never been before he became a Christian. Now, nearly every other month, they had the minister, who preached in three churches in the area, over to dine with them. He wasn't married and Liberty kept hoping he'd find a nice young lady to marry. Women weren't plentiful in the west. Her twin's best friend, Daniel, wasn't married yet, either. Danny the Doctor, she laughingly called him. He had lived with Alex until his family grew too large. Danny had moved out and found a place of his own.

Libby sat up and looked around the room. It was homey and pretty. Taupe colored wainscot covered the walls about three feet up and warm, dark, honey-colored trim divided the wainscot from the upper walls. Creamy color, with pictures of seascapes, graced the upper walls. The bookcase had a few books and bibelots that picked up the creamy sand and taupe colors. A large vase, filled with red roses, sat alone near the windows on a round table with a creamy marble top streaked with the exact color of the wainscot. *How did Abby ever find a table like that? It's gorgeous.* Liberty decided it was time to go downstairs.

Abigail was a bit concerned about the girl who'd come in last evening, Katie…Katie McKenna. She wondered what circumstances led her to run away.

Abby heard the bell clang and went to the door of the mission. A delivery boy handed her a telegram. She thanked him and went to a small side room she used as an office. After reading its contents, Abigail was upset. She prayed, *Lord, please protect and keep Matthew safe. Elijah sent this, first thing this morning. It's nearly time for dinner. What took the telegram so long to get here? Where could Matthew be? I wonder if Elijah sent a telegram to Liberty? I suppose he has.*

Bessie had left about an hour and a half earlier to begin dinner at the house. Abby gathered up her satchel and a heavy sweater. She looked out the window and saw it was beginning to rain. She wanted to get home before it began to pour. *The rainy season isn't over yet,* she thought with a sigh.

A slight commotion at the kitchen door, which opened to the back courtyard, drew her attention. She saw Kirk talking to the girl, Katie, as they came into the mission. Seeing the natural charm of the Bannister men, she smiled inwardly. *I do so love that young man!* She entered the kitchen as the two young people entered the other end of the room. She walked with outstretched arms toward Kirk, who walked right into them. He gave her a hug and kissed her cheek.

"Abby, how are you?" He straightened up, as Abby wasn't a tall woman.

"Oh, Kirk, how happy I am that you're here! I see you've already met Katie. I was just getting ready to head home. I'd like you both to come for dinner," she said impulsively. "Katie, perhaps you'd like to freshen up while I talk to Kirk. I've had a telegram I need to show him."

Caitlin, a bit bewildered at the friendliness of the people in front of her, had assumed Mr. Bannister to be a handyman, but these two certainly seemed on friendly terms. Cait rapidly assessed her options and decided she'd be more comfortable with Kirk and Abigail than with the three women who resided at the mission.

"I'd be pleased to join you for dinner if you will just give me a few minutes." She smiled at Abigail thankfully and wondered at the smile that hovered on Abby's lips.

"Of course," Abby responded, eyes twinkling. She was beginning to realize this girl was someone of means. *She dresses so similar to Liberty that it tickles the cockles of my heart. She seems quite well-mannered. Perhaps she's in mourning to wear all black like that. I can't wait to talk to Elijah. He always seems to have a better perspective on people than me. It looks like he'll be home tomorrow morning. How I do miss that man when he's gone. It's as if part of me is missing.*

Caitlin, with a backward glance at Kirk, headed up the stairs, wondering if it was imagination or did Kirk reek with charm. She was amazed Fire would allow Kirk near. She reckoned he had to be trustworthy. Horses always know.

She washed up and looked in the mirror. Her gray eyes, rimmed by thick curling lashes, looked shadowed, darkened by grief. She made sure her hair was still smooth and changed her blouse, which she'd also worn the day before, into a fresh one. She sat for a few moments to give Abigail Humphries time to talk to Kirk Bannister. Her thoughts swung again to Fire. She was shocked her stallion would allow a stranger near him but not the stableman, Joey. Mr. Bannister said Fire whickered to him. She wondered if Fire would let Kirk ride him.

Abby ushered Kirk into her little office.

"Kirk, please sit down. I want you to take a look at this. I received it minutes before you came in with Miss McKenna."

Kirk took the telegram and read it quickly. He looked at Abigail in astonishment and consternation.

"But he left three days ago. Where is he? Abby, I think you should know that Liberty came with me. She's at your house and wanted to talk to Elijah. We didn't know he'd be away. I see by the telegram that he's staying with Alex. It's not my story to tell but given the situation, you should know Liberty's pregnant. She only found out yesterday because Conchita told her. She's been sick every morning for over a week."

Abigail gasped and tears came to her eyes. *How blessed Liberty must feel. It was the one thing I wanted all my life and now God has blessed Elijah and me with Liberty and Alex and all Alex's children…and now, Liberty. Oh, Elijah will be elated. Thank You, Father, thank You for all these grandchildren. I feel barren no more.*

Kirk could see Abigail was overwhelmed by the news of Liberty's pregnancy.

"It's such a surprise, isn't it?" he said. "I can scarcely wait until Matthew hears the news. He will be dumbfounded by it, I'm sure. Don't worry about Matthew. He's in God's hands, after all. We both know God will take care of him. I think I'd rather not have Liberty know about Matthew just yet, at least not tonight. I want her to get a full night's rest. Perhaps we could tell her in the morning. There's nothing to be gained by telling her tonight, anyway."

"I agree. I know you came down here to help with some repairs, but there's nothing here that is an emergency. I think you should go home with Liberty tomorrow, perhaps try to trace Matthew's tracks."

"I think you're right. That would be the best plan. I can't understand him not letting Alex know he wasn't coming. Something's definitely wrong, but I have a gut feeling Matt's all right."

"Kirk, I'm quite concerned about this girl, Miss McKenna. I know she's hiding from someone, and the more I talk to her, the more I think she's come from a good background. I want to help her, but if she's run away and people are looking for her, I don't know how safe she is here. I don't think she realizes that people will look for her here at the mission. We may not be so well known outside of Marin County, but more and more people are beginning to know about us and our work here. Have you looked at her hands? Her speech and demeanor are gracious, but her hands look strong and calloused, as if she's used to hard work. It's a conundrum to be sure."

"Have you seen her horse, Abby?"

"No, but Joey told me it's a nice one."

"It's not only a nice one, it's a beautiful stallion, a gorgeous roan, and not a cheap ride, I can tell you that. The girl is not poor, not with a horse like that one. She wants me to try riding him."

"I wonder about her. If she is hiding, mightn't she be safer at the Rancho? Anyone who's looking for her will be sure to look here. What do you think? Do you think Liberty would mind having a young woman around the house?"

"I think she'd enjoy it. Since Sally Ann married, she's missed having a woman around, except Conchita, of course." He stood. "We'll keep Elijah's information about Matthew quiet for tonight. Tomorrow's soon enough for Liberty to know. Also, I think you should ask Libby before inviting Miss McKenna to the Rancho. She's been pretty tuckered out lately and might feel she has to entertain her. I know I could say yea or nay. After all, it's my home too, but it's Liberty who would have to amuse her. Let's see how it goes during dinner. Is that all right with you?"

"Perfectly fine with me. I just thought of something. Let's have Elijah tell her since the telegram said he'll be home first thing in the morning. Liberty is quite close to Elijah. It's as if she were his daughter. It would be best coming from him."

The two of them nodded their heads in agreement and relief. They left the little office and found Katie waiting for them at the kitchen table.

Kirk scrutinized the girl carefully and saw the shadows under her eyes and a bit of a droop to her lips. He wondered what the girl had been through recently. *She doesn't have the look of one who'd sit around and mope.* He looked at her hands, surreptitiously, because of Abigail's comment. *The nails are short but clean. Abby is right. Her hands have been used to hard work. Well, we will have to see what the evening has in store for this young woman. I feel somehow protective of her, but it certainly isn't every day I see a woman with a gun strapped to her hip who looks like she could shoot it. Reminds me of Liberty, even the way she dresses.* He smiled inwardly. *She's a regular Annie Oakley.*

Abigail handed the young woman a rain hat, but the girl said, "Thanks, but mine is used to being wet." She jammed her wide-brimmed hat onto her head, looking much like Liberty with her black split skirt and long boots. The main difference was she wore a black blouse where Liberty most always wore white.

They headed out the door and down the rain-drenched street, walking the few blocks to the Humphries' house. Chatting amicably until they arrived, Abby led the way into the front door. Caitlin and Kirk both took off their hats and shook them out before entering, wiping their feet on the mat. The house opened into a wide hall. The front foyer, lit by a chandelier, had a beautiful coat tree where they hung their hats. The Humphries had a selection of house slippers for guests, and Caitlin took off her wet boots and socks and slipped her feet into soft fur-lined slippers. She could feel the ambience of contentment in the very walls of the house.

She looked with pleasure at the large parlor on her left. It was understated elegance. Instead of a door, there was a huge arch at least three doorways wide. It was a grand room with a huge bay window, which made the room appear even bigger when they walked into it. The far wall had a large fireplace with a beautifully carved oaken mantel above it. The accoutrements perfectly complemented the room. Two ornately carved wingback chairs, the upholstery a pale green, matched the pillows of the settee that separated the wingbacks facing the fireplace. A cheerful fire burned in the grate to ward off the chill.

"What a beautiful room! It looks newly done. Have you recently refurbished it?" Caitlin loved the homeyness, yet felt the elegance. *There is peace here. What brings the feeling of peace to this room?* Before Abby could answer, Cait heard quick footsteps coming down the hall, and a beautiful woman entered. Her steps quickened even more when her eyes lit upon Abigail.

"Oh Abby, I hope you don't mind unexpected company." Liberty threw herself into Abigail's arms, which enclosed her in a long, thorough hug.

"Libby, child, you know you're always welcome." She pulled back and said, "Liberty Bannister, meet Katie McKenna."

Caitlin held her hand out to shake Liberty's, and her heart sank as she thought, *Mrs. Bannister—she must be Kirk's wife.*

"I am glad to make your acquaintance, Miss McKenna."

"As I am yours, Mrs. Bannister."

Deep gray eyes looked into moss green and liked what they saw. Caitlin covertly looked Liberty up and down, assessing her attire and demeanor, and appreciated the effect. There was an instant kinship, a feeling they'd known each other for a long time. Caitlin had never in her life had a close female friend except for Sweeny.

Until eighteen months ago, Liberty had few friends and those only from boarding school.

Drinks were on a sideboard and Abigail graciously poured out apple juice, raspberry lemonade, or blackberry juice according to the tastes of her guests. They went to the chairs before the fire. Libby and Kirk sat together on the love seat. Caitlin and Abby sat facing each other across the span of the coffee table.

Kirk took a healthy swallow of his apple juice. "Miss McKenna has offered to let me ride her stallion, Fire." He turned to face Liberty. "You should see him, Libby. He's a gorgeous gray roan. I don't think I've ever seen a more beautiful horse in all my life."

Caitlin beamed. "You're most welcome to call me Katie. I have never seen Fire take to anyone the way he did you, Mr. Bannister. Joey McClintock came in to feed him, and he wouldn't let him anywhere close. He won't even touch his food if anyone else is around. Fire will bite, too. Why, he nearly took the fingers off one of my ranch...ahh... one of my..." Her voice trailed off. "I never was very good at duplicity." She smiled ruefully at the other three, who gaped at her.

Chapter XIII

Thou shalt not steal.

EXODUS 20:15

CAITLIN FELT THE HEAT of a blush rising up her neck and suffusing her cheeks. She gazed back at the three people staring at her. *I've never been good at untruths,* she thought.

"I'm sorry…I suppose I may as well tell you why I'm here. It will take some of the pressure off me, since I've never been good at dissembling." She looked again at the three people seated before her and knew, somehow, she could trust them.

"I came to the mission because I overheard a threat made on my life. I was in a stall, bottle feeding a newborn calf whose mother couldn't nurse. I was on my knees, and I'm pretty sure it was my brother-in-law and one of our ranch hands who were discussing how to get rid of me. I'm not totally certain. You see, my da died a few days ago and…" Tears suddenly filled her eyes.

Liberty went to the girl and pulled her into her arms. She embraced the younger woman with all the love she could pour out. Tears stood out in her own eyes as she felt the girl's bereavement and sorrow.

"I'm so sorry, Katie…so sorry."

"Caitlin, my name is Caitlin Kendall McCaully. My da was the only one who ever called me Katie."

"Not the McCaully Ranch up in Sonoma County by Santa Rosa?" Kirk asked.

"Why, yes…do you know it?" Cait responded. She pulled a handkerchief out of her sleeve and wiped at her eyes and blew her nose. She was embarrassed by her outward display of emotions. It wasn't normal behavior for her.

"Who doesn't know it? Everyone north of San Francisco knows it. It's one of the largest cattle ranches in northern California. Well, Caitlin McCaully, welcome." Kirk grinned at her.

Cait smiled and dropped her eyes. *I would be attracted to a married man. Goodness, I've never felt this way in my entire life. His look turns my knees to jelly. I like his wife, though. She seems very sweet.*

Thomas entered the parlor and announced, "Dinner is served."

Abigail said briskly, "Let's go eat. I have a few things I'd like to say, but it can wait. Oh, Thomas, meet Katie McKenna. She's a new girl at the mission."

"I've met her, ma'am." Thomas winked at Caitlin. "We's jest not met formal like. I'm pleased to make your acquaintance, miss."

Caitlin, never one to make class distinctions, stuck out her hand. "I'm pleased to meet you, too, sir." They grinned at each other. Thomas left to help serve the meal.

Elijah and Abigail had several servants who were well liked, well paid, and well appreciated. Abby's personal maid had been working for them for a little over a year. Plechett was a single woman in her thirties. Born in France, she was petite and efficient. Liberty always enjoyed conversing with her in French whenever she visited the Humphries' house. Abby had grown to love Plechett and the feeling was mutual. Elijah had also wanted another person as an all-around help, someone who could not only help Joey McClintock groom the horses but could help serve or do whatever else was needed in the household. He'd hired Jim Pipkin, who could do almost anything from repairs to even cooking…if Bessie ever left her kitchen. He loved his job and lived over the stables in a neatly kept apartment. Everyone called him Pippie, which he secretly adored. He'd never told Elijah about his past, and Elijah had never asked. Pippie and Thomas enjoyed good talks and sometimes checkers or chess in the evening. They'd become good friends.

Abigail took Kirk's arm, Liberty took Caitlin's arm, and the four of them entered the dining room together. Kirk and Abigail were both dreading Elijah having to tell Liberty tomorrow that her husband had gone missing.

Jared Hart rode over to the McCaully Ranch. He wanted to have a talk with his brother, Jethro, who was assistant foreman. He didn't want to work, but he was beginning to think it was the only way to get his hands on some money. He wondered if Jethro would give him an advance. His head ached abominably.

He rode to the big house and thought he'd get Mrs. Dunstan to give him a cup of coffee to clear his head. Jared hitched his horse and, going up the stairs, let himself in.

He called out, "Anybody here?" Duney came out of the kitchen wiping her hands on a towel.

"Why, good morning, Mr. Hart." She smiled at Jared. "Can I help you with anything?" Duney knew the rest of the family didn't care for Mr. Hart, but he was part of the family, and she would do her best to make him feel welcome.

"Hello, Mrs. Dunstan, would you mind rustling up a cup of coffee for me?" Jared was on his best behavior.

"You're in luck. I just made a fresh pot. Mr. Ewen usually comes in round about now, and I try to have a pot ready for him. Mrs. McDuffy went into town to shop for a few things." She bustled around getting a cup and pouring Jared one.

"Here you are, Mr. Hart." Duney smiled as she handed him the cup.

"Thanks—think I'll just go sit in the library and enjoy this."

"Certainly, Mr. Hart."

Jared left the kitchen and made his way softly but rapidly to the library. His subconscious mind took in the fact that the room was beautiful. Walls of a soft salmon color stood in stark contrast from the dark mahogany of the mantel, shelves, and desk. A fire burned low in the grate. Four wingback chairs all sat facing the fire in a semicircle with a low, square table between them and the fire.

Jared made a beeline for the desk and sat down. He yanked open the bottom left drawer. Reaching into the back of it, he drew out a small satchel. He opened it and his eyes widened. Quickly, he stuffed the large amount of money into his shirt front, shoved the satchel back into place, and closed the drawer. He heard footsteps coming down the hall so he grabbed for his coffee cup, leaned back into the chair, and hurriedly put his feet up onto the desk.

Ewen walked into the library, and Jared allowed his feet to drop to the floor, but the thud was muted by the thick Belgian carpet that covered much of the hardwood floor.

Ewen didn't like Jared Hart at all. He was the opposite of his hard working brother, Jethro, who was nearly indispensable.

"What are you doing here, Jared?" Ewen bit out the words.

"Well, now, that's a fine how-do-you-do. I was thinking about asking my dear brother for a job, but I guess I'll pass. Where's Cait?"

"I have no idea."

"Is she out riding fence then?"

"No, she cleared out, and by my way of thinking, you're the reason why." Jared was shocked. "Cait's gone? Well, where she'd go?"

"I told you I have no idea. She was very closed-mouthed about where she planned to go or what she planned to do. Now, I'm asking you, again, what're you doing here?"

"An' I told you, I was thinking about working for my brother. I don't expect you'd allow that," he said sarcastically, "so I guess I'll just mosey on home." He stood slowly and headed for the library door, hoping the money in his shirt wouldn't rustle or fall out. "See you another day, Ewen." He walked out of the library and out of the house, his cup of coffee only half drunk and left sitting on the desk.

"Farewell." Ewen wondered why the man had come to the library. *Why sit at Mac's desk rather than in one of the comfortable chairs by the fire?* He walked to the desk and sat where Jared had been sitting. *Does he know about the payroll cash?* Ewen opened the drawer wide, he saw the flattened satchel, and his heart sank. *Payroll is due this Friday. Guess I'll ride into town and withdraw some of my savings. I can't prove Jared took it, but there'll be a reckoning with him on the morrow.* He decided he was in need of that cup of coffee he knew was waiting for him. He picked up Jared's cup and headed to the kitchen.

Jared felt as if the money were burning his skin. *I can't believe I took it, but what other options do I have? None, that I can see, or I'll be a dead man. Well, I'll just pay it back later.* He sneered at himself. *And just how will I be doing that when I don't have two cents to rub together?*

The day was gorgeous, signaling the rainy season was on its way out. The sky was as deep a blue as it had ever been, seamless, embracing a sun that shone brightly. The fresh air had warmth to it, making a body feel it was time to do away with coats.

Jared scarcely noticed the good weather. He rode up to a secluded spot on a hill and dismounted. Opening his saddlebag, the young man pulled the money out of his shirt and arranged it carefully as he counted it. He meticulously placed it into his saddlebag. It was enough to cover his entire debt and more. *Maybe I can win some of the money back.* He fastened his saddlebag and headed to McGregor's Saloon. He wanted to get the money paid before any of McGregor's men came looking for him, or Aidan found out about his debt.

A couple days had passed but Conor Innes was no closer to knowing his identity than when he first awakened at the Pindar's house. He did, however, feel he was beginning to make some headway with the men. *There's definitely bad blood between John and Rhys. They're at loggerheads*

over something. My bet is that Rhys is up to something along with his inseparable sidekick, Jeb. John feels something's not right but doesn't know yet what it is. I'd like to ask Sneedy, but a body doesn't go asking about another man's trouble. Guess I'll have to find out some other way.

"Sneedy, I heard mention at lunch today that we're all working together next week. What's that all about?"

"Waal now, looks as if this afta noon we'll start rounding up the calves, separatin' 'em from their mamas. Next Monday mornin' we're gonna start brandin' 'em. It's a real time-consumin' job an' a lot a work. We'll be glad for you, seein' as how you got all that experience an all." He grinned at Con, taking the sting out of his words.

Conor hoped he did. *I sure hope I have all that experience and all…I can recall seeing cattle stretched out like the sea in my mind. I'm pretty sure I know my way to rope a calf. I can remember having a contest with…? Whoever it was, he loved to rope, I do remember that. Lord, if You want me here to continue searching out whoever it is who threatened Miss McCaully, I'll be glad to do it. I do think You want that, but please help me recover my memory.*

Elijah arose early the next morning before the household was up. He'd said his good-byes the evening before. He shaved and dressed quickly, hoping to be away before anyone else arose because he wanted to make the first ferry across to Sausalito. He closed the bedroom door behind him and on quiet feet walked down the stairs. It was still dark. Although he was familiar with the house, he'd lit a taper as he didn't wish to trip over a toy or make a noise. Entering the kitchen, he lit a wall sconce and blew out the taper. Hard rolls and salami sandwiches were already made up in the cooler, and he stuffed them into his satchel. Elijah relit the taper, blew out the sconce candle, and went into the little room off the kitchen with the light in his hand.

To his surprise, Xander was there sitting on the floor playing with the puppies. A fat satchel lay beside him. He looked up at Elijah and grinned from ear to ear.

"Good morning, Granpajah. Mama and Papa said if it's all right by you, I kin come with you for a week or so. I have my clothes and workbook and other stuff I need in my satchel. I could help you carry the puppies. Is it all right? You kin say no if I'll be a nuisance, but I'd love to give the puppy to Aunt Libby. I've even saddled Blaze for you and Red for me. And…I's gonna ask you if I kin take one more of these puppies and give 'em to Granpa and Great Granny. Can I…huh?" Xander knew he was pushing to the extreme. He looked up at Elijah a little pathetically.

Elijah found this amusing because deep in Xander's eyes was the knowledge that Elijah could not refuse him anything within reason.

"Of course, if you're sure it's all right with your mama and papa, I'd love to have you with me. I was planning on riding up to visit Liberty and her papa and granny anyway. You'll be welcome company." He stooped and gave Xander a big hug that was returned in full. He was glad Xander was in the room. He, in truth, didn't know which puppy was his. They put on their coats, and Elijah took the puppy Xander handed him.

"Is this one mine?"

"Yes, and I'll take the other two. I yam glad they'll have nice homes an' I won't have to worry about them." He grinned at Elijah as he stuffed one puppy on top of his clothes and carried the other wriggling puppy under his arm. They went outside feeling the awesomeness of a fresh new day.

The air felt cool as wetness hit their faces like a blanket. A thin line of light was beginning to creep up on the eastern horizon as fingers of light began to shed their rays, filtered by a bed of fog that lay over the city. It wasn't as dense where they were, but they would be riding down into it. Elijah checked the girth on both horses.

"You did a fine job, Xander, and thanks for saddling up. It saves some time." He held the satchel and Xander tried to mount holding the other. He made it after three attempts, Elijah shouldering up the boy's rear to help him over the top.

"Whew, I made it. Bet it'd be easier if we had one more satchel. I kin hang the one with my clothes in it and carry another one of the puppies in the other. D'ya mind, Granpajah? There's one hangin' right by the back door."

"No, I don't mind." Elijah headed over the cobbles to the door. He grabbed the satchel and wondered if they were going to make the first ferry. He was grateful Xander had saddled the horses. They put both puppies into the satchels and hung the one with clothes over the pommel. Elijah climbed on Blaze and they started for the ferry. Elijah's puppy was inside his coat and squeezed up comfortably against Elijah's middle.

CHAPTER XIV

Be sure your sin will find you out.

NUMBERS 32:23b

CAITLIN LAY IN BED THE NEXT MORNING and wondered about the change in plans. She, in truth, was not used to someone else making plans for her. Not sure whether she liked the feeling or not, she lay thinking about the events of the evening before. Dinner had been delicious. Bessie wasn't simply a cook; she was a chef. Roast beef that had been stuffed with green peppers and dotted with onions throughout, with a scrumptious gravy over a bed of rice, was eye pleasing as well as palate pleasing. Abigail sat at the head of the table in the beautiful dining room. She'd been placed on Abby's left and Liberty on Abby's right, which was a position of honor. Kirk sat next to Liberty. There had been much banter between the two and Cait, who had witnessed few relationships beyond that of her sisters, enjoyed the fellowship. She felt a strong attraction to Kirk. It was an unusual feeling, and she was sorry he was Liberty's husband. After Abigail said the mission was becoming quite well-known for harboring women in need, Liberty had invited Cait to stay at the Rancho, a vineyard in Napa. She stretched and thought about how going to the Bannisters' Rancho would be beneficial.

For one thing, she'd be able to ride Fire freely on their property. If anyone came looking for her, the Bannisters assured her she'd be protected. At a distance, she'd look like Liberty to any inquisitive eyes. A second positive was that it would be closer to her own ranch and close to the mail box she'd opened. *I wonder if I should simply not worry about the threat and go home. It's not Jared I worry about. I know where the threat is there, at least I'm quite certain it's Jared. My main worry is, who else is involved? Will I be able to recognize the threat from someone else? I don't think so.* She wondered about the closeness she witnessed in the people with whom she had dined. *I do like what I see in these people. It's as if they have that same peace I saw in Da before he died. Whatever it is…I'd like to have it.*

Liberty Bannister seemed quite a woman. She not only spoke intelligently, she acted kindly. Abigail had broached the subject of Caitlin going to the Rancho when she saw how well the two young women got on together. There had been an instant rapport between them, and Caitlin had been surprised another woman could be so interesting. Most of Cait's encounters with other women had been boring, vapid discussions about clothes or the weather but nothing of any import. Cait considered the dinner a success. Scintillating conversation on a wide variety of topics sprinkled with humor and warmth. *Yes indeed, I like what I saw.*

Jared slept easier that night, knowing none of McGregor's men would be coming after him. He'd been able to resist gambling the rest of the money. There wasn't a whole lot left over, but if he could stay away from McGregor's, he'd be all right. The temptation was to gamble the money in hopes he'd win the other back and replace it before anyone found out it was missing. *The problem with that is, I haven't had such good luck, lately. I'd probably lose all of it. I know Ewen will know it was me if he finds it's gone missing. I hope that doesn't happen before I can replace it.*

Jared's temper was more even as the pressure of his debt was gone, but he felt guilty about the money. He climbed out of bed and looked down at his still-sleeping wife.

They'd had quite a row last night. He'd had too much to drink. He'd been celebrating, on his own, the payback to McGregor. Aidan had been upset that her husband's attention wasn't fixed on her the way it used to be, and she was tired of him drinking every night. They didn't have much in common these days. Jared wondered if they would have much of a future together. He didn't like clinging women and felt Aidan had become possessive, clinging to him like a noose around his neck. Dressing quickly, he made his way downstairs.

He walked into his kitchen and encountered a shock. Ewen was sitting at the round oak table, drinking a cup of coffee. He was talking to Cassie as if they were old friends. *Well, guess I'm in for it now. I had a feeling he'd find out, but I didn't reckon it'd be this soon. No sense bluffing my way out of it. I can tell by his eyes he knows it was me.*

"Good morning, Ewen. What are you doing here?"

"Maybe it's a fine morning for you, Jared. I think you know why I'm here. Get a cup of java and we'll go to the study where we can talk." Ewen spoke abruptly and stood as Cassie silently handed Jared a cup of coffee.

I don't like the sound of this, but I don't want to rile Ewen either. If Aidan finds out about what I've done, I'll be out of this house and on my keister in a hurry.

The house was Aidan's free and clear. Mac had given it to her without Jared's name on the title when they were married last year. The dwelling was situated on the edge of Santa Rosa, the county seat of Sonoma. Santa Rosa was quite populated for a western town and was steadily growing. Mac had bought the house without Aidan's knowledge but quite sure his daughter would love it. It was a beautiful home with the feel of money in its every floorboard. Jared liked the prestige it gave him with the townsfolk.

The two men went to the study and Jared closed the door after them. He hoped Aidan would not make an appearance until after Ewen left.

He didn't feel up to making an excuse as to why Ewen would make an appearance at their house. Jared gestured for Ewen to sit down, which he did, obviously feeling comfortable and putting Jared off balance.

"You know why I'm here."

"Yes, as a matter of fact, I do."

"Well, I've thought about this long and hard, young man. I spent an uncomfortable night, but I think I've come up with a solution."

"And just what would that be, Mr. Carr?" Jared almost sneered.

"Okay, Jared, you can have it your way, in which case I'm turning you in for robbery. We've had quite a rash of those around here lately. I'm sure the sheriff would hope to connect you to all of them. Or, you can start showing respect in your attitude. Do you still have the money? Can you give it all back to me right now?"

"No, I don't." He spoke curtly.

"Well, I've been thinking. You can work off your debt at the ranch, and I'll say nothing, or I can simply turn you over to Sheriff Rowe. I understand you two have had your differences. I'm sure he'd love to make an example of you. Take your pick but don't take overlong. I won't be waiting forever before I take action. On second thought, perhaps I should just turn you over to your brother and the rest of the ranch hands. After all, you stole the payroll due them tomorrow."

Jared's eyebrows flew upward and his eyes widened. His brother could be a formidable enemy, and the men who worked for McCaully Ranch were hardened and tough. They'd string him up as soon as look at him for stealing their money. There was a certain code among most cowboys, and integrity and honor ranked high. His brother, Jethro, didn't have the time of day for him.

"I won't have to take any time at all to think about it. I'll work for you." He reached into his middle desk drawer and pulled out the remaining money.

"Here's what's left of what I took." He handed the money to Ewen, who didn't bother to count it. "I'll work off the rest of it. I needed cash to pay off a debt."

Ewen ignored his comment. "I'll expect you after lunch…today. You will eat, sleep, and work at McCaully's until you pay off your debt. You're not allowed in the main house and I'll make sure McDuffy and Duney know it. If I have any problem with you, I'm telling you straight up, I'll be turning you in for robbery. You'll work for McCaully's until every last Morgan dollar is paid. I hope you're clear about what I'm telling you."

He arose and began to head for the study door. "You can spend your free time however you wish, but you'll pull your weight on the ranch, or else. No idle threats here, just the plain facts of the case. See you after lunch in front of the barn." He left.

Jared stared as Ewen shut the study door quietly behind him.

It was still early when Elijah and Xander rode up to the house. They were able to make the first ferry after all. Elijah dismounted, putting his little puppy down. He helped Xander by taking the two puppies from him and setting them on the ground, where they ran in circles, sniffing new scents.

"I can't believe we're here already. I'm terribly hungry. How about you, Granpajah? Are you hungry yet?"

"Uhhm, I'm quite hungry. We had a little problem eating those hard rolls, didn't we?" He grinned down at Xander, who grinned back.

"Yes, sir, it's hard to eat when ya gots the puppies to care for. I love hard rolls, cheese, an' salami. Can we have it for breakfast?"

"Yes, we can. I like it too. Maybe we'll add a little butter to it, what do you think?"

"My mouth's watering already."

Pippie came around from the back of the house. He happened to be looking out his window, drinking coffee in his apartment over the stables, as the two had ridden up.

"Good morning, Mr. Elijah…morning, Master Xander.

"Good morning, Pippie. Nice to see you, and I appreciate your taking care of our horses. We have empty stomachs."

"Well, looky here, looky here. What is this, Xander?"

Xander stood tall, lifted his chin, and answered proudly, "Our Daffy whelped seven puppies, Pippie. That's funny…puppy, Pippie."

"That does sound strange." He smiled at the boy with affection in his eyes. Xander was a regular visitor at the Humphries. "They sure are cute little things. How old are they?"

"They's nearly eight weeks old. I wish we could keep 'em, but we can't."

The puppies had all done their wees. Elijah still wasn't sure which one was his. They all looked the same to him. Xander unerringly picked up Elijah's puppy and handed it to him. He handed one to Pippie, and all three made their way to the back door.

Plechett opened it and gasped when she saw the puppies. She smiled widely.

"Oh, my, wait till the madam sees this! She's in the kitchen, sir." She swallowed before asking, "Are you keeping all of them, sir?"

"No," Elijah whispered, "just this one." He held a finger up to his lips, and his bright blue eyes sparkled with mischief. The four walked quietly down the hall toward the kitchen. They peeked in and saw Abby, Liberty, Kirk, and a strange girl eating breakfast. Elijah sat his puppy on the floor and motioned to the others to do the same. Plechett put her hand over her mouth to keep from giggling aloud. The four stood, watching to see what would happen.

All three puppies gamboled into the kitchen. One grabbed the ear of the puppy in front of him. They began to wrestle and tumbled under the table…a loud growl, a yelp as pointed teeth bit an ear too hard, and all three crashed into Liberty's legs. It happened so fast. Liberty upended her plate as she stood with a yell. Abby and Caitlin jumped up, and Kirk bent to look under the table. He laughed as he saw the culprits of Liberty's distress.

Liberty laughed too, as did Caitlin and Abigail. All three giggling women hunched on their knees and began pulling the puppies apart and cuddling them. Abigail looked toward the kitchen door.

"What are you thinking, Mr. Elijah Humphries?"

Elijah pushed Xander in front of him for protection.

"Oh, Abigran…I talked him into a puppy. We have seven in all. Daffy whelped seven. Can you believe it?" He counted on his fingers. "We gave one to a neighbor. One is going to Uncle Daniel, and one is going to Aunt Maggie. Now you kin have one, Aunt Liberty kin have one, and Grandpa and Great Granny kin have one. Then, I onlys have one left." He eyed Caitlin, seeing a soft heart.

"What's yer name?"

Caitlin smiled. "Right now, it's Katie. Do you think I could have that seventh puppy?"

"Do you have a yard where she could run around?"

"Yes, I do…a great big yard."

"Are you a friend of Aunt Libby's?"

Caitlin glanced at Liberty, who nodded her head slightly.

"Yes, we are friends. In truth, today I'm going up to the Rancho for a few days."

"Oh…you'll have a good time up there. All right…you kin have one. My papa's gonna be coming up here next week…ta Aunt Libby's, I mean. Granpajah, kin you send Papa a telegram and tell 'em ta bring the runt up here with him?"

"Yes, yes, I'll do that after we eat. Let's go wash up."

Pippie headed out to take care of the horses. As he shut the door, he realized Joey had come over from the mission.

"Good mornin', Joey…your timing is perfect." He smiled at his friend. The two took the horses to the stable.

In the kitchen, Bessie wiped up the mess on the table. Abby mopped the wooden floor. There was much laughter and chatter as they cleaned up. The puppies were helping, licking the floor clean under the table. Abigail laughed as she tried to push them away so she could swipe the wood with a wet cloth. As soon as Xander removed one puppy from the spot, another took its place.

Abby suddenly remembered she needed to talk to Elijah. She must let him know they hadn't yet told Liberty about Matthew. She pushed off her knees and hoped to waylay him before he said anything about Matthew, but it was too late. Elijah had reentered the kitchen, speaking to Liberty as he came in.

"I'm sorry about Matthew, Liberty. We'll find him...I'm certain we'll find him."

Liberty took one look at Elijah, her eyes widening and her pupils dilating as the import of his words engulfed her. She turned white as a sheet and Caitlin, who saw her blanch, moved quickly behind and caught Liberty as she fainted.

Caitlin lowered Libby to the floor. Bessie fetched a cold cloth to press on Libby's brow, and Abigail left to find some smelling salts.

"Who's Matthew?" Caitlin was trying to figure out why Liberty would faint at such news.

"My brother...Libby's husband." Kirk said the words softly as Bessie laid the cold cloth on Liberty's brow.

Kirk's reply was overshadowed by Caitlin's concern for Liberty. She knelt and loosened the neck of Libby's blouse but as she did, his words sank into her consciousness. Caitlin's face flushed red while her mind raced. *He's not married to her. Kirk's not married to Liberty. Oh, my, oh, my goodness.*

CHAPTER XV

A man shall eat good by the fruit of his mouth:
but the soul of the transgressors shall eat violence.

PROVERBS 13:2

"IS LIBERTY ILL?" Elijah asked. Kneeling down, he picked up Liberty's hand and patted it, real concern in his eyes.

"No," Kirk said, glancing at Elijah, "she's pregnant."

Ah, thought Caitlin, *that's reason enough to faint, and hearing about her missing husband that way.* She looked over at Mr. Humphries, and a frown tightened her lips. *He could have been a bit more circumspect... pregnant or not.*

Elijah sat down heavily in a chair and stared at this young woman who'd thought never to have children.

Xander was scared. He'd never seen anyone faint dead away like that. He was scrabbling, trying to round up the puppies and get them out of the way.

Abigail returned and passed the salts under Liberty's nose. She came to as the ammonia stung her nose lining. Opening her eyes, she was shocked and embarrassed to find herself on the floor.

"Why, I've never fainted in all my life."

"Oh, Aunt Libby, you scared the brat right out of me."

"You never are a brat, Xander." She smiled wanly up at the young boy. She sat up with the help of Caitlin and pressed a hand to her brow.

"Sorry, I...Matthew's gone missing?" She stood too quickly and a wave of dizziness hit her. She swayed and Caitlin helped her to a chair.

"You never told her?" Elijah looked unbelievingly at Abby and Kirk.

Kirk replied quickly, "There was nothing to be gained by telling her last night, except for her to get no sleep."

"I thought you could tell her, Elijah. I knew you'd get home early today." Abigail made no excuses.

Kirk said, "I'd decided to ride up to Napa today and get our Sheriff Rawlins on it right away. I also thought I might try to retrace Matt's steps. He was going to ride up to the Hendersons'—"

"Hendersons'!" Cait interrupted. "Do you mean the Merlot wine Hendersons? Why, they live just a hop, skip, and a jump from the ranch. They aren't home. They've gone south until late spring." Caitlin was doing some fast thinking. *Poor Mr. Humphries...I misjudged him. He's terribly upset that Liberty hasn't been told. I think I know why Kirk looks like Conor.*

"You're saying your husband's gone missing?"

"Yes, he left to go up to the Hendersons' and then was going to go to my twin's house in San Francisco. Evidently, he never got there."

"How long has he been missing?" Caitlin was quite sure she knew the whereabouts of Liberty's husband.

"For five days. He wasn't due home until tomorrow."

"I'm so sorry, Liberty, I didn't mean to spring it on you like that. I thought you already knew," Elijah said. He was still upset about her fainting. It wasn't like her.

"No." Libby looked accusingly at Kirk. "I know you're trying to protect me, but I don't want to be cushioned from anything. I never have been, not in my entire life, and I certainly don't want to start now."

Caitlin looked at Libby admiringly and said, "I don't want to stir up too much hope, but I think I know where your husband might be."

All eyes shifted her way in total surprise.

"I thought you looked familiar, Kirk. I hired your Matthew the night before I left the ranch. He arrived that evening with Doctor Addison in time for dinner. He…" She looked at every face and swallowed. "He doesn't know who he is."

Liberty and Abigail gasped.

"He'd been hit over the head and robbed up near the Galways' mine. My brother-in-law is Gavin Galway. One of his miners, a Mr. Pindar, found him on the road and took him home. It was fortunate that Doc Addison stopped by the Pindars' house on his way home from Vallejo. He nursed Matthew. Evidently, he'd been unconscious for over a day. He told me he felt fine, except his head hurt abominably.

"I hired him that evening to try to find out who on my ranch wants me dead. I overheard my brother-in-law and one of my ranchers discuss how to get rid of me."

Liberty sat down heavily.

"What does this man look like?" She didn't want to get her hopes up.

"Well, he looks a bit like Kirk here, except Kirk has lighter hair. Conor's hair…excuse me, but we made up the name Conor Innes so my foreman would be more amenable to me hiring a complete stranger. Ewen, my foreman, is quite partial to the Irish. Anyway, Conor has darker brown hair and deep-set blue eyes. He has a peaceful air about him. I think Kirk is taller by a couple inches."

"Did you notice his gun? He had the butt specially made…it's a one of a kind."

"No, I had my cook give him a gun. He had nothing except the clothes he wore, his holster, and his horse…a piebald mare. I'm hoping he can rope a calf. The men will start cutting the calves out and branding them on Monday."

"With the piebald, it's Matthew all right. It explains why no one's heard from him. About roping," Kirk said proudly, "Matthew is better than anyone I ever saw roping a calf, 'cept me, of course. We used to have contests all the time…and he owns a piebald mare. I think you are most likely correct in your assumption. It's Matthew."

Elijah spoke up. "Well, let's talk while we eat. Xander and I haven't had breakfast. I have it right here in my satchel." He rummaged in his bag. "Come on, Xander, let's sit down and eat. Maybe we could get these puppies put out in a stall for a bit. Do you think that would be all right?"

"Yup, Granpajah, I'll take them out to Pippie an then we's kin eat. I yam hungry. Miss Bessie, duya think I could have some hot chocolate milk…pul-lease?" He batted his eyelashes at Bessie, his big gray-green eyes sparkling with good humor now that he knew his Aunt Liberty was all right. For her to have a baby was no big thing…his mother had five and was on her sixth.

"Yes, Master Xander, I'll fix you some right now."

Elijah looked around. "Where's Thomas?"

Abigail angled her head toward her husband. Her voice changed and she enunciated clearly, "He's been *invited*, by Nelda, over to the Hancocks' house for breakfast. Nellie's planned a feast for him. Since you were away, I figured he could take some time off."

"Oh, Abigail, my girl…are you matchmaking again?" Elijah laughed at Abby's machinations. She was forever plotting how to put certain people together. He left the kitchen to wash up, again, after holding a pup. Xander and Kirk carried the three puppies to the barn.

Caitlin stared after Kirk. *Why do I feel so thankful he's not married? I have never, in my entire life, been attracted to a male. I like men a lot more than women, but attracted to any of them? Never! And Liberty Bannister? I have a strong feeling she will be different from any woman I've ever met. There's something about her that emits peace, despite her fainting spell. I like her. I'm going to find out what it is. I think Abigail, Elijah, and Kirk have it, too.*

Aidan came back from riding just before lunch. She was surprised to see Jared dressed in denims and checkered shirt. He wore a brown leather vest and his gun was strapped to his leg.

"Where are you going?"

"I've been feeling bored. I've decided to work on your *sister's* ranch for a while." He knew his remark would bring a spurt of anger to his dear little wife. His comment was meant to rankle her. She resented the fact that the entire ranch now belonged to Caitlin.

"What...are you turning over a new leaf, Jared?" she asked with a sneer.

He ignored her question but responded, "I won't be coming home most evenings. I'm going to bunk with the men."

Aidan looked at him with shocked eyes. "Why ever would you do that? If you're going to work over there why don't you sleep in the house? Are you having a fling with my little sister? Is that why you're going over there?"

"I said, I'm going to bunk with the men. Besides, your little sister isn't there. She headed out the day after the will was read and hasn't been heard of since." He continued to collect his things, stuffing some into a shaving kit and the rest into a satchel. He looked around for a bedroll and found one crammed into the back of the clothespress.

"Caitlin's gone? Why ever would she leave when she just inherited?" Jared ignored her question. He didn't answer because he didn't know.

"I'm going to have lunch and then I'll be off. I'll probably be home Saturday evening but don't arrange any dinner parties for me."

He didn't want to say he'd probably be dead on his feet. He'd been living a life of leisure and was not used to physical labor. He knew he was a show off, but he would need to pace himself if he was going to keep up with the men. Jared was taking Ewen's threat seriously.

Conor Innes awoke slowly. He didn't want to open his eyes. His dream had been so real, and yet, all he could remember were beautiful moss green eyes looking at him full of love. The face was a blur. His mind tried to go back, to remember. Usually, the result of too much searching was a raging headache. The headaches were less and less bothersome. During the day, he would sometimes have a quick flashback…something he was doing would trigger a quick memory. He simply couldn't hang onto it and make it grow into total remembrance. He felt frustrated.

Father, I don't mind working here. I promise to stay and help find the cause of Miss Caitlin's worries. I would, however, like to know who I am. I need your peace about all this. Help me ferret out the truth of what's going on here at McCaully's. I reckon I should go report my own robbery to the sheriff. I don't think Doc Addison did that or I would have had a visit by now. Help me, this day, to be pleasing to You, dear Father. Amen and amen.

He thought about God and how His greatness was manifested in every part of nature. He knew some people were straying from truth, worshiping the created rather than the Creator. He prayed that he would love God with a pure heart, one not tarnished by willful disobedience. He needed a Bible. He was used to reading a portion of scripture every day. *How can a body grow to know God more and more if they don't read what He Himself had men write? God inspired men to write so we can know His ways, His goodness, and His love. Help me walk in Your truth today, Lord.*

The men were beginning to awake. Dawn was fast coming over the horizon. Conor stretched and sat up, swinging his legs over the side of the bed. He stretched and scratched his chest, grinning inwardly. *Reckon scratching my chest is better than Eli over there scratching his buttocks.*

He donned his clothes and was ready for breakfast. It was most always fairly quiet until the men had consumed some coffee. As he started for the door, Rhys shouldered him hard, going the opposite direction. Conor grunted as he spun sideways. The roughness was on purpose and Conor knew it.

Instead of shoving Rhys back, he asked, "Room too small for you, cowboy?" As he spoke, he could sense all movement around him come to a halt, but his eyes were watchful of Rhys and never left his face.

"Why'n't ya watch where you're goin', you greenhorn?" Rhys spoke in an ugly tone.

Conor knew to back down from the man would be a sign of weakness. On the other hand, he didn't want to tangle with a bad-tempered cowpoke unless he had to. He pushed Rhys, who was blocking his way, knocking him sideways with his own shoulder. He strode swiftly toward the door that was being opened by Ricardo.

"You better watch it, cowboy," Rhys yelled as Conor reached the porch.

Jethro was coming up the steps and heard Rhys yell. He took one look at Con's set face. His new hire was barely containing his anger.

Conor strode to the mess house, Ricardo trying to keep up.

"You handle that *bueno*, Con-nor. You savvy the man, no? He one bad *hombre*, that one. I theenk you feet in here ver' nice. I'm glad for you to be in our crew, *sí*."

Conor turned and smiled at the Mexican who was so agreeable, sensing the goodness in him.

"So, because I'm part of John's crew, is that the reason behind Rhys' ugliness?"

"May beee, I doan know. He just one bad *hombre* an' you doan want to rile heem too much."

Jethro entered the bunkhouse, which was uncommonly quiet, and stepped up to Rhys.

"You got a problem, cowboy?"

"Nope, nope I ain't, but I ain't likin' your new hire neither. Thinks he's bettern' anybody else."

"Well, keep your nose to yourself, Rhys. He's not part of your crew, but I've seen him draw. He's faster than anybody I've ever seen. You mess with him, you'll be lucky he doesn't draw a bead on you, son. You wouldn't last two seconds going against a man like him. Listen up, men…I like that man. He's a hard worker and minds his own business. He's now part of this outfit so get used to it. I came out here ta say we have a new hire. Ewen's hired Jared for the roping. He doesn't have a lot of experience, and it's none of my business as ta why Ewen hired him. He'll get no preferential treatment from me because he's my brother… nor will he be treated any differently by any of you boys. Now, go get some breakfast…there's work to be done."

Jethro's eyes met John's and winked. He knew Rhys was bad news but couldn't seem to get to the bottom of the trouble. He'd had a good talk with Ewen, who said to keep Rhys on until the man became unmanageable.

John responded to the wink by looking down quickly to hide his amusement. The altercation between Rhys and Conor had been a deliberate ploy by Rhys to get himself embroiled in a fracas. Rhys must be involved in something really bad, but John didn't know as much as Rhys credited him with knowing. Whatever it was, Rhys seemed scared he'd be found out. John looked up at Jethro. He was a fair-and-square boss.

Liberty felt embarrassed. "I've never swooned in my life," she said to Caitlin. "The closest I ever came to it was when Elijah informed me that my late husband had cut me out of his will. Armand will never know it, but it was the best thing that could have happened to me."

She said to Elijah, in jest, "That's some effect you have on me." She giggled when she saw his face.

"Sorry, Liberty. It didn't cross my mind that these two," he said, looking meaningfully at his wife and Kirk, "would be too fainthearted to tell you about Matthew, no pun intended."

"Kirk is right. I probably would have spent a sleepless night. Instead, I slept quite well. And now, I think it's time that we got our things together and were on our way."

Chapter XVI

Envy thou not the oppressor, and choose none of his ways.

For the froward is abomination to the LORD:

but his secret is with the righteous.

PROVERBS 3:31-32

LIBERTY, CAITLIN AND KIRK prepared to ride to the Rancho. Both women had an easy time gathering their things as neither one had much to pack.

Kirk said, "You stay here, Liberty. We'll go down and saddle up and be back by to pick you up." He could see she was tired. Perhaps it was the fainting, but she looked weary to him.

"I'm ready to go, and I am quite capable of walking the few blocks to the mission. I'm not ill, Kirk, I'm pregnant."

"Well, I've never seen someone swoon before, and it was a bit frightening," he responded.

"Frightening…it scared me to death!" Xander had been frightened seeing his Aunt Liberty out cold like that. He had a chocolate mustache he was attempting to lick off.

Elijah hugged the young boy to himself and wiped his mouth on a napkin.

"I am glad you're staying with us. You can help Abigran and me train the puppy to go outside."

"Didn't I tell you? I started working with the puppies when they were four weeks old, and they're all trained. They'll scratch at the door if they need to go out. If that doesn't get your attention, they start whining. Then, if you don't pay attention, you're in trouble. I started timing 'em with Papa's extra watch. They need to go out about every two and a half ta three hours, but after you feeds 'em, they need to go out right away." He beamed proudly at everyone.

"That's tremendous news. I'm so proud of you." Abigail had been dreading the thought of having to train the puppy. She felt more amenable to having one knowing it was already trained.

Kirk said, "I guess we need you to go out to the barn with us. You can show us which puppies go with us. I reckon you're going to have to keep Elijah and Abigail's puppy busy today. He's going to be one lonely puppy with his mama and siblings gone."

"She," Xander corrected, "she's a she. I mean, a girl puppy. I'll go show you which ones you need to take with you." Kirk, Caitlin, and Xander went to the barn. Liberty turned to Abigail and hugged her.

"Thanks for having me. I feel this trip has been providential. If I hadn't met Caitlin, I wouldn't know where to begin to look for Matthew. We can only pray he'll be all right. Having amnesia sounds frightening, doesn't it?"

Abigail replied, "He's in the Lord's hands, after all. Perhaps it's all part of God's plan…for him to find the culprits who are threatening Caitlin. Perhaps there was no one else that could have helped to find out who's behind it all. Trust God, Libby, there's a purpose in all this."

"I know Abby, I know, and you're right. I hadn't thought of that." She turned to give Elijah a big hug. "I'm so thankful for you. You're as dear to me as my own papa. It's strange that I've known you longer. You were the instigator of my freedom. I don't believe I'd ever have left Boston without your help. Thank you, Elijah Humphries." She kissed his cheek.

Elijah's eyes teared up as she spoke. "You are a blessing to Abigail and me," he replied. "We're delighted about your news. And here you thought you couldn't have children. How God has blessed you with a wonderful husband and now a baby. He will continue to bless you, my girl. I do love you." He hugged her back.

The others had returned with the puppies.

"See this one, Aunt Libby? He's got that smudge on his nose. That's the one I picked out for you. Grandpa and Great Granny get the other one. Today, Granpajah an' I will telegram Papa to bring the other pup for you, Miss Katie." Xander was proud he had given away all the puppies in such an expedient manner.

Kirk shook his hand. "Xander, you're a born businessman. I'll help your Aunt Libby with the puppy. He will be a welcome addition to the Rancho. Maybe next year by this time, I'll have my own house built. Then I can have one of Daffy's next litters." He ruffled Xander's hair and and hugged him.

Everyone said their good-byes. Kirk and Caitlin, each carrying a puppy, and Liberty, with just her satchel, headed for the mission. When they arrived, they peeked in on Janne, who was making breakfast for the other two girls. Caitlin couldn't even remember their names. She'd been so exhausted when she met them. She could only remember Janne, the blonde one.

"Hello, everyone." Liberty spoke gaily. "We're setting out for the Rancho, but I thought you might like to see my new puppy." Caitlin took the puppy out of the satchel and the girls wanted to hold and pet it.

Kirk was eager to be on their way. The morning was nearly half gone already.

"I'll saddle Pookie for you, Libby, while you visit." He handed the other puppy to Janne.

Caitlin followed him out, merely saying, "Good-bye, everyone."

Fire whickered as they entered the dimness of the stable. Caitlin saddled him while Kirk saddled Queenie and Pookie. He led his two horses out and hitched them to the rail outside the barn. Fire stamped impatiently. Cait soothed him, led him into the bright sunlight, and handed the reins to Kirk.

"Do you want to try riding him now or wait?"

"I'll ride him, if he'll let me." His face glowed with pleasure as he took the reins and moved to stand right in front of Fire. He reached up sure hands to scratch Fire's cheek. Fire raised his head up and down and nuzzled Kirk under his arm. The stallion pushed gently at Kirk.

"I think you're jesting, Katie McCaully. This horse is as gentle as a lamb."

Caitlin was astounded at Fire's behavior. "He's never even done that to me. What is it with you, anyway?" *You've charmed me,* she thought, but said aloud, "You've charmed my horse, and he seems to adore you. And…he's not as gentle as a lamb. I'm not jesting. You'll see differently when someone else is around. I…" Her voice trailed off as she heard a door bang.

Kirk felt the horse stiffen as Joey McClintock came out of the house. Fire backed a step, flattened his ears, and glared at the newcomer with wide eyes and nostrils flaring.

"Reckon you're not jesting…what a change. I haven't seen him like this."

Joey made a wide berth around the yard and went into the barn with a softly spoken good morning to the two of them. Fire stood alert a few moments, as if ascertaining the man wasn't coming back out of the barn.

Kirk readjusted the stirrups, as he was longer in the leg than Caitlin. He threw a rein over the stallion's neck and stepped into the stirrup as Fire stood quietly, waiting for him to mount.

"It's truly incredible. He's only let my da and me near him. Ever."

Liberty came out of the house and the horse stood still but not stiff. Liberty knew better than to startle the stallion and she talked softly as she headed toward Pookie.

"Oh, Caitlin, he's gorgeous! What a beautiful horse! He's absolutely lovely."

Fire stomped his foot and pawed at the cobbles, his neck arched proudly. Apparently he wasn't upset by Liberty's presence, either.

"Well, my stars, I don't know what it is you Bannisters have, but I like it." Cait mounted Queenie, and Libby handed her one of the puppies. She climbed on Pookie, easily mounting, with the other puppy in the satchel. Wheeling Pookie around, she started to head out, but the stallion was having none of it. Liberty figured he wouldn't permit a mare in front of him. He pushed Queenie aside, took the lead, and sedately led the way out to the street. Kirk grinned at Liberty as his horse squeezed by.

Jared Hart was introduced to John, Drew, Ricardo, Sneedy, and Conor. He nodded to each one but said nothing. He recognized a couple of their faces, but Jared didn't know any of them.

Ewen had taken a real shine to Conor and wanted Jared to work with him. He hoped Jared would stick to Conor like glue. He knew from his encounters with the new hire that a bad partner wasn't going to influence Conor. His hope was that Conor would influence Jared. Mackenzie McCaully had nearly detested Jared. A blood-sucking leech around Miss Aidan's neck, is what he'd called him. Now Ewen had a real hold over Jared, and he was going to use it to the hilt. He would make a man out of him yet.

Conor was surprised at this stroke of luck. Sneedy had been his partner, but Jethro had been told to pair Sneedy with Ricardo. The two men were putting up fencing about one hundred yards away...working toward Conor and Jared. Conor was secretly glad he'd been paired with Jared. Now he could assess the younger man first hand...perhaps even see which ranch hand was his accomplice. He covertly studied Jared as he helped him, showing him how to dig holes for posts and string barbed wire.

Jared didn't talk much but tried his best to do a good job. He broke out in a cold sweat when he thought of how he could end up in jail or kicked out of the house.

Ewen rode out in the late afternoon to see how things were progressing. He rode a big bay, a gelding that had to stand close to seventeen hands high. Conor had not seen many horses that stood so tall. Ewen climbed down from his bay.

"How's it going, boys?"

"Well, pretty good I'd say," Conor answered. Jared barely looked at Ewen. "Jared here is a quick learner. Faster picking it up than I was the other day. I think we're going to work together just fine, sir." Conor looked across at the boss, knowing he was feeling them out.

"That true, Jared? You going to be able to work with Conor Innes?"

"Yes, yes I am. I'll be able to work right well with this man, I reckon." Jared was surprised at the warm glow he felt inside from the praise Conor had given him. He wasn't used to someone making positive comments about him. Both men continued to work as Ewen stood watching. It was a good match, and Ewen hoped Conor could turn Jared around.

Stepping into the stirrup, Ewen climbed onto the great horse with ease. He turned his gelding and spoke once more. "See you men later." With a nod, he put his spurs lightly to his horse's sides and was off.

Conor said, "I'm new here, too. You must know the boss personally."

"Yeah, I know him." Jared's reply was curt, and he kept right on working.

Conor thought, *At least he's not trying to act superior because he's married to the owner's sister. I got the impression he was a loafer. Guess I thought wrong. He's working hard enough. He must not want me to know his relationship to the McCaullys.*

Conor didn't try to press Jared for any more information. *Got to build up some trust before I try to figure all this out. Sure would help if I knew who I was.*

Kirk, Liberty, and Caitlin rode up to the Rancho and arrived just before dusk. The long drive from the start of the property to the house never failed to remind Liberty of the first time she'd set eyes on the Rancho. It had been too dark to see much, but the house had been lit up like a party.

She remembered having the feeling of coming home. She still felt that way. Even though she'd built a house and lived in it for a year, she continued to feel as if this was home. She almost felt like a visitor when she visited her papa and granny even though she designed most of the house and chose the colors and furniture. This Rancho was home.

Liberty wished she could ride to Caitlin's ranch immediately. She wanted to see if it really was Matthew and if he'd know her. She prayed he'd remember who he was.

The two women dismounted and as they did so, Diego came out of the barn.

"Welcome home." He looked curiously at Caitlin. *She dress much like Mees Libbee. Looky, looky at that...she haf a gun like Mees Libbee too, strapped to her leg...uhm uhm. She a gun-sleenger.* Diego smiled at his thoughts, grinning widely at the newcomer. *She ees ver-ry pretty.*

Liberty grinned at Diego, having seen his eyes widen at the sight of Caitlin's gun.

"Diego, meet Caitlin McCaully. Caitlin, this is Diego Rodriguez, our foreman. He's our 'can do anything man' and friend."

"Pleased to meet you, Mr. Rodriguez." Cait nodded and stuck out her hand to shake Diego's, which pleased him. He took her hand and shook it warmly.

"Eets nice to meet you, Mees McCaully."

"Look, Diego. Look what I have here from Xander." Liberty pulled the puppy out of the satchel and handed it to the startled foreman. "This is the newest member of our family. Isn't he adorable?" Liberty giggled at the surprised look on Diego's face.

Diego laughed at the wriggling puppy. Caitlin put the pup she was holding on the grass. He immediately ran in circles, his nose to the ground. He scampered to the edge of the stable yard, where grass grew, to do his business. Diego put Liberty's puppy down, and he ran to join his brother, his tail wagging nonstop.

Fire began to prance, lifting his head up and down. He didn't seem to want Diego so close. Kirk slipped off the magnificent horse.

"I'll brush Fire. You can have the other two horses, Diego. This one's pretty skittish."

"*Sí*, I can see eet. Conchita, she haf the good cheeken *enchiladas*. Eet smell so wonnerful in the keetchen."

Diego led the two horses into their stalls as Liberty and Caitlin picked up the puppies and headed for the house. Kirk waited until Diego was in a stall brushing Queenie before leading Fire into the stable. He put the animal in the farthermost stall from the door so he wouldn't be disturbed. Opening the stall door, he let Fire smell it before leading him in. The great horse went in easily. Kirk scooped a few cups of oats, giving the horse a bit of a treat. Unsaddling the big roan, he picked up a couple curry combs and brushed down the beautiful stallion. Fire seemed to enjoy himself. Kirk stroked the stallion and talked to him in a soft voice that was full of admiration.

"Yes, ol' boy, I think we have this mutual admiration society going on here. I like you and you like me. Yup, a mutual admiration society of two." He turned his head and spoke softly to Diego. "I need to talk to you when we're finished."

"Eets about Meester Bannister, *sí?*"

"Yes, it is," Kirk replied.

Diego hummed as he brushed the two horses, and Kirk crooned to Fire.

When the two had finished, Kirk straightened up the tack room as he spoke to Diego.

"Miss Caitlin is a guest here, but my guess is she will only stay the night. She was at the mission in San Rafael. Her father died this past week and she inherited. Evidently, someone wants her out of the way. She said a threat had been made on her life. That's one reason I'm going to ride over to her ranch. You know that bad feeling you've been having about Matthew? Seems like you have a good reason to have it. We're pretty sure Matt was robbed and left for dead on his way to, or from, the Hendersons'. He has amnesia and doesn't know who he is. Liberty and I are riding up to McCaully's tomorrow to see if it really is Matt and if we can find out who wants Miss McCaully dead. I'm going to leave you in charge here. I plan to stay and help with the calf branding, which starts on Monday."

Diego nodded in agreement and could only hope Matthew would be at McCaully's. He crossed himself when Kirk had said Matt had amnesia. Diego would pray for him.

CHAPTER XVII

Who can find a virtuous woman?

For her price is far above rubies.

PROVERBS 31:10

LIBERTY OPENED THE DOOR of the Rancho and ushered Caitlin inside.

"Please follow me. I want you to meet Diego's wife, Conchita." She headed straight for the kitchen. Cait walked much slower, looking around in appreciation of the beauty mixed with a homey charm. The house exuded a feeling of peace. On her right was a great room that looked inviting. *It's the same feeling I get from these people. They're comfortable, joyful, and full of confidence. There's love between them and certainly an openness I've never experienced before. I've never thought about it, but I suppose not having a mother, I missed out on the more expressive parts of relationships. Da never was one to hug us girls or show much affection.*

As Caitlin strolled to the kitchen, she watched Liberty walk toward a short Mexican woman with a shining black braid hanging down her back.

"Conchita, did you miss me? Look what I have from Xander." Liberty put her puppy down and hugged the woman, whose dark eyes glowed.

"*Si,* Mees Libby, I mees you. How you feeling?"

"I wasn't sick this morning," Liberty replied proudly, as if she had something to do with it. Conchita felt a puppy lick on her leg.

"They ees sweet puppies!" She knelt on the floor to pet them and looked curiously beyond Liberty to Caitlin. She straightened and wiped her hands on her apron. The puppies ran around, exploring.

Liberty drew Caitlin forward and introduced the two women.

"Caitlin, this is one of the most amazing people you'll ever meet in the whole world, Conchita Rodriguez. Conchita, meet Caitlin McCaully."

Conchita gazed at the girl whose eyes looked bruised from sorrow. Caitlin stuck out a hand to shake, but Conchita felt an overwhelming compassion and instead of taking her hand, she gathered the girl to herself and embraced her as if she were her mother.

Caitlin took an unsteady breath and began to cry as if her heart would break. Caitlin had never had a mother and the tenderness of Conchita was her undoing. The tears took her by surprise, but she couldn't help herself. Her shoulders shook with sobs. She grieved the loss of her da. In truth, all she wanted was to go home and lose herself in work.

"Ah, Mees Caitleen, God is good. He weel give you strength to bear whatever troubles your heart." Conchita continued to hug the girl as if she could soak up some of the sorrow.

Liberty's heart sorrowed for Caitlin, knowing she must have loved her father very much. She would be devastated to lose her papa or Elijah. She hoped she could help Caitlin in some way and share with her the love of Christ. Liberty rubbed the arm that had been broken; it ached. She knew the weather was changing.

Caitlin pulled back from Conchita, wiped her eyes with the back of her hand, and pulled a handkerchief out of her sleeve to blow her nose.

"I'm sorry. I don't know what's the matter with me. I've never done that in my entire life."

"You've just lost your father, you're quite certain someone is plotting to kill you, you've left your home and ranch in fear, and you don't know what's the matter with you?" Liberty smiled at Cait, but her green eyes were serious.

Conchita looked startled by what Liberty had said.

Liberty patted Conchita on the back. "My goodness, it smells good in here. We're having *enchiladas*, aren't we?" Without waiting for an answer, Liberty went on to caution Conchita. "By the way, we're not telling anyone else Caitlin's real name. We're calling her Katie. She's a guest here unless she decides to come with me tomorrow. I'm going to her ranch. We think Matthew is there working as a ranch hand, but he doesn't know who he is."

"Meester Bannister doan noh who he ees?"

"No, I mean, yes...he doesn't know who he is. He was hit over the head and robbed. Caitlin is pretty sure he's Matthew, but we don't even know that for sure. Elijah was at Alex's house but came back to San Rafael this morning. He said Matthew never showed up at my brother's and never telegrammed to cancel, either. Kirk is going to try to track him down. If it proves not to be Matthew at Caitlin's ranch, I think we should hire the Pinkerton's. We must pray and believe that God has us all in his hands. Kirk and I will head up there tomorrow."

Kirk entered the kitchen. "Hello, Conchita, mm, smells good in here. I'm hungry."

"You all wash up an' I weel serve. I theenk you come home thees night, but I not sure. I gif Lupe and Luce off today. They go veesit their *tia* and *tio* in San Franceesco."

Liberty said, "We can dish up ourselves. Don't set the table...we'll all just get our own. Oh, but it does smell so good! I'll show you your room, Cait, and you can wash up in there." She grabbed the jug of fresh water that sat by the back door and headed down the hall.

Kirk whispered into Conchita's ear, "Liberty fainted this morning. I hope you make her go to bed early. She has a mind of her own, that woman." He kissed Conchita's cheek. "You are the mainstay of this house—you do know that, don't you?"

"I weel try to get Mees Libbee into the bed early. An' I theenk we all important to thees house, but *gracias*, Meester Kirk, *gracias*." She patted Kirk's arm and turned away, her eyes misted over, touched by Kirk's words.

Kirk found an old blanket and took it outside the French doors of the kitchen. He folded it several times and placed it in the corner next to the house. A slanted, red-tiled roof stretched back as far as the house itself, held in place by columns. The width of the roof extended about fifteen feet wide. It was perfect for parties and provided shelter from the sun and rain.

He found a battered tin pan and pumped water into it for the puppies. The courtyard was perfect for them as it was entirely enclosed by a stucco wall. He asked Conchita for some leftovers. Spanish rice with chunks of beef was put into a dish and the puppies ate hungrily. He went back in to see if there might be any bones the pups could chew on. He snagged two soup bones out of the cooler and returned to the patio. As he stood watching, it began to pour rain. First, huge droplets hit the cobbles not covered by the tile roof. In less than a minute, the downpour drenched the courtyard, flattening flowers around the fountain in the center. Kirk stood watching the deluge and thought about Caitlin. *Well, Lord, I thank You. I know I need a Christian wife...I won't be unequally yoked, but I believe that won't be a problem. I plan to be the spiritual priest of the home as Your Word desires every man to be. Prepare her heart, Father, to accept You and the love You so readily give us. Thank You, again, for bringing that woman into my life.* Kirk had never thought to fall in love so completely, but Caitlin captivated him. It was the deep, satisfying, commitment type of knowing this was right. Content the puppies would be comfortable, he went inside to wash up.

Liberty led her unexpected guest to the room she herself had occupied when she had come to the Rancho two years ago. It was a beautiful room painted an airy yellow that made the entire space look sunny. French doors, all glass, led to the outside. The doors had a curtain that pulled to one side, matching the ones at the large windows. It was fresh and warm. There was a fireplace, but it wasn't lit. The mantel above it was a dark mahogany. Above the mantel hung a picture of a field of daisies.

The bedroom reminded Caitlin of her own yellow one, only hers was wallpapered with sprigs of daisies on it.

The room darkened as clouds rolled in and blotted out the blue they had enjoyed on their ride to the Rancho.

"Thank you, Liberty, for being so gracious. This room reminds me of my own at the ranch. It's yellow too, with daisies." Her eyes misted. *I must be tired. I'm too emotional. I can't remember ever feeling this way.* "I love the yellow. Look, it's going to rain, and yet in here, it still feels as if the sun is out."

Liberty replied, "I know. This is the room I stayed in the first night I arrived from Boston a little over two years ago. It was during the rainy season, but this room never seems dark or depressing."

Liberty thought back to the heavy darkness of the rooms of her old house in Boston. She'd had Elijah's old firm take care of selling it. It held horrible memories. Liberty had dealt with her feelings, but she found just one time of laying everything out before God wasn't enough. When any bad feelings arose she handed them over to God. Her heart held neither bitterness nor concern about the past. It was over. And, with God's help, she was determined to keep it that way.

She led Cait to the little room and showed her the commode. She set the jug next to the sink. It was cheerful, but Liberty was thinking of putting in the newer flush toilets. It would be a huge renovation, but it would be worth it once it was done.

"When you're ready, come straight to the kitchen. We eat in there. You don't have to change for dinner, either. We are fairly informal unless we're entertaining the mayor, minister, or some bigwig. I need to go wash up. Is there anything else you need?"

"No, this is perfect, thank you."

Liberty left and Cait sat in a chair for a minute to collect her thoughts. *Liberty will ride up to the ranch tomorrow. I'm glad. I want to go home. Think I'll see if Kirk will stay on and help with the branding. He'd be another set of eyes and ears and could keep tabs on his brother. That Conor is his brother is a foregone conclusion in my mind. He looks just like him. If I stick close to Liberty, Kirk, or Con, oops, not Con…Matthew, I should be all right. Perhaps Liberty could be my guest for a week or so. I'll ask her at dinner.*

Caitlin let herself out the French doors and thought the vineyard beautiful. It was a private little patio, so she quickly divested herself of her split skirt and shook it out to rid it of any dust. She stood watching as it began to rain. She'd always loved the scent when rain first fell. She took a clean blouse out of her satchel and donned it. Fastening the tiny jet buttons up the front, she checked her reflection in the mirror. My hair is a disaster. She washed up and quickly rebraided her hair, letting it hang down her back much like Conchita's. Caitlin pinched her cheeks for a little color and felt she was ready to eat. Her stomach was rumbling. She took a deep breath and went to the kitchen. Kirk was already there, but Liberty was not.

Caitlin felt the color climb into her cheeks as she walked into the room.

Kirk leaned against the double doors that led to the courtyard and perused her lazily.

Conchita felt a charge in the atmosphere and with sharp, black eyes saw the look on Kirk's face. *Uhhm, I know someday a woman weel come. She knock heem off hees feet. Sí…thees ees the one.* Conchita laughed inwardly. *This one weel not be the easy woman for Meester Kirk, no. Thees one weel make Meester Kirk dance.* She observed the girl carefully. *I theenk she ees good girl. Praise be to You…Dios del Padre.*

Liberty entered the kitchen. "I'm famished—let's eat."

The four made a circle and joined hands. Kirk clasped Caitlin's hand and felt a warmth climb straight up his arm. His heart began to pound harder. *I can hardly believe my reaction to this girl. She's upended my world.*

Liberty thought Kirk would pray, peeked to see him preoccupied, and said, "I'll pray. Thank You, Father, that You have watched over our family. I thank You for protecting Matthew. Keep him safe, dear Lord. May we all be guided by Your hand. Father, thank You for Caitlin. We pray for Your provision and safety over her. Help her, Father, to know Your comfort during this time of bereavement. Thank You, now, for this food. We pray this in the matchless name of Christ our Savior. Amen."

Caitlin smiled at Liberty. "Thank you, that was beautiful." Her hand tingled from holding Kirk's.

"You're welcome. Come and dish up. You'll enjoy Conchita's *enchiladas.*"

Dishes were stacked at the end of the counter. Conchita handed one to Caitlin and had her begin dishing up.

"You weel like thees, Mees Caitlin, ees good food. An' you, Mees Libbee, you must eat for you and the babee."

Caitlin was endeavoring to keep her thoughts on the food, which smelled wonderful, but she was acutely aware of Kirk standing behind her.

"This looks wonderful. I haven't had Mexican food before. Our cook, Duney...rather, Mrs. Dunstan, is Irish." Cait dished herself a generous helping.

"You like the cold tea? Or, we haf the apple juice. What you like to dreenk, Mees Caitlin? I get eet for you." Conchita set some glasses out and waited to pour.

Liberty pointed to a bowl with chopped-up tomatoes. "One word of warning, Caitlin, this side dish is salsa. It has *jalapeño* peppers in it and is delicious but spicy hot. You eat it with the *enchiladas*...but sparingly, until you get used to it." Liberty grinned in remembrance. "My friend Maggie choked on it the first time she had it. She took a huge mouthful, not realizing it is truly hot."

"You go ahead, Liberty. Ladies first. I'll wait until you dish up." Kirk was trying his best to keep his eyes off Katie. *That's what I am going to call her, he thought, it's what her da called her and seemingly no one else. Well, I have no doubt in my mind this is that forever kind of feeling that's come over me. I've never in my life felt so protective or bowled over by a female. I am in love, completely, overwhelmingly, totally, utterly...I could go on and on. This is it, Kirk Bannister. This is the woman to have and to hold until death do us part.*

CHAPTER XVIII

Set me as a seal upon thine heart,
as a seal upon thine arm:
for love is strong as death.

SONG OF SONGS 8:6a

AFTER HE DISHED UP HIS FOOD, Kirk walked slowly across the kitchen and sat next to his future wife. That she was, he had no doubt. If she already had a beau it was simply too bad. She was his. He explored her face with intense eyes.

Cait caught his look and her gray eyes gazed into his. It was as if time stood still. She felt confused and looked down. *Is that look what is in my own heart? Am I imagining more than I should?* She raised her head to glance at him but found his eyes still on her. A flush crept up her neck, but she couldn't look away. Caitlin had always been honest, and her gaze back at Kirk was open and true.

Liberty, busily eating, suddenly became aware of the stillness, and with a fork of food halfway to her mouth, saw something precious and private. She looked away…embarrassed by what she'd seen. Her green eyes glanced at Conchita, who was standing at the counter grinning as if she personally were responsible for what was happening between Kirk and Caitlin. Liberty grinned at Conchita, but the other two didn't even notice.

The moment passed but an unspoken agreement forged between Kirk and Caitlin. She was in deep mourning. Death had taken her father, who'd been the man in her life. She'd thought to mourn for years, but everything had changed. She knew in her heart she would always miss her da, miss him deeply, but she'd found her man…a man to love 'til death do us part…*love is as strong as death…now, where have I heard that?*

It was nearly eleven at night. The man dressed all in black wore two guns, the holsters strapped to both hips. It was dark and his clothing was chosen purposely. He didn't care for anyone to see him. He rode to the east border of the McCaully property, slid off his horse, and waited for two men to show up. His black horse and clothing made him indiscernible and he blended in with the darkness of night. The stars were sprinkled here and there but mainly shrouded in the thickness of clouds. The rain had come and gone but would not be long in coming again.

He looked up and stared toward the direction of hooves approaching swiftly. *Good. I don't have to wait all night for them to show up.*

Two riders, barely noticeable except for the sound of hooves and jingle of harnesses, rode up and dismounted quickly. They were silent, no greeting given.

The man in black spoke as if he were the boss. "Glad you could make it. Have you heard anything more on the McCaully girl?"

"No, sir, she's vanished inta thin air. I cain't get away durin' th' day to search for her. I'm thinkin' we need the Pinkerton's in on this. I jest don't know where she's gone. No one at th' ranch knows where she is by my reckonin'."

His accomplice stood in the darkness, not saying much. He pulled out a cigar, cut the end, and lit it, puffing at it several times to get it going. He observed the other two with veiled eyes. He was in on this operation, but he didn't say anything to the man in black. *I own the cowboy, but him...reckon I'll wait and see. I don't trust him, and he certainly shouldn't trust me.*

"No!" said the man with two guns. "We're not bringing anyone else in on this. It's too big. I'll be paying you both a goodly amount next week. I took some samples into a surveyor's office in Napa, and it's the real stuff. We've got to get rid of the McCaully girl and orchestrate things to go our way. Keep your eyes and ears open. It won't be long before we're mining freely."

The man who smoked the cigar said, "By the way, you better stop robbing lone men on the road. It's a huge blunder, believe me. That's about the fourth one now, and we don't need any lawmen around here breathing down our necks looking for you. Watch your step. Do you hear me?"

The man in black nodded. "Yes, I hear. I'll tell my men to stop." His cold eyes seemed to glow in the dark. He fondled his right gun butt and liked the feel of it. His man had given it to him after the last robbery. It was custom made and had a grip like none he'd ever seen.

The man who smoked the cigar and the cowboy climbed on their rides, not realizing the man in black considered them extra baggage. He needed them for the time being, but the cowboy was being forced into this and the other—the other was greedy. The man with two guns couldn't afford to have too many men know who he was. He'd get rid of these two, one a cowpoke and the other a man of some repute in Santa Rosa. *Once their usefulness is over, so are their lives.*

Conor had found a Bible in the small bookshelf that resided in a corner of the bunkhouse. It was squeezed in beside some classics. He'd pulled it out and was now lying on his top bunk reading Proverbs. It was a book someone had told him to read on a regular basis. He could see bright blue eyes that spoke of God's love. He could almost recognize the face. It danced on the fringes of his memory but when he tried to grasp it, the face eluded him. He could hear the man's voice in his mind's ear saying to him, "I read a chapter in it every night. It's a book to live by."

Jared was in the next top bunk, lip curled in disdain. *How could anyone read that drivel? It's boring.* He heard Con chuckle and wondered at it.

"What's so funny in there? I thought it was a book with a bunch of don'ts and very little do's."

"Oh, I find this humorous. Listen to this: It is better to live in a corner of the roof than in a house shared with a contentious woman."

"That's the truth." Jared thought about it for a second and chuckled aloud. "I can see why you think it humorous, except I sometimes *have* a contentious wife, and I can see the truth in those words."

"There's a lot of those tidbits of wisdom in Proverbs. I remember one I read that's similar. I don't know it word for word, but it says something like, a nagging wife is like a constant dripping."

Jared chuckled again. "Isn't that a form of torture? I think I remember reading something about the Spanish Inquisition and dripping water was something that wore on a man's nerves. I see how a woman could be compared to that. My wife isn't a nag. She just doesn't talk, maybe for days on end, if she's angry with me."

"Well, that isn't healthy either." The two men talked together for quite some time. Jared couldn't remember the last time someone stirred his thinking like this man. He was a balm; he emanated peace. *Peace... that's something I've never found.*

Conor said to him, "Would you care to go for a walk with me?"

"Sure, I'd like to stretch my legs."

The two men went out and walked around the corral. It had rained and they could smell the wet dirt and a few not-so-pleasant odors, but the dust had settled.

Connor said to the younger man, "I'd like to share something I found about a year and a half ago. Please hear me out."

"All right by me."

"Before I start, I want to tell you that my name's not Conor Innes."

"What? Why are you goin' by another name?"

"I was robbed and beaten and almost died last week. I don't rightly know who I am. I don't know if I have family looking for me or where I hail from. I do know one thing though."

"Well, what's that?"

"I know that I'm a Christian. I have a personal relationship with Jesus Christ, and it doesn't matter who I am. God knows who I am. I can't rightly explain it, but I have a deep-down peace and contentment that the struggles of this world can't touch. It's like having a king and being subject to him, but He takes care of all the storms life brings my way if I let Him. I can see you are a hurting man, Jared. You long for something and wanted your wife to fill that longing but she can't, she never could. Only Jesus can."

"You're right about that. I thought being married to Aidan would satisfy my gut...would take away the feeling that I don't belong or I'm not worth much. It did for a while, but it didn't last."

"I know...nothing does, except a personal relationship with Jesus Christ."

"Well, how do I get that?"

"The first thing you do is to repent of your sins, the things you know you've done wrong, and then you ask Jesus to come into your heart and take over."

"I'm ready...right now."

Doc Addison had knocked on Sheriff Rowe's door every single day since dropping Conor Innes off at the McCaully Ranch.

Sheriff Rowe was sick of hearing the complaints Doc Addison set forth. There had been three men beaten and robbed on the Sonoma road before Conor. He made the fourth. The sheriff believed the general population of the town of Santa Rosa was quite happy with the way he operated. He heard a complaint or two, but for the most part the fine citizens were content, mainly because they were jejune. They simply didn't know anything. The doctor, the mayor, and several prominent citizens were not happy. They were aware shady deals had been made, payoffs to those who agreed with the politics of Sheriff Rowe. Some council members voted on controversial issues the way the sheriff asked in return for personal favors. Nothing was done overtly to upset the townspeople but corruption lay at the heart of it.

Doc Addison had enough of nothing being done. He mounted Blondie and decided to take a ride to Napa. He knew Sheriff Rawlins. *Something has to be done. Someone's going to get killed the way things are going. I've had four men, counting the one who can't remember his name, that I've treated for head injuries after being robbed. I think Sheriff Rowe is too busy with other things to even care.* He rode south at a gentle lope. In truth, it wasn't such a long ride. He felt disappointed to find Sheriff Rawlins was out. He wrote a long missive and left it on the lawman's desk. He headed back to Santa Rosa worried about the rash of robberies.

Kirk went to the barn to saddle up the three horses. Diego was there already and had saddled up Pookie and Queenie. Kirk slapped the foreman on the back.

"Diego, you are one fine *hombre*. Thanks for saddling up the horses. I'll send a telegram and let you know if it's Matthew or not. Miss Caitlin seems to think it is. Reckon I'll stay there, at least until the branding's finished. I'm hoping to find out who's causing problems on her ranch. If I don't, I plan to bring her back with me, but I don't think she'll be too willing."

Fire was shaking his head up and down and had whickered twice. Kirk went into the stall with a carrot in his hand and offered the horse the treat. He stroked the fine animal and spoke softly to him. Fire put his head on Kirk's shoulder. It surprised him mightily that this horse was so loving toward him. He saddled Fire up and led him out where Caitlin and Liberty were already waiting. The two women were dressed so alike he had to grin. They'd already breakfasted.

"I need to run inside and get my satchel...I'll be quick." Kirk strode to the house. First, he went to the kitchen to tell Conchita they were leaving. He checked on the puppies but saw Lupe and Luce had everything under control. He grinned at the two playing with the pups.

"I can see Conchita's going to have trouble getting any work out of you two today." They laughed up at him from the patio floor.

"Dose two...I weel haf the trouble now," Conchita laughed her explosive laughter. "They weel take good care of the puppies, you no haf to worry about that."

"Yes, I'm sure they will," Kirk replied. "I don't know when I'll be back. I'll be gone at least the week, if not longer. Alex is supposed to come up Sunday, I think, but he'll be staying at Liberty's Landing. Take care, Conchita." He kissed her cheek.

He went to his room and opened the bottom drawer of his chiffonier. Pulling a tiny velvet bag out of a small box, he stuck it deep into his denim's pocket. He grabbed his satchel and headed to the barnyard, surprised that Katie was on Queenie.

"You're not going to ride Fire?" He looked up at the woman whose clear gray gaze was upon him.

"No, I hope we get to the ranch by lunch time. I'd love for the men to see you come riding in on him," she said with a huge grin. "I believe it will be a priceless moment. None of those men can get even close to Fire, even when he's in the paddock or tied to the hitching post."

Kirk checked the girth and mounted Fire. "Don't know why he loves me, but the feeling's mutual."

The three, with a wave to Diego, headed for the McCaully Ranch.

John and Drew decided to ride out together. They wanted to see if there were more cows that needed rounding up after breaking through the fence the week before. The McCaully Ranch had more than a thousand acres that had never been fenced in. The two men knew some of the cows that had plowed through the fencing had calves that needed branding. They rode by Jared and Conor to let them know where they were headed and then on down the fence line to Ricardo and Sneedy.

"We're headin' out to th' crick...Diablo Ridge. Should be back by lunch. Jest wantin' ta see iffen we have calves needin' ta be rounded up." Drew was more talkative than John. The men nodded to each other and the two on horseback wheeled around and galloped off. They slowed to a canter but had quite a ride to the creek and didn't care to miss lunch.

Meanwhile, Jared worked steadily alongside Conor Innes, surprised at himself. He'd been working for a couple days, but he was enjoying the labor. He and Conor talked about politics, history, favorite books...a variety of subjects while they strung fencing. Conor also told him how to grow spiritually. They would read the Bible together in the evenings and talk. Jared had never had a male friend.

The work at McCaully's was hard, but Jared was beginning to realize why these men were content. To work hard and achieve something gave more pleasure than a fast greenback at the gaming table ever did. Jared had never had much self-worth. His mother had died when he was five and his father had married a woman who had no time for him. His father was always gone, but there had been plenty of money and no responsibility as he grew up. Jethro had chores but Jared never had. He'd never truly worked a day in his life. Jared hadn't realized that a man's self-esteem was tied up in his work. One thing he now knew in his heart of hearts...Jesus was the way to real contentment and peace.

Chapter XIX

Thou shalt not kill.

EXODUS 20:13

JOHN AND DREW rode for a long while, finally pulling up at the creek. Drew wondered who else was there and pulled up on the reins.

"Whoa," he said and stopped to point out the tracks to John. A gunshot rang out, catching him full in the chest. Several more shots were fired in rapid succession. Drew fell off his horse, his hands clutching his chest. He felt air whoosh out of his throat and knew his lung had been hit.

John leaped off his horse and pulled Drew into the scrub oak to take cover. John fired back but couldn't see where the shots were coming from. Drew was trying to staunch the flow of blood with his own neckerchief.

"I gotta get you to the doc right away. D'ya think you kin ride?"

"Don't think so." Drew gasped, "I'm hit purty bad." His breathing sounded ragged. John didn't know what to do. They could try to ride out, but he wasn't sure Drew could ride. He couldn't lift him up to carry him on his own horse because Drew was bigger than he was. On the other hand, if Drew didn't get help…he was sure to die.

Lunch time was fast approaching. Conor and Jared had expected John and Drew back by now. Ricardo and Sneedy rode up as the two fence workers were collecting their tools.

"Ya'all seen John an' Drew?"

"No," Jared replied. "How far were they riding out?"

"Only to the crick by Diablo Ridge," Sneedy said. "Think I'm gonna ride out thar. I'lls be foregoin' lunch I'm a thinkin'. It ain't like John ta be late nor Drew ta miss a meal."

"I'll ride with you, Sneedy. I expected them back too. John told us they'd be back before lunch." Conor liked John and hoped everything was all right.

"I'll go with you." Jared didn't hesitate, not wanting to be left behind if Conor was going.

Sneedy turned to Ricardo. "You kin tell Mr. Jethro where we is. An' Ricardo, you take a good look-see cause I want ta know iffen anyone else is a gone fer lunch."

"*Si*, I weel do eet." Ricardo wheeled his horse around and cantered toward the ranch.

"Let's be a goin' then." Sneedy didn't want to waste time. He could almost smell trouble.

John had staunched the flow of blood, but he was quite sure Drew was not going to make it. Blood bubbled on his lips and his breathing became increasingly labored. The shots had ceased, which seemed strange. The two men were still hidden in the thicket, but John had no doubt that whoever had fired on them could find them easily enough. He sat with Drew's head on his lap and tried to make him comfortable. There was no way he could pick him up and carry him. He lost track of time, but the sun was nearing its zenith. It had to be close to noon.

He sat thinking about the young man whose head was cradled in his lap. Drew couldn't be more than twenty-five years old. He'd been working on the ranch for the past five years and the two of them had grown quite close.

John had lost a younger brother to scarlet fever years back and had taken to Drew when the young man had been hired on. There was much about Drew that had reminded him of his dead brother.

John said he didn't believe in God but he whispered, *"Please, God, don't let him die."*

It had been quiet for some time. The only noise came from Drew's labored gasps for air. In sharp contrast were the birds chirping in the trees.

"I ain't gonna make it, John," he gasped. "I want you ta have my belongins…I got no family, no kinfolk no more. I know where I'm a goin', John. My sweet Jesus'll be a waitin' fer me."

"Hush, Drew. Someone'll miss us and be here soon." John knew the younger man was dying. Drew gasped one more time for air…he was gone. John held the man's head close to his heart and cried great racking sobs for a young life needlessly taken. He wiped his eyes on his sleeve and vowed to find whoever had done this wicked deed.

"I'll find 'em Drew…I'll find 'em if it's the last thang I ever do." He sat there for some time when he heard horses approaching. He wiped his eyes again and stood to see who had arrived. It was his crew, save Ricardo. He hailed the men with his hat, waving it in the air.

The men were silent when they saw Drew. They dismounted and John related the shooting to them. "Alls we wuz doin' wuz mindin' our own business lookin' fer calves. Drew pulled up an' wuz gonna say somethun ta me when all hell broke loose. It don't make no sense. There weren't no more shots. No one came gunnin' fer me."

Conor spoke for all the men. "I'm sorry, John. I know you were like a brother to Drew."

John, with the help of Sneedy and Jared, draped Drew over the back of his horse. John held the reins in his left hand, and the men rode silently back to the ranch.

Sneedy wondered if Rhys had anything to do with this. If he did… he was a dead man.

Kirk, on Fire, led the two women up to the McCaully house. They rode past the barn and bunkhouse, but instead of riding into the stables beyond the barn they turned toward the house.

Several men came out of the chow hall and gaped when they saw a man other than Mac riding Fire. Hank, one of Manny's crew, went back inside to tell the men that Miss Cait was back and a strange man was astride Fire.

More men crowded onto the porch of the chow hall to take a look.

"Waal, would ya look at thet. Why, I'd not believe it iffen I hadn't seen it with my own eyes. It's hard ta believe an' I'm a lookin' right at it." Hank spat a stream of tobacco juice over the railing. "Thet's some fine hoss, an' I hain't never seed no one on 'em 'ceptin' Mr. Mac or Miss Cait."

The men stood talking and stared as the two women and the man hitched the horses to the rail. As they watched, the three grabbed their satchels and disappeared into the big house. The ranch hands speculated a few minutes about Fire and how unfriendly the stallion was. Several had personal experiences with the horse, thinking they could convince the roan to be friendly. They wondered who the man was who sat Fire so easily.

Manny looked toward the range and saw John...leading Drew's horse. He bumped Ricardo's arm. "Look."

Several others turned. All talking stopped when they saw Drew draped over his horse. Every man there liked Drew. He'd been a hard-working cowboy. A lot could happen to a man riding the range, but none there considered murder.

Ricardo ran to the bunkhouse to tell Jethro the crew looking for John and Drew had arrived and that something had happened to Drew. He also informed his boss that Miss Caitlin had returned.

Jethro, who'd eaten earlier, rushed outside. He saw the men riding in and strode out to meet them. Jethro already mourned in his heart for the young cowboy he could see slung over his horse. *Wonder what got 'em? Did he get thrown, or a rattler get 'em?* Before the others approached, John hurriedly related to Jethro what happened. Jethro turned to survey the group on the porch. *Jeb and Rhys went into town for the lunch hour.*

I sent Eli and Mosey into town for some more staples for fencing. I know there's bad blood between Rhys and John, but enough to kill a man? Reckon I'd better go to the big house and tell Ewen and Miss Cait. She worked a lot with Drew. This is bad...this is real bad.

The men crowded around John.

Jethro turned to Conor. "Con, come on with me up to the big house." He knew Ewen and Miss Cait would be grieved and he wanted Conor's peaceful presence with him.

Caitlin had seen the men standing on the chow hall porch as they rode up to the big house and had grinned inwardly. Several ranch hands had tried to befriend Fire, but he'd never let anyone closer than ten feet. She still marveled Fire had taken to Kirk as if he'd known the man all his life. Kirk sat him easily and held the reins firmly but with a light hand.

As they went in the front door, Mrs. McDuffy met them in the spacious foyer.

"Welcome home, Miss Caitlin." Mrs. McDuffy had always favored Miss Cait over the other two girls. She'd help to deliver her and because Ryanne had died having her, Duffy had helped to raise the girl.

Caitlin replied, "Thank you, it's good to be back." Drawing Liberty forward, she made introductions.

"This is Liberty Bannister, and this is her brother-in-law, Kirk Bannister."

The two newcomers shook hands with Mrs. McDuffy. It warmed her heart these folk were so friendly. She looked carefully at the two and wondered if she'd seen Kirk before.

Cait added, "They'll be staying here for a week, maybe longer. Are the guest rooms ready?"

"I can sleep in the bunkhouse," Kirk said. "I'd prefer it." He did some fast thinking. He'd need to be with the men if he were to flush out information. He also wanted to stick close to Matthew.

Caitlin said, "Duffy, could you let Duney know we'll be wanting lunch? I'll show Liberty to her room. And Kirk, you can wait in the parlor or follow Duffy to the kitchen and meet Duney."

Caitlin started up the stairs as Sweeny came flying down.

"Oh Miss Cait, Miss Cait, you're back! How are you? Oh Miss Cait, I'm so glad you're back." Sweeny loved her mistress, and her heart overflowed with gladness. She'd never, since coming to work for the McCaullys, been away from Cait even overnight. The family had taken trips once in a long while, but Sweeny had always traveled along.

Caitlin hugged her faithful servant. "I missed you too, Sweeny." Taking Liberty's hand, she made introductions. "Liberty Bannister, meet my servant but also my friend, Helen Sweeny. Kirk Bannister, this is Sweeny, my faithful companion. Liberty is Kirk's sister-in-law."

Sweeny bobbed a curtsy and murmured, "Pleased to meet you, I'm sure."

Liberty said, "It's a pleasure to meet you, Sweeny. Cait has told me what a wonderful woman you are." Her gracious words warmed Sweeny's heart.

Kirk said, "I'm pleased to meet you, ma'am. I have a feeling we're going to be friends." He grinned as his eyes glanced to Caitlin, who blushed.

Sweeny saw it and grinned at Mr. Kirk. "I do hope that's true, sir."

Duffy viewed the introductions with interest. She wondered if this young man was Miss Caitlin's beau. She eyed him closely and nodded her head, but she would withhold any opinion until she knew what kind of man he was. Mr. Hart had been charming but had turned out to be a stinker.

"Mr. Bannister," she said, "please come with me, and perhaps Duney will give you an appetizer." Mrs. McDuffy led the way to the kitchen, Kirk and Sweeny behind her.

Cait said, "Come on, Liberty. I'll show you to your room." She climbed the stairs as she talked with this woman who was fast becoming a real friend.

"I'd like you to peek in at my room first. You'll see why I liked the room I slept in last night." She opened the door to her suite and Liberty walked in, admiring the sunshine yellow room. Sprigs of daisies were scattered on the wallpaper as well as on two plush yellow chairs and the cushions of a rocking chair. French windows opened to a balcony that overlooked the back gardens.

"Oh, this is lovely, Caitlin. I can see why the room last night reminded you of this. It's nearly the same shade of yellow, isn't it? It is beautiful."

"Thank you. I'll show you your room so you can wash up." Cait led Liberty down the hall. They passed one door and Cait opened the next. The room was unique, done in cream, sage green, and brown. The wainscot was painted dark brown topped with stripes of cream, green, and brown. The trim was all cream. A chocolate-colored love seat sat under the windows that faced south.

"This is really different. It's a tasteful mix of colors." Liberty liked the blend of greens and browns on a background of cream in the duvet cover and chairs.. Caitlin showed her the commode and washroom.

"You can wash up in here and I'll meet you downstairs."

Caitlin returned to her rooms to freshen up. Running lightly down the stairs, she reached the bottom as Jethro and Conor walked in the front door. With one look at their set faces she knew this wasn't a friendly meeting. She scrutinized Conor and was amazed how much Kirk resembled him.

"Jethro, Conor, what's wrong?"

"Where's Ewen? We need to talk to him and you, right now." Jethro's face was stony and his lips were set in a thin line.

"I don't know. I just got here."

Cait heard footsteps on the landing and turned to see Liberty at the top of the stairs.

Liberty started down but stopped halfway when she saw Matthew. He hadn't seen her yet. She descended slowly as she focused her eyes on her husband.

Conor felt the stare and looked up to see the moss green eyes he'd dreamed about in a face he thought he must know but simply couldn't remember. She was gorgeous and looked at him with eyes filled with love and apprehension at the same time. As he stared at her, his eyes clouded with disappointment. He had thought when he saw the owner of those green eyes that he'd remember who he was.

"Liberty, this is my assistant foreman, Jethro Hart, and one of my hired hands, Conor Innes. Men, this is Liberty Bannister of Bannister Vineyards." Caitlin emphasized the name Bannister and watched Conor to see if he reacted to Liberty or the name Bannister. She saw nothing to indicate he recognized either. Caitlin felt let down. She'd been hoping that when Conor saw Liberty his memory would return.

"Pleased to meet you, ma'am," Jethro said. He turned to Caitlin. "I need to talk with you right away, alone. Con, wait here and see if Ewen shows up. I'll be right back."

Caitlin said, "Let's go to the library. We can talk there."

The two of them excused themselves and walked into the library, closing the door behind them.

Chapter XX

Fret not thyself because of evil men,

neither be thou envious at the wicked.

PROVERBS 24:19

WHEN CAITLIN HAD INTRODUCED THEM, Conor had stared at this green-eyed woman.

Bannister...Bannister...I know that name. Conor Innes isn't my name...is it Bannister?

Conor gazed at this woman and held out his hand. "I know you, don't I? I can't remember, but I have dreamed of your eyes over and over again. I know that I know you. How's that for an introduction?" He smiled, but it didn't quite reach his eyes. Frustration at his lack of memory filled him. *How could I forget a woman like this? She's beautiful with that copper-colored hair and those gorgeous eyes.*

Liberty, dressed in a split skirt and blouse, with a waist tiny enough for a man's hands to span, took his hand and felt the electricity travel up her arm from his touch. She looked deep into his blue eyes and willed him to remember.

"Yes, yes, you do know me. You're Matthew Bannister, owner of Bannister Vineyards. Even more importantly, you're my husband." Tears started in her eyes, but she blinked them away, not wanting to embarrass Matthew more than he already was. It was awkward for both of them.

Something in Matthew recognized her touch. "I got hit over the head, and I can't recall much of anything that matters. I've been praying I'd at least find out who I am. You, Liberty Bannister, are an answer to my prayers."

Matthew stared at this beautiful woman but felt stiff. He knew awkwardness was not a familiar feeling. *Should I kiss her? I know her, she's my wife…yet, I don't know her…I don't know her at all.*

The moment was taken out of his hands as Kirk stepped into the front hall. He stopped dead when he saw his brother, and a big grin spread over his face.

"It is you, Matt!" He strode to his brother and gave him a quick bear hug.

"Heard you've been having a hard time of it." He looked closely into Matthew's eyes. "I'm your brother…Kirk. I can see you don't remember me but rest assured, we'll find the best doctors and get you taken care of. That's a promise."

Matthew felt an impression of closeness, a unity of blood ties, but he still had no memory.

"I can't leave here yet," he responded. "I made a promise to God I would see this thing out. I'm trying to find out who's the threat to Miss McCaully and today we've had a real bad time of it. One of the men I've been working with, Drew Collins, rode out with our crew leader, John. They were looking for stray cows with calves—we're supposed to start branding on Monday. They were shot at, and Drew was killed just a few hours ago on McCaully property. That's what Jethro is telling Miss McCaully right now. I don't know where Mr. Carr is. He's the foreman. But, we need to ride for the sheriff and also scout around where the shooting took place. We'll see if we can get any idea who did this or why. We need to go while it's still daylight. If it rains tonight, it could wipe away any evidence we might find."

Caitlin turned toward Jethro once they were in the library and wondered what was so important. He seemed so serious.

"What's so dire, Jethro…?" Her voice trailed off as she looked at him.

Jethro stared at Caitlin, deep sorrow shadowing his eyes. "Cait, there's no easy way to say this. Drew's been murdered."

"What?…Where? When?" She collapsed into one of the solid leather chairs. She wasn't sure her legs could hold her. *Drew, the gentleman cowboy who was always so courteous to me.* "I rode wit him only tree days before me da died."

Jethro knew she was distraught. She only spoke with a brogue when she was disbelieving or stunned or funning with someone. Jethro knew her well…he was half in love with her. He'd never let himself go because it was hopeless. Cait looked at him as if he were an older brother, and she had nothing but disdain for Jared.

"It happened today on McCaully land. John and Drew rode out to Diablo Ridge to find some calves for branding on Monday. When they got there, Drew started to say something to John and they were fired on. Drew caught the first bullet in the chest, knocking him off his horse. John drug him into the thicket, but there were no more shots. John couldn't get him up onto his own horse to carry him back. He just sat there holding him till he died."

"Oh, how awful! Has anyone gone to get Sheriff Rowe?" Caitlin paced around the library as her mind raced.

"No, John came in with Drew just after you got here. Conor, Jared, and Sneedy rode out, skipping lunch, to find John and Drew. This has just happened, Cait…there's been no time to do anything."

"Jared…Jared's working? Jared's here on the ranch…working?" Caitlin raised her voice. She could scarcely believe it.

"Yes, Ewen hired him a few days ago. He paired him with Conor, and truth to tell, he's doing a fair ta middlin' job. He works steady and hasn't even tried ta come up ta the house."

Caitlin's legs nearly buckled at the news of Jared, and she sat down again. *Drew is dead and Jared is living right here on the ranch. Wonder if he did it...wonder if he killed Drew? I don't trust Jared as far as I can throw him. Why in the world would Ewen hire Jared?*

"Jethro, send someone into town to get Sheriff Rowe and Doc Addison—he'll need to fill out a death certificate. Get a group of men together, men you can trust, and ride out right now. Go to Diablo Ridge and see if you can see where the shooters were. There are caves in that ridge where a body could hide out."

Jethro kept quiet because Cait was still thinking.

"I'd like you to take John so he can show you exactly where and what happened. I don't want John left alone. In truth, I want you to take Conor, Sneedy, and my new hire, Kirk, to ride out with you. That way, with the new hire, you'll have someone who isn't distracted by too much knowledge."

"You've hired another man?"

"Yes, just for the branding—says he's good with a rope. If he doesn't pull his weight, well, you can fire him." She looked at Jethro seriously. "I want him put into John's group. It'll help take up some of John's attention. If I know John, he's going to go gunning for anyone he thinks might have done this dastardly deed. He's loved Drew like a brother. I hope Rhys stays out of his way for the time being. If I know John, he'll shoot first and ask questions later."

Tears formed in her eyes and ran down her cheeks as she thought of Drew. She'd worked many a time with him, and he'd regaled her with stories and anecdotes that had made time fly. Unlike some of her other ranchers, she'd known Drew well. Her da had hired him five years ago. He'd been one of a kind, and Caitlin was sorely going to miss him. She pulled a handkerchief out of her sleeve, wiped her eyes, and blew her nose. She felt no embarrassment crying in front of Jethro. He was almost family.

How could two brothers be so different? She wondered. *What made them so different? Why in the world would Ewen hire someone he knows hasn't done a lick of work in his life?*

Cait looked her assistant foreman straight in the eyes. "Jethro, I'll take care of the funeral arrangements. Liberty Bannister will help me.

You need to let all the men know there will be a wake tonight. Keep a sharp eye out. I wouldn't like to think any of our men could be involved, but you know as well as I do that there's been bad blood between John and Rhys. And Jethro, tell me the truth. Is it okay having Jared work here? Did Ewen say anything at all to you before hiring him on?"

"Nah, Ewen never says much about decisions he makes. He's been the one riding out and checking on Jared. He seems to be working hard enough. I haven't been around Jared all that much since he's been here. I don't want any of the men to think I might favor him because he's my brother."

"I can understand that. I have a confession to make, but only to you. The man I hired, Conor Innes, has amnesia. He can't remember who he is. Doc Addison gave him the name Conor, and Maisie gave him Innes as a last name. The idea was that having an Irish name would put him in good stead with Ewen."

"Conor doesn't know who he is?" Jethro's eyebrows climbed up his forehead. He felt shock that the easy going, peaceful man must be roiling with questions. "He seems so content. I have to say that's a real shock an no mistake! How'd he end up here? He really doesn't know who he is?"

"No, he was bashed over the head and robbed. I guess he nearly died. Doc Addison nursed him and then dropped by here on his way home to see Da, not knowing Da died. Conor was with the doc when he came that evening. That's why Con ended up here. I hired him after dinner that night. Although he has amnesia, by now I reckon he knows his name."

"How's that? I mean, how would he know his name now?" Jethro was confused. "There's too much happening and too much information in a short period of time. You know, Cait, I certainly am not one to like fast changes." Jethro was methodical, a man who liked to think things through before moving on to deal with something else.

"He knows who he is because that was his wife I introduced you to. I would imagine by now the new hire has come out of the kitchen. Kirk Bannister is Con, rather Matthew's, brother. I don't know if he's going to want to be called Matthew or Conor, but he's the owner of Bannister Vineyards in Napa."

"I've heard of it. Will he be leaving us? I'd hate to see that. He's a calm presence with the men. He keeps his temper in check and is a good example." Jethro wondered if a man who worked grapes could rope a calf.

"He and his brother, Kirk, will stay and help with the branding. We need every hand we can get. Drew was one of our best ropers." She stood. "Now, where's Ewen?"

"He rode off afore lunch an' I haven't seen hide nor hair of 'em since. I thought maybe he'd be here at the house. I didn't look to see if his ride is still gone."

"Well, you better send for the sheriff and Doc Addison right away. Then, go and see if you can find out what happened at Diablo Ridge. I expect Kirk and Con, I mean Matthew, will want to grab something to eat first. Come on and I'll introduce you to Kirk. I think you'll like him. He's got that same peaceful air about him as his brother." She led Jethro out the library.

"You fool! You crazy fool! You told us you didn't want anyone breathing down our necks, and here you go and shoot one of McCaully's men." The man, dressed in brown, turned from the cold-eyed man to the cowboy, anger clipping every word. "Get some sage brush and cover the tracks coming up here. There'll be no mining nor pay for us for some time now. We're going to have to lay low."

He faced the shooter. "What did ya shoot 'em for anyway? You know as well as I do they were only looking for calves." He turned again to the cowboy, whose hands were shaking. "Don't you leave a single track coming up here, you hear me? Put some sage in front of the cave entrance. I've got to go…people will be looking for me." He took out a cigar and lit it, thinking it might calm his nerves. "That's all I need…a cowboy who's been shot."

The shooter stood watching with cold eyes as the man dressed in brown lit his cigar. The killer's heart was black with evil. He stared as the cigar-smoking man climbed on his horse and rode carefully down the ledge.

The cowboy asked, "Did you know they were looking for calves afore you shot 'em?"

"Yes, I knew. I wanted this operation slowed down a bit. You imagine Deke your boss, but I'm the one calling the shots, not Deke. I took samples into an assayer's office in Napa a few weeks ago. It's a good quality of gold. I waited for McCaully to die. Deke would like to go ahead, but Caitlin McCaully is in the way. I plan to deal with her before we move forward. This gold's been here a long time, and it's not going anywhere. It's like ol' Ben Franklin once said, 'Patience is a virtue, virtue is a grace, and both put together make a very pretty face.' I have found the virtue of patience in my line of work. It always pays off in the end."

The cowboy was afraid of Deke, but he was more afraid of this cold-hearted demon who could shoot someone for no good reason. *He shot Drew with no regret at all. He's a cold-blooded man, and I'm right sorry I ever got tied up with this mess. I sure hope Drew isn't hit bad.*

Mosey and Eli rode into to the ranch with Rhys and Jeb. Ewen was still nowhere to be found.

Ricardo was trying to figure out who had been gone for the last couple hours. His heart mourned Drew as he ticked off men on his fingers. *Eli's whole crew has been gone—Mosey, Rhys, Jeb, and Duke besides Eli himself. I need to tell Sneedy. Eets too many peoples gone. Maybe the trouble's not from McCaully Ranch. Maybe eets some other mens shooteeng Drew.*

John was sitting in the chow hall. He didn't want to eat but needed some food. He smiled sadly, thinking of how Drew would always tell him eating solved everything. Drew had never passed up a meal that John could remember.

Manny, Sneedy, and Hank sat with John. No one was talking; no one had to. It was a tacit agreement that John was not to be left alone. They all mourned Drew. Manny had wanted him on his own crew, but John had kept the young man's loyalty, loving him like a brother.

Ricardo wanted to talk to Sneedy but not in front of the other men. Mr. Ewen still had not shown up. Ricardo was beginning to think back. Mr. Ewen had been gone quite a bit lately—going into town. Ricardo didn't like the direction his thoughts took. *Surely, Mr. Ewen could not be involved een any of this mess, or could he?*

CHAPTER XXI

In whom we have redemption through his blood, the forgive-
ness of sins, according to the riches of his grace.

EPHESIANS 1:7

CAITLIN AND JETHRO JOINED KIRK, Matthew, and Liberty in
the parlor.

A blush rose to Caitlin's cheeks as she introduced Kirk to Jethro.
"Kirk Bannister, this is Jethro Hart, my assistant foreman. Jethro, Kirk
Bannister of Bannister Vineyards." She turned to Matthew.

"So, Conor Innes, can we drop the name and call you Matthew?"

"Yes, I would appreciate it. I still can't remember anything of real
import. God answered my prayer. I wanted to know who I am and now
I do. I don't have to worry that family are out there somewhere looking
for me. Thank you, Miss Caitlin, for finding my wife and brother, but I
still plan to stay here and see this thing out."

"You are most welcome, except your brother and wife found me."
Cait didn't elaborate. She said to Jethro, "I wanted Conor here, rather
Matthew, to find out who has made a threat on my life. I wa—"

"Someone made a threat on you, Cait?" asked Jethro, stunned. "Who
would do such a thing, and why?"

"I don't know. It happened after Da died, before the funeral. I was in a closed stall bottle feeding a calf whose mother couldn't nurse. I overheard two men talking about how to get rid of me." Caitlin was sorry she'd started this conversation. Jethro was, after all, Jared's brother. She did some quick thinking, knowing what the next question would be.

"Do you know who it was? Have you any idea?"

"I'm not a hundred percent certain, so I'd not like to accuse anyone just yet. I hired Matthew to try to ferret out any information, to get close to the men and see if he could find someone who's disgruntled for some reason." Caitlin added, "Kirk asked if he could do the same." She turned to the two Bannister men. "I'd appreciate it if you two would go with Jethro. Ride out to the ridge and see if you can find any traces of who might have done this. I'll ask Duney for some fried chicken or something you can eat while riding. Kirk, since we don't know what you'll encounter, you'd better take Queenie and not Fire. I'll brush him down and feed him. Please excuse me." Cait hastened to the kitchen to fetch something for the two men to eat.

Matthew put his arm around Liberty's shoulders. "I'll still be staying in the bunkhouse. We need to find out exactly what's going on."

"I understand. I'd like you to find out who is responsible for making threats on Cait. It would be frightening to think someone you work with could want you dead." Liberty gazed up at Matthew while she talked. She liked the feel of his arm around her.

Jethro said to Matthew and Kirk, "You two wait here for Caitlin. I'm gonna get a couple men to ride for Doc Addison and Sheriff Rowe. Not that the sheriff will do much. He's a lazy man with too much responsibility an' nothin' ever gets done because of it." Jethro walked out the front door just as Ewen was coming up the step.

"Bad news, Ewen. Let's go inside." Jethro turned, frustrated he would have to explain again when there were things that needed done.

As Ewen and Jethro entered the house, Caitlin returned from the kitchen with chicken wrapped in newsprint for Matthew and Kirk. She handed the chicken to the two men and said, "That'll give you a bit to eat until you can get a full meal." She blushed as her fingers touched Kirk's.

He looked down at her. "Thanks, Katie, this will tide us over." He looked at Matthew and asked, "You have water in your canteen? Mine's filled up from this morning."

"Yep, I'm all ready to go. Thanks for the chicken, Miss Cait."

She said to Jethro, "I'll tell Ewen what's happened. You all need to get going. Oh, excuse me, Ewen, this is Kirk Bannister of Bannister Vineyards, and this is his sister-in-law, Liberty Bannister. I've hired Kirk to help with the roping, and Liberty will be my guest for a while. Liberty, Kirk, this is my foreman and right-hand man, Ewen Carr."

"Pleased to meet you, Mr. Carr. I've heard a lot about you." Kirk reached out to shake Ewen's hand. Liberty also shook his hand and murmured a greeting.

"Pleasure to meet you, but have we met before?" Ewen looked into Kirk's deep-set blue eyes, which seemed familiar to him. He glanced at Jethro, but when he noticed Conor, he suddenly realized why Kirk looked familiar.

"You two boys related?" he asked, nodding at Conor and Kirk.

Caitlin replied, "It's a long story. I'll fill you in." She turned to the three who were leaving. "See you men later. There will be a wake tonight. Jethro, I'd like a report before then, if possible."

Ewen's anger was obvious. Cait could see he was upset with her orders and for cutting him off, but enough time had been wasted. The men needed to ride out to the ridge before it rained.

Kirk turned to Liberty. "Keep a close eye on Katie, won't you?"

"Of course," Liberty replied. She reached up and kissed Matthew on the cheek. "You take care, Matthew Bannister," she said, her green eyes serious. She added, "Now that I've found you, I don't want to lose you again!" She smiled to lessen the import of her words.

Ewen asked, "What in tarnation is going on here, anyway?"

"Reckon you should be here when I'm not," Caitlin said. "Where have you been, anyway? I'll answer your questions soon as these men are on their way."

Before Ewen could formulate an answer, Jethro said, "We'll give you a report as soon as we get back from the ridge, Miss Cait."

He settled his hat on his head and followed Matthew and Kirk out the front door.

"Think I'll get Manny and Hank to ride into town." Jethro was thinking out loud.

Matthew said, "That's a good choice. Those boys cared about Drew."

"I know. Most of these men are open and true blue, but not all." Jethro had never liked Rhys, but Ewen had hired him. Rhys was a good worker, but he wasn't sociable and had caused several fights among the men. Ewen said to keep him on and see if it worked out. Rhys had been working on the ranch for nearly a year. Jethro was worried John might go gunning for Rhys.

Kirk stopped at the hitching post. Fire whickered, which surprised Jethro to no end.

"That horse friendly to you?" he asked in astonishment. Jethro had been in the bunkhouse and hadn't seen them ride in. He took another look and realized the stirrups were down...much longer than Cait needed.

In response, Kirk dug into his pocket and found a lump of sugar. He gave it to the stallion, who flicked his tail appreciatively, delicately taking it out of Kirk's hand.

"Well, I'll be jiggered! I never would've believed it if I hadn't seen it. I've never seen another man close to him, 'ceptin Mac, of course. You must have the right something, young man."

Matthew stood watching with a smile on his lips. *From what I just witnessed, I think he's got the right something for Miss McCaully, too. I feel as if I know him even though I have no memory of our relationship. It must be close or he wouldn't have hugged me when he saw me. My wife is gorgeous. Lord...now that I know who I am, I'd like to get my memory back. Please help me.*

Kirk said, "I'll meet you by the stable. I need to adjust the stirrups on Queenie." He took his canteen off Fire and hooked it onto Queenie's saddle as he spoke.

Jethro and Matthew went to get their rides. Jethro stopped by the bunkhouse to tell Manny and Hank to ride into town. It was quiet when he entered. All work had suspended, but Jethro didn't like that idea. It gave a man too much time to rub shoulders and tempers.

"Manny, Hank, I want you boys to ride into Santa Rosa and get Sheriff Rowe and Doc Addison. The rest of you boys get back to work...I don't remember tellin' any of you it was a holiday." He looked at them, knowing most were mourning Drew. He didn't believe any of these men would kill another man for no good reason.

"Sneedy, you're to ride out with me, and John...where's John?"

"John's in the barn with Drew," Manny answered. He was buckling on his gun belt. Hank was putting on his vest.

"Anybody with him? I don't think he ought ta be left alone for a while." Jethro was worried that if John did much thinking, he would go after Rhys and there was no proof Rhys was involved yet.

Manny replied, "Frank's with 'em. Come on, Hank, let's go."

The rest of the men gathered their things to finish the afternoon work, but there was none of the usual banter.

Sneedy followed Jethro and Matthew to the barn. The three men entered the quiet dimness of the stable. Frank and John were sitting together in a stall shoulder to shoulder next to Drew, who had been placed on a bed of straw covered by a blanket.

"John, I'm so sorry. I know how much you cared about Drew." Jethro spoke softly. The stable seemed almost a holy place.

Drew had been a Christian and often spoke to John about the love of Christ. John had never seen a need to follow a belief that someone had died for his sins. He used to laugh at Drew and say, "All my friends are gonna be in hell...why would I want to go to heaven?"

John sat mourning his friend. He could remember Drew's reply to his laughing comment. *Ya'll might be thinkin it's a jest, John, but hell's no joke. Hit's a place of eternal torment, an' I'll be a tellin' ya straight up, hit's a lonely place. Ya'll won't be seenin' none of yore friends thar, thet's fer certain. All's thet's good we knows here, comes from God Almighty, an' friendship an' all, hit comes from th' Lord. Hell…why hit's a loneliest, darkest hole, an' ya caint even be imaginin' how bad it is.* John's eyes teared up in remembrance.

Matthew looked at the dead cowboy, knowing his spirit was gone. Matthew and Drew had talked a bit about their relationship with Christ.

He said to the other men, "Drew's probably walking hand in hand with Jesus, looking at his new mansion in glory." Matthew hoped he could bring comfort to their hearts by his comment.

Jethro said to John, "Manny and Hank are riding into Santa Rosa for the sheriff and Doc Addison. I'd like you to ride out with Sneedy, Matthew, Kirk—who's a new hire—an' me. We're gonna scour that area where you were shot at. See if we can find out who did this. D'ya feel up to it? We'd like to go afore it rains and washes away any trace of the shooter."

"I want more'n anythang ta find out who done this dirty deed. Shore, I'm up to it, but who's Matthew?"

Matthew replied, "I'm Matthew. I got hit on the head and don't really know who I am, but I guess my real name's Matthew."

Frank and John stared at him as they stood. John pulled out his kerchief and blew his nose. He was ready to do whatever was needed to find Drew's killer.

Jethro turned to Frank. "I'd like you ta help up at the house. Miss Cait's gonna have the wake tonight and she's gonna need help setting up the parlor. You go up an' ask her what you can do. She'll be eating lunch now, so give it about a half hour or so. You also need someone ta help you move Drew up there when things are ready. Get Jared afore he rides out to work, tell him ta stay around an' help you." He nodded to John. "Let's be going, we have work ta do."

When Ewen had arrived at the ranch, he hadn't been surprised that Miss Caitlin was home. He'd seen Fire tied to the hitching post. He now watched silently as Jethro, Conor, and the new hire, Kirk, walked down the front steps.

Caitlin gave a brief explanation to Ewen but left out Matthew's amnesia and how she'd met the Bannisters.

Afterward, Ewen went upstairs to clean up for lunch. He knew he was late. He brushed off his new brown shirt—there was dust from the road in the creases. *So much can happen in such a short space of time. I feel frustrated not knowing what's gone on this morning. Drew's dead, and for no good reason. And Conor, how is he tied up in this? Why call him Matthew?*

Downstairs, Caitlin decided she wasn't hungry. Knowing Drew was dead had blunted her appetite, but she realized Liberty must be famished. Cait had heard when a woman was pregnant, she ate for two.

"Come on, Liberty, let's go to the kitchen. I want you to meet Duney, my stupendous cook, and we need to eat." Cait led her new friend to the kitchen.

"Duney, this is Liberty Bannister. Liberty, this is one fine cook, Duney. She's really Mrs. Dunstan, but I'll allow you to call her Duney." She grinned at the cook and Liberty. "I'm hoping you'll become a familiar face around here, Liberty."

Liberty shook hands with the cook. "I'm happy to make your acquaintance, Duney. Caitlin has told me splendid things about your cooking. I'm looking forward to tasting it for myself." Liberty liked the looks of this older woman. She had honest, twinkling blue eyes.

Mrs. Dunstan replied, "I'm glad to meet you. Is it ma'am, or miss?"

"Ma'am, but please, call me Miss Liberty. That's what I'm used to. It's what my cook calls me."

"All right, Miss Liberty. I'm supposing you two are hungry. I have fried chicken, mashed potatoes and gravy, and some coleslaw. I made a pie for dessert. Mr. Ewen is supposed to be back for lunch. I wonder what's holding him up?"

"He's back, Duney. He's upstairs washing up. I just had a talk with him in the library."

Duney said, "I'll clear the extra place setting. I set a place for Mr. Bannister, but I understand he's riding out."

"Yes, he is. I'll pick it up. I can see you're busy in here," Liberty said. "After all, it's my brother-in-law who was supposed to eat there. Umm, it smells delicious in here. I'd like to learn some of your favorite meals, Duney. I've been taking lessons from our cook and am becoming quite proficient, at least in Mexican dishes I am."

Duney looked at her sharply. "You're learning how to cook?"

"I echo that question only adding a word," Cait said. "Why are you learning to cook?"

"Well, in the beginning, I thought I might have to know how, but it became so much fun I couldn't stop. I love making food taste good and having people like what I cook. It's an achievement. I went to boarding schools in France and Switzerland and never spent any time in a kitchen until I moved west a couple of years ago." Liberty continued, "Why, I didn't even know an onion could make you cry until I started cooking." She laughed and Duney laughed with her.

"An onion can make you cry?" asked Caitlin. The other two women chuckled.

"See what I mean, Duney? That's what comes from never being in a kitchen."

"I see, Miss Liberty, I see. It is an admirable thing for you to learn to cook." Her eyes twinkled brightly at the younger woman.

Chapter XXII

The lips of the righteous know what is acceptable:

but the mouth of the wicked speaketh frowardness.

PROVERBS 10:32

EWEN STROLLED INTO THE KITCHEN a little out of sorts. He was hungry and too much had happened this morning. He wondered what the sheriff would do and if he would find out anything. He rather doubted it.

"Where did they put Drew, in the stable?"

"Yes, it's why I haven't stabled Fire yet," Caitlin answered. She glanced at Liberty who was listening in. "I just went out and put him in the corral. I'd like Drew laid out in the parlor. We'll have a proper wake tonight. Liberty can help me with the funeral plans. She will be our guest for this next week. We do need to have Doc Addison look at Drew and fill out a death certificate. I wonder..."

"What...what do you wonder, Miss Cait?" Ewen looked at the young woman closely. *What does she suspect?*

Caitlin explained to Ewen about Matthew's amnesia and what had transpired. She went on to relate what she was thinking.

"For one thing, I know that there's been more men than Conor, I mean Matthew, robbed recently. When Doc Addison dropped him off, he told us Matthew was the fourth that he knew about. Perhaps the robbers are staying in one of the caves up on Diablo Ridge."

"Why would they do that?"

"It's a good place to hide out."

"Is that where Drew was shot?" Liberty asked the question because the atmosphere in the dining room had become tense. She didn't know what was going on but hoped she could ease the feeling.

"Yes, Drew was shot at the creek that runs at the foot of Diablo Ridge. The ridge, the creek, and miles beyond is all McCaully property, but it's not fenced in. If robbers are hiding on McCaully land, I want them found."

"But, Miss Cait, you don't know that for sure," Ewen said.

"No, I don't know for sure, but I can make sure, can't I?"

"Yes, I suppose you can," he said heavily.

"After lunch, can you please get Abbot and Frank to move Drew into the parlor? I'll have it ready for his body." Cait teared up again thinking about Drew.

Liberty said, "I'd be glad to help you get the parlor ready, Caitlin. I know this has got to be hard on you, but first, do you think I could take a nap when we finish here? I'm exhausted. That was an emotional moment seeing Matthew. It's so strange that he doesn't know me. I knew the day after he left that something was wrong. Our foreman did, too."

Ewen asked, "You're from Bannister Vineyards? I bought a few bottles of their Merlot about a year ago, but I haven't drunk any of it. I've heard Bannister's wine is getting better every year…that so?"

Liberty grinned at the older man. "It's not only true, it's verifiable."

Ewen took a closer look at the young woman who was Conor's wife. *She's not pretty, she's gorgeous.* Winged eyebrows arched over fantastic green eyes and her smile was sweet.

His frosty blue eyes warmed. "We'll simply have to find out this evening. I'll break out a bottle, and we'll try it."

"It's a deal. Now, if you two will please excuse me, I really do need that nap." Liberty left the dining room.

To Caitlin, the room felt empty without Liberty's energizing presence.

"Now, Caitlin, will you please tell me what the devil's going on? Where did you meet the Bannisters? Why have you hired Conor's, rather, Matthew's brother? And, do you have any idea what the blazes is going on around here? I want some straight answers."

Manny and Hank rode into Santa Rosa. It took nearly an hour to cover the distance between the ranch and town. Overhead, the sky was a pristine blue, not a cloud marring its perfection. Rolling hills with scrub oak or a stand of arbutus and maple dotted the landscape. Wildflowers in a beautiful array spread their blanket of beauty over the hillsides as the rain and warmer weather motivated the plants to new life.

Manny thought how strange it was that nature remained beautiful, ignorant of hearts that mourned or the finality of death. He remembered back to when his own mother died. It had seemed to him that the sun should stop shining or the creek should stop its flow of water in respect for his mother's passing.

He looked over at Hank and said, "You go lookin' for Doctor Addison, and I'll be a lookin' for Sheriff Rowe. I'm givin' you the better job," he said with a grin. "No tellin' where the sheriff is, but I'm gonna start at McGregor's. I'm thinkin' thet he's got a dry mouth. Seems like I heerd a body kin always find the sheriff belly up ta the bar. In truth, you may have the harder job. The doc could be out deliverin' a baby or caring fer some poor sick person. We kin meet back here soon's we find our quarry." He waved at the front of the bank. There were two benches, one on either side of the door, where a body could wait comfortably.

"All right by me," Hank answered. "Sooner we get back, the happier I'll be. I'm not likin' what's bin happenin' at th' ranch. Tensions air a runnin' too high. Thet Rhys, I don't think he'd out and out shoot Drew, but I kin see John gunnin' fer him iffen he gets smart with that mouth of his. Thar could be more killin' afore this is over."

Manny nodded in agreement. "Let's git to it, then." They dismounted and tied up in front of the bank, looping their reins around the hitching post. Doc Addison had an office next to the bank almost directly across the street from McGregor's.

"See y'all shortly," Manny said as he started across the street. Hank nodded.

John rode a little ahead with Sneedy beside him. He didn't want to talk. Sneedy, who was usually garrulous, rode quietly beside him. John was thinking hard about who could have done such a thing. *I know some of the men are worried about me gunning for Rhys, but I got more sense than thet. I'm not about to go after a man till I knows it's the man I'm a lookin' fer. Thet'd be jest plain stupid. I might be a lettin' the real culprit go free iffen I was ta do thet.* He couldn't think of anyone who might have a grudge or hard feelings against Drew. *Maybe they was a gunnin' fer me an' missed.*

Jethro rode with Matthew and Kirk. The talk was banal until Jethro asked Matthew what he thought of the entire mess.

"Well, I reckon I don't know. Drew was a good man. I can't see any of the McCaully outfit gunning him down. I know Rhys and John have a problem with each other, but for Rhys to shoot Drew—no. Drew and John were together. He'd have gone for John instead."

"That's exactly what I've been thinking, but go ahead, I wanna hear what else you have ta say."

"I think this is about a lot more than a couple men not getting along. You heard Miss Caitlin. She heard two men talking in the barn when she was in a stall with the door closed. They didn't know she was in there, which was a good thing. There must be much more to this than simply bad tempers or bad blood between two men. No, I think there has to be something quite large at stake. What that is, I have no clue. If Miss Caitlin were to die, who would inherit?"

Jethro looked at Matthew, speculation evident in his eyes. He paused before answering.

"Well, if she were to marry, it'd be her husband, but long as she's not married the land would be split between Maisie and Aidan, her two sisters. Whoever is after Miss Cait only has to get her out of the way, then the two sisters, and after that, their husbands…not an easy task."

"If you don't mind me asking, would they keep the land or sell? Your brother, would he go after the land? Would he be willing to get anyone out of the way for money? Is he an honest man?" Matthew wanted Jethro to share his feelings about his brother.

Jethro pulled up his horse. His lips thinned into an angry line at the question. He took a big breath, ready to be speak in an explosive voice. Kirk and Matthew pulled up also, but Matthew was not angry or at all hostile. His look back at Jethro was simply questioning.

The air whooshed out of Jethro, who felt tired. He'd lain awake nights trying to figure out Jared. He'd never done a lick of work in his life and was now working contentedly. Jethro knew Jared hated Caitlin. His gaze was troubled, but he knew these two men would be discreet.

"A year ago, Jared tried to kiss Caitlin just afore he was ta marry Aidan. As far as I know, Cait never told Aidan about the attempt, but she did try to persuade Aidan not ta marry Jared. Jared has hated her ever since, and he's done his best ta get Aidan ta hate her, too. That's the long and short of it. What he's playing at now, I can only guess at. He's working and I never saw him ever do that, not in my entire life."

Matthew said, "He's doing a good job working, too. I've enjoyed having him as my partner. He hasn't said what his reasons were for joining the McCaully outfit, but in all honesty, I believe he's enjoying himself."

Kirk, who'd been sitting quietly listening, had been doing some thinking. *If I was to marry Katie, whoever is after her will have to come after me, too. That might just be a good plan, to my way of thinking.*

John and Sneedy were getting too far ahead, so the three men stopped talking and rode to catch up.

The five men didn't want their horses to muck up the area where Drew had been shot. Rather than riding to it, they splashed downstream about a hundred yards and tied up their horses.

Nearing the spot on foot, Kirk spied where Piggypie had come across—Mathew had shoes made for all the Bannister horses with a B stamped into each shoe. Kirk saw two other sets of prints that must have belonged to Sneedy and Jared.

Matthew pointed to the imprints in the mud. "These are our prints, mine and Sneedy's, and see there, that's Jared's horse. His shoes aren't marked." Matthew nodded to John and Jethro.

Sneedy said, "Yep, those air mine. We come across the crick right here when we seen John a waving his hat at us."

They walked a few yards further up creek and John pointed across it.

"Thet's where me an' Drew comed across. Drew pulled up as soons we crossed th' crick. He started ta say sumptin' and then he wuz hit full in the chest. I figgered th' shootin' came from up thar." He pointed to a ledge on the cliff near the top.

Matthew and Kirk surveyed the ground as Jethro and John scanned the ledge. Matthew looked at Kirk and pointed out the obvious. Kirk nodded, for he too had seen tracks made by five horses. Matthew already recognized Drew and John's tracks. McCaully's had two slant marks stamped into the shoe of every McCaully horse. It was their brand minus the M. The other two men examined the ground and John looked surprised.

"Well, I'll be jiggered. I'm guessin thet's what Drew wuz meanin' ta point out ta me when we wuz fired on. Three other sets of prints thar an' one of them McCaully's. Let's go back an get our horses and follow 'em. Let's sees where they lead."

Hank found the doctor in his office catching up on paperwork. The smell in the office was overwhelming. Used as he was to clean fresh air, he was sensitive to any smells not of nature. He felt like taking his neckerchief and putting it around his nose but didn't want to offend the doc.

"Doc, we got some bad news at McCaully's. One of our ranch hands is daid, an we needs you to come out an take a look at th' body."

"I'm sorry to hear that, son. What happened? Did a rattler get him?"

"No! He wuz murdered, Doc. Out an' out murdered right on McCaully property."

Doctor Addison had already begun packing his medical kit, mentally thinking what all he might need, but he paused in shock and stared at the younger man.

"Murdered! Someone murdered a McCaully ranch hand? It's not the new man, is it?" The doctor had done some quick thinking. Perhaps robbery hadn't been the motive for Conor Innes' bashed head.

"Nah…it was Drew Collins. I don't think you be a knowin''em, Doc, but he's daid and someone kilt 'em. He wuz shot full in the chest with never no warnin'. Manny's gone ta find Sheriff Rowe."

Doc Addison said, "I saw Rowe go into McGregor's 'bout a half hour ago. I've been trying to get him to do something about the robberies we've been having around here. We've had four men bashed on the head and robbed, and Henderson's and Fitzsimmon's houses were robbed. Nobody was hurt but valuables were taken, and the hired help in both places said they didn't see nor hear anything."

"Don't know nothin''bout that, Doc, but Jethro asked us ta come git you, and we needs ta be gettin' back ta the ranch."

"All right, just let me pack up a few things, not that I'll need much, but I might just end up spending the night." He grabbed the nightshirt he kept in a bottom drawer for emergencies and laid it on top of the paperwork he'd need for a certificate of death.

"We'll be a waitin' in front of th' bank when yore ready, sir." Hank started for the front door. The smell of carbolic, alcohol, and other medicinal pongs made him lightheaded, and his stomach lurched at some unidentifiable odor.

"I'll be there shortly." The doctor was still in a bit of shock from hearing the news about a murder. He was having trouble collecting his thoughts.

Murder…murder on McCaully Ranch. What could have happened? Wonder if I should try riding to Napa again. I don't trust Sheriff Rowe to do much of anything. He may ride out there and act professional, but to find out who did it, no. I have no faith in him at all. Sheriff Rawlins, on the other hand, is true blue. He can find out who did it if anyone can. Wonder if this is at all connected with the rash of robberies we've been having? Someone needs to take charge and get to the bottom of this!

CHAPTER XXIII

Though a sinner do evil an hundred times, and his days be prolonged, yet surely I know that it shall be well with them that fear God, which fear before him.

ECCLESIASTES 8:12

MANNY HAD NO TROUBLE FINDING SHERIFF ROWE. He had on a uniform of sorts, all in brown. His shiny tin badge pinned to his shirt pocket flap made him look official. He was, as Manny had thought, belly up to the bar downing a whiskey as the tall cowboy pushed through the double swinging doors of McGregor's.

Manny stood a moment, surveying the room. The sheriff turned to look at the newcomer as he plopped his glass onto the counter. He plugged his cigar into his mouth, his eyes squinting through the haze of smoke at Manny. McGregor stood on the sheriff's left and the priest, in his long black gown, stood on his right, talking to him. The priest also noted Manny when he entered the saloon.

There were several men sitting at tables; some played cards. Two other men were at the bar but as the swinging doors opened, they'd turned to look at the newcomer, too.

Manny didn't like the feel of the atmosphere in the tavern. It almost felt as if time were suspended. The hair on the back of his neck prickled. He let his gaze slide to the sheriff, who didn't know Manny. But Manny knew him.

He did some quick thinking and announced to the room in general, "Guess th' man I'm a lookin' fer ain't here." He turned on his heel and retreated out the swinging doors. Taking his hat off, he wiped his brow on his arm in relief. He couldn't for the life of him think why he felt the way he did, but going back outside gave him a sense of safety. *Now, why th' blazes would I be a feelin' this way? I knows, fer some reason in my gut I knows, thet I wuz th' enemy in thar.* He wiped his brow again before replacing his hat.

He let his eyes rove slowly down the street and saw Hank waiting for him in front of the bank. His spurs clanked on the wooden planks of the sidewalk as he strode down and crossed the street in long strides.

"You find the doc?" he asked Hank.

Stepping up to the bench, he looked at Hank but didn't sit down. He wanted to be gone from here. Hearing a noise on his left, he saw Doctor Addison coming out of his doorway, a big key in his hand to lock his office. Manny strode toward the doctor, not waiting for Hank's reply.

Hank trailed after him, wondering what the big hurry was.

Doc Addison scanned the street over the shoulders of the two men who were approaching him. He saw Sheriff Rowe come out of McGregor's, looking around until he spotted the three standing together. Rowe glanced away when he saw the doctor watching him. *Now that's interesting. He doesn't want me to know he came out searching for McCaully's man? Why? What's going on here? I thought Manny was supposed to get Sheriff Rowe to go with us.* Doctor Addison looked at Manny with a question in his dark brown eyes, waiting for him to say something.

"Hello, Doc." Manny shuffled his feet a bit and looked at the wood-planked sidewalk, embarrassed and at a loss to express the evil he'd felt in the saloon.

Hank asked, "Couldn't find the sheriff?"

"Yeah, I found 'em, but I didn't bother him none 'bout the trouble at McCaully's." Manny tried to explain. "Hit wuz the most ungodliest feelin' I ever had. I'm not jestin'. I swear thet saloon closed in on me. When I walked in thar, th' hairs on the back of my neck stood up, an' I felt as if I wuz lookin' death right in th' face. I cleared out without sayin' nothin' ta the sheriff. I felt as iffen I wuz the enemy, an' I'd be gunned down fer askin' fer 'em."

Hank looked at Manny in surprise. Manny was their crew leader, and he wasn't given to imaginations or fear. Hank had seen Manny kill a cougar, standing his ground as the cat leaped toward him. Manny was a brave man. If he sensed danger, then it was not a figment of his imagination…it was real.

Doc sighed and simply nodded, as if he agreed with the cowboy.

"Let's be on our way then, but don't look up when you turn around—Rowe is watching us right now. He doesn't know either one of you boys, does he?"

"Nope," they both responded, surprised at the doctor's words. They turned, without glancing across the street, to get on their rides.

The doctor and cowboys rode down Main Street and as they neared the saloon, the sheriff flipped his cigar over the hitching post, staring as they passed by. The priest had come out of the saloon to join the sheriff at the rail. The doctor tipped his hat to the two men but didn't stop. He had the distinct impression explanations weren't needed. When they reached the last building, Manny kicked his horse into a gallop and Doc Addison hoped his faithful palomino could keep up.

Liberty stretched and rolled onto her back, staring at the ceiling. *So, my husband doesn't know me. Does that mean we start all over? I know he felt uncomfortable and frustrated. Father, please help him regain his memory.* She sat up, and pulling her grandfather's watch out of her pocket, she thought, *Guess I had a snap this time. I always feel better with a quick nap. I feel groggy and tired when I take a long one.* Feeling refreshed, she arose and readied herself to go downstairs.

Meanwhile, Caitlin had told Ewen almost everything. She explained why she hired Conor and that he had amnesia. She related overhearing someone talking about getting rid of her, and why she left the ranch and had gone to the mission in San Rafael. He'd asked her who she had overheard, but she said she didn't know.

As Liberty walked into the dining room, Ewen and Caitlin looked up. "I thought you were going to take a nap." Cait looked carefully at Liberty and saw the bruised look of tiredness was gone from under her eyes.

"I did, thank you. The bed is quite comfortable." She smiled at the look in Ewen's eyes. "I call it a snap. I only need about ten minutes for a nap. I feel revived and ready to go."

Caitlin said, "I've heard when you are first pregnant, you are tired and take naps. I reckon it must be true."

"Yes, I've heard that too. I would appreciate it if you didn't let Matthew in on the news. I'd like to see if he recovers his memory first. He seemed frustrated enough without the added knowledge of becoming a father." Liberty added, "You see, we thought I couldn't have children. This is such a miracle. I'm hoping he recovers before he knows about it. I know he wants to see this thing out, but when the threat on your life is over," she said as she nodded to Caitlin, "I plan to get Matthew to the best doctors money can buy. My twin's best friend is a doctor, and I'm hoping he will know how to treat Matthew or know someone who can."

There was a banging noise in the foyer and Caitlin jumped up, wondering if the men were back as she ran to the front door. The surprise on her face was evident when she saw her sister.

"Aidan! What are you doing here?"

"Jared told me you weren't here! Reckon he lied to me. I have decided, little sister, that since Jared is here at the ranch, I'm going to be here too."

"Jared told the truth. I haven't been here until just before lunch. You are more than welcome to be here. We've had quite an upset today—"

"Where have you been?" Aidan cut in, not believing her, but the tightness in her shoulders eased a bit. She had imagined all kinds of things.

"Visiting a friend. Come on to the dining room and meet her. She'll be here for a few days." Cait hoped Liberty wouldn't say anything about them meeting only a couple days ago.

Aidan's eyes widened. She didn't think Cait had any friends unless they were her ranch hands or Sweeny. *This should be interesting— some masculine looking female, I have no doubt.* She set her case down, dropped her satchel by the stairs, and followed Caitlin to the dining room. As she entered, she saw the most gorgeous woman she'd ever seen. Automatically straightening her back, Aidan felt diminished. She never had been one to look at a person's character, only the outward appearance; hence, Jared. *Wonder if Jared's seen this woman? She's exquisite.* Caitlin made the introductions.

Ewen looked on with amusement. He could almost feel Aidan's discomfiture.

Liberty surprised Aidan by standing for the introduction.

"Aidan, how nice it is to finally meet you." Liberty smiled and sensed a great deal of tension in the younger woman. She tried to put her at her ease and gracefully held out her hand to take Aidan's. "Caitlin's told me so much about you and your sister. My, Cait does look a lot like you, doesn't she?"

"I'm happy to meet you, too, Mrs. Bannister—Bannister, isn't that a vineyard over in Napa?" Aidan was impressed. Liberty was beautiful and quite charming.

"Why, yes, have your heard of it?" Liberty was surprised. Matthew hadn't pushed marketing it yet, but Bannister's was becoming a well-known vineyard.

"Yes, I have some of your last Merlot. It's quite delicious. Cait here doesn't drink wine. Did you know that?" Aidan was trying to determine if this woman really knew her sister.

"Yes, I know. Most of my friends don't drink wine, but I was raised in a quasi-French home and had wine mixed with water when I was about five. It's a common practice with the European influence, you understand, and my father is a vinedresser."

Ewen and Caitlin watched the interchange and were amazed at the charm and easy-going manner of Liberty Bannister.

Ewen liked what he saw and hoped her feminine ways would rub off on Caitlin. He had no idea Liberty was a sharpshooter and could ride as well or better than Cait.

Ewen spoke up for the first time. "So, let me understand, Aidan. You're moving in, is that correct?" He was certain Jared had not explained the sudden employment at the ranch. If Aidan were aware, she'd have kicked him out lock, stock, and barrel for his thievery. Aidan was a straight shooter, and although she acted spoiled, her main problem had always been insecurity.

Aidan looked at the foreman through veiled eyes and said, "For the time being, yes." She didn't want Liberty to know she suspected Caitlin of being with Jared.

"Have you eaten?" Caitlin suddenly realized if Aidan had ridden from Santa Rosa, she'd probably had no lunch.

"No, I haven't and I'm famished. Which room am I in? I'll go wash up before I eat."

"Your own rooms, Aidan. I'll let Duney know you need to eat."

"Yes, and I want Jared to know I'm here so he can dine with us here at the house."

"Jared is a ranch hand, at present, and won't be dining with us." Ewen spoke with an authority that brooked no argument. It shocked Aidan and the other two women. He continued, "Neither will your husband, Matthew," he nodded at Liberty, "nor his brother, Kirk. They'll be eating at the chow hall like the rest of the men. No special favors. It causes tension and ill feeling, and I reckon we have enough of that right now as it is."

Aidan looked indignantly at Ewen, but she knew better than to contradict him. Mac had always been adamant that Ewen was in charge of the ranch hands, and if he laid down the law, the girls were to abide by it.

Liberty was relieved. She didn't want the strain of trying to keep up conversation with a man she knew was uncomfortable in his own skin. Time was needed in her situation.

Caitlin, on the other hand, was quite disappointed and tried to cover it. She had looked forward to spending more time with Kirk. Ewen was right and she also said nothing to contradict him.

Matthew was an excellent tracker. He'd been following the tracks and suddenly they disappeared. He held up his hand to halt the other riders and pointed to the last of the tracks. The other men had no experience in tracking and thought this was the end of it.

Matthew said, "It'll be difficult, but I think we can still trace the trail—looks like someone brushed the dirt to cover up the tracks. See where they've been swept away? Most likely, they didn't get every print, and if we're careful, we'll find a print here and there. It'll take time but let's walk. Most of the time when you sweep away prints, the sweep is as evident as the prints themselves."

The men dismounted. Matthew knew that most likely the shooters had kept to the main trail, which led up the mountainside. He was right. The going was slow, but the ranch hands could see Matthew knew what he was about.

Kirk could track, too. Matt had taught him years ago. Matthew had learned from a Coast Miwok Indian, and Kirk was glad his brother had taken the lead.

The ledge that circled over half of Diablo Ridge was about forty feet wide, but there were only about three ways to go up. Because the ridge was on McCaully property, most folks didn't know the other two ways.

Sneedy was breathing hard from hiking the steep trail. When they reached the ledge, Matthew pointed out a partial hoof print to the left. He knelt to take a better look. It was the same as the one by the creek. The men were quiet. No one felt like talking. They headed left on the ledge but didn't get back on their horses.

Jethro said quietly, "This ridge is riddled with caves. It'd be easy to miss what we're looking for." Everyone agreed.

Matthew nodded. "They most likely have it covered up with scrub brush, so we'll have to be careful not to miss it—that is, if they're even using a cave."

Sneedy, still wheezing, said, "I bin thinkin' they'll be a shootin' from whare's they could sees us below. Mebe th' place we're a lookin' fer is down thar just a bit." He pointed farther down the ledge, more in line with where John and Drew had crossed the creek.

John said, "I'll be bettin' Sneedy's right. We'll look fer th' straight shot down ta where we was."

Matthew continued to walk methodically as he looked for openings in the hillside. They found two that were not deep and were not covered. No prints or swept dirt marred their entrances. As they searched on, John and Sneedy checked out the steep drop toward the creek area. The entire hillside was densely covered by pine, oak, sycamore, buckeye, and manzanita. The underbrush was thick, but the ledge itself was a rocky outcrop that jutted out, clear of any growth except scrub bushes where the steep hill began to climb again.

John pointed downward at the same time that Matthew pointed to the rising hill.

"There," Matthew said, "that's where the trail goes."

"An' thet's a clear shot ta where we was at th' crick." John pointed where the creek lay, at least fifty yards downward. He bent and picked up an empty shell casing, holding it up so the others could see.

"Guess I'll hang on to this. Mebe it's th' bullet what got Drew."

CHAPTER XXIV

Enter not into the path of the wicked,

and go not in the way of evil men.

PROVERBS 4:14

WALKING THE HORSES HAD BEEN A GOOD IDEA. The men could see where the shooters had swept the trail clean, but the sweeping of leaves and tree debris had lead straight to the side of the hill. An opening was covered with sage brush and a big bush with leaves that were beginning to wither.

John, eager to discover why anyone would ambush them, had pushed the branches aside and stepped into the cave. He stopped to let his eyes adjust. The others followed. The cave looked deep and the entrance was at least four feet wide. It was the biggest they'd seen yet.

"Anyone got a light?" Jethro asked. He knew Sneedy must have some matches because he carried the new type in a small case to light his rolled cigarettes.

"Yup, I got some." Sneedy lit the match using his thumbnail to strike the end. It flared and they could see lanterns and other paraphernalia a few feet in on one side. Kirk picked up one of the lanterns and Sneedy lit it. He struck another match and lit two more lanterns. The cave went deep into the middle of the hillside.

"Well, would ya' looky there," John said as he pointed to some pickaxes. "We got us a regular gold minin' equipment stash right here on McCaully property."

Jethro held one of the lanterns high over his head and started into the recesses of the cave. He held the lantern close to the side wall and could see where some mining had taken place. The wall had a wide line of a rusty red color with varying degrees of yellow.

"Ah," Jethro said with a sigh, "and right here on McCaully's. We've got gold, folks, real pay dirt, you might say. Reckon they were afraid Drew saw the tracks down by the crick, lost their head, and started shooting. Maybe we need to put off the branding and have men stationed here to guard the stuff that belongs to Miss Caitlin. I'll talk to Ewen about it." He nodded to John and Sneedy. "You boys know cattle has been a losing operation the last few years. Gold would put this ranch back into shipshape. Reckon someone else thought they could get at it without anyone being the wiser.

"You all know Miss Caitlin hightailed it out of here the day after the reading of the will. She heard a threat made on her life while she was in the barn, down on her knees, feeding a baby calf. Two men were talking of how they could get rid of her. I'm telling you because someone thinks they can get the property. My guess is, whoever it is figures Miss Aidan and Miss Maisie wouldn't come back here to live on the ranch—that they would sell it. We have at least one traitor and maybe more working on this ranch."

John and Sneedy looked shocked that someone would want to kill Caitlin.

Kirk waited until Jethro finished before he made his intentions known. "I'll tell you fellows straight up, I plan to marry Miss Caitlin fast as she'll let me. That'll be two people to get through before this ranch goes to someone else. I'm thinking it would be a good thing for all the ranch hands to be gathered together with the Galways and the Harts and let every blamed one know that if Katie and I don't survive, the other two sisters will split the land and keep it for their own. That would make at least six people the murdering thieves would have to do away with before they could get their hands on this gold."

Jethro was shocked this man planned to marry Caitlin. *How long has she known Bannister? Reckon it don't matter—when a man loves a woman that's the end of it. Glad I like his brother so well. He's got ta be a good man with that kind of influence around all the time. His thoughts turned to his own brother. On second thought, maybe he isn't good. I'll wait afore I form an opinion about him.*

Jethro said aloud, "That's a good plan, Bannister. I'm thinking once the thieving murderers find out we're on to 'em they'll have ta quit. On the other hand, gold is a strong incentive for some, an' they won't give up till they got it. Interesting thing I've learned is that once they get what they want, they're still not satisfied."

Matthew looked at the four men before him. "That's because the Lord Almighty put a craving in the heart of a man to worship, but the desire to worship is only satisfied when we worship God. Trouble is, most men never find out what it is their heart is yearning for. They can worship a woman, and she will never measure up to God; she can't. Or, they worship money or gold or power. None of those things will satisfy the way worship to God will. Only when we do that are we truly satisfied."

Kirk was proud of his brother and the truth he related to the men. "That's so true, Matt. I know what you are saying is true from first-hand experience."

Sneedy asked Matthew, "Is yer name Matthew or is it Conor?" He looked at Kirk. "Why you keep a callin' 'em Matt?"

"Because he's my brother. He got hit on the noggin by robbers and still doesn't know who he is. He's the owner of Bannister Vineyards in the Napa Valley. His horse, Piggypie, evidently wouldn't let the men near her. They stole Matthew's money, gun, and worse—his memory."

Doctor Addison was proud of Blondie. She'd made the trip to McCaully's in good shape. Manny and Hank tied up at the hitching post along with the doctor. As uncomfortable as it was for them to enter the main house, they led the way up the steps with the doctor trailing behind. Before they could knock, the door opened and Mrs. McDuffy bade them enter.

"Please, come on in boys. Doctor Addison, I'm glad these two found you. I know Miss Caitlin is hoping to talk with all of you. I think the parlor would be the best place. Come this way, please." She led them into the elegant parlor. "Please be seated. I'll let Miss Caitlin know you're here." She went in search of Cait.

The two cowboys were afraid to sit for fear of dirtying the furniture, but the doctor had no such qualms. He plopped on the settee with alacrity, glad for the softness after the hard leather of his saddle.

"Sit down, sit down, Miss Caitlin won't mind a bit of dust from the road." He eyed the two men with a cheerful air that did not match the seriousness in his eyes. The good doctor was worried. He knew in his heart of hearts that the sheriff of Santa Rosa was a bad man. This day had confirmed it.

"While we wait for Miss Caitlin, I'd like you to relate to me again, Manny, exactly what you felt and saw when you went into McGregor's. I know McGregor's is a bad place to begin with. Several men have met with evil in there. Is that what you're talking about?"

"Nah, hits hard ta explain, Doc." Manny was embarrassed. All he wanted right now was to be working a fence or riding the range. His surroundings set him on edge, and the question made him wonder if he really was imagining things, yet he knew he wasn't.

"I'll tell you both straight up, I wuz a lookin' death straight in th' face. Hit was a cold, wet sort of feeling, an' hit didn't come from th' room. Hit comed from the direction of the sheriff. He wuz a lookin' like ol' Satan hisself...black an' evil. I knew in an instant thet I wuzzent gonna say a word to 'em. I'm surprised, even now, thet he didn't comed after us."

Doc Addison looked this true-blue cowboy in the eyes and saw honesty and a bit of fear. He said heavily, "I believe you, young man, I believe you. I've been thinking for some time that the sheriff is up to no good, but I didn't think it stretched more than paying people to keep their mouth shut about his politics. I suppose I should have known better."

Caitlin entered the parlor with Liberty. She was glad for the peaceful presence Liberty exuded. Aidan, although not asked, came too. Ewen had gone to check on the men and get the story about Drew from someone other than Cait.

As she started to greet the doctor and the two cowboys, there was a knock at the front door. Mrs. McDuffy was already there asking Frank what it was he wanted.

Cait hurried to the door and saw Frank, bareheaded, wringing his battered Stetson in his hands.

"I cleaned Drew up an' dressed 'em in his Sunday go-ta-meetin' clothes. Mr. Jethro, he wanted me ta bring 'em up ta th' house. Said we wuz havin' th' wake ta night." He shuffled his feet, not because he was uncomfortable around Miss Caitlin but because he hated being in the big house. McDuffy left for the kitchen.

Caitlin squeezed Frank's shoulder and said, "Thank you, Frank, for all your help. I know this hasn't been easy for you." She turned away from him for a second and swallowed hard, but the tears welled in her eyes anyway and rolled down her cheeks. Her voice quavered as she said, "I can scarcely take it in. I don't know a soul who didn't like Drew." She took a handkerchief out of her sleeve and dabbed at her eyes and blew her nose.

"Yeah, me neither. Cain't be seein' anyones thet'd want 'em daid." Frank's eyes misted over, seeing the tears in Cait's. "Thing is, Miss Cait, it weren't no accident, neither. I'm hopin' John keeps his haid. Iffn he goes gunnin' fer Rhys, we could end up with mor'n one daid cowboy here at McCaully's. I'm a hopin' we find the real culprit, an' fast."

Caitlin nodded at Frank. Her eyes mirrored the worry she saw in his.

"I've thought of that too. Rhys has always ridden John hard. I don't know why, but I don't think he'd shoot a man, either. Besides, if he did, it wouldn't be Drew, it'd be John. I want you to bring Drew up here and lay him in the parlor. Tell the men we're having the wake for him tonight. Thanks for getting him ready for it."

Frank muttered, "You're welcome, Miss Cait." He slipped his mangled hat back onto his head and turned to leave.

Manny strolled to the front door. "Come on inta th' drawin' room, Frank. Hank, th' doc, an' I were jest about to converse with Miss Cait here. You kin come on in an' be a listening, too."

Frank took a deep breath, removed his Stetson, and followed Caitlin and Manny into the parlor.

The doctor and Hank had stood when the three women had entered the room, but Liberty ended up introducing herself because Cait had hurried to the door.

Liberty continued to talk as she tried to put the cowboys at their ease and explain her presence at the same time. "I'm Liberty Bannister." She held out her hand, first to the doctor and then to the cowboys.

"What are you doing here, Doctor Addison?" Aidan asked, not realizing the ranch had a dead cowboy.

"Well, I came to take a look at Drew Collins and write out a certificate of death since we have no mortician in all of Santa Rosa County. I'd also like to find out a bit more about the situation here. How's your amnesia victim, Miss McCaully?" the doctor asked Caitlin.

Before Caitlin could respond, Liberty asked, "Are you the doctor who nursed him?"

"I am," Doc Addison responded, curiosity in his warm brown eyes.

"Thank you, sir, for caring for him and bringing him here. I'm his wife, and would like to know your prognosis of his case."

"Ah...now I'll be able to know his true name. He's a very obliging young man—doesn't look Irish, though." His eyes twinkled. He liked the looks of this young woman. It was not merely that she was beautiful. He knew, simply from meeting her, that she had a personal relationship with Jesus Christ. It emanated from her, and he discerned her sweet spirit. Only one time in his life before had he met someone that exuded the Holy Ghost in this manner. Evangeline, his late wife, had that same sweetness of the Holy Ghost. He'd snatched her up and married her within two months of their meeting. Everyone who knew the doctor knew he and his darling Evangeline had been inseparable. She'd been a nurse, and the two had worked together.

Liberty's green eyes sparkled with life as she spoke to the physician. "His name is Matthew Bannister," she said, "owner of Bannister Vineyards in Napa. He was on his way to, or from, the Hendersons' when he was beaten and robbed. I suppose you know more about that than me. Matthew doesn't recognize me, but he did remember my eyes, which is a start, I suppose. Caitlin was visiting and put two and two together when she met his brother, who looks much like my husband. When she found we were missing Matthew, she was fairly certain she knew where he was. I'm thankful she's such an astute person."

The doctor smiled. "Yes, Caitlin's an intelligent young lady. And, Mrs. Bannister, I believe he'll make a full recovery with time. These kinds of cases are difficult to assess, but the fact he remembered something about you is a good thing. He knew his horse's name, spoke it automatically. I would recommend you take him to a specialist who deals in head trauma problems. There are some good doctors in San Francisco."

"I plan to do that as soon as Caitlin is safe. Matthew won't leave here until he finds out who made a threat on Caitlin's life and gets the problem cleared up," she answered. "He's committed to seeing this thing through."

The men and Aidan looked with shocked eyes at Liberty as she spoke. None had known of the threat on Cait's life.

The doctor remembered when he'd come to dinner with Conor that Gavin had pressed Caitlin for a destination that night. She had not given him a straight answer, and the doctor had not thought to ask her why she was leaving so soon after Mac's death. Now he knew. Someone had threatened her.

Aidan stared at Liberty and thought, It couldn't be Jared, could it? *I know he drinks and gambles, but I don't think my husband would murder someone...* Aidan put the thought out of her mind. She knew Jared hated Caitlin for telling Aidan not to marry him, but she didn't think he'd stoop to killing anyone. *He wouldn't, would he? I am confused about so many things. I hate my life.*

Chapter XXV

Evil pursueth sinners:
but to the righteous good shall be repayed.

PROVERBS 13:21

WHEN THE DOCTOR AND TWO COWBOYS rode past Sheriff Rowe and the priest in front of McGregor's Saloon, two other men had come out and stood not far from the sheriff. They talked as they watched the three riders leave town. The sheriff could hear a bit of their conversation about Mac McCaully passing away.

Sheriff Rowe spoke genially to the black-robed priest. "I'm going to ride out to McCaully's after I finish up a few things here in town. I have some paperwork to catch up on. Don't know if you know any of the McCaully outfit, but I recognized that cowboy who came into the saloon. He's one of the crew leaders—comes in every now and then to buy supplies for the ranch. I see they came in to get Doctor Addison. Think I'll ride out and make sure everything's okay. Do you want to ride out there with me?"

The priest smiled and shook his head. "No thanks, Sheriff, I have some things I need to finish up at the church, and I've been invited to the Sheridan's for dinner. Please give Miss McCaully my regards and tell her I was sorry to hear about her father's passing. At her request, I visited him a few days before he died."

"I'll do that," the sheriff said pleasantly. He tipped his hat to the padre.

Matthew and the other cowboys rode back to the main house. It was nearly dusk by the time they pulled up.

Jethro said, "I'd like all of you to accompany me. Miss Caitlin is waiting for an accounting of what we saw today. I'd imagine the ranch hands are getting ready for the wake."

The five men went up the stairs and without knocking, Jethro entered the front foyer. He peered into the parlor and saw Drew already laid out there with chairs ringing the entire perimeter of the large room. Jethro pulled out his pocket watch and saw the time. Cait was most likely eating dinner.

"You all go to the library, and I'll find Miss Caitlin." He cut across the parlor to the dining room. "I'll get Ewen, too."

Matthew led the way to the library. It was where he'd been hired. The other men followed him. Kirk and Matthew sat comfortably in two of the leather chairs. Matt gestured to the other two chairs.

"Might as well sit a spell and make yourself comfortable. Man's gotta relax now and then." He smiled at John and Sneedy as he tried to put the two cowboys more at their ease.

He continued to talk. "The first night when I arrived here, the doctor and I were invited to dinner. Miss Caitlin hired me after Doc Addison gave me the name Conor. Her sister, Maisie, gave me the last name of Innes so Ewen would take a shine to me."

"Yep, he shore do like the Ireesh," said Sneedy, who was still worried. "I bin a thinkin' there has to be at least one ranch hand who's a traitor. Wonder if it's Rhys? Fer some reason, I don't be a thinkin' it is. I knows it's none of the crew I'm on, an' I'm a thinkin' it's not Manny's crew, either. Thet leaves Eli's crew. There's Eli, Mosey, Duke, Rhys, and Jeb. Land sakes, it's hard ta think any one of'em would kill a man, specially a man like Drew."

Sheriff Deke Rowe climbed onto his horse. *Guess I'd better see what the McCaullys have found out about this whole thing. Wonder if those cowpokes could see the tracks going up to the cave? Stupid of Flint to lose his head like that and shoot the cowboy. That will slow things down a bit. Wonder if he really did lose his head? He's a cold one and no mistake. On the other hand, that cowpoke Dawkins, I've got him by the nose and can lead him wherever I wish. I paid his gambling debts and now I own him. He sure didn't want to be mixed up in this, but I'll make a rich man out of 'em and he'll be grateful I did. McGregor would have lynched him had I not stepped in and paid his debt. I don't know how loyal he is, but until he pays me back, he's mine. Wonder how bad Flint hit that McCaully man? I'm thinking he did it on purpose, but why?*

The sheriff headed out of Santa Rosa. The town was beginning to light up with lamps in storefronts, and the few street lamps the town could boast were casting an aura of light across the main street. Dusk was quickly turning to dark, but the sheriff knew the road well. He set his horse to a steady canter.

Caitlin, her guests, and her hired hands entered the library. The four men already seated stood when the women joined them.

"We were just about to have a meeting in the parlor," Caitlin said. "This is a better idea, but first, where is Sheriff Rowe?" She held Jethro's glance. "I did ask you to send for both of them, didn't I?"

Manny cleared his throat. "Miss Cait, I'll be a tellin' you straight up, thet sheriff is bad news. I started to get 'em, but he was a standin' thar in McGregor's, belly up ta th' bar, lookin' fer all he wuz worth like ol' man Satan hisself. I never said a thang to 'em, I wuz thet skairt. I jest acted like th' man I'm lookin' fer weren't there, an' I left. I felt like if I said a thang to 'em, he'd a shot me daid right then and thar."

Caitlin's eyes widened at the import of his words.

There was an uncomfortable silence, broken when Doc Addison cleared his throat and said, "He's been up to no good, Miss Cait.

I knew he was paying some of the city elders to look the other way for certain things he's done, but I never thought he'd be involved in a mess like this, until today. He's a bad one and no mistake."

Sneedy said, "Trouble is, Miss Cait, we's gots us at least one or more traitors on th' ranch. I cain't say as ta who it is, but I knows thet thar was one McCaully horse with the shooters. I've been a thinkin' mighty hard, an' I'm a figurin' it's gotta be someone in Eli's group, mebe Eli hisself. I don't like ta be a blamin' someone when I don't rightly know."

"Thanks, Sneedy, we won't go bandying about what you've said in here. Does anyone know where Ewen is? I thought he'd want to be in on this conversation."

"I seed him headin' out when I comed up ta th' house, Miss Cait. He talked ta th' boys ta see what we be a knowin' about th' shootin', an' then I seed him riding off." Frank had wondered where the foreman was going when it was getting dusk and the wake would be starting before long.

Kirk stood to give Liberty the leather chair next to Matthew. She smiled and mouthed thanks to him. Aidan sat down opposite her, and Caitlin took the desk chair.

"That's very strange," Caitlin said. "Used to be he'd hardly leave the ranch, and this is the second time he's ridden off today. I wonder why?"

Sheriff Deke Rowe rode at a steady canter toward the McCaully Ranch. He was barely discernible dressed as he was all in brown. He sat his black mare comfortably.

The stars overhead shone in abundance, and the sky had been cleared of rain clouds by a freshening breeze. The moon had arisen in radiant glory, a fat sliver in the inky blackness of the heavens. It lit his way with a soft glow, but he didn't notice. He ruminated on what he would say when he arrived at the ranch. He needed some excuse for his presence there.

Suddenly a shot rang out and he tumbled from his horse. He clutched his shoulder as pain seared through him. It burned as if on fire. Shocked but maintaining a presence of mind, he crawled off the road and hoped he could hide, but the landscape was rolling hills with short scrub and flowers. There was nothing he could hide under or behind. He lay still but drew his gun as he heard the sound of hooves pounding toward him. He cursed his horse, under his breath, standing there as if purposely to give him away. He was ready to shoot until he saw who it was.

Ewen Carr jumped off his horse when he saw the man lying next to the road. He was shocked to see the sheriff. He lay in plain view, a shining star on his chest reflecting the moonlight. He drew his gun to be ready in case the shooter fired again.

Kneeling on one knee, he asked, "Are you hurt bad? I heard the shot and knew someone is up to no good. We've had a rash of robberies on the road, as I reckon you've heard."

"It's just a shoulder wound," the sheriff gasped. "I'm mighty thankful you rode up when you did. I have no doubt they'd have come to finish the job. Wonder if you could help me, Carr? I was on my way to McCaully's because I've heard some strange goings on. I know the doc is there, an' I'm sure he can patch me up."

Ewen took his neckerchief off and balled it up to staunch the wound, which was bleeding profusely. He couldn't see well as it was so dark.

"The hole in your shoulder's high. I'm sure you'll be all right, but you're losing a lot of blood. I'll get you back onto your mare and head back to McCaully's. I need to be there anyway." Ewen spoke as he took the sheriff's kerchief to try to bind the makeshift bandage in place.

"What are you doing heading into town this time of night?" The sheriff was curious. He'd seen Ewen in town half a dozen times in the last week.

"I was riding into town to get you. I think you need to be at McCaully's and see what's been going on. I didn't talk to 'em, but when I saw Manny didn't come back with you, I figured he couldn't find you, so I decided to hunt you down." He helped the sheriff to his feet and steadied him as he swayed. "Sure you can ride?"

"Yeah, I'm sure." Deke Rowe felt lightheaded from the loss of blood and shock. He was bleeding profusely. *Flint wouldn't shoot me, would he? I reckon he would. Then he could get all the gold for himself. I didn't plan on murder when I started this thing. I'll tell Dawkins he'd better be careful. He'll end up dead, most likely. I know I would've if Ewen hadn't happened by.* The sheriff was beginning to feel faint.

Another shot rang out, and then another. Ewen returned fire, but not knowing where to shoot, he aimed at the bluff above them, thinking it would be the best place for a man to ambush someone on the road. He shot at the bluff's edge, methodically shooting across its top. No more shots rang down.

"Let's be going, then," the sheriff said hoarsely, unsure how long he could ride. Ewen helped the sheriff onto his horse. Sheriff Rowe sagged forward, leaning over the pommel and onto the neck of his horse.

The man standing on the bluff that overlooked the road cursed his bad luck. He'd thought to go down and finish the sheriff off. He spoke aloud to himself. "Now, Rowe's alerted. I have no doubt he'll know I did it. Well, it's my misfortune he's not dead, but I'll get him another day. I'm not about to share the gold with a bumbling sheriff nor a cowpoke who has no backbone."

The library was beginning to feel overcrowded and stuffy with so many bodies in it. Liberty, feeling queasy, stood to open a window, but Matthew, knowing her objective, opened it for her.

He smiled at this woman who was his wife. Her shoulder brushed against his and he felt as if he'd been scorched. *We must have a mighty strong attraction to each other for her to affect me this way. She looks tired. Sure wish this business was over, and I knew my past.* He took her hand, kissed her palm, and folded her fingers over as if to hold his kiss. She looked up, her eyes full of love for him.

Kirk, watching them, smiled to himself.

Cait asked, "Jethro, did you find out anything at Diablo Ridge?" She wanted to hurry this meeting along as the rest of the men would be coming in soon for the wake. "I wonder why Ewen isn't here? He should be here listening to all of this. Does he know the sheriff might be part of this mess? And, who would shoot Drew? Do know who did this?"

Jethro, who'd been sitting in the back of the library, stood to address those present.

"We know why, but we don't know who, Miss Caitlin. There's a mine up on the ledge, and to our reckoning, it's a gold mine."

"Gold!" Aidan gasped.

Cait paled, stunned.

The doctor and cowhands were surprised. The look on their faces was disbelief, yet every one trusted Jethro, who continued to talk.

"All the men who rode out with me agree. We believe samples have been taken. There's lanterns, picks, and other paraphernalia for mining in that cave. There was a clear spot to pick off Drew from the ledge where the cave is located. Matthew—most of you know him as Conor—is an excellent tracker. He led us straight to the cave."

Frank, Manny, and Hank stared at Conor, who was now Matthew, and wondered what the blazes was going on.

"So," Caitlin responded, almost breathless from shock, "you think whoever did this is after gold on McCaully property?"

Jethro nodded. "All of us who rode out believe that. There's evidence that the mine's a mother lode. Perhaps we could get Gavin to come out and look at it or take some samples in to have it assayed."

"Wonder, if the sheriff is involved, how he found out about the gold?" Doctor Addison asked. He could scarcely credit the sheriff with murder. "A man will do strange things for gold, but it's hard to believe the sheriff would murder a man."

"I wonder if we should question Eli's crew?" Jethro asked. "Perhaps we can get to the bottom of this if we can find out which man, or men, is involved in it."

Cait said, "I think that's a good idea. It sounds as if the men are coming in now. Does anyone else have anything else to say?"

John spoke up. "I want ta find out which one of Eli's crew is involved in such a deed. I don't rightly care who it is. I want thet man a hangin' fer what he done."

Chapter XXVI

When the wicked are multiplied, transgression increaseth:
but the righteous shall see their fall.

PROVERBS 29:16

AFTER JOHN USED THE WORD hanging, it was silent for a moment, each person reflecting on the dead man in the parlor and which cowboy might be involved. John stared at the floor as tears filled his eyes.

Jethro said firmly, "I don't want this business to go any further than this room. I need Ewen to be apprised of this before we proceed. I mean it, Manny, Hank, John, Frank, Sneedy…it's gonna be hard to keep your traps shut, but that's exactly what I'm saying until Ewen knows. For sure, we don't want to be giving a hint that we know anything, or we'll lose the advantage we have."

Manny answered for the four other men, "We're a hearin' you, Jethro, and we knows how ta hold our tongues."

All five stood, wanting to get cleaned up a bit before they joined the other men who were already gathering in the parlor. They walked out of the library.

Kirk and Matthew followed them out but not before Kirk had given Caitlin a long look that pinked up her cheeks. The doctor, always aware of undercurrents and what was going on around him, noticed the interchange and smiled inwardly, knowing Caitlin had found her man.

Jethro said, "I need to clean up and change my shirt." He was still curious about how long Caitlin had known Kirk, but he didn't have the nerve to ask. He left, wondering where Ewen was.

The parlor was well lit. Sconces reflected their quiet glow in the large mahogany framed mirror. The occupants of McCaully Ranch turned out in full force to pay their last respects to Drew. The doctor filled out the death certificate.

Food had been set out as well as refreshment. Had not the oak table of the dining room been so sturdy it would have groaned with the weight of it: Pies, cakes, open-faced sandwiches, meats, salads, and an assortment of cheeses covered the long table. Plates, silverware, cups, glasses, juices, and coffee were spread over the surface of the sideboard. It was a night to remember and reminisce a life. Memories of Drew were shared, most with a chuckle, as the dead man had brought joy to so many.

The French doors to the dining room had been thrown wide open. The men loaded their plates and returned to the parlor to honor their dead friend. Everyone at McCaully's except Sweeny, McDuffy, and Duney were planning to sit in the parlor for the wake.

Eli's crew were seated together. Jethro sat across the room looking at each of them surreptitiously, trying to figure out who might be a traitor to the McCaully outfit. The only one he had a problem with was Rhys.

This evening, Rhys sat quietly, feeling sorry he'd been so hot tempered with John and his crew. He stared at John, who was looking at the floor, knowing the man was hurting. Rhys had no idea someone in his crew was tangled up in the whole affair. He looked over and saw Caitlin and another woman talking to each other as they began to dish up their food. Rhys wondered who the woman was and why she was at the wake.

Suddenly there was a banging at the front door. It was flung open, and Ewen staggered in under the weight of the sheriff.

The men in the room couldn't see what was going on because the door from the parlor to the front entry was shut. Kirk and Jethro left the parlor. Kirk was the first to get to the sheriff's side. He put a steadying arm under the man's shoulder, taking some of the weight off Ewen. The sheriff was nearly unconscious from the loss of blood.

Caitlin, followed by Liberty, hurried to the foyer.

Cait said to Ewen, "Take 'em to the room off the library whir we had me da." Her eyes flew to Kirk's.

There was too much going on and Kirk was uneasy. He didn't know the injured man was the sheriff, but two men being shot in one day was more than enough.

Ewen said, "Caitlin, stay with the men in the parlor. We'll take care of this."

Kirk nodded. "Those men will guard you with their lives."

"I agree, Miss Cait," Jethro said. "Sit with Manny."

Liberty had appraised the situation and headed for the kitchen to ask Duney to heat some water. The doctor opened the doors to the library. He knew which room Cait was talking about. He'd been there often enough to check on Mac when he became too weak to use the stairs. He crossed the room ahead of the three men and threw open the heavy door to a large office that had been converted to a bedroom.

"Get a couple towels out of there," Ewen nodded toward a huge mahogany armoire.

Doc Addison grabbed several towels and a flannel sheet. Quickly pulling back the bed covers, he and Jethro spread them out so the sheriff wouldn't bleed all over the bed linens. Kirk pulled off the sheriff's boots while the doctor unbuttoned his shirt. The sheriff started rambling but was soon unconscious.

"He's lost a lot of blood, Doc. I was headed into town and heard a shot. I knew of the robberies we've had recently and figured whoever fired the gun was a robber, but he was nowhere close to the sheriff. I think he fired from the bluff and I got some shots off after he fired on me. The sheriff said if I hadn't come along the man would've come to finish him off."

"Didn't get into town to see Hannah then?" The doctor was busy working on the sheriff and didn't see Ewen's reaction, but Kirk did.

Ewen looked at the doctor, shocked. "You know about us?"

"Why, yes, though I'm the only one she's told. She is my dead wife's sister you know—said you haven't set a date yet."

Ewen looked a bit discomfited as Kirk, who looked on, grinned from ear to ear.

Jethro thought to himself, *So that's where he's been getting himself off to. I was beginning to worry about him, but it makes sense. I think he's been sweet on Miss Hannah for a long time.*

Ewen answered the doctor, "N-no…no, we haven't set a date. I was thinking June. She wants to make her own wedding dress, her being a seamstress an' all. Neither of us has ever been married. I waited till Mac was gone. Figured I needed to stay here as much as possible to help Caitlin."

"I know you've waited a long time." The doctor glanced at Ewen. His gaze swung toward the grinning Kirk. "When will you be marrying Miss Cait?" he asked with a smile at Kirk's astonishment.

"As soon as she'll have me," Kirk answered promptly. He smiled back at the doctor and grinned at the dazed look on Ewen's face.

"Miss Caitlin's going to marry you, son?" asked Ewen, disbelief evident in his voice.

"I believe so," Kirk replied, "and the sooner the better. Then the thieving murderers will have to do away with two rather than one."

"Did she say she'd marry you?" Ewen was still disbelieving. Caitlin had never looked at a man let alone fallen in love with one.

"Nope, I haven't asked her yet, but Katie'll marry me. We have an unspoken agreement, but it's going to be spoken before this night is out. I made up my mind today that sooner is better in this case. It'll be a form of protection for her."

Jethro nodded. "That's true, I understand your desire to hurry this thing, and yet, whoever is behind this would have to get through Caitlin's two sisters and their husbands before they could get the land."

Kirk replied, "Yes, but the two sisters could easily sell. My understanding is that neither of them is interested in ranching."

Ewen said, "Hm, that's true, neither one of the girls ever cared at all for ranching. If Caitlin were out of the way it wouldn't take long for the sale of the ranch, providing there were buyers ready and waiting."

"Precisely what is needed," Kirk said, "is a big meeting, family and ranch hands together, so everyone would understand that the two sisters will never sell. Now that gold's been found, I'm quite certain that would be the truth."

"Gold? What're you talking about, cowboy? Gold on McCaully Ranch?" Ewen was flummoxed.

"Yes," Jethro replied, "we believe it's why the sheriff's been shot. We're speculating, but we think he's involved in trying to get rid of Caitlin. At least one of our men, most likely someone in Eli's group, is involved. There's one other person, maybe more, but we have no idea who."

Ewen felt overwhelmed with the information. He replied to Kirk, "I could get a wire out to Mr. and Mrs. Galway tomorrow morning. I'll talk to Miss Cait about it and see what she says before I proceed. I think you're right. A big meeting is in order."

"Thank you, Ewen Carr." Kirk hoped he'd be friends with this man who was so important to the ranch. It seemed a bit strange to him that a man who'd been single for so long would fall in love. *I reckon love is no respecter of age.* He left the room to go in search of Caitlin and make his wishes known. He was sure she would agree. *Last night her eyes told me she feels the same way about me as I feel about her.*

Doc Addison was doing some thinking about the man lying on the bed. *I'd bet Blondie's beautiful tail that the sheriff has been done in by a partner who wants all the gold to himself. Wonder if our cowpuncher will talk when he finds the sheriff was shot?*

The sheriff was still unconscious. Doc took his wrist and felt his pulse. It surprised him that it was racing and thready.

"Wonder if Rowe has a weak heart? This may not be an easy fix. His heart's pumping hard, too hard. It's trying to get more blood, but it can't. He's lost too much. I know a few doctors who'd stick leeches on him and take more out." He shook his head at such stupidity.

Ewen, standing at the foot of the bed, said, "The bullet went clean through. I didn't think about there being any complications."

"Neither did I." Doc took off his frock coat and rolled up his sleeves. "I'll be right back." He went to the kitchen to tell Duney to heat up some water, only to find a huge pot already boiling.

"You're a wonder, Duney." He smiled at her in appreciation.

"I can't take the credit for it, Doc. Miss Liberty told me to heat some water. She's in the dining room, right now, making up a plate for you. I like that girl—she's thoughtful. Be a good influence on Miss Cait, that's for sure."

"Yes, she seems level headed. I like her, too. She has quite a presence about her."

Aidan had gone upstairs to change her clothes into something more appropriate for the wake. She was sorry to hear about all the problems that had befallen Caitlin and thought, *I jumped to conclusions when there's no basis for them. Here, I vowed to be a better sister to Cait and when the moment presented itself, I sneered and nearly accused her of having an affair with Jared when I know the two can't abide each other. What's the matter with me, anyway?*

Aidan entered the dining room, and all the men stood. Jared looked at her with shock. He'd not supposed she would come to the ranch.

She looked at him nervously, afraid he'd be angry and think her possessive.

He got up, took her by the arm, and led her down the hall to Caitlin's sitting room. Kicking the door shut behind him, he thought to himself, *Ewen or no Ewen, I need to talk to my wife.*

When Jared kicked the door shut, Aidan thought he was angry and looked at him piteously, tears welling in her eyes. Before, when they had arguments, she never cried. She would yell or scream or simply not talk to him for days on end, hoping the silent treatment would make an impact on him, but it never did. Now, she was tired of being alone in their big house. At the beginning of their marriage, it had looked to be a house of love and laughter. Aidan was tired of her wretched marriage. She felt Jared didn't want her. If he did, he'd come home at night to be with her. She'd gone around to different businesses and paid off all his debts, but she felt it was useless. She was at the end of her rope and her eyes, full of misery, looked at Jared.

"Aidan, I'm not angry with you, not at all. I do need you to know in the short time I've been here, I've changed. Please believe me when I tell you, I'm a different man." He led her to a chair and sat on the ottoman to face her.

She stared at him, her eyes widening.

"I want you to hear me out, and then you can decide what you want to do. I know I've been a cad, a bounder, a sot, and I don't know what else…oh, and a losing gambler. I was in over my head at McGregor's. I received threats on my life if I didn't pay up. That's why I begged you for money…I was scared. I was so scared and desperate that I rode over here and stole money out of Mac's desk."

Aidan gasped and her eyes turned cold and hard.

CHAPTER XXVII

I will even betroth thee unto me in faithfulness:
and thou shalt know the LORD.

HOSEA 2:20

JARED SENSED AIDAN'S BURNING ANGER. "Let me finish—
please. It was payroll money. Ewen made it up out of his own money
and threatened me into working off my debt here at the ranch. The
thing is, though, it's the best thing that could have happened to me. I
got paired up with the new hire. He's a man that walks around with
peace in his soul no matter what's happening around him. I liked what
I saw. He told me about living life the way we were created to live it,
and I accepted Jesus as my Savior. I can feel the difference. I can see
the difference, and there's a peace in my being I've never known in
my entire life. I thought you could fill the void, but I was asking the
impossible. I now know my Creator in a personal way, and I know I'm
different from what I was. I wanted to confess all this to you before I
tell you that I have also come to realize that I love you. I don't think I
ever did before, or at least realized I did. You were an amusement, an
avenue to a nice house and money, but I grew tired of you, not because
of anything you did but because my focus was on the wrong things. I've

been a selfish fool and have been praying it's not too late to make it up to you. I want to have children with you. I never did before as you well know, but now, I want to live a good life and grow old with you, Aidan. Please forgive me. Please, give me the chance to prove I've changed." Jared got down on one knee. "You're not to pay off the debt to Ewen, either. I will work it off and be the better man for it, but I want you to know, I love you until death do us part."

Tears began to roll down Aidan's cheeks. This was what she had always wanted. She had seen the difference in Jared immediately when she walked into the parlor. She could forgive him anything if he could leave the drinking and gambling alone.

"I can forgive you, Jared, but I believe you're right. You do need to work out the debt by yourself." She looked at him closely to see if he would be angry with her comment…to see if he meant what he said.

He looked grateful at her agreement, and his eyes gleamed bright with unshed tears…thankful for her forgiveness.

Aidan said, "I went around town and paid all that you owed to different businesses. I don't like the thought of owing anybody anything. Got that from my da, I reckon."

Jared said, "I need to apologize to Cait for my actions. I was so worried you'd listen to her and not marry me, and then I was plain downright ugly trying to put a wedge between the two of you. You must know she loves you."

He stood and pulled her to her feet. "I love you, Aidan. Thank you for your forgiveness. I promise to cherish you for the rest of my life." He took her into his arms and kissed her gently and then deeply, with more passion. His arms tightened around her, and she felt safe and cherished as she never had before. She kissed him back in full measure. Her arms crept around his neck and she molded herself to him.

"I love you too, Jared…so very much."

As Kirk entered the parlor, he saw Liberty sitting next to Matthew. The two were deep in conversation, and Matthew held Libby's hand in his. Cait was sitting next to John. Neither one was conversing, but Kirk felt the two were consoling each other. Eli's crew still sat together. Rhys was staring at the floor, his brow wrinkled in concentration, but Jeb was crying, the tears rolling down his cheeks. Kirk had a quick moment of insight. He put his hand on Jeb's shoulder and gave it a squeeze.

"Jeb, would you come outside with me for a few minutes—I'd like to talk with you." Jeb followed him out the door, his shoulders shaking with uncontrollable sobs.

Jeb Dawkins had, at one point in his life, planned to be a schoolmaster. That long-ago desire flashed before him, and he wished he'd have pursued it. He pulled out a large kerchief from his back pocket and wiped his eyes and blew his nose, but the tears continued to roll down his weathered cheeks.

Kirk got right to the point. "You know how Drew was killed, don't you?"

Jeb looked at him with scared eyes. "I'm a dead man if I say a thing about it."

"You may be a dead man if you don't. Do you know the sheriff is here? Fact is, follow me." He led Jeb back into the house.

Jeb was wondering what Kirk knew and why the sheriff would be here at McCaully's. He'd been thinking it'd have been a lot better to let McGregor's henchmen string him up than to have the sheriff own him, body and soul. He'd cared for Drew…loved his lighthearted jests and his serious eyes when he spoke of something important. *Now, he's dead an' I'm a party to it. I don't know if I want to talk to the sheriff, either.*

He followed Kirk across the library and watched silently as Kirk opened a door. What he saw almost made him want to vomit with fright. The sheriff looked as if he were dying. Mesmerized by the sight, Jeb walked slowly toward the bed.

The sheriff had regained consciousness but knew he was dying. His ticker was plum worn out. He saw Jeb and grimaced with pain.

The two men stared at each other, but Jeb was quite certain he knew who'd shot the sheriff. It scared him right down to his boots. He began to quiver with fear.

"Better...for you...to tell them...the truth," the sheriff whispered brokenly. "He'll get you...he'll get you, if you don't." Sheriff Rowe gasped for air.

The doctor looked down at the sheriff with pity in his eyes. "I know you're Catholic, Deke...you want us to get Father O'Flannagan for you?"

The sheriff's eyes had closed but they flew open at the doctor's question. He didn't need to answer. Jeb answered for him.

"You do, and the sheriff's a dead man. It's the priest that did this. It's the priest that killed Drew. He's no priest at all. He's an outlawed gunslinger come up here from Texas. His two church helpers are bad, too."

Sheriff Rowe closed his eyes again now that the truth was out.

Doctor Addison was shocked. "I can scarcely believe it. The priest is behind all this? Father O'Flannagan is head of this operation to get control of McCaully's?"

"Yep, he's the one that wants to get rid of Miss Cait. Day after Mac died he came waltzing into the stables as if he were born in it. Told me he was gonna get rid of Miss Cait out on the range or right there in the stable. Said he could hit her over the head with a horseshoe and throw her into the stall with Fire and no one would be the wiser. They'd all think it was her horse that did it.

"I stuck to her like a burr the whole day of the reading of the will. I watched to make sure O'Flannagan wasn't around. I was scared but glad when I found out she'd run away.

"Flint told me today he planned to marry her, and I was to take orders from him, not Sheriff Rowe. I owed McGregor's. Sheriff Rowe bought my debt, and I've been working and doing whatever he said. But that Flint, why, he shot Drew for no good reason. He shot 'em just like he was doing target practice. He did it on purpose. The sheriff here told me there'd be no killing and I believed 'em. It's the priest that isn't a priest, Flint O'Flannagan, and his men who are the ones who've been robbing people around here. His heart's as foul as Satan himself."

Kirk decided right then and there that he and Cait were getting married…tomorrow. *I'd better let her know and Matthew, too. Figure what I'll do is give my portion of Bannister Vineyards to Matt with the provision that I get twenty percent of all sales. He can buy me out, I suppose. I'll have to think that through. He'll have children now who can inherit. I've always loved roping and ranching. I'll love the life here, and it'll be my pleasure to get this place back into shape.*

"Come on, Jeb, we're going back to the wake." Kirk touched the man on his arm.

The sheriff roused enough to say, "I'm sorry, Dawkins…for getting you…into this mess." His breathing was becoming more and more labored.

Jeb nodded, not knowing how to respond. He moved to open the door and Kirk followed him out.

Ewen looked at the sheriff with saddened eyes. He remembered a sermon he once heard when he was a little boy back in Ireland. All he could remember of it was: "Silver and gold have I none." *You have neither silver nor gold and look what your evilness has brought you, Deke, death and not the life you could have had.* He turned away, his thoughts straying to the woman he'd fallen in love with. *Hannah said she wouldn't set a date until I realize I need Jesus. She knows I'm honest enough not to fake an acceptance. I've heard of that happening. The man says he's made a commitment, and then…well he hasn't got Jesus, but he's got the girl. Looking at the sheriff makes me know I'd better do some reading of the Good Book and make up my mind. I always thought I was so self-sufficient, but I'm beginning to know otherwise. I have a feeling Liberty and Matthew Bannister and Kirk all have what Hannah has and Drew had. Why didn't God spare Drew if he loved him so much?*

"Doc, I have a question for you." Ewen didn't look sheepish. He simply wanted an answer.

"What is it?"

"If God loved Drew so much, why didn't he spare him? Why didn't he protect him from the bullet?"

"That's a good question, Ewen. I'm not certain I know the answer." The doctor said a quick prayer for help and clarity.

"I reckon, Ewen Carr, we don't realize how glorious heaven is. We don't live as if we have a passion to see Jesus. We have no concept that taking us out of this world when we're a believer is an act of mercy. It takes us out of all sorrow and hurt." He looked sagely at the foreman. "We think of heaven as the goal and forget that heaven is only a reward. Jesus Christ is the goal. To live, to serve, and to worship the One who sacrificed all so that we can have a relationship…a personal relationship with God Almighty, that's what we were created for. God wants us to have relationship with Him. Only then are the desires of our hearts satisfied." He heard a groan behind him. The sheriff had heard everything Doc Addison had said.

The sheriff gasped, "Lord forgive me…don't deserve it…but forgive me…come into my heart." Tears slid from the dying man's eyes, wetting the pillow, but a look of wonder and peace came over his face. "Yes…yes, I'm ready…" He gasped one last time and was gone.

Ewen looked on in astonishment. The doctor had seen deathbed confessions many times over, but they never ceased to stir his heart.

"Is that all? I mean…will he go to heaven if he didn't have time to serve Jesus?"

"Yes, yes he will. We are not serving God to get to heaven…Jesus paid the entire price for that, which is what the sheriff just obtained." He closed Deke's eyelids and pulled the sheet up over his head. "We serve because we love Jesus and want to delight Him in all we do. I keep wondering what all we're going to do in heaven, but I can tell you one thing—we won't be sitting on a cloud with a halo on our heads being bored to death. We're going to be busy, but it's going to be the most joyful busy. We can't begin to imagine it. Perhaps, if we haven't learned to worship God, it'll be one of the first things we learn how to do. I don't rightly know." The doctor paused.

"I just had a thought. Wonder if we could get the priest out here to pray for the sheriff. We could set a trap for him and let everyone in on it except the priest."

Ewen thought for a minute. "That might not be a bad idea. Perhaps we could set it up so Miss Cait goes out to the stables with him and he tries to get her to go with him. We'll have to talk to Kirk and Caitlin and see what they think about it."

Caitlin, without looking up, knew Kirk had entered the parlor. It was as if he emitted an aura she recognized without looking. She watched as he perused the room. He nodded at her, and the look in his eyes warmed her heart. He crossed to where Eli's crew members were sitting. Jeb had been weeping profusely and Cait felt sorry for him. She saw Kirk tap him on the shoulder and whisper something in his ear. The older man stood and the two went outside. She wondered at it. *Is it Jeb who's involved with all this? Perhaps the sheriff related the entire story and Jeb is a part of it. Or, maybe Kirk is sorry for Jeb because he...* Her thoughts were interrupted by the appearance of her sister and Jared.

Aidan and Jared entered the parlor looking like newlyweds. *Goodness! I've never seen that look on Jared's face before, or on Aidan's, either, for that matter.* Aidan sat next to Rhys, where Jeb had been sitting. Jared walked to Caitlin, his feet soundless on the plush Belgian carpet.

"Caitlin, I'd like to talk to you for a few minutes, in private, if that would be all right with you."

She glanced at him in surprise, which turned to a look he couldn't fathom...almost like fear. He looked at Cait questioningly. He nodded to Aidan, who led the way to Cait's sitting room.

Caitlin followed them down the hall but sat in a wingback chair where she could view her sister and brother-in-law at the same time. She'd scream the house down if they approached her. Since the reading of the will, she was wary and on her guard. Her hand crept down to feel her trusted firearm strapped to her hip. Because of all the goings on around the ranch, she hadn't even wanted to attend the wake without it. She knew she was scared but didn't want it to show.

CHAPTER XXVIII

He that diligently seeketh good procureth favour:
but he that seeketh mischief, it shall come unto him.

PROVERBS 11:27

"**I HAVE SEVERAL THINGS I NEED TO TELL YOU,** Caitlin. The very first thing is an apology, which I hope you'll accept. I am very sorry for my past behavior. I've been every sort of a fool, literally a real fool. At first, I was afraid you'd convince Aidan not to marry me. You were right, though—I was not marriageable material. I have been a selfish lout, but no more. I am sorry for any grief I've caused you by trying to separate you from Aidan. I did all I could to try to turn Aidan away from loving you, but I never could. She loves you dearly. If you've thought otherwise, it's because of me."

"Why are you telling me this? Why the change now?" Caitlin, her voice even, was still on her guard. She'd never trusted Jared and she didn't plan to start now.

"I'm telling you this because I am different. I know this will sound mawkish in light of all that's gone before, but I have accepted Jesus Christ as my Savior. Believe me, it's not sentimental drivel. It's real and it goes deep, to the core of my being. I now have a peace in my heart I've never known before. Life is all about relationships. When we die and stand before our Creator, all that's going to matter is our relationship to Jesus Christ and our relationship to others…all others. We can't pick and choose who we wish to be nice to. We are to love others as ourselves. Again, I am sorry for any torment I've caused you."

"Where did you hear this? When did you become a Christ follower?" Caitlin had a feeling she knew the answer before he spoke but the idea excited her. This is what her da had found. This is what Liberty and Kirk had, and even Doc Addison.

"I saw the peace Matthew Bannister carried around within himself. He's not like any other man I've ever known. Just a few nights ago, I accepted Christ when Matthew talked to me. I am not jesting when I say it has changed me. I will never be the kind of man I was before."

Cait looked at Jared with questioning eyes. "Can I accept Christ, too? What I mean is…may I ask him into my heart right now? I know what you are talking about, Jared. I saw Da change before my eyes. I have seen what Kirk and Liberty have, and I want it. With all my heart I want it."

"Me too." Aidan broke into the conversation. "I want it too. I've been selfish and jealous and insecure in who I am. I want the peace I see in you, Jared." Tears formed in her eyes and rolled down her cheeks. "I'm so tired of trying to be strong."

Jared took her into his arms and kissed her lightly on the lips. "I'll try to be the strong one. I've neglected you so long, it's no wonder you're tired." He knelt. "Let's all kneel right here and pray. You pray for forgiveness of your sins. Repent of the things you know you've done wrong. I learned from Matthew that repenting means turning away from and heading in the other direction. It doesn't mean simply being sorry…it takes an act on your part to reject living the way you did before. You ask Jesus to come into your heart and take over."

The two girls knelt, one on either side of Jared, right there in Caitlin's sitting room, and prayed together. Tears streamed down their faces. When they were finished, Cait spoke up.

"I don't feel any different. Maybe it didn't work for me."

"Matthew explained that, too." Jared hugged both women. "Being saved isn't a feeling. It's a faith. Some people really feel a change and have all this emotional hoopla. I have to confess, I did. I still do. I feel like I'm walking on a cloud, but some people don't feel any different at all. It's not the feeling that counts, it's what Jesus did for you on the cross and your belief that you are now His servant, His subject, but most of all, His beloved."

Caitlin could accept that, and she couldn't wait to tell Kirk.

When Kirk had gone to the parlor and seen Katie gone, he asked John where she was.

"She went down th' hall with Jared an' Miss Aidan."

"Thanks." Kirk turned to leave. Seeing Jeb sit with Eli's crew out of the corner of his eye, he felt sorrow for the man. Jeb had made poor choices that got him caught up in murder. His choices had forever changed his whole life.

Kirk went down the hall and tapped on the sitting room door.

Jared said, "Come in."

As he closed the door behind him, Kirk felt as if he was intruding, but the atmosphere was peaceful. He smiled at the three standing so close to one another.

"Am I interrupting something?"

"No, you're not interrupting anything. You can, however, greet your new sisters in Christ." Jared was grinning from ear to ear.

Kirk was amazed. "You've accepted Christ as Savior?"

Caitlin answered, "Yes, I don't feel any different, but yes, I have. Aidan and I both prayed." She smiled at him, glowing. Aidan and Jared stood watching the interchange.

"Many people don't feel any different, Katie. I didn't. It's not about feeling. It's about believing," Kirk responded with joy in his voice and eyes.

Calling Caitlin "Katie" brought raised eyebrows. Jared's eyes slanted to Aidan and he winked.

Kirk's use of "Katie" warmed Aidan's heart. Her da had called his youngest Katie.

"Do you want us to leave? Are you wanting to talk alone?" asked Aidan. Her eyes looked innocently into Kirk's.

"No, it's fine if you wish to stay." He grinned at Jared and Aidan. "This way, I've got witnesses." Taking Caitlin's hand in his, he knelt on one knee.

"Katie...Caitlin Kendall McCaully...will you do me the honor of marrying me? I love you, the until-death-do-us-part kind of love. I would like to spend the rest of my life showing you that I do." His heart was pounding so hard he felt he wouldn't hear her answer. It was one of those decisions he'd thought about when looking at Jeb, a decision that would forever change him, but he welcomed it.

Stunned, Cait's throat tightened and she doubted she could talk. *He does love me! How can this happen so quickly? What's even more surprising is that I love him—I truly love him,* she thought wonderingly.

Kirk waited for a reply with bated breath. It seemed an eternity before she found her voice.

"I...I accept...with all my heart, I accept." Tears filled her gray eyes.

Kirk stood and reached into his pocket.

Not caring that her sister and Jared were looking on, Cait put her hands on Kirk's shoulders and kissed him. It was quick, light, and sweet. Kirk smiled into her clear eyes.

"Katie, I not only want to marry you, I want to marry you tomorrow morning."

Stunned again, she gasped.

Aidan looked at Kirk, shocked.

Jared, putting two and two together, knew it was to protect Cait from the threat made on her life. Aidan had told him about it not more than a half hour before.

Kirk dug deep into his pocket and pulled out the velvet bag. He upended it, and a ring dropped out into his palm.

"This was my mother's," he said, and slipped the ring on her finger. It was a beautiful sapphire surrounded by diamonds and fit her finger.

"Tomorrow? You want to get married tomorrow? I don't have to go through the agony of deciding colors and patterns or a wedding dress?

I accept! I wholeheartedly accept." Caitlin was an outdoor girl. She'd always preferred denims to a dress. Her da had insisted on dresses for Sunday dinner, or when anyone else was invited to supper, but otherwise, Cait could be found in denims.

It was Kirk's turn to be surprised. "We can have the big wedding later, if you like."

It struck Caitlin why he wanted to marry her so quickly. *He thinks to protect me by this. It won't work…whoever wants me dead will try for him, too.*

"Maybe we should wait. Tomorrow is too soon, don't you think?" Caitlin felt tired yet energized by this man who loved her.

Kirk looked deeply into her eyes and saw worry for him.

"Nope, tomorrow's not soon enough," he replied. His eyes reflected his love for her and her cheeks became rosy, but she couldn't look away.

Jared said, "I think we'd better be going back to the wake, Mrs. Hart. Will you accompany me?" He held out his arm, smiling into her sapphire gaze.

Aidan took his arm, and they started to leave but Kirk said, "Wait— can you wait a minute? I have something I want to share with you. It's a very private matter." He put his arm around his Katie's shoulders, pulling her closer to his side as if to protect her.

"We found out just a while ago who is behind the threats and Drew's death."

Cait stiffened under his arm, but he squeezed her and continued. "Sheriff Rowe is dying in the little room off the library. Evidently, Jeb got himself into trouble with gambling debts at McGregor's."

As he spoke, Jared tightened Aidan's hand against his side, looking at her with saddened eyes. The revelation hit Jared a little too close to home.

Kirk said, "Sheriff Rowe paid Jeb's debts and then made Jeb a party to his perfidious schemes. Jeb helped find the gold and has done jobs he's more than ashamed of."

"Did he shoot Drew, or did the sheriff?" Caitlin asked, dreading the response.

"Neither," Kirk said grimly. "Evidently, your Father O'Flannagan isn't a Father. He's not a priest at all. He's a gunslinger from Texas. I'd like to get with Ewen and figure out a plan. O'Flannagan has two henchmen. They're the ones who robbed Matthew. Oh…Matthew needs to be in on this too."

Kirk looked at the floor, puzzling over how to bring a resolution to the situation. It was quiet as the three watched Kirk and wondered what he was thinking.

"I can't seem to think right now. Reckon it could be because I'm getting married tomorrow." He grinned hugely as he hugged Katie closer to him.

Jared said, "Whatever you plan, please let me in on it. I need to get back and sit with the men." He stood at the opened door, waiting for Aidan.

She hugged Caitlin. "Best wishes, little sister. I'm very happy for you. I am sorry I've been so mean. It will never happen intentionally again." She kissed Cait's cheek and held out her hand to shake Kirk's.

"Congratulations, Kirk…I'm happy for you. Have you seen her in her denim trousers yet?" She grinned at his look of surprise and headed to the door where Jared took her hand and gently pulled the door shut behind them.

Once they were in the hall, he said, "Your eyes are more beautiful than Cait's new ring." Jared took his wife in his arms and it was a while before they made their way back to the parlor.

"You wear denim trousers?" With one eyebrow raised, Kirk smiled down at this girl he was going to love till the day he died. He pulled Caitlin into his arms. She fit just right. He kissed her forehead. "I love you," he said. He kissed her left cheek. "I love you." He kissed her right cheek. "I love you." Taking her head in both hands, he kissed her lips gently.

Cait put her arms around his chest and hugged him. She kissed him with all the love welling within her. She could feel the quickening of his heartbeat.

He took her by the shoulders and set her back a couple steps and looked deeply into her eyes. "We will have to finish this tomorrow." His eyes were serious, the blue darkened with passion.

"I love you, Kirk Bannister. I think I fell in love with you in the stable in San Rafael. I am so excited and happy. I...I was feeling so alone mourning my da, wanting to be back here, and uncomfortable with staying at the mission. I felt miserable. I never thought to fall in love, and here you walk into my life and sweep me off my feet after sweeping Fire off his feet! I know we have much to learn about each other, but you're going to have to teach me exactly what it means to be a Christian. I like and admire what I see in your sister-in-law, Liberty, and in your brother as well as you, of course."

He took her hand and kissed her fingertips. "I happily accept the role of teacher. And, I'm going to love being a cowboy."

"Can you really rope a calf?" she asked, laughing.

"Just you wait and see. And now, my dear wife to be, I think we should honor Drew and go to the wake." He kissed her lips lightly and led her out the door.

As Jared and Aidan made their way into the parlor, so did Ewen, Jethro, and Doc Addison. The three had talked at length about what they would present to the men, but in the end decided to play it by ear. They agreed they wouldn't divulge Jeb Dawkins' name. The man was deeply grieved that Drew was dead. Even though he hadn't pulled the trigger, Jeb expressed overwhelming remorse at having an association with the man who'd killed Drew.

The talk in the parlor ceased as the five who entered found chairs.

The silence was uncomfortable. Several men shifted in their chairs or shuffled their feet. Abbot cleared his throat as if he was going to ask a question, but as soon as he looked at Jethro's face, he changed his mind. Manny scooted over to allow Jared and Aidan to sit together.

"Thanks, Manny," Jared said with a smile. "It's been a few days since I've seen my beautiful wife." He still held Aidan's hand.

"No problem," Manny replied, "I'm a movin' over for Miss Aidan, not you." He punched Jared lightly on the shoulder to let him know he was liked as well. "Always did have a soft place in my heart for her."

Aidan patted Manny's shoulder. "Thanks, Manny, you're a good man." She sat between Jared and Manny and looked around the room. The chairs were nearly all taken.

Realizing Jethro wasn't going to make any announcements, the men sat chatting to each other. The atmosphere in the room, although respectful, lightened. A jest would be spoken or some story about Drew's pranks, and light laughter could be heard.

CHAPTER XXIX

O give thanks unto the LORD; call upon his name:

make known his deeds among the people.

PSALM 105:1

THE MEN'S CHATTER DIED DOWN and the atmosphere in the parlor changed again. Everyone could feel something brewing.

Jared touched Aidan's arm. "Have you eaten yet?"

"No, and I'm famished."

The two strolled to the dining room.

Ewen followed Aidan and Jared through the open doorway and loaded up a plate, too. He'd watched the doctor eat from the plate Miss Liberty made up for him while the sheriff lay dying. It had nearly turned his stomach. Now, he was hungry.

Jethro also filled his plate but glanced across the table at his brother. Jethro wondered at the look he saw on his brother's face. He went back into the parlor and sat down next to Sneedy.

Pouring himself a cup of coffee, Ewen smiled across the table at Jared. "I feel in need of something a bit stronger than coffee." Quietly, he added, "Glad I got to you before the sheriff did."

"I know," Jared replied. "Kirk told Aidan and me all about it. I'm thankful, too. I know I'd have taken the sheriff's offer, and I'd not be standing here tonight. I'll tell you one thing, though—you couldn't have done anything better for me than to get me out here working. I believe you also had a good idea in pairing me up with Matthew. I'll be grateful to you until the day I die. Your decision to have me work off my debt out here at McCaully's has changed my life."

Ewen was shocked. *Where's the pouting, poor-me man I've always thought Jared to be? A man can't change that fast, can he? He's talking plainly, and in front of Miss Aidan, too. Isn't he afraid she'll kick him out on his ear when she finds out about stealing McCaully money?*

"What's come over you, Jared?" Ewen glanced quickly at Aidan, but she was busy choosing a piece of chicken as if the conversation was an everyday pleasantry.

"Guess you could say the Holy Ghost got hold of me, Ewen. I'm a different man than I was a few days ago, an' I've got you to thank for putting me on the right track. I haven't talked about this to Jethro yet, but I will."

Ewen's eyes widened at the import of Jared's words. *Think I'm getting bombarded on all sides by this Holy Ghost Jesus message. First it was Hannah, then seeing that Con, er, Matthew and how peaceful an' all he is. Listening to the doc and hearing him an' the sheriff, I'm thinking I need this, too. I'll talk to Hannah about it, or maybe I'll do it on my own like the sheriff.*

They headed back into the parlor, Ewen trying to clear his mind of everything but the business at hand. He could scarcely believe the change in Jared. It was astounding. The change was a testimony to Ewen's heart and he knew he longed for more than he now had.

He sat next to Doc Addison, eating methodically, deep in thought as he considered what he should say to the men. Finally, setting his plate aside, he leaned forward, clasped his hands between his knees, and cleared his throat. All talking ceased as the men realized Ewen was ready to tell them what was going on.

"We're going to have a meeting right here, where Drew is lying. You all know his spirit's gone, but we honor him by our presence here tonight. I want this meeting right here so's we can figure out a plan for catching the murderer. We now know who it is." He got right to the point.

John jumped up. "You know who it is? Who th' blazes is it? I've had enough of this pussyfootin' around. I want ta see some action."

"I'll get to that in a moment, but first—"

"First, we're all meeting here tomorrow morning," Kirk interrupted him, "because Miss Caitlin and I are getting married…tomorrow, first thing. Perhaps some of you don't know, but there was a threat made on Katie's life and I mean to protect her. She's agreeable, and we'd like to marry as soon as we can get a minister out here tomorrow morning." He nodded to Ewen. "Sorry to interrupt but to me, that's the first order of business."

Ewen looked at Kirk, his eyes serious. "I can understand that—and frankly, I agree. To protect Miss Caitlin is of the utmost importance. Everything else is secondary." He nodded to the men. "It's the reason you haven't seen her around here since the reading of the will. She ran away to take sanctuary. She overheard threats made on her life, and she didn't know who she could trust around here."

The men looked astounded that anyone would make threats on Miss Cait's life. Some would protect her with their lives. A couple men eyed Kirk, wondering what kind of boss he'd make. Would the two of them stay and run the ranch or sell off McCaully's? A few smiled about having Caitlin marry, but John wanted to know who the murderer was.

"Let's have it, boss," he said.

"All right, but hear me out before any of you jump up an' decide you're going to do something about this." He looked around the circle of men, with Aidan, Caitlin, and Liberty sitting there, too.

"Sheriff Rowe is dead in the other room."

Liberty gasped at the bluntness of his statement, but Ewen continued to talk.

"He paid off a gambling debt at McGregor's for one of you boys, and in the process, owned you. If he hadn't paid off the debt, believe me, you'd be dead. The sheriff confessed before he died. He didn't plan on anyone shooting Drew. The understanding was that there'd be no killing. There's one more man—well, three, but one in particular—who is the ringleader and the truly bad one…the one who shot Drew, with no compunction, no regret, but worse, no reason."

"Get on with it, boss, tell us who th' blazes it is!" Rhys, frustrated, had a short fuse. He'd had several long looks by men from other crews that made him feel as if they thought he might have something to do with Drew's death.

Ewen continued, "You need to know the man is an outlaw. He's a gunslinger from Texas that's been posing as the priest in Santa Rosa."

"Father O'Flannagan? You talkin' about Father O'Flannagan?" Mosey asked. "He ain't a priest? Why, I've gone in ta talk ta him fer confession round 'bout once a month. He ain't a priest? Well, I'll be jiggered." Mosey was upset. He'd bared his soul to a man who probably laughed at him when he left the confessional. "Dad gummed that man! He's probably been laughin' up his sleeve at me."

"More ta th' point, what we gonna do with 'em?" John looked around the circle of men. He saw the misery in Jeb's eyes and realized he'd been the one bought off by the sheriff. He knew, too, how awful it was when a man got addicted to something. His own pa had been addicted to drink. He was a good man unless he was under the influence. Those times, he'd beat his wife and kids, always in a rage when he drank too much. He'd be so sorry afterward. When he'd broken John's arm in a drunken stupor, that'd been it. John had run away from home.

Doc Addison said, "We've thought of a plan but wanted to run it by you boys first and see what you think. All of us probably have a different idea."

Ewen said, "We wanted to know if we should use Caitlin as bait. We would have the priest—I hate even calling him that. It dishonors the sacred office. What we were thinking is that we would have O'Flannagan out to say an intercessory prayer for the sheriff. O'Flannagan wants to get Caitlin alone, anyway. He'd like to kidnap her and get her to marry him."

"But why would th' man want that? Beggin' yer pardon, Miss Cait." Rhys didn't understand it. "Why would the man be wantin' ta force Miss Caitlin ta marry him?"

Jethro answered, "For the same reason they didn't want anyone poking around Diablo Ridge. We found a gold mine up there that looks to be a mother lode. I'm talking lots of gold. That man...that evil man wants control of McCaully's to get at the gold. He figured Miss Aidan and Miss Maisie would sell the land if Miss Cait were out of the way. I'm sure he was correct. The sheriff was up to his neck in this whole affair. Our cowboy was only in it to pay off his own debt. So, the long and short of it is, O'Flannagan is planning to force Caitlin to marry him to get at the gold, or he plans to kill her outright."

"Over my dead body," Kirk said.

Doc Addison said, "Hopefully, they'll be no more dead bodies. We'd like to avenge the death of Drew. By capturing this gunslinger, we would be doing a favor to the community of Santa Rosa, the Catholic Church, and fulfill John's wish to get this man. Exposing him for what he really is will benefit all of us. He has two men who work for him at the church, but they're robbers. They're the ones responsible for bashing Conor here over the head. Conor is Matthew Bannister, owner of Bannister Vineyards in Napa. These men robbed him not only of his possessions but of his memory as well."

The men sitting around the room looked at Matthew as if he were a different person.

He looked back at them, a peaceful smile on his face, and said, "I may have found out who I am, but I still have no memory of my past. I get snippets here and there, but for the life of me, I can't pull up anything of my life before waking up from being robbed."

"It'll come, Matthew, don't struggle with it, it'll come," the doc said easily.

Ewen said, "Our plan is that we let Miss Cait go with this O'Flannagan to the barn...not the stables. She can say she wants to show him the new kittens in one of the mangers. We'll have men stationed there.

"Maybe Miss Cait will get him to talk, but we don't really need anyone more than our cowboy who told us. He witnessed Drew's shooting. We need to keep him safe. I have no doubt O'Flannagan will want him dead. Our cowboy's the only one I know who's privy to what that cold-hearted, false priest has done."

The doctor nodded toward Caitlin. "It was O'Flannagan you heard talking in the barn with our cowboy. You were right that someone made a threat on you, Miss Cait." The doctor looked grimly down at the floor for a moment, then continued, "Our cowboy was watching the entire day of the reading of the will to make sure you were safe, and that O'Flannagan was nowhere near the premises. He was protecting you, Miss Cait."

Caitlin felt ashamed for having thought it was Jared. She was glad she'd never spoken of it to him. He'd hated her, but that was because of his own insecurities. He'd never have killed her. She bowed her head and stared at the carpet, afraid that if she looked at anyone, they would know her thoughts.

The ranch hands looked at each other, wondering who it might be, until Jeb spoke up on his own.

"It was me, boys. I'm the one who gambled at McGregor's. They were ready to string me up and the sheriff, why he steps in an' pays my bill. I didn't know he was bad till he asked me to spy on the ranch. I was to report to him if anyone knew about the mine. I didn't know at the time that Flint O'Flannagan was involved in anything. The sheriff thought he was the boss, but it was O'Flannagan who was calling the shots. I can't tell you all how sorry I am. I loved Drew an was in the cave when O'Flannagan shot down at John an' Drew. He felt no remorse, nothing a'tall."

Tears ran down his cheeks as he confessed. His shoulders shook silently with the pain and grief he held within. He took a deep shuddering sigh, glad to have unloaded the heavy secret he'd been carrying.

John said, "It weren't your fault about Drew, Jeb. Gettin' into trouble with McGregor wuz your fault, but I don't know anyone in this room what wouldn't take what the sheriff offered you. It was a way out, but most of us is findin' th' easy way out ain't no way out a'tall. Shootin' Drew wuz the loathsome-hearted O'Flannagan's fault, an' we'll get 'em. Fer sure, we'll get 'em. I say we string 'em up."

Ewen said, "Well, I say we devise a solid plan afore we go getting the man out here."

"Maybe I could ride in early an' get the minister," Kirk said. "We could have a quick wedding and then ride for O'Flannagan."

The men all started talking at once, each one having an idea. There was much discussion, and plans were laid for the next morning. They talked long into the night as they sat thinking of Drew and finalizing exactly what each man's job would be the next day. It was decided that Eli's crew would go out and guard the trail going to the cave on Diablo Ridge. That would get Jeb off the ranch and safe from O'Flannagan's gun. With the sheriff dead, Jeb was the only witness to the gunslinger's involvement with murder. Jeb swore he never let Sheriff Rowe or O'Flannagan know there was more than one way up Diablo Ridge.

Ewen said, "Rhys, tomorrow morning, instead of guarding the ridge, I want you sitting on the bluff that overlooks the road. You can watch to see if the gunslinger makes his way out here afore we're ready for him."

The men decided to call it a night, and the wake broke up as the tired cowboys went to the bunkhouse. For some, sleep was elusive.

CHAPTER XXX

Let your speech be always with grace, seasoned with salt, that
ye may know how ye ought to answer every man.

COLOSSIANS 4:6

LIBERTY SLEPT FITFULLY, awaking off and on during the night. She lay thinking about the events of the evening. It had been late when she'd finally gone to bed. Lighting a taper, she looked at her grandfather's watch. It was two thirty. She lit a candle with the taper and poured herself a glass of water. Sitting with her pillows plumped behind her, Libby felt wide awake. *Father, You are so holy; I praise You. I am thankful for Your sacrifice…holy, holy, holy is the Lord God Almighty, Who was, Who is, and Who is to come. Thank You for Your holiness. Lord, I have so many requests. I don't like to keep asking you for things. I'd rather sit and contemplate You and Your goodness, mercy, grace, and compassion, but I pray Caitlin is as sweet as she portrays herself to be. Kirk has fallen in love completely. He is head over heels in love with the girl. I guess I'm concerned that he'd marry an unbeliever. Your Word tells us to not be unequally yoked. I married an unbeliever in obedience to my parents and was sorry for it for thirteen long years. Now, I'm happier than I've ever been in my entire life.*

I pray too, my Father, for Matthew. Please let him regain his memory. I pray for Jeb, Lord…life is difficult. The choices we make, the things we do can live with us for the rest of our days. I pray he comes to know You and Your forgiveness. He is grieving for his part in all this. I pray he can lay it at your feet…and his habit of gambling. Father, I understand I cannot control other people or their choices. I pray my choices would be pleasing to You. Help me to love others, not through the eyes of the world but through spiritual eyes that are seeking to love as You love. I love You, Father God. She continued to pray and finally fell asleep when the first streaks of dawn appeared over the horizon.

Aidan lay in her old bed, feeling as she never had in her entire life. She fell asleep with the deepest contentment in her heart she had ever known.

Caitlin didn't sleep so well. She could scarcely believe she was to be married in the morning. Her thoughts jumped from one thing to the next and back again. She began to pray and ask for protection for her betrothed. She lay a long while before sleep overtook her.

It was still dark when Kirk rode to Santa Rosa to get the minister. The sun was just beginning to break over the eastern horizon as he made his way into town. Glorious rosy pink, orange, and yellow colors blended into harmonious triumphant praise to their Creator as they streaked across the sky above the foothills. He rode Queenie in case anyone should see him. He certainly didn't want to cause undue speculation by riding Fire. The air was fresh and clean. Kirk could smell in the air that it would be a good, clear morning with rain later in the day.

"Red sky at night, sailors delight; red sky at morning, sailors take warning," he softly quoted. *Don't remember who made up that ditty. It's been around for a long time, but I'll bet it came from Jesus saying about the same thing.*

Caitlin had given him directions to the house on the edge of town. He slowed to a walk when he came to the first abode. It was on the east side, so he wouldn't have to ride down the main street through town. It was a modest cottage nestled among trees and shrubs with a flower garden that teemed with color. Through the trees on the right side of the house, past a picket fence in dire need of paint, was a small, quaint white church. He glimpsed a worn path across the middle of the cottage's yard toward the cemetery that separated the church property from the house.

Sliding off Queenie, Kirk fastened her reins to the hitching rail and went up the cobblestone walk. He hoped someone was an early riser and wouldn't make too much of a fuss. He knew it was an imposition, and yet, without exaggerating, Kirk felt it was a matter of life and death. Hesitating because of the early hour, he curled his hand into a fist and rapped lightly on the door. He waited and started to knock harder, but the door opened by a little girl not more than five years old.

"Have you come to take the kitten?" her big blue eyes welled with tears. "Mama says we can't have all the kittens, only one. I love all of 'em an' I named them Shadrach, Meshach, and Abednego, an' I don't want anyone to take 'em."

"No." He smiled down at the little redhead with freckles all over her face. "No, I've come to ask your pa for help. We already have a litter of kittens at McCaully's. They were born in a manger in the barn."

"Oh, that's all right then, c'mon in." She wiped her nose and tears away on the sleeve of her dress. "Pa's already drinking his coffee. You have to be quiet, though. We have a new baby, and Mama and the baby are still sleeping." She held her forefinger up to her lips, and her voice dropped to a mere whisper. Opening the door wider, she beckoned him to enter.

Kirk took off his hat and followed her to the kitchen, which was located at the back of the house. The little girl was barefooted and padded down the hall, her feet quiet on the pinewood floor.

"Pa, we have company," she said proudly.

Her father was reading his Bible and hadn't even looked up. "Yes, Deborah." But he didn't register her comment.

"Reverend Mr. Babcock, we have company," she said a little louder and quite formally.

The minister's head jerked up as he looked at the man directly behind his daughter. He was nearly the same height as Kirk and as he stood abruptly, he almost knocked over his chair. He made a grab for the chair's back as it started to topple, top heavy because his frock coat hung from it, and smoothly set it upright on all fours.

"I'm sorry, guess I wasn't paying any attention." The minister looked to be in his mid to late twenties. Unruly curls of sandy blonde hair covered his head. In contrast, his eyebrows and lashes were dark. He had a deep groove in his right cheek and good humor seemed to lurk deeply within his greenish-hazel eyes.

"How can I help you, sir?" He seemed off balance, discomfited.

Kirk tried to put the man at his ease. "I know it's early, Reverend Babcock, and what I have to tell you is a long story. The short of it is that I'd like you to come out to McCaully's and perform a wedding."

"Who are you?" The minister asked.

"Sorry...name's Bannister, Kirk Bannister. I hail from Napa and I'm marrying Caitlin McCaully." He reached out to shake the minister's hand.

"Well, now, that is a nice surprise. When do you plan to have the ceremony?"

"As soon as you can saddle up your horse and ride out there with me." Kirk didn't want to waste time with explanations, but knew he'd better say something to motivate this man or he wasn't going to budge.

"Sir, it's imperative that we get going as fast as possible. I'm going to say something to you that is shocking but true." He turned to the little girl. "Could you please go get one of the kittens so I can look at it?"

Deborah skipped to the back door and headed for the toolshed.

Kirk turned to the minister. "The priest here in Santa Rosa is not a priest. He's a gunslinger from Texas and last night he murdered Sheriff Rowe."

Reverend Babcock began to fasten the top buttons of his shirt as fast as his fingers could fly. He reached for his cup of coffee and gulped it down. Grabbing a plain cravat lying on the table, he tied it into place faster than

Kirk had ever seen. His frock coat was hanging on the chair back, and after tucking his shirt into his trousers properly, he hurriedly put it on.

"Let's be going then." His eyes had darkened at the thought of a gunslinger posing as a priest. It clarified a few things; mainly, why the man would never meet with him. The so-called priest had been openly hostile, and the two men who worked for him were downright nasty.

"Sorry, I know I'm the one in a hurry, but I must wait for your Deborah and her kitten." Kirk smiled ruefully.

It pleased the man of cloth to no end that this man was thoughtful, not wanting to hurt his little girl's feelings.

"I'll go saddle up while you meet one of the kittens from the fiery furnace." He grinned at Kirk. "I read the story from Daniel to her only a week before the kittens were born. She named them. I'll meet you out front at the hitching rail." He went out the back door, murmuring something to his daughter as she came in.

The little girl had all three kittens in her apron. The mama cat trailed behind her, tail held high. "Look here, mister, I brought all of them for you to see."

She carefully sat on the floor, still holding up her apron. Gently lowering the kittens to the floor, she looked up at the man with the kind eyes and held up one of the kittens.

"This un's Meshach, he's a tabby, and this,"—she held up an identical kitten,—"is Shadrach, also a tabby. The one with the smudge on his nose is Abednego. I don't know what kind of kitten she is. Thanks for taking the time to look at them. My pa says you're in a hurry, so you best go. It's wise not to keep Pa waiting. Bye, mister."

"Bannister, my name is Mr. Bannister. Pleased to meet you, Miss Deborah, and thanks for showing me your kittens. Bye now, I don't want to keep your father waiting either." He patted her head and left the kitchen with long strides down the hall, gently closing the front door behind him.

Flint O'Flannagan woke up slowly. The sun was shining brightly, but he couldn't see it. There was only the brightness through a crack in the thin dark curtain. *Another day without rain. We must be nearly over the rainy season.* He had decided last night, before falling asleep, to ride out to McCaully's today. Knowing the sheriff would never divulge information about the mine, Flint knew he could better assess the situation from there. If Sheriff Rowe was incapacitated, he'd be sure to get into the room where Rowe was lying. He'd simply put the man out of his misery. *A pillow will do quite well, I believe. Think I'll take Miss McCaully for a ride. I could always leave her tied up in one of the caves on Diablo Ridge, better yet, at the bottom of the ridge with a broken neck. Guess I'd better tell Kaufman and Beekers where I'm going. Ah, it's early. I'll most likely be back before they get around. I'll leave a note on my desk.*

People were just beginning to get up when the minister and Kirk passed under the huge arched sign of the McCaully Ranch.

The two men hadn't talked much because they rode at a gallop most of the way. When they reached the long drive to the house, Kirk pulled up his horse to a walk. He wanted to cool off Queenie before their arrival. Reverend Babcock pulled up his horse as Kirk began to speak.

"Mr. Babcock, I am wanting to marry Miss Caitlin because I love her. It is also for protection. Gold has been found on this ranch by O'Flannagan and the sheriff. They were planning a way to get rid of Miss McCaully and hoped the ranch would go up for sale. The two other sisters would most likely have sold out as soon as they could. O'Flannagan shot the sheriff last night and Ewen just happened to be near enough to help out. Rowe should have been all right, but he lost too much blood and evidently had a weak heart. One positive outcome is that the sheriff accepted Christ as Savior before he died. Doc Addison was explaining to Ewen Carr about becoming a Christian and the sheriff, lying on the bed, accepted Christ right there." Kirk grinned at the minister.

Stephen Babcock felt a warmth toward this young man. *He must be close to the same age as me. Wonder if he'll live here at McCaully's, or will he take Miss McCaully off somewhere else?*

"I'm glad to hear about the sheriff…better late than never, I always say." He continued, "I take it you're a believer?"

"Why, yes, I am. So is Miss Caitlin as of last night. Seems her brother-in-law, Jared Hart, led both his wife, Miss Aidan, and Miss Caitlin to Christ."

"Jared Hart?" the minister could hardly credit it. "You're saying Jared Hart is a Christian?"

"Yes, my brother led Jared to Christ and he's been discipling him, too." Kirk grinned hugely at this man who looked so nonplussed.

Stephen Babcock swallowed as the thought of Jared Hart, gambler, rabble rousing drunk, and who knows what else…was saved!

"Praise the Lord." The minister grinned. "Sounds as if you've had a revival going on at McCaully's! Well, the Lord be praised!"

"Yes, we've had a small revival, but also a death. O'Flannagan murdered one of the cowhands yesterday as well as the sheriff. My intent is to marry Miss McCaully and let O'Flannagan know the jig is up, that he's been found out. We'll have to arrest his two companions at the church, too. They're the ones who have been robbing people around here. They robbed my brother and he's been left with amnesia. He can't remember a blamed thing about his past."

"Yet, he led Jared Hart to Christ?" the minister asked.

"Yes, yes he did."

"Well, by my reckoning, having amnesia is worth a soul any day of the week," the minister said as they arrived at the house.

CHAPTER XXXI

I will greatly rejoice in the Lord, my soul shall be joyful in my
God; for he hath clothed me with the garments of salvation,
he hath covered me with the robe of righteousness,
as a bridegroom decketh himself with ornaments,
and as a bride adorneth herself with her jewels.

ISAIAH 61:10

KIRK **STARED AT THE MINISTER IN SURPRISE**. "Reckon I didn't think of that, but you're right. Having amnesia is nothing compared to leading a soul to the glory of the cross. I have a feeling we're going to have some good talks in the future. I'll enjoy attending your church, I'm sure."

Stephen flushed and replied, "I think you're right. We will have some good talks. Truth to tell, I've missed having a man I can bounce ideas off and have good fellowship without having to worry about whether he approves of everything I do. I think you may be that man, Kirk Bannister."

The two climbed off their horses and shook hands as if sealing a pact. They quietly entered the house, but it looked as if everyone was up. Kirk led his guest through the parlor, stopping to explain about Drew, whose body still lay in the room.

"This is the other man who was murdered yesterday, Drew—"

"Collins," the minister said, "it's Drew Collins, a fine young man." Tears sprang in the young minister's hazel eyes at the tragic death of this kindhearted cowboy. He squeezed his eyes shut for a moment and said a quick prayer for John, Drew's sidekick. Drew had told him how he was praying his friend John would accept the Lord. Stephen Babcock made a mental note to be sure to speak to John and encourage him.

He wiped his tears on his sleeve, reminding Kirk of the reverend's little girl.

"So, you knew him?"

"Yes, he was a regular attender at our services. He would often work on his day off helping some of our older folk with needed repairs around their houses. As I said, he was a fine young man."

The two men passed through the parlor and entered the dining room. Some of the household were already eating. Kirk didn't see Katie, although Liberty was there. Also seated were Ewen and the doctor. Liberty sat with a beautiful yellow robe wrapped around her, but after taking a closer look, Kirk could see she was exhausted. He was concerned for her.

"Good morning, everyone. This is Reverend Stephen Babcock of Santa Rosa. He's the minister who's going to marry Katie and me as soon as we can get everyone together. I'd like that to be as soon as possible. I'm going out to round up the men."

Ewen looked a bit sour. Going to bed later than usual, plus the fact that he hadn't slept well, made him cranky. He'd lain long into the night pondering all that had happened and the actions of those who said they were Christians. He felt at odds with himself, and it wasn't a comfortable feeling.

"I'll take care of the men." He took a long look at Kirk. *Well, he said last night he was going for the preacher. He certainly didn't let any grass grow under his feet this morning. Wonder what kind of man he is and what kind of boss he's going to make? If he's marrying Miss Caitlin, will he lord it over everyone? Will he take my advice at all?*

He had no idea as he stared at the younger man that he would love him as the son he'd never had. He swallowed down the last of his coffee, nodded at the young minister, and headed out to the bunkhouse.

Reverend Babcock looked over at Doc Addison, a huge grin on his face. "Good morning, Micah, we missed you in services last week."

"Thank you, I missed being there. How is your new son doing anyway?" The doctor grinned right back, his eyes twinkling.

"Best baby boy ever born, I'd say. We named him Micah, just so you know." He clapped the doctor on the shoulder. Doc teared up at the honor.

"Please, Reverend Babcock, sit down and have some breakfast," Liberty, even with smudges under her eyes, looked devastatingly beautiful. Her green eyes looked at the sandy-haired man and wondered what kind of minister he was. His eyes were gentle and kind looking.

"Yes," said Doc, "please sit. You had quite an early call this morning."

Liberty started to get up to wait on the minister. She'd been quite sick this morning and was drinking tea to try to settle her stomach. She didn't feel like moving but as she pushed back her chair, she felt a hand on her shoulder gently holding her in place. Startled, she looked up to see Kirk shaking his head.

"You just sit there, little mama. I'll get him something to drink." Turning to the reverend, he asked, "What would you like? Have you only had coffee? Would you like some breakfast?"

"I'll have whatever you're having, and I prefer coffee over tea, please."

The minister sat across from Liberty. He could see the sweetness in her eyes and wanted to know more about her. He loved meeting new people and sensed this woman was special. "Do you have other children, Mrs....?"

"Bannister," Liberty said. "I am Kirk's sister-in-law. I don't know how much he told you, but no, this is my first baby and I'm keeping it secret from my husband, Matthew. He's been a ranch hand here at McCaully's because he was robbed and beaten and doesn't know who he is. I'd like to get him some specialized medical help and see if he recovers before I share my news with him."

"Bannister…Bannister, for some reason that name seems familiar to me. When Kirk introduced himself it rang a bell, but for the life of me I can't place it." Stephen Babcock wasn't one to forget a face, or a name for that matter, and he was discomfited that he couldn't recall why he knew the name Bannister.

"It's because of Bannister Vineyards, most likely. My husband has been producing a Merlot for the last couple years." Liberty smiled at him charmingly.

Doc Addison asked, "So, when Kirk rapped on your door this morning, were you up yet?"

"Yes, as you very well know, we have a new baby who was up most of the night…so was Helen. I heard Deborah get up early and go out to check on the kittens. That was it for sleeping. So, yes, I was up and no, I hadn't had breakfast."

Kirk returned from the kitchen with two plates loaded with eggs, bacon, potatoes, and toast. Duney, holding open the door for him, had been appalled he would go into the kitchen and serve himself, but he assured her at his house that was how mornings were run. He turned to the sideboard and poured two cups of coffee.

"You like it black or with the trimmings?" he asked Stephen.

"Black, thanks," replied the reverend. "You seem very calm to be marrying in, let me see"—he tugged at his fob chain, pulling out a beautifully engraved watch piece—"most likely less than an hour."

"Yes, I am. I don't believe before last night I would have felt so at peace. But now that Katie's acknowledged Christ as her Savior, I have no qualms at all."

"Caitlin has asked Jesus to be her Savior?" Liberty was flabbergasted. "When did that happen? Oh my goodness, that's marvelous! I was praying last night—no, early this morning—that she'd make a commitment. I praise God for that! Think of all the rejoicing in heaven, and…" She smiled, her green eyes sparkling. "All those angels singing for joy!"

"Yes, it must be quite a sight." Kirk smiled at her. "Just last night, Jared talked to Katie along with Aidan and led them both to a saving knowledge of Christ. You see, Matthew led Jared to Christ and has been mentoring him," Kirk said.

Liberty took a lacy handkerchief out of her robe pocket and wiped her eyes. *Oh, Father, how grateful I am for Your infinite love. Bless this day for Kirk and Cait. Thank You. And, because of Matthew's lost memory, three people have come to know You! How grateful I am for Your providential care.*

"Where is Katie, anyway?" Kirk asked.

"You'll not see her until the wedding. Sweeny and Aidan are helping her. I've been feeling too woozy to be of any real assistance, so they kicked me out." Liberty smiled wanly at the three men sitting across from her.

Kirk, who had finished his breakfast, guzzled the rest of his coffee.

"You stay here and keep Liberty company." He nodded to the minister and the doctor. "I need to talk to Matthew." He grabbed his hat off a chair and headed for the door, yelling as he went, "All right, everybody better be ready in quarter of an hour…no longer!" The door slammed after him.

"Quarter of an hour!" gasped Liberty. She stood, smiled graciously at the minister, and nodded to the doctor. "I hope you enjoy your breakfast. I need to get dressed, which won't take long as I only have what I brought with me." She walked out of the room as befit a lady, but when she was out of sight, the two men heard her running toward the stairs and could hear her taking them two at a time.

The doctor grinned over at Stephen. "Decorum out the window." He chuckled.

"Out of sight, out of decorum," the reverend said.

"Yes, women are a strange breed, are they not?" Stephen thought of his own Helen. "Men underestimate them, you understand. We, for some reason, think they are the weaker sex, and yet, I believe that is only physical. Mentally, I believe women to be quite astute, at least my Helen is. She can also discern many things that pass me by. Mark my words, there will come a day when women will finally realize the position Christ gave them."

"As long as they are obedient to scripture, I have no quarrel with that," The doctor said. "I have seen homes, however, where the woman usurps control. Instead of the man being the head of it, she rules the roost, and it most often ends up being a place of chaos. Christ gave man headship over the home for a purpose. He is to be priest…to spiritually guide his household in the ways of God. When he relinquishes that leadership, there is imbalance. I'm not a theologian such as yourself, but it is what I have observed," the doctor said earnestly.

"Oh, I agree with you one hundred percent," Stephen said. "The husband and wife each have a role to fill in a marriage. I heard a man say to me one time that he was definitely the head of his home, but his wife was the neck that turned it."

Both men laughed, their conversation interrupted by Ewen coming in the door. The ranch hands followed him in. They were dandied up with their hair smartly slicked down, each decked in his best clothes.

Ewen said, "We'll be having a memorial service this afternoon, but I'd like you four boys to please take Drew out to the stable and put him on that hay bed you made, John." He nodded to John and then to Ricardo, Sneedy, and Rhys.

Rhys glanced quickly at John to see if he objected to his help, ready to decline if he did, but John seemed fine with it. The rest of the men started to line up the chairs in rows with a center aisle.

Upstairs, Caitlin was getting ready. The night before, Cait and Sweeny had gone up the narrow attic stairs and found Cait's mother's wedding dress in a huge trunk. Taking the gown back to her room, Sweeny helped Cait try it on. It fit perfectly, lengthwise, and although very snug at the waist, it would serve her well. The fake silk flowers on the veil were crushed, but Sweeny said that was no problem and she could fix it. The shoes in the bottom of the trunk were too small. Caitlin could barely squeeze her foot into one of them.

"The dress is long and full enough, no one will see your shoes anyway," Sweeny said, comforting Cait. She had taken the veil to her room to work on it so it would be ready by morning.

Now, both Aidan and Sweeny were fussing over Caitlin.

Sweeny said, "We can be thankful the dress fits. That's the main thing. If you'll consent to a corset, the dress will fit your waist better too. You won't have to worry about it tearing."

"I hate corsets," Cait said.

Aidan was smoothing out the dress for Cait. She hadn't worn her mother's dress, wanting the seamstress, Hannah, in Santa Rosa to make one for her.

"You have to wear a corset, Cait. You could tear out the side seams without it. It'll keep your spine straight, too," Aidan said.

"I won't be wearing the dress very long—just long enough to get married. I hate corsets," she said again.

"I know, I know," said Sweeny, "but I promise I won't lace it up too tight." She held it out to Caitlin who, with a huge sigh, took off her nightgown, slipped on her camisole, and wrapped the dreaded corset around her middle.

"I can scarcely believe you're getting married today," said Sweeny as she laced up the corset.

"In truth, I can't either. I knew, however, the first moment I saw him walk into Fire's stall he was someone special. It didn't take me more than an hour to realize I was extremely attracted to him."

Aidan said, "He walked into Fire's stall? Oh, my goodness! I can't get close to him at all. That is amazing!"

"Oh, Aidan, Sweeny, I love him. It's fantastic, marvelous, perhaps irrational and absurd, but I do! I do!" She laughed. "I'm going to be saying that in less than an hour...I do!"

Aidan and Sweeny rejoiced with Caitlin.

"Turn around, Miss Cait, I need to get you ready," Sweeney said.

Aidan said, "The dress looks lovely on you, Cait."

There was a tap on the door and Liberty peeked in her head. "I'm going to get dressed as fast as I can. Kirk said we're having a wedding in fifteen minutes." She closed the door and went to her own room. She was now used to dressing herself and quickly divested herself of her robe and nightdress. Liberty hadn't brought anything except her split skirts and blouses. She looked ruefully at her wardrobe and dressed in her normal attire, wishing she'd brought something a little fancier. Still feeling a little nauseated, she went to the kitchen for some plain toast to settle her stomach.

Aidan finished helping Caitlin and ran downstairs to see if it was time to start the wedding.

Hank had a violin on his knees, planning to play a song for Caitlin as she walked down the aisle between the chairs. Ewen said he was going to give her away. The chairs were filled with the men.

Stephen Babcock nodded yes to Aidan's question. Both Duney and McDuffy had gone out and cut flowers, filling all the vases they could find to decorate the room. All was in readiness for a wedding.

CHAPTER XXXII

And Adam said, This is now bone of my bones,
and flesh of my flesh: she shall be called Woman,
because she was taken out of Man.

GENESIS 2:23

AIDAN HEADED UP THE STAIRS to tell Caitlin it was time. "Everything's ready, Cait, and everybody's waiting. Oh, sweetheart, you look absolutely beautiful, and I love you!" She threw her arms around her younger sister, gave her a big hug, and kissed her cheek.

Sweeny also hugged Cait. "You look pretty as paint, dear girl."

Aidan wasn't finished. "Cait, I want to say, again, I'm sorry for all the nasty things I've said and done to you. I do love you. You are my precious little sister, and I hope we have a wonderful relationship in the future."

"Me too, Danny, me too."

Surprise and pleasure glowed in Aidan's eyes. She hadn't heard that nickname for years, but she had always secretly loved it. She knew, too, that Caitlin using it meant there were no hard feelings. She grabbed one of Caitlin's hands and Sweeny grabbed the other. The three hugged before going out the bedroom door.

Sweeny and Aidan ran lightly down the stairs while Caitlin waited at the top for Hank to start the music. Aidan found a chair in the front row, and Jared came to sit next to her. Sweeny hurried to the kitchen to see if there was anything more she could do for Duney and McDuffy, but all was ready.

Duney, finding out the evening before that Caitlin was to be married, had stayed up and made a cake.

Sweeny gasped when she saw it. "You've outdone yourself, Duney my girl. It's beautiful!"

"McDuffy helped me frost it this morning. That Liberty girl wanted to, but she has morning sickness and looked quite peaked. I made her sit down with a cup of tea." She gave a last look around the kitchen, wiping her hands on a towel. "I guess we're ready then." The three women went to the parlor and found seats in the back so they could sit together.

Liberty was sitting with Matthew in the front row, but when the minister and Kirk came in, Matthew stood next to his brother. Aidan also stood, as Caitlin had asked her to be matron of honor.

Ewen turned and nodded to Hank to start playing. Ewen then looked up at Caitlin and motioned for her to come down the stairs. Hank usually played the fiddle at barn dances, but his violin could just as quickly become a formal instrument. He'd had lessons growing up and was quite adept. He had chosen Pachelbel's *Canon in D Major* especially for Caitlin. It was a difficult piece, but he knew it from memory.

The music was sweet and tears stung Liberty's eyes.

Jared stood and everyone followed suit, all turning to watch as Caitlin made her way down the stairs.

Ewen's face had softened upon seeing Caitlin look so much as her mother had so many years ago. His thoughts flitted back to nearly thirty years before. He and Mac had come over on a ship from Ireland and had fallen in love with the same girl. Mac had won Ryanne's heart. Ewen had never looked at another woman until he'd met Hannah Danielson. He swallowed the lump that had formed in his throat. Caitlin could have been his daughter instead of Mac's. He took Cait's hand, lovingly placing it on his arm, and the two started up the center aisle.

A surprised impression flickered across Kirk's mind. *She's in a wedding dress.* But thoughts fled as he caught her gray eyes on him, trusting, nothing hidden, full of love and promises for the future radiating from within her.

He returned the look in full measure. *I will love and cherish her until the day I die.* His thoughts began to splinter. *She caught me by surprise... never thought I'd fall in love like this. Goodness, she's tall...almost as tall as Matt. She's beautiful. Reckon I didn't realize she's so beautiful. I was looking more at her character. There's something about a new Christian...they glow, or is it love for me? Oh, Lord, help me be the spiritual leader You desire me to be. Help me to love her wholly and seek her good.*

The music stopped and Kirk stepped forward to take his bride off Ewen's arm. Before he did, Ewen took Caitlin's veil and threw it back over the tiny fresh roses Sweeny had sewn to it. The silk flowers had not been salvageable.

The foreman kissed her on both cheeks. "This," he said as he kissed her left cheek, "is from me. And this," he said as he kissed her right cheek, "is for your da. He'd be so proud of you, Caitlin." He looked deeply into her eyes. "You look just like your mother, so very beautiful." He stepped back.

Caitlin was startled as realization dawned within her. *Ewen was in love wit me muther! I niver knew until just now.* Her thoughts settled back on Kirk. *I love him. I hope I can measure up to his expectations. What does he expect in a wife? I can't cook, I can't sew, I don't drink, I'm not thrilled about dancing. In truth, I don't know what he sees in me, but I can see that he loves me. It's in his eyes...but he doesn't know me!*

Stephen Babcock asked the gathering to be seated.

"Dearly beloved, we are gathered here this day..."

The ceremony was beautiful. The young minister stopped talking and had communion for the couple as he explained that the two would now drink from the same cup. He asked Cait and Kirk to kneel and those gathered to bow their heads. He sang "Jesu Joy of Man's Desiring" in the clearest, most beautiful tenor voice anyone in the room had ever heard. Several men cleared their throats as the passion for Christ came through in the purity of his voice. It caught at their heartstrings. Aidan and Liberty had tears streaming down their cheeks.

There was no ring exchange. Cait was wearing the ring Kirk had put on her finger the night before.

The ceremony proceeded and when Stephen pronounced the couple man and wife, a loud knock sounded on the door. Several jumped at the jarring sound.

Mrs. McDuffy, who sat in the back row, answered it.

It was Rhys, from Eli's crew. He'd been astride his horse on the bluff overlooking the ranch and road.

"He's a comin'," Rhys said excitedly, "O'Flannagan's a comin'. Ya got lessen twenty minutes ta git yerselves ta where ya'll wantin' ta be."

Caitlin said, "All right boys, keep your heads and—"

"You all know your job," Ewen interrupted her. "Eli, get your crew over to Diablo Ridge, we need to protect the mine but more importantly, Jeb. Manny, your men will be around the corral looking natural-like, as if you're working. John, get your crew stationed in the barn, out of sight. Now, hop to it."

While he was talking, Caitlin kissed Kirk quickly on the lips and was gone, hurrying up the stairs to change. Liberty and Aidan followed her up. Some of Aidan's clothes still hung in her clothespress, and she was dressed in a beautiful blue gown that brought out the blue of her sapphire eyes. Aidan needed to change, too.

Liberty, thankful she had on her normal attire, was still feeling rumbly in her tummy. She took a deep breath and silently prayed for the events that were about to take place. Before going to help Caitlin, she strapped on her gun belt and checked for bullets. She quickly went to Cait's room.

Unbuttoning the back of Cait's gown, Liberty said, "You looked absolutely beautiful—stunning as a matter of fact. Can you believe it? You're married! You are now my sister-in-law." Liberty gave Caitlin a big hug, trying to take the bride's mind off the man who wanted to kill her.

"You know, I didn't even think of that," Cait said. "We're now sisters! I know we're going to be such good friends. Can Kirk really rope?" She giggled at her own question.

Liberty laughed as she helped Cait divest herself of the wedding dress and corset. "He can rope anything he aims for, believe me. He roped me one time when I was going from the stables to the house. In truth, I gave him a length of rope the first Christmas I was at the Rancho because he loves to rope everything."

Cait laughed at the thought of Kirk roping Liberty. She donned a clean, checkered blouse and pulled on her denim trousers and leather boots. She strapped her gun belt on and looked up to see the admiring look on Liberty's face.

"I like your denims. I never thought of wearing trousers. My, but you look grand. I want some of those. Wonder if Matthew would mind?" Liberty grinned at the long slim legs on this girl. *She's going to keep Kirk guessing for the rest of his life. It's exactly what he needs. She's perfect for him.*

Cait straightened. "Let's be going. I think we ought to go to the kitchen and wait to see what happens."

"Let's tell Aidan what we're doing," Liberty said.

"I suppose I'd better, because she won't be ready. She takes a long time with her toilette. I'll bet anything she won't be half dressed," Cait said a little disgustedly.

She tapped on Aidan's door and was taken aback to find Aidan dressed and ready. Earlier, Aidan had absconded with one of Cait's split skirts. She had on her riding boots and a lovely flowered blouse. The three women grinned at each other.

"I told Liberty you wouldn't be ready. I apologize!" Cait said. She'd never seen Aidan looking so carefree or confident. "Goodness, Danny, you look marvelous!"

"So do you, Katie, me luv…wi'd bitter be a getting' away, me sweet." Aidan dipped into a heavy brogue.

Liberty laughed. "I had several English friends but no one Irish when I was in boarding school. I like the accent…although I had to translate it in my head."

Caitlin laughed but sobered quickly. She was becoming nervous and a bit frightened. Liberty saw her look and knew what was needed.

"Wait just a minute." She took the two women's hands in hers and said, "Let me pray." All three bowed their heads as Liberty spoke to their Father.

"Dear Heavenly Father, we ask Your protection upon the McCaully Ranch this day. We need Your hand of deliverance and ask that the enemy be brought down, not by our skill, but by Your mighty hand. I pray special protection upon Caitlin Bannister"—she squeezed Cait's hand—"and upon Jeb Dawkins. Lord, please, may we find favor in Your sight. Be with us this day. We leave the outcome in Your all-knowing care. In Your mighty, precious name we pray. Amen."

"Amen," Aidan and Cait said together.

Cait added, "Thanks, Liberty...I needed that. I was starting to feel awfully nervous. I am going to have to learn to rely on God and not myself."

They hurried out of the bedroom and down the stairs to the kitchen.

Everything was back in place. Ewen went upstairs. The doctor and minister were in the room with the sheriff and had opened the windows. It had begun to smell.

Entering the parlor, the women saw the flowers had been removed and chairs put back. As they reached the kitchen they heard the cowbell by the front door ring its low gong. McDuffy started for the door.

Ewen had positioned himself a quarter of the way down the stairs and as she opened the door, he slowly began to descend the rest of the way.

"Well, Father O'Flannagan, what a pleasant surprise," said Mrs. McDuffy. "Why, what brings you out here to McCaully's so early? Come in, please, come on in."

Ewen reached the bottom of the stairs and acted surprised. "Good morning, Father O'Flannagan. Guess I'll second the question. What brings you out here so early?" He reached out to shake the gunslinger's hand but, in truth, wanted to hammerlock him. "Come in, sir, please come right in."

Listening from the kitchen, Liberty believed McDuffy and Ewen should go on the stage. She thought their acting was perfect.

"Good morning. I spent the night in Vallejo and am just now returning. I took the earliest train. Thought I'd see how you all are doing at McCaully's since Mr. McCaully died. I also thought, perhaps, I could get a cup of coffee. I know you, Ewen Carr, are a Catholic, and I was wondering if you would be interested in visiting me for confession. I've never seen you there or at church."

"No, no…I'm not Catholic, yet it is providential that you came by this morning. We have Sheriff Rowe in a room. He was murdered last night and in need of intercessory prayer, Father."

Caitlin had gone around from the kitchen and headed down the hall to the front entry. "Father O'Flannagan, why, how nice to see you again." Cait had never realized his eyes were so cold. He smiled, but it didn't reach his eyes. It gave her the shivers.

"Miss McCaully, it's good to see you, too. I am sorry to hear about the sheriff, though. We've had a rash of robberies. Perhaps the robbers went too far. I told the sheriff he needed to investigate and find who was committing these heinous crimes."

"Yes, I've heard four men have been bashed over the head…horrible business, isn't it? Come on in and sit a spell. I'll get some coffee, or would you like to go out with me and see our new litter of kittens first?" Cait asked innocently.

His eyes glittered. "If you'd be kind enough to show me, I'd like to see those kittens," he said easily.

"Please excuse us, Ewen. I want him to see Henry and her darling kittens." She smiled, but it didn't reach her eyes either.

Flint didn't notice—he was doing some quick thinking.

"We called her Henry before we found out she was a female," Cait said. "Now, it's short for Henrietta." She knew she was talking fast, but she always did that when she was nervous. She concentrated on keeping the brogue out of her words. "They're in the barn. Come, Father O'Flannagan, and I'll show you." She headed out the front door and down the steps, intending to go to the barn.

Flint was right behind her. He glanced around, but seeing no one between them and the stable, he took Caitlin by the arm and steered her toward the stable instead of the barn.

"What are you...?" She started to pull away until she felt the hard barrel of a revolver in her ribs.

"Just head for the stables, little girl. You an' me...we're going for a ride," he said and jabbed the revolver a bit deeper into her ribs while still holding her arm with his left hand. He had on his cassock and his gun didn't show, but neither did his hand.

CHAPTER XXXIII

No weapon that is formed against thee shall prosper;
and every tongue that shall rise against thee in judgment thou
shalt condemn. This is the heritage of the servants of the LORD,
and their righteousness is of me, saith the LORD.

ISAIAH 54:17

THIS IS IT. I knew it wasn't going to be easy. All right, Caitlin Kendall McC...Caitlin Kendall Bannister, I am now a believer...do I believe Jesus can save me or not? Yes, I do believe He can save me. Jesus, I am asking You to save me from this man. He is evil and wants to do me harm. I am putting my trust in You. Please protect me. Caitlin took a deep breath and felt much better. She believed in miracles...what had happened to Jared, Aidan, and herself was a miracle. Her heart still beat fast and she was scared, but the debilitating fright was gone.

"We're going to saddle up your little pony and take a ride." His laugh was wicked.

Matthew and Kirk were in the barn with their eyes fixed on the front door of the McCaully house. The two brothers stood looking through a crack between a couple boards. Kirk had stacked some bales of hay to hide behind when Katie entered the barn, but the brothers saw Flint grab Cait's arm and steer her toward the stables. They saw her start to pull away. Matt realized the gunslinger was holding a gun in his right hand under his cassock. Matt's lips thinned, and out of the corner of his eye he saw Kirk fingering his own gun.

"Let's go," he whispered. "We'll slip out the back and run for the stables."

"Right by me," Kirk whispered back.

"Wait here," Matthew said to John, Ricardo and Sneedy, who crouched behind a separate stack of hay. "They're heading for the stables."

The two men ran lightly over the smooth dirt of the back of the barn. Sidling up against the barn wall, Matt took a quick peek around the corner, motioning with his hand for Kirk to wait.

He whispered, "Wait...wait...now!" The two made a mad dash for the back of the stables and, scurrying along the stall doors, sneaked into a stall next to Fire just as Cait and Flint walked in. The dimness, after the bright light outside, nearly blinded them, but their eyes quickly adjusted.

Fire was standing head up, not moving. His tail swished once and then he stood still as stone, not a muscle twitching.

"Saddle up your horse, girl...and be quick about it!" Flint spoke gruffly and was still holding her arm, but his gun hand could now be clearly seen.

Matthew saw it and grabbed Kirk's arm, who looked at him questioningly. Matt patted his gun, then jerked his thumb at Flint O'Flannagan's. Kirk's eyes widened as he suddenly recognized Matthew's gun. *Matthew recognized his gun...I'd like nothing better than to put a bullet into this evil man...maybe two bullets, one for Matt and one for Drew.*

Flint held onto Cait's arm and walked her to the tack room. He let go and stood with his gun aimed at her. The outlaw watched her every move. She took her saddle off the saddle stand and lugged it back to Fire's stall. Her horse stood at full attention as if he sensed all was not well with Caitlin. Fire was facing his manger, away from the stall door, but he knew someone was there. Throwing the saddle over the side of the next stall, Cait saw a movement and her eyes widened. She took strength from the fact that Matthew and Kirk were crouched in the corner of the adjacent stall. Kirk had laid a finger on his lips. She blinked twice in acknowledgement and tears started in her eyes. She brushed them away as she grabbed Fire's saddle blanket.

She opened the stall and slipped up next to her horse to throw the blanket on him. He pawed hard at the straw, and Cait pulled the blanket back off him. It was a bad sign. She could feel it in her gut.

In a harsh guttural voice, Flint asked, "What the tarnation do you think you're playing at, girl?" He moved into the stall with Cait and shoved her hard out of his way so he could saddle the stallion.

Caitlin, thrown off balance, tried not to crash into Fire. Flint stepped back out of the stall as the girl stumbled heavily. She made a grab for a side slat, but still off balance, hit her temple on a board and knew no more as she slid down the side boards.

Matthew, gun drawn, had beat Kirk to position himself behind Flint as the outlaw began to move into Fire's stall.

An unearthly scream rent the air as the horse kicked out. Matthew was flung across the wide alley of the stable, thrown by the force of Flint's body being propelled into his. Hitting his head on a support beam, Matthew was knocked unconscious.

Flint was lying face down at Kirk's feet. Kirk turned him over and wished he hadn't. It was a sight he'd not soon forget. Fire's hoof had penetrated Flint's skull and where his eyes should have been was only flesh and bone. He dragged the man into the stall across from Fire's and knelt next to his brother. He felt Matt's neck for a pulse. Gladness filled him as a steady throb met his searching fingers.

He ran to check on Caitlin, praying the stallion had missed her coming down from his kick. "It's all right, boy. It's all right." Kirk crooned to the shivering roan. He knelt and felt Katie's ankles, calves, thighs, ribs, and arms, talking aloud to the horse. Katie seemed all in one piece.

Men were running into the stable from both ends, and Kirk pointed to the stall where he'd drug Flint. It was still open and they could all see he was dead.

Kirk said, "Caitlin's Fire protected his mistress." He stroked the horse, glad the problem had been taken out of their hands. He was emotionally done in. He picked up his bride, who was still unconscious. Fire nuzzled her hair and blew softly on her face. Backing out of the stall, Kirk headed for the house, staggering a bit. Katie was no lightweight. Before he got to the front gate, Caitlin's eyes opened and her arms crept around his neck.

"Oh, Kirk, I was so scared...what happened?" She could feel the steady, even thump of his heart and was thankful to be alive and in his arms.

"Katie, me darlin', it's all right." Kirk was trying for an Irish brogue but missed the mark. Cait giggled. He set her down but once her feet hit the ground, his arms tightened and hers slid up his back as she hugged him. They kissed, deeply, passionately, with a gratefulness they were both alive.

Liberty and Aidan came running out of the house, followed by Ewen, Doc Addison, and Stephen Babcock. Sweeny, Duney, and McDuffy weren't far behind.

"Matthew needs help. He's been knocked unconscious," Kirk said, holding his Katie close to his side.

Liberty flew across to the stable as if on wings. Falling to her knees, she cradled Matt's head in her arms.

"What happened? Will he be all right?"

Ricardo answered her, "Si, hees heart, eet ees strong, mees. He weel be fine."

Sneedy said, "My guess is that thar stallion kicked the Father here, and he went a flyin' into Matthew, a knockin' 'em against the post."

"He's no priest, sir—he was a very evil man," Liberty said.

Doc Addison came in. "Not again...I just doctored him up a short time ago," he said as he pulled the legs of his trousers up a bit to kneel gingerly and examine Matthew, making sure nothing was broken. "Guess he suffered another blow to the head. It's not broken open this time, though."

Matthew opened his eyes and saw moss green ones staring back, concern for him etched in their depths.

"Liberty, I love you." His eyes adjusted and he saw men standing around them. "I'm all right. Think I'm in for another headache, though." Helping hands lifted him up off the floor. The doctor stood, dusting off his trousers.

Matthew said to Liberty, "It's strange, but I don't remember. Did I tell your father I was going to Henderson's? And, what are you doing up here at McCaully's, Liberty? For that matter, why am I here? Guess I don't recollect getting here, but I seem to recall everything else, at least I think I do."

"It's a long story, Matthew. Let's go back to the house." Liberty took his arm, grateful to God for restoring her husband.

"Is Kirk married or is that a dream?" he asked.

The men started to laugh.

"It's for real, young man," the doctor said. "Got married just this morning."

Memories came flooding back into Matthew's consciousness. "Ah… and Flint O'Flannagan…what happened to him? Last I remember, I was pointing a gun at his back."

Jethro said, "He's in there. Seems as if Caitlin's Fire took care of our problem."

Matt walked over to the stall and reaching down, picked up his custom-made revolver. "This," he said, "is mine." He looked down at O'Flannagan. "The good Lord must have known there'd be no repenting here." Taking Liberty by the arm, he led her out the stable.

EPILOGUE

I have fought a good fight,
I have finished my course,
I have kept the faith

II TIMOTHY 4:7

THE DAY HAD BEEN A LONG ONE. Kirk had more than proven himself an excellent calf roper. Drew had been their best roper but Kirk surpassed him. The men were surprised to see the young man rope and tie up a calf's legs in short order. None had ever seen it done so quickly and were surprised that he'd never bragged about his capability. They would readily accept this man as boss. Jethro was impressed, but Ewen could scarcely credit it.

"You grow grapes? Why, young man, that is a waste of good talent… you were born to be a rancher. You've outdone yourself, son." He slapped Kirk on the back and his eyes gleamed with pleasure. Kirk would be his new boss. The thought crossed his mind that Caitlin could hardly have done better. He'd felt so badly losing his lifelong friend, Mac McCaully, to cancer. He'd mourned deeply, but the tie that had bound the two men together was now severed. It was as if the connection he'd had to Ryanne was also severed. He'd been faithful to her memory all these long years. Now, he had fallen in love and would marry. He had made a commitment to follow Christ the night before last. He'd told Hannah all about it the day before, after church. They would have a June wedding. Hannah had agreed to move to McCaully Ranch and take up residence there. She could take in sewing there as easily as anywhere else.

Ewen was proud to have Kirk married to Mac's daughter. The young man was a hard worker and knew what he was about. He also felt life had taken on new meaning and that great days lay ahead for all of them.

Doctor Addison had stayed on for a few days on the pretext he wanted to see how Matthew and Caitlin were doing. Both had taken a blow to the head. In truth, he stayed on because he felt as if these people were his family. He had his mother in Vallejo, but they'd never been close. She hadn't wanted children. He and his own dear wife had not been able to have children. Now, the doctor continued to check on his mother every few weeks as she was getting up in years. But he was hungry for the kinship of family and the affection these people seemed to have for him.

Yesterday, the day after the death of Flint O'Flannagan, Caitlin and Kirk, Liberty and Matthew, Jared and Aidan, along with Ewen and the doctor, rode into town to go to the church where Stephen Babcock preached.

When they entered the church, Ewen spied Miss Hannah Danielson and excused himself to sit with her. The rest found a long pew where they could sit together. It was a wonderful service of thanksgiving and praise. The congregation sang with gusto and the newcomers were made to feel right at home. The message was about laying one's burdens at the feet of Jesus. Liberty thought it quite good and was glad Kirk and Caitlin would be going to a church where the truth was taught.

After the service, Caitlin invited Stephen and his family out to the ranch to have dinner with them, but they had declined as Helen was still feeling the effects of having a new baby and no sleep at night.

It was now Monday evening and everyone was relaxing in the

backyard. Two patio swings, several chairs, and a couple tables sat on a cobblestone patio under a huge grape arbor. Dinner was over and they were waiting awhile before having dessert.

Matthew pushed off gently with his foot to keep the patio swing in motion, his arm comfortably draped around Liberty's shoulders.

Liberty leaned toward Matthew's ear and said quietly, so no one else could hear, "I am so thankful your mind has returned to normal. It was quite uncomfortable being married to a man who didn't know me. I've done that before, you understand."

"You need to forget Armand. You belong to me, my sweet, lovely wife. I hope we can erase those horrible memories. In a way, it's what Saint Paul said, forgetting what lies behind, I press on toward the goal…you know the verse. I wonder how long it would have taken me to remember everything if I hadn't gotten hit on the head again?"

"I don't know, but I'm thankful I don't have to wait for you to get your memory back because I want to tell you about a miracle." Libby's tone was almost hushed.

He kissed her lips. "What miracle are you talking about?" He looked deeply into her eyes, a smile lurking in his own. He had a feeling this woman would never cease to surprise him. *How I love her!*

"Oh, I suppose it's the one I have growing within me…we, Matthew Bannister, you and I, are going to be parents."

Shocked, he laid his hands on either side of Liberty's face and gazed intensely into her green eyes.

"Are you sure? I thought you—"

"Couldn't have a baby?" she supplied. "I thought I couldn't, but evidently it wasn't me. It was Armand. Oh, Matthew, I'm so excited and thankful." Tears flooded her eyes, wetted her lashes, and spilled down her cheeks. "We're going to have a baby!"

Matthew picked Liberty up and lifted her high above his head, in front of everyone. He whirled her around and around as he laughed up into her face. Liberty laughed down at him and sparks flew. He stopped, eased her to the ground, and kissed her. He picked up a spoon and dinged his glass of apple cider. "Hello everyone, your attention, please."

He dinged the glass a couple more times and said, "I know we already have your attention." He squeezed Liberty to his side. "But we have a big announcement to make. We are going to be parents. Liberty is expecting a baby. It is a miracle for us and we'd like you to share in our joy."

Everyone began clapping and chattering about babies.

Jared looked at Aidan and said, "We probably will too, before long, don't you think, sweetheart?"

She smiled back, fluttered her eyelashes at him, and replied demurely, "Why, thit is dapendin' entieerely upon you, I'm sheer." She dipped into a brogue.

McDuffy peeked out the back door and announced, "Company coming, thought you should know...three riders."

"Who could it be?" Caitlin wondered. She and Kirk went through the house to the front door. There, trying to tie his horse to the hitching rail with one hand, was Xander, a puppy tucked under his other arm.

Caitlin looked at the man who was Xander's father. *Goodness! A male replica of Liberty, and surely the other man is her father?* Amazement flitted across Caitlin's face at the close resemblance these two men had to her new sister-in-law. She and Kirk went down the walk together to greet the newcomers.

There was much backslapping as introductions were made. Caitlin liked the looks of Liberty's family and she welcomed them.

"I came up from San Francisco to get my son, Xander, who insisted you wanted a puppy, Miss McCaully," said Alex Johnson.

"Nope!" said Kirk.

Xander's face fell and Alex looked in surprise at Kirk. His gray-green eyes moved to Miss McCaully.

"You don't want the puppy?" he asked.

"Why, yes, yes I do," she answered, her face wreathed in a grin.

"What are you saying, Kirk?" Alex looked intently at him.

"I said nope, because it's not Miss McCaully, it's Mrs. Kirk Bannister!" Kirk grinned at Liberty's brother.

Both Liberty's father and twin looked at Kirk and Cait, dumbfounded.

"Yer saying yer married ta her?" asked Xander, jerking his thumb at Caitlin. "Whoopee, Uncle Kirk's married!" He carefully placed the puppy in Caitlin's waiting arms and, slipping one of his arms through hers, he walked her to her own front door. "So, Aunt Caitlin, yer not gonna be faintin' like my Aunt Liberty, are you?"

Caitlin laughed down at the precocious boy while color suffused her cheeks. "No, at least not right away, anyway."

"It's nice to see you again, Aunt Caitlin, yous just gonna love this puppy. She's gonna be a bit lonely, though. She's been playing with her brothers and I know she's gonna miss them. We've been staying at my grandpa's house and I got to play with his puppy and yers. I'm glad you married Uncle Kirk. I heard Granny say he needed a good woman. I think you must be a good woman." Xander rattled on as they walked through the house, charming Caitlin with his observations. When he reached the patio he spied his Aunt Liberty.

"Aunt Libby, how are you? I'm so 'cited to be here. Yer not gonna faint again, are you?" He gave Liberty a big hug. "Papa and Grandpa were worried about Uncle Matthew and I think yous forgot to send them a telegram saying yous found him."

Liberty's hand flew to her mouth. "Oh, I did forget. We've had so much happening around here."

Matthew stood and put his arm around his father-in-law's shoulder, introducing the newcomers to Doc, Ewen, and Hannah. Caitlin, still cuddling her puppy, said, "Guess what, Xander? Tomorrow we're going to ride to a gold mine. How would you like that?"

"A gold mine? Jumpin' long johns, I'd love it!" He looked at his papa a little sheepishly.

Alex said to his son, "I told you, you'd have fun if you came up to the ranch. Your Uncle Kirk tells me they are branding cows until two o'clock and then riding out to the gold mine tomorrow. Isn't that exciting?"

"Yep, it is...but what's more exciting, is that Aunt Caitlin is Uncle Kirk's wife...nothing kin beat that!"

Kirk, not caring that all eyes were on him, pulled his Katie to himself and kissed her soundly, on the mouth. "That's right, nothing can beat that!"

Tory's Father Preview ~ Chapter 1

Be merciful unto me, O LORD,

for I cry unto thee daily.

PSALM 86:3

"**AND WHAT DO YOU SUGGEST, GEORGE?** Am I simply to walk into Brighton's residence and say, 'Oh, by the way, sir, you may be marrying a murderess?' He'd demand evidence. I would too, if I were him. We've looked for…ahh, let me see…it was back in seventy-three, wasn't it? Here it is, already the fall of 1875. We've been looking into this for nigh unto two and a half years, and we can't find any substantial proof."

Christopher Belden, chief detective for the Boston Police Department, felt it was time to step down. He was tired. George Baxter, his right-hand man, was the brightest mind in the department. He felt George was ready to step into his position.

George Baxter stared bitterly at Belden.

"Bradley Burbank's sister, Mrs. Hadley, has been down here countless times demanding an investigation. She is quite certain her brother was murdered, even though the coroner ruled it an accident. I fully agree with her, but we've hit a dead end. There are no witnesses, no one yelling foul play except Mrs. Hadley. She says her brother stopped seeing the Vickers woman about a month before his demise. That's what sparked the fuse. According to Mrs. Hadley, her brother told her the Vickers woman was mentally deranged. It was the reason he stopped seeing her. Burbank breaking off the relationship evidently made Mrs. Vickers furious."

"Well," replied Christopher, "you know the saying. 'Hell hath no fury like a woman scorned.'"

George, his voice sounding harsh, said, "We know she killed her husband, and we're quite sure she killed Bradley Burbank, but how can we prove it, sir? And surely someone should tell Brighton to watch his back and what he drinks."

The Boston Detective Agency had hit a dead end trying to tie one Mabel May Vickers with the murder of her husband and that of her male friend, Bradley Burbank.

The day was bleak. Rain threatened all morning, and the sky finally decided to spill its contents. Torrents streamed down rooftops. Gutters rapidly overflowed, making little rivers down the sides of the cobblestone streets. Thunder crashed and lightening streaked the sky as it stretched out crooked fingers across the heavens.

The girl, curled up into a ball of misery, lay on a settee in her own sitting room, her head cushioned on a pillow as tears streamed unchecked down her cheeks.

It's a perfect day for crying, she thought. *Looks to me like God's crying too. Oh, I just know Papa's going to be sorry once he marries that woman. I just know he is. Frankie thinks so too. She doesn't like her either, but she doesn't say so. I can tell that woman hates me. I see it in her eyes. I'd like to run away, but where could I go? Oh, how I miss Mama! What in the world am I going to do? That woman is mean. Why can't Papa see it? Maybe I could go live with Aunt Olivia. Wonder, would Papa even allow it? No, I don't suppose he would, but that woman looks at me as if I were a spider she'd like to squish. Oh, what am I going to do?*

Victoria Lynn Brighton was eleven years old. Wise beyond her years, she could see where the household was headed with a new Mrs. Brighton at the helm. Her papa had met the woman at a dinner party and felt sorry for her. He'd begun seeing her about three months before, but already they had decided to marry. The wedding was on the morrow.

Mrs. Mabel May Vickers was a widow with three children. There was a girl, thirteen years old, and two boys, one eleven and one seven. Victoria had been told to be nice to them, but no one had told them to be nice to her. The younger of the boys, Henry, had spilled an inkwell all over her favorite floral-print chair and her Turkish carpet.

Victoria's mother had turned the nursery into a sitting room for her since there'd been no more children after Tory. Her books and special things were there. Henry, the seven-year-old, was spoiled, in Victoria's estimation. He hadn't even apologized. The girl, Madeline, acted supercilious and had broken the spine on the locket Victoria's mother had given her for her tenth birthday. It had a tiny daguerreotype of her mother and father on one side, and her mother and herself on the other. Madeline had apologized, but it had been out of the corner of her mouth, and Tory didn't think she meant it. She'd asked her papa to get it fixed, but it was still lying on his chiffonier.

Madeline, at thirteen, had not been sent to boarding school. Victoria had asked her papa why, and he'd said Mrs. Vickers had insufficient funds, so Madeline went to day school. The boy Victoria's age, Charles, was the nicest. He was a bit quiet but observed everything that went on. When he spoke, which wasn't often, Victoria listened because he was smart.

Victoria's mother, Laura, had died nine months earlier. Victoria was supposed to be kept innocent of the cause, but she was best friends with their housekeeper, Mrs. Franks. Frankie, Tory lovingly called her. She'd filled Tory in on all the details. Her mother had gotten pregnant again, but this time when she lost the baby, an infection had set in and she'd died from it. Tory had been desolate and inconsolable. The only time she felt halfway fine was when she rode her horse, Commotion. Then, she could forget.

Victoria, still curled up, thought bleakly about Mrs. Vickers. Her deep-set blue eyes had icicles in them. They looked coldly at her, and her smile looked more like a grimace, her lips pulled back from perfectly straight, small teeth.

Tory sat up, staring bitterly at the stained carpet, trying to think how she could escape being around Mrs. Vickers. Life would be different beginning tomorrow, with a new Mrs. Brighton in charge. Tory dreaded it.

Learn more about *Tory's Father* at:
MARYANNKERR.COM

56681999R00175

Made in the USA
Charleston, SC
29 May 2016